Books by David VanDyke:

Stellar Conquest Series:
First Conquest
Desolator: Conquest
Tactics of Conquest
Conquest of Earth
Conquest and Empire

Books by B. V. Larson:

Undying Mercenaries Series:
Steel World
Dust World
Tech World
Machine World
Death World
Home World
Rogue World
Blood World
Dark World

Flagship Victory

(Galactic Liberation Series #3)

by

David VanDyke
and
B. V. Larson

Copyright © 2018 by Iron Tower Press.

ISBN-13: 978-1980726081
BISAC: Fiction / Science Fiction / Military

Illustration © Tom Edwards
TomEdwardsDesign.com

Part I: Defender

The evil, soul-crushing Mutuality had been overthrown by my Liberation. My troops and followers, my brave men and women, Straker's Breakers, aided by allies such as the Unmutuals, the Ruxins, the Sachsens and many defectors, now stood victorious astride the trash heap of history that was its collectivist paradise. No longer would its tyranny hold more than a thousand worlds in thrall. The New Earthan Republic was born.

Next, I would turn my attention to my former regime and nation, the Hundred Worlds. Long the enemy of the Mutuality—though their common citizenry was kept from this knowledge—the Huns were already seizing territory from our Republic and seemed unwilling to consider peace between the two great empires of mankind. Therefore, with the help of faithful friends and allies, I resolved to force them to talk.

But before I could implement my intentions, before I could set my plans in motion, before I could even begin my honeymoon with my new wife—the commander of my fleets, Carla Straker née Engels—the insectoid Opters intervened. They'd first tried to addict me to their nectar. Next they utterly

1

destroyed our largest shipyards at Kraznyvol. Now we raced to
Murmorsk, to confront the Nest Ships there.

- A History of Galactic Liberation, by Derek Barnes
Straker, 2860 A.D.

Atlantis: Capital of the Hundred Worlds
Carstairs Corporation Headquarters
One year ago

The Hundred Worlds consisted of a bright cluster of stars, rare jewels in the velvet black of space.

These star systems had become Humanity's home, even if Old Earth still made the claim of origin. Like many other human-occupied systems Earth was under the sway of the alien Hok, the soldiers of the Mutuality. It was unrecognizable to any independent, civilized person.

At the center of the Hundred Worlds, like a blue gem in a treasure chest, the planet Atlantis shone brightest of all. Unlike Earth, Atlantis bustled with energy and industry. She was the economic and political crossroads of the Hundred Worlds, and she served them all as their capital.

On Atlantis, all things met, all paths intersected, and all power was conglomerated.

Megacorp owner Billingsworth M. Carstairs VI told himself these unassailable truths every day of his rich life.

Carstairs had commanded a host of underlings to gather for a high-level executive meeting. He always started such meetings wearing a stern frown, even when he was happy. His father, Big Bill Carstairs, had taught him that trick as a child. "Start from a position of dissatisfaction, my boy," he'd said, "and your employees will work all the harder to please you. They'll cherish your every smile, which you can then bestow like rare gifts."

Big Bill had been right, may he rest in peace. Over the last decade, Carstairs Corporation had grown from the third largest conglomerate in the Hundred Worlds into the biggest—it was now double the size of any other megacorp.

The best part was the old man had had the decency to die before retiring, turning over his controlling interest to his son and namesake, Billy.

Of course, nobody outside the Carstairs family called him Billy anymore. Not if they wanted to keep their jobs.

The power of Carstairs meant Billy had Parliament Ministers in his pocket and plenty of fat government contracts. In fact, they'd just given him one of the fattest, which was why he had called today's meeting.

Stepping into the meeting chamber, Billy heard the room fall silent for a moment. All eyes fell to him, and his frown deepened in response.

"Welcome, sir!" his CEO, Romy Gardel, gushed as she moved aside from her position at the head of the table.

As his most trusted underling—and lover on demand—Gardel knew he was in a good mood, despite his forbidding appearance.

"Thank you, Romy," he said. "Everyone take your seats. Ladies and gentlemen, I have good news. The Defense Committee has approved funding for the Victory project. In fact, they were so impressed with the prototype, and so worried by the *unfortunate* military disaster at Corinth," —here Carstairs released a broad, genuine smile and a chuckle, prompting sycophantic laughter from his underlings— "that they doubled the budget and tripled our potential bonus for commissioning the lead ship on time."

"No constitutional problems?" asked Mike Rollins, the corporation's senior legal advisor. "How did they get around Section 4.3?"

"The Declaration of Rights?" Carstairs chuckled again. "The Supreme Judiciary provided an official opinion that anything less than a full brain is mere tissue, with no more human rights than a transplanted heart or kidney, as long as it was harvested legally. A few tweaks to the Involuntary Organ Donor laws—necessary for the war effort under the Loyalist Act, you see—and thousands of brains become available, as long as they've lost certain vital functions, the poor souls. One slip of a scalpel and, 'oh my, how unfortunate,' with a generous settlement for the families, of course."

The Board members briefly changed their expressions to match Carstairs' own, a moment of crocodile-teared sorrow.

Carstairs continued, "The Loyalist Act gives the government all the authority it needs to identify and confiscate

4

the remains for research purposes, and to classify all that research, does it not, Mister Rollins?"

"It does."

"So we're cleared to proceed." Carstairs clapped his hands in satisfaction. "If these new flagships prove successful, not only may they allow our brave forces to achieve new gains, but the program can eventually expand to the civilian sector, where Victory-style AIs can be used for a wide variety of applications." He frowned significantly at Rollins. "Our patent suites are comprehensive?"

"Unassailable, sir," the attorney said. "Oh, eventually other megacorps will find a way to legally use brain parts to create stable AIs, as it's the only approach that has ever kept a machine AI from madness, but the comptrollers tell me we'll have a good fifteen years of market dominance."

"And undoubtedly a large rise in the value of everyone's stock options." Carstairs clapped his hands once more. "Excellent! I'll expect weekly reports on the project. Carry on." He turned to go, and then looked back over his shoulder. "Oh, Romy, drop by my office when you're done here."

"Yes, sir," she said with just a hint of extra color in her perfectly cut face. Carstairs found that money and power were always the best aphrodisiacs, and since he'd just promised Romy more of each... well, best to strike while the iron was hot.

Very hot.

He also had the latest pharmaceutical aphrodisiacs available, guaranteed to produce maximum performance with minimum side effects.

His executive bedroom was about to get a workout.

Chapter 1

Murmorsk System, New Earthan Republic

Admiral Derek Straker, mechsuit pilot and self-styled Liberator of humanity, gripped the backrest of Commodore Carla Engels' command chair. He stared at the enormous hologram projected above the battleship *Indomitable's* gargantuan bridge. It showed a bewildering swirl of warships locked in mortal combat.

Indomitable had just arrived at Murmorsk, the recently overthrown Mutuality's—now the New Earthan Republic's—second-largest fleet base and military shipyards. Straker and Engels both expected the strange insectoid Opters and their carrier-like Nest Ships to strike there next, after apparently destroying the larger, main base at Kraznyvol.

Their guess was right.

Straker's hope, that *Indomitable* and other Republic forces could catch the Opters in the act, had panned out. His message drones had directed all available warships to assemble at Murmorsk and engage at the senior commander's discretion. *Indomitable's* slow sidespace transit speed meant she arrived well after the other ships.

"Who's in command of our forces?" Straker asked.

Tixban, the ship's octopoid Ruxin sensors officer, replied, "It appears Commodore Gray has assumed that position."

Straker saw Engels nod with satisfaction. Despite a rocky start, the crusty, older Ellen Gray had become a solid sister-in-arms to them both.

"Highlight enemy battle positions," Engels ordered.

Tixban brushed his subtentacle clusters across the console, refining the hologram view to illustrate his words. "Six Opter Nest ships are grouped here, about halfway between the star and the edge of flatspace. Their combat drones are approaching the inner planets and shipyards."

"How many drones?"

"At least fifty thousand. There may be more. I am still collating data."

Straker's brow furrowed. "Hell... Fifty thousand... How can we fight that many?"

Engels stood to walk closer to the hologram. "During transit here I studied all the data we collected. Individually the drones are weak. Many of them are no more than a small fighter with an expendable pilot and one weapon, usually a beam of some sort. I believe those are crewed by the dog-bees, the least intelligent kind of Opters. The next, less numerous class up is a larger fighter, probably piloted by the antlike technicians you saw. These have a mix of two or three small weapons. More punch, more survivable. Above that, they have attack ships comparable to ours, with single larger weapons, likely piloted by wasp warriors."

Straker grunted in acknowledgement. "What forces do we have?"

Tixban highlighted the icons. "Commodore Gray's flagship, the super-dreadnought *Correian*. Five dreadnoughts, nineteen battlecruisers, thirty-five heavy cruisers, sixty lights, and over four hundred escorts from destroyers down to corvettes. Everything that could converge from nearby systems."

"Attack ships?"

"Forty-five, from the local forces, along with two monitors and a handful of escorts. They also appear to be trying to launch some of the warships under repair, but they're unlikely to make them battle-ready soon enough."

"Those attack ships won't last long. The monitors may survive... How long until the Opter forces hit them?"

"Two hours."

"And Commodore Gray's ships?"

"About three hours until her fastest ships can join the battle."

Straker slammed his palm on the chair's back. "And there's no way for *Indomitable* to reach the fight in time."

"No," said Engels. "We need twelve hours minimum simply to reassemble the sections." The battleship, too large to

7

transit through sidespace in once piece, had to break apart into sixteen sections every time it traveled from star to star.

"Damn it all, we can't just sit here aboard *Indomitable* as spectators!"

"We have no other choice," said Tixban.

"Oh, yes we do. Indy? Zaxby?" Straker called into the air, presuming the artificial intelligence Trinity would be listening. The AI inhabited the destroyer formerly called *Gryphon*, docked with *Indomitable's* prime section.

A voice that *sounded* like Indy—the machine part of the group-mind—replied. "I am not Zaxby or Indy anymore. I am Trinity now, Admiral. How may I serve?"

"How quick can you get me to the fight?"

"Trinity is the fastest ship present in the system. I estimate I can reach the forward edge of the battle area within two hours, if you board me within the next seven minutes."

"On my way."

Engels was already turning to object. "What do you think you can do out there that Ellen Gray can't, Derek?" she hissed, moving close. "You're not a fleet commander."

"Exactly, so I'm not needed here. I can't just sit on my ass. You're the naval officer. You get *Indomitable* traveling inward as fast as you can. Assemble on the move. Trinity will keep me safe while I observe our new enemies up close."

"Observe," she scoffed. "You can't observe anything more than sensors collect. Send in Trinity on her own if you need data. You don't need to risk yourself."

"I have to get in there," Straker insisted.

"I will keep him safe," Trinity assured Engels. "I also am interested in observing the Opters up close and adding to my data stores." That sounded more like the Zaxby part of the triumvirate being. with Indy AI

"There you go." Straker pecked Engels on the lips. "Gotta run, hon. See you on the other side." He left her fuming.

As he jogged toward the flight deck, he called into the air, "You still wired into *Indomitable's* nervous system, Trinity?"

"If you're asking if I'm still connected to the shipboard network—I am."

"Tell Redwolf to grab my go-bag from my quarters and meet me at the airlock. Then pass to the flight deck to prep my mechsuit. I'll walk it aboard."

"There's no need," said Trinity. "I am even now loading it into my cargo bay, having anticipated your desire to bring it along."

Straker changed direction toward the airlock. "Great. Be there in a minute."

At the portal from *Indomitable* to Trinity, Sergeant Redwolf stood in his battlesuit, a duffel in each hand.

"What's in the other bag?" Straker asked as he came to a stop.

"My own gear, sir."

"I don't need you along, Red."

The man's black eyes darkened further. "Ain't I your bodyguard, sir? And your steward?"

Straker thought about it. "I guess you are, aren't you? Okay, good to have you along."

Redwolf's planar face almost cracked a smile. "Glad to hear it, sir. I wouldn't want to have to fibertape you and carry you aboard." He entered Trinity ahead of Straker.

Straker snorted and followed. *Damned battlesuiters. Think they can do or say anything and get away with it. Kinda like mechsuiters.*

When he reached Trinity's compact bridge, he was surprised to see a young, platinum-haired, ethereally beautiful woman standing near the empty command chair. "Please, Admiral, sit," she said. She wore an ice-blue skintight poly-suit that left little to the imagination. A sleek headset hugged the back of her skull like a piece of high-tech jewelry.

Straker couldn't help but take an appraising look before forcing his eyes to move above her neckline. "And you are?"

"I am Trinity," she said, with a knowing smile and a lift of one perfect eyebrow. "I used to be known as Doctor Marisa Nolan. My body has been rejuvenated and my mind has been integrated."

Straker's jaw dropped. "You're that creaky old woman?"

"I *was*." She turned left and right, showing off her body to best advantage. "I retain all of my personality and memories, so I'm still vain enough to appreciate being a knockout again. I was quite the heartbreaker in my younger days."

"I imagine…" Straker said, mentally reminding himself once again that he was happily married. "Feel free to wear something a little less…"

"Sexually arousing?"

Straker made an exasperated sound. "Forget it. Let's get underway."

"We're already accelerating at maximum, Admiral," she replied. "Interacting with you socially takes only a tiny percentage of my attention, so there's been no delay."

Right. She was just as much a part of Trinity as Zaxby or Indy, though it was hard to remember that right now. "Good. Fine. But seriously, you make it difficult for me when you act this way—like a Tachina clone."

The Marisa-body's face fell. "I take your point, and I apologize."

She turned and walked out. Maybe she was merely doing as he asked, or maybe she had her feelings hurt. If so, she needed to grow up. A rejuvenated hundred-year-old woman should know better, even if she did share a brain with a teenaged AI and the nonhuman Zaxby.

Nolan looked just as good from behind. Straker shook his head and thought of cold showers. When that didn't work, he mentally superimposed Carla's image on Marisa's, and then turned his face to the main holoplate. "Give me a view of the upcoming engagement."

"Of course, Admiral," said Indy's disembodied, decidedly non-sexy voice.

The holoplate showed a swarm of Opter drones. Well, technically not drones, as they had pilots, but they were likely to operate as drones—expendable extensions of the Nest Queens' will, so he called them drones. The swarm approached the inner worlds in a disciplined mass, heading first for the largest and most densely industrialized planet of Murmorsk-4. This was a small gas world, and the main shipyards were on the moon called Beta-2.

Dozens of other facilities, on smaller moons, supported the shipbuilding and repair operations. Skimmer booms tens of kilometers long dropped from the lower moons, dipping their probes into the soupy atmosphere, sucking up valuable gases. Complexes thrust upward from the surfaces of other, larger planetoids, space docks and mining facilities and agricultural domes, all the marks of orbital industry.

Murmorsk-3, a green world, held the balance of the system's population. The two planets happened to be almost in alignment, at their closest approach, perhaps forty million kilometers apart.

The enemy should strike M-4, the most heavily defended, first. If they won there, the weak defenses at M-3 were unlikely to stop them. Straker wondered whether the Opters would exterminate the civilian population, or merely conquer them. Green worlds were valuable—populations less so. Did the bugs prefer subjects, or genocide?

If what they'd done at Kraznyvol was any indication, they'd leave nothing alive.

Ellen Gray's fleet was farther away from the targets than the incoming enemy, stretched into an oblong blob with one end pointing toward M-4. Those lead ships would reach the battle site in about three hours. The back end of the blob would reach M-4 in five hours, according to the annotations on the holoplate.

As Straker watched, one-sixth of the enemy began to separate and head toward M-3. One Nest Ship contingent out of six? Probably. And why? Did they hope to divide the defenses?

Straker wondered what drove these Opters. Glory? Competition among themselves? Did each Queen keep score, or did they cooperate fully and unselfishly? He put these questions to Trinity.

"Hello, Admiral," said Zaxby as he ambled onto the bridge. His headgear had become even more compact than the last time, a wireless interface to the rest of Trinity. "We sense that you would prefer to speak to our Zaxby body."

"I like to speak to someone I can see, that's all."

"You could see Nolan."

"I could see a little too much of Nolan, thank you very much."

11

"That would seem to be your failing, not ours," Trinity-Zaxby said.

"If biological urges are failings, we're all hopeless—including you."

"Touché. To answer your questions, the Opters within each Nest are truly one collective society. You may think of each Nest as an individual group-mind, headed by one Queen."

"You mean they're telepathic?"

"Not at all. But like a flock of birds or a school of fish, they are so attuned to one another that they seem to share one mind, and they do use brainlink technology comparable to ours. Unlike humans, though, they have no taboos about networking brains electronically, so when it's convenient, they do so."

"And the Nests? Do they form bigger group-minds?"

"Many Nests may compose a Hive, but they do not seem linked. Nests almost always cooperate effectively, like ships in a fleet, but I have seen indications of the occasional disagreement. However, we should not depend on any division within their ranks."

"I'm just trying to get a sense of them. So they do keep control of their own bugs and drones? They're not interchangeable?"

"No," said Zaxby. "Each Nest has its own pheromones, markers, and genetic quirks."

"What happens if a Nest Queen dies?"

"There are queens-in-waiting, but there would be disruption in the command structure."

Straker stroked his jaw. "So that's a weakness."

"No more than losing a human military commander would be."

"What happens if a Nest Queen loses too many forces? Will others turn on her and, I don't know, take her territory?"

"Occasionally, but not routinely. There is a natural limit to what one Nest Queen can control. Hive Queens act like feudal monarchs, with their subordinate Nest Queens owing them allegiance."

"Is there something above a Hive Queen?"

"There's a senior queen with an untranslatable name. Mutuality databases assigned her the designation 'Empress.' There's very little information on her, though."

Straker moved closer to the plate. "I need something right now. Something I can use. Something we can do here—you and me, Zaxby—uh, Trinity—to help us win this battle. We can't afford to lose our largest remaining shipyard system. Can we... hack them or anything? You're an integrated AI now. You were a good hacker before. You should be a super-hacker now."

Zaxby preened. "I *am* a masterful-hacker, but hacking requires access, or at least proximity. I can't hack from light-minutes away. I need to attack their cybernetic systems in realtime from short range. They are unlikely to simply watch as I do that, though, so the safest way is to join the fleet and become one target among many, mutually supporting with Commodore Gray's escorts."

"Okay, so rendezvous with them."

"We are on course, and will join them in approximately one hour."

Straker paced back and forth. "Gray's lead forces will be an hour late, though, right?"

"Correct."

"Will the M-4 defenses hold?"

"My simulations say they will have lost fifty percent effectiveness within the first hour."

"But Gray's forces are going to arrive piecemeal, spread out, rather than in one hard wave."

Zaxby zoomed in on the future battle zone and extended his predictions. "Correct. Our lead elements will sustain heavy casualties."

"How heavy?"

"Approaching one hundred percent, if they fight to the death."

Straker's eyebrows lifted. "That's not feasible. They won't fight to the death anyway—not these former Mutuality forces, and I wouldn't want them to. What if we pull the lead elements back and thicken up, delay our arrival by, say, half an hour to an hour?"

"Effectiveness rises proportionally with delay, but the defenders are dying at an equal rate. I have run every standard simulation, and Commodore Gray's tactics appear to be nearly optimal."

"And do we win?"

Zaxby frowned. "The final outcome is firmly within the margin of error."

"Meaning it's a toss-up."

"Yes. And both fleets will be devastated no matter what."

Straker smacked his palm repeatedly into his fist. "We have to find a way to break through. Zaxby, you must have ideas. I remember you saying you used to come up with crazy schemes and your superiors would shoot them down. Now I need a crazy scheme—something that will give us a big win."

"Finding a hack is my best chance. If I can disrupt many drones, the odds could swing heavily in our favor."

"What about hacking the Nest Ships?"

"They're farther away, and they won't let me sneak this ship within hacking range."

"We can if we use underspace…"

Zaxby's two nearest eyes narrowed doubtfully. "Even if they do not have detectors, they are unlikely to leave us unmolested once we emerge. If you wish to make an underspace attack, it would make more sense to simply deploy float mines. We might be able to destroy one or two of their Nest Ships before the others scatter on random courses."

A sudden thought struck Straker. "What happened to Indy's objection to killing?"

"It is still there, but it has been subsumed among the three of us. We find it permissible for us to kill creatures of an alien enemy which seems bent on destruction and death of our people."

"Good. Maybe we should put you guys in charge of *Indomitable* again."

"We would politely refuse. We find this ship-body to be much more flexible."

"But it's so small! Think of the facilities you'd have aboard the battleship!"

"You seek to tempt us." Zaxby turned one eye away to glance at his console. "We can always scale up. For now, speed and flexibility is better than raw power."

"Do you have any more technological tricks up your sleeve?"

"None usable on such short notice."

"What about using float mines on the drones?"

"We might kill a few dozen—perhaps even hundreds—but this would have negligible impact on the battle."

"And it's impossible to float a nuke directly inside a Nest Ship?"

Zaxby spread his tentacles. "I've explained this before. It's completely possible to float the warhead—but it won't detonate properly unless it emerges in vacuum. The presence of atmosphere will cause trillions of molecular interactions that will disrupt the precise timing needed. You will have, at best, a dirty bomb. On a vessel as large as a Nest Ship, that will hardly bother them at all. Contaminating a Nest Queen may cause disruption—but then again, it may not. Imagine a human commander who was irradiated and knew she would die, but not until days after the battle. She would not shirk her duties. And there must be contingencies in case a Queen is incapacitated."

"Dammit. There must be some way…"

Redwolf stepped onto the bridge, his battlesuit boots clanging loudly on the deck. "I put your gear away, sir."

"Thanks, Red." Straker gestured at the screen and sighed. "We're trying to come up with some clever trick to win this battle… or at least reduce our casualties. We're about to get hammered."

"I'm just a grunt, sir. If I can't shoot it or screw it, I salute it or paint it." Redwolf took a step forward and removed his helmet to better look at the screen. "Speaking of getting hammered… too bad we can't board those Nest Ships with our suits."

Straker snapped his fingers. "Maybe we can. Zaxby?"

"The possibility exists, but the probability of success is low."

"Why?"

15

Zaxby ticked off reasons on sub-tentacles like fingers. "We have to sneak up on them, and we don't know if they have underspace detectors. If we do, we need to emerge long enough to take a final reading, yet not be seen. If we manage that, we would need to gamble that the target Nest Ship doesn't move on final approach. Most importantly, we don't have precise interior plans. We don't even know if the Opter ship you visited was representative of others. You said it seemed modular, so we can't be assured of the layout. Emergence in atmosphere is dangerous enough: if you appear congruent with a solid object, you will die."

"The Queen was in the center, and the center was pretty big. That would be our target. You have the data from my debriefing, right?"

"Of course."

"Assuming we don't get spotted, what are the odds of me emerging safely?"

"No better than fifty percent."

Straker considered it. He *wanted* to take the gamble, get in there and fight. But fifty-fifty...

"Boss," Redwolf said, "That's nuts. I mean, if it was for the win, maybe it would be worth a coin flip, but we'd only be taking out one of their ships. And do we even know that would affect the battle? Their attack forces probably got their orders. They ain't gonna just bug out."

"Despite his hideous pun, I second Sergeant Redwolf's misgivings," Zaxby said. "You'd be reversing your Pascal's Wager."

"Little upside, big downside." Straker felt like punching something. "You're right. It's too big a risk. So we're back to the hacking... but it seems like we could do more, now that Trinity is a warship again. You three brainiacs need to come up with something."

Zaxby smiled, more naturally than he used to, it seemed to Straker. The Ruxin was getting better at mimicking human body language, probably because of being brainlinked to Nolan. "Actually, I do have one idea."

Chapter 2

Straker and Trinity, approaching Murmorsk-4

"We're in position," Zaxby said from his helm console. Trinity didn't actually need a hands-on pilot, but the Ruxin seemed comfortable there, and ran his subtentacles restlessly over the control inputs, like a poker player shuffling chips while waiting for play to start.

The main holoplate showed the Murmorsk-4 defenses already heavily engaged with—and losing to—the Opter drone swarm. They were furiously defending the valuable shipyards, but it was just a matter of time before they would be overwhelmed and dismantled by the enemy's thousands of small craft.

Thousands more were incoming. They'd passed beyond M-4 and now formed a thick plane of battle barring the New Earthan fleet from relieving the defenders. Trinity was embedded among Commodore Gray's lead corvettes, just moments from engagement.

This forward edge enjoyed the right of first blood as the small ships opened up with their primaries. For almost a minute they slashed and burned dozens of enemies without suffering return fire, for the Opter drones had much shorter ranges. As a destroyer, Trinity seemed a monster alongside the tiny corvettes, but she joined them with her superb suite of defensive weaponry—defensive in the sense of it being optimized for antimissile use, which made it perfect for this work.

The corvettes continued boosting at flank speed, but began maneuvering randomly. Combat sims had shown they would survive longer if they continued to gain velocity and to dodge as they entered the heart of the swarm. This gave them a slim chance to win through, rather than none at all—which was what slowing down would have meant.

"You gonna insert into underspace?" Straker asked, fingers gripping the arms of his captain's chair.

"Never fear, Oh Great Liberator. Our timing will be impeccable," Zaxby replied.

"Because it looks like we're getting—"

The universe cooled, a telltale sign of underspace insertion, and Straker immediately cranked up the heat on his pressure suit. The holoplate showed the same icons, but Straker knew they were predictions, not hard sensor observations.

Trinity steered toward the nearest, densest cluster of Opter drones. "Hack-mine away," Zaxby said. "Rerouting."

Straker watched as Trinity altered course toward another cluster. When she was just in front of that group, Trinity dropped another hack-mine.

He itched to demand Trinity pop out of underspace in order to see if the hack-mines were working, but that would be pointless. Once deployed, the tiny, stealthy devices, converted from a variety of probes, mines and missiles available in Trinity's stores, would broadcast highly invasive, broad-spectrum information attacks.

If they worked, some of the enemy drones would be disrupted, rendered combat-ineffective for at least as long as it took for them to clear the malware. If it worked well, the Trojans, worms and viruses might even cause the Opters to attack each other.

This was the idea the Zaxby-Trinity meld had come up with, the only way to hack the Opters without simultaneously exposing Trinity to mass attack or giving warning of the attempt. The downside was, Trinity couldn't test out attacks and evaluate the enemy's responses. The hacks were shotguns in the dark of cyber-linkspace. Popping up and looking at them wouldn't change anything.

And if the hack-mines didn't work, at least Trinity could pass through the swarm and try to help the defenders of M-4.

Nineteen more of the devices floated up from underspace before Trinity passed the blockers and Straker was confident enough to insist they emerge. The seconds before the holoplate updated seemed agonizingly long.

When the new information caused the image to ripple and change, Straker stood and cheered. Far more of the speeding corvettes than expected had survived within the swarm—

18

perhaps half of them. Behind them, each slower class of ship in its own wave—frigates, then destroyers, then light cruisers and so on—had smashed deep into the blockers, remaining combat-effective for far longer than the simulations predicted.

"Get me a comlink to Gray on the flagship," Straker said.

"Comlink to *Correian* established, audio only."

The sound fluttered and burst with the static of the battle. "Gray here. Make it fast, Straker. I'm damned busy."

"The hack-mines seemed to have worked."

"Thanks, yes. They disrupted thousands of drones. Pat yourself on the back. Anything else?"

Straker ignored the prickliness. The older woman had never quite adjusted to such a young man in supreme military command, but she was far too competent for him to take her to task about it—at least in public. He didn't want fawning sycophants anyway.

"We're heading in to help the defenders," he said. "Follow as soon as you can. Anything critical to report?"

The big flagship, with its coordinating staff of hundreds, had a lot more ability to process sensor data, intelligence, and comlink reports. When Gray answered back, she didn't disappoint him.

"The shipyards on Beta-2 are the critical core of the facilities," she replied. "That's where the defenders will make their last stand. Everything else is secondary. Save that, and we can call it a win—or at least, not a terrible loss. Once that's secured, we'll work outward."

"What are the reports from M-3?"

"They're holding. I believe the swarm sent there was a pinning attack, meant to keep their local forces from aiding M-4. Focus on Beta-2. That's my professional opinion."

"You're the fleet officer, not me," Straker said, trying to give the commodore her due. He knew how annoying it was when the boss tried to second-guess and micromanage a competent subordinate. "See you at Beta-2. Straker out."

"Comlink ended," Zaxby said. "You know, Derek Straker, I particularly like Commodore Gray."

"Oh? Why?"

19

"Not only is her exterior a lovely shade of chestnut that I find aesthetically pleasing, but she doesn't take any guff from you."

"Take any guff, huh?"

"I believe that's the correct expression."

Straker smiled. "Yeah, I respect her. I know she'll tell me what I need to know, rather than be a yes-man."

"Oh, yes, I can see that. I can, yes." Zaxby blinked one eye.

"You're insufferable now that you have instant access to an Earthan language database on your brainlink."

"If you want to know *suffering,* try living among an alien species your whole life."

"You could have gone back to Ruxin now that it's liberated."

"And miss all this? Pish-posh."

Straker snapped his fingers. "Back to work, squiddly."

"There's no need for slurs." Zaxby turned up the place where his nose would be and shut up—exactly as Straker had hoped he would.

With the main display now updated in realtime, Straker could do nothing but watch as Trinity's icon crawled across the intervening space and the minutes ticked down. In that time, he tried to make a decision.

Should he order Trinity to attack from long range, darting in and out, drawing many enemy drones away from the main battle? Or should they descend into underspace and emerge among the defenders, to stiffen their defense?

Unfortunately there were no more hack-mines—and it was possible the enemy had already observed the results and had taken countermeasures anyway. Trinity still had plenty of float mine warheads, though, converted from the relatively useless shipkiller missiles she usually carried. No missile would survive the thousands of beams that the swarm employed, and would have to detonate early, killing only a few. Better to drop nukes among them from underspace, if it came to that.

It occurred to Straker that the swarm tactics of the Opters rendered useless nearly one-third of the weaponry of the typical human fleet—the missiles. Railguns were also less effective until point-blank range, as tiny craft dodged them easily. Beams were still effective, but the small size and maneuverability of the targets made up for their lack of armor.

"Zaxby, make a note for the next message you send to your brainiac buddies. We need a new class of ship, or at least a new weapons loadout for escorts, optimized against our new enemy."

"Do you not mean Opter-mized?" Zaxby laughed, a little too vigorously.

"Now who's making hideous puns? Just do it, will you? Perform some studies, run some sims, come up with recommendations."

"It may not matter."

"Why?"

Zaxby rolled an extra eye around to fix three on Straker. "Because at this rate, we may soon have no shipyards."

"You're trying to be a smartass. That's a good point, but, we have hundreds of small yards, usually for building freighters and local attack ships. Include that in the study. I need some kind of... liberty ship."

"Liberty ship?"

"Access your historical database from Old Earth, twentieth century, World War Two, United States of America. Their Liberty Ships were freighters, but the principle is the same. A ship that can be built quick and cheap. Something with a small crew, very simple, and effective mainly against these drones. Everything else should be sacrificed for combat effectiveness—crew comfort, unneeded sensors, extended comms. Something like a super attack ship, or specialized corvette. Something we can build by the thousands."

"I will send it out on the next message drone." Zaxby tapped at the console. "Admiral Straker, I need to know our tactics. Do we attack from outside, or pass through to help defend?"

Straker stroked his jaw as if thinking, but he'd already decided. If his main role was to inspire his forces, he couldn't very well snipe and pick at the enemy from the outside. Only by putting himself in with the defenders would he stiffen their spines and, just maybe, this would urge Commodore Gray's forces on to greater efforts.

21

"We go in. Get a good reading and set course to emerge somewhere protected, but close to the fight. We'll need to orient and update, and then help out where we see they need it the most."

"Aye aye, Liberator."

"I'm surprised you're not concerned that we'll be killed."

"Given that Opter drones are too small to mount underspace detectors, we maintain the ability to escape at will."

"We won't be exercising that option. In fact, make sure you don't even mention it. Nobody's going to be inspired by a Liberator who has a backdoor out of the fight."

"Methinks I could not die anywhere so contented as in the king's company, his cause being just and his quarrel honorable."

Straker growled, "Methinks Shakespeare is becoming all the rage. Didn't he also say something about the king being responsible for all those arms and heads chopped off in battle?"

"So he did… Fortunately, I can regrow arms, though not a head. Well, at least not without assistance. The upgraded rejuvenation bay might be able to do it, if the brain were preserved. In fact, I—"

"Do you mind paying attention to what's going on around us?"

Zaxby huffed. "Our mind has sufficient capacity to pay all the attention needed, as we're cruising in empty space right now. My full focus won't be necessary until we emerge in the midst of combat."

"Fine. How long will that be?"

"Approximately fifty-six minutes."

"I'm going to suit-up."

Zaxby's eyes widened and spun with surprise. "You're going to wear your mechsuit?"

"Why not? I'm no tactician, and I can brainlink in to your sensor feed. Better than sitting here yakking with you."

"Of course, you feel powerless. The mechsuit will counteract that sensation. However, please take care not to damage the cargo bay with your random flailing."

22

"I don't flail—especially not randomly," said Straker. "Just make sure I can control the cargo bay functions on command. You don't want me to have to blast my way out from inside."

"I shudder to think."

Redwolf followed Straker as he headed for the cargo bay. "What's the plan, sir? We gonna drop on somebody?"

"I'm not sure yet, Red. By the way, how'd you like to train as a mechsuiter?"

Redwolf grinned through his open faceplate. "Thought you'd never ask, sir."

"I can't guarantee how well you'll integrate with the mechsuit. It really depends on how you brainlink. Some just can't. But at least you can run the Sledgehammer on manual, now that Karst turned traitor."

"I wish I'd killed that scumbag motherfucker when I had the chance."

"You and me both, Sergeant. In fact, you have my express permission to shoot him on sight, though I'd rather have him in my brig under interrogation. I have the feeling there's some interesting info in his head." The door to the cargo bay opened in front of him as the Indy portion of Trinity monitored his movements.

Inside, his mechsuit lay on its back, its clamshell torso hatch open to allow access. Straker stripped off his pressure suit, stored it, and then hopped up onto his fifty-ton combat rig. He rolled into the reclining conformal cockpit and plugged in his brainlink. That plus the manual activation code brought the monster to life.

Soon, his world expanded. He seemed to simultaneously stand inside a shrunken cargo bay, his body and senses now congruent with the man-shaped mechsuit, and also to see beyond, outside Trinity and into the void. He tested the datalink feed and made sure he was able to open and close the external doors and control the air pressure.

Once he was sure Redwolf was sealed and ready in his battlesuit, he lowered the atmo to near vacuum. Then, he waited, watching, until Trinity approached the swarm attacking M-4 and its orbital facilities. A short few minutes in underspace brought them to the battle for the moon, Beta-2.

23

They emerged into a silent storm of chaos and confusion. Thousands of drones swooped and fired, spinning and dancing in evasive patterns that reminded Straker of flocks of birds or schools of fish, so coordinated that they appeared to share one mind.

Above him loomed a besieged monitor, an enormous local defense ship second in size only to an asteroid fortress, or to *Indomitable.* Clearly, Trinity had emerged here in order to shield herself with its bulk.

Hundreds of the monitor's point-defense weapons fired, rippling and lighting up the area with fireworks. Where beams were revealed by the dust they illuminated, Opter drones were speared and knocked out. Where railguns fired, the projectile streams, although launched at high velocity, almost never hit anything. The drones slipped aside like fish dodging the teeth of sharks.

"Worse than I thought," muttered Straker. "Two-thirds of our weapons are useless."

Trinity added her firepower to the local fight, and soon had opened a bubble that provided welcome relief to the monitor. The drones were obviously targeting its beam emplacements, surgically disarming the big ship piece by piece.

In her former incarnation as the destroyer *Gryphon,* Trinity had been built for this kind of work—a hunter and killer of anything smaller than herself. Add to that Indy's AI precision and Zaxby's years of service at a weapons console, and kilo for kilo she was the deadliest anti-drone ship in human space. She knocked out hundreds of the craft within the first few minutes of the fight, before they drew back to stay out of her most effective range.

From time to time the monitor would launch a missile and detonate it at minimum range. These blasts would catch a handful of drones that couldn't flee fast enough, but this was a mere desperation measure. There weren't enough missiles in its inventory to make much difference to this kind of enemy.

"Vidlink for you, Liberator," Straker heard Trinity say in Indy's machine voice.

"Put it through."

24

A realtime picture of a large bridge appeared in his optical cortex, a man in a commodore's uniform sitting in the flag command chair. "Pearson here, aboard the monitor *Rhinoceros*. Admiral Straker—Liberator—is that you, sir?"

Straker set his feed to show his face. "It's me, Pearson. Pardon the view, but I'm suited up right now."

"You're a sight for sore eyes, sir, and that ship you're in is a vicious little thing, but we can't hold without help. Lots of help."

"Commodore Gray's inbound with the biggest fleet we could gather, but she's fighting her way through her own shitstorm. We have to hold until she gets here."

"We'll do our best... but sir, we've lost most of our sensors and eighty percent of our beams, and these damned critters already landing on our hull and breaching. It's only a matter of time before they chew through our armor."

"Do you have marines aboard?"

"Not enough. They all got stripped for other sectors when... begging your pardon, sir, but when we were fighting against you."

"Understood. Do you have any other escorts?"

"No, sir. My other monitor *Hippopotamus* is down and my attack ships didn't last long. We're all that's left. When we go, Beta-2 goes."

"Hang in there, Pearson. We'll try to scrape them off you. Straker out."

Below Trinity and *Rhinoceros* squatted the main shipyards the monitor was trying to protect. Ground-mounted weapons in armored turrets fired upward into the swarm, but there simply weren't enough of them. Capital beams designed to cut ships in half vaporized individual drones, but even on their lowest settings and fastest recharge times, this was overkill, swatting flies with sledgehammers—and it was wasteful of energy and time.

Now and then flights of missiles would launch from the moon's surface, but most of the time they would be picked off long before killing any targets. Railguns fired intermittently, and with some effectiveness, as it appeared the ground

25

installations had access to submunitions, clusters that would burst and catch the dodging drones in spreads.

But as Pearson had said, the cloud of drones was pulling in tighter and tighter, and at the edges of the rocky plain on which the shipyards sat, Opters were already coming in low over the horizon, nap-of-the-surface, in order to avoid the defenses and deploy armored vehicles to assault.

Armored vehicles... finally, something Straker could attack.

"Trinity," Straker said, "as soon as Red and I jump, orbit *Rhinoceros* and clean off her hull. Pop in and out of underspace if you need to get out of a jam. Try to keep this monitor functional, because when she dies, the shipyards will die with her."

"Jump? To the surface?" came Zaxby's worried tones. "Have you gone mad?"

"Probably. Message all friendlies please not to shoot the 'suiters, okay?" Straker cued the outer doors to open. "Redwolf, you ready?"

"Right behind your mad self, sir."

"Go." Straker launched out the opening and began falling slowly in the low gravity—too slowly, a miscalculation. He rotated head-down and used his landing thrusters to speed up— just in time. A hex of six drones dove toward him, blazing with their lasers.

Jinking with bursts of his suit jets, Straker aimed and fired his force cannon. The needle of armor-piercing plasma ripped one drone to shreds. He added his gatling to the mix, but the other five dodged the stream of bullets. They were simply too quick at this range.

Firing the gatling had an unintended consequence, though. Throwing reaction mass upward sped him toward the ground. Impact warnings flashed in his HUD, supplemented by his mechsuiter's senses and instinct. He somersaulted to put his feet down and opened up his retros just in time, slamming to the rocky, uneven surface of the nearly airless moon.

Beam strikes punched holes in the terrain around him.

Chapter 3

Straker stayed low on the surface in his mechsuit, with Redwolf beside him. He ran in shallow bounds, his stabilization system and his experience keeping him from flying upward in arcs that would eliminate his ability to dodge.

A mechsuit wasn't an aerospace fighter, even if it was of comparable size. He had to stay low and use the terrain, the huge rock formations and the pits, the buildings and mining sites scattered around the complex. In this, the smaller Redwolf actually had the advantage.

The battlesuiter skipped along behind him, and Straker wondered briefly what Redwolf could do in a fight where every combatant vehicle outmassed him by a factor of ten or more. Normally battlesuiters operated in squads or platoons, their numbers, cooperation and ability to hide in cover making up for their size.

But Straker could hardly have refused him coming along. He wasn't sure Redwolf would have followed such orders anyway.

Straker reached an ore processing facility, layered with pipes and girders and conveyors, and sheltered beneath it. Lasers peppered the area around him, and he returned fire deliberately and precisely, taking out three of the six attackers. Redwolf fired his own beam rifle upward to unknown effect.

The enemy return fire hit the pipes and gas leaked out, creating a cloud that provided concealment. At this, the three remaining drones broke off and retreated. A ground defense beam speared one on the way up. After that, they posed no threat to Straker and his sidekick.

"Why don't they come down and swarm the surface?" Redwolf asked.

"They will. I think Trinity surprised them. She's like having a dreadnought in the hull of a destroyer, at least for

27

point defense. I'm guessing they're concentrating on her and *Rhino* before they come down in a mass."

Redwolf pointed. "I think I spoke too soon."

Straker turned to look where he indicated, toward the horizon. He could see dust kicked up by a line of vehicles advancing toward the shipyard facilities—hundreds of them, he thought. Optical zoom confirmed it: small, six-wheeled combat cars, backed up by light tanks. Just above and behind them hovered fighter drones. "They landed them beyond the horizon for a ground assault. I doubt our defenders are ready for this kind of battle. They don't have enough troops, and most of the turrets are optimized for anti-space."

"At least it's our kind of battle, sir."

"My kind of battle, Red. You can't possibly survive in the open against that many. This is my specialty."

"But sir—"

"I see a pillbox over there," interrupted Straker. "Run to it and defend. Do what infantry does best—hold your ground. Try to link up with friendlies. They have to have at least a few troops, even if it's just the security forces. You're better off helping them. Now go! That's an order."

"Aye aye, sir." Redwolf turned to sprint across the broken, rocky terrain.

Straker put Red out of his mind and began to run to his right, for the left end of the approaching enemy line. Standing toe-to-toe with such mass was a fool's game. He'd hit them from the flank and attempt to roll them up by ones and twos.

This nearest enemy formation, equivalent to a battalion of seventy or so vehicles, had chosen a relatively flat area with a road running down the middle, the best approach possible over the rough ground. Even so, it slowed them down as they tried to keep good formation.

The rough ground would be Straker's advantage. Staying low, he worked his way to the end of their line and let them go past.

His first kill was their leftmost overwatch fighter drone, and then another which turned to try to sniff him out. He wasn't sure what their response would be to this, for every military force had its own doctrine. He was hoping it would be the reaction of a natural flying creature, with a dog-bee or wasp pilot—to send in the aerospace forces.

He was right. The other ten close air support drones raced toward him, directing suppressive beam shots that struck rock all around him, sending up clouds of dust and gas from the vaporized stone.

This was exactly as he'd hoped. With his own multi-spectral sensors, he could easily see through the clouds, while the enemies were hindered and their beams were attenuated.

He picked off three before they backed up and diverted the armored vehicles.

Five down, sixty-some to go.

Two platoons of six vehicles each—one of wheeled scout cars and one of tracked light tanks—spread out and moved to surround his position. Rather than let them do so, he scurried to his right and tried his gatling against his lighter opponents.

The penetrators sparked against the material of the scout car, and then dug in as he extended the burst at a single spot. The vehicle slewed and rolled, smoke pouring from its burning carcass.

This was good news. It meant he had two weapons that could kill them instead of only one.

He put a force-cannon bolt into the tank behind the burning car, and it too brewed up, plasma shooting from every crack in its broken shell. The weapon was made to take down heavy tanks much larger than these, after all.

Straker raced ahead through the gap he'd created, splitting his targeting and firing left and right. The uneven ground allowed him to hit the soft underbelly of a car with his gatling for an easy kill, and his force-cannon bolt sliced through the side of a tank like it was made of cheesecake.

These Opters make poor ground warriors, he thought. They lacked heavies, missile tracks and battlesuiters compared to human forces—at least in this place. Maybe they had different force structures when planning on taking and holding ground. Perhaps this battalion was the equivalent of a few ship's marines, hastily thrown together to try to take advantage of a weakness in the human defense.

And they'd never faced mechsuiters.

Well, he'd school them now.

Racing in an arc, Straker used the rocks and pits to keep solid ground between himself and anything not a target. This was one of a mechsuiter's greatest strengths—his near-perfect situational awareness on the battlefield. The combination of mind, brainlink and combat-optimized SAI made his maneuvers as natural as a footballer maneuvering for position on a field, instinctively placing himself to best advantage.

As he did, he picked off his enemies two by two. In less than a minute, he'd eliminated both platoons.

Seventeen vehicles down, more than fifty to go.

Straker imagined what his enemies would do next. They had to be surprised and concerned that one opponent had already wiped out so many of their combatants. In their place he'd take no chances. He'd turn his entire force and try to surround and trap the mechsuiter before tackling further defenses.

Reversing course, Straker ran back the way he came, slipping out of the trap as the Opters tried to extend and encircle. As he did, he picked off three more cars and two more tanks, and ducked back among the rock formations.

Twenty-two down.

He became aware of activity above him—close above him, not the main space battle taking place kilometers higher. He sent out an air-defense radar pulse and identified two six-ship hexes of the largest enemy fighters, the ones that approached attack ships in size. Unlike the smaller drones, these had weapons that might severely damage or destroy him in one shot.

Those blasts started falling all around him, blowing rock into the sky and shaking the ground. He worked himself deeper into a small canyon and narrowed the arc where they could reach him. Glancing beam shots fell hot on his skin, but his field reinforcement and his superconducting layers shrugged off the heat.

For now.

Okay, they'd called in air support.

Well, he had some on-call air support of his own.

"Straker to Trinity," he said. "I need you to clear my skies. Can you pop over here?"

"Aye aye, sir," came Zaxby's voice. A moment later, Trinity exploded into existence from underspace, emerging for no more than two seconds. In that time, twelve hard-driven secondary beams skewered the twelve attack fighters, leaving them tumbling and falling to crash into the surface.

Before the first one augured in, Trinity had disappeared again, and Straker marveled at what an AI-controlled warship could do. Her triple brain made Straker and his mechsuit look slow. He shivered with the passing thought that perhaps it was a blessing all AIs before Indy went mad. If they hadn't, they might have transformed, or even replaced, humanity in ways he wasn't sure he'd like.

Perhaps they still would, if Indy could be reliably replicated.

But until then, the universe belonged to organic life—and organics fought over territory. That meant at least this little corner of the galaxy would remain comprehensible.

Before the dust of the crashes settled, Straker raced at his enemies, using the confusion to shield him from their sensors. Disrupting unit cohesion was another specialty of mechsuiters—although he admitted that didn't work on these Opters as well as it did on human troops. Even more so than Hok, the insectoids kept calm and fearlessly executed their plans. They could be surprised, but it didn't seem their morale could be broken. They probably had very little individual sense of self-preservation.

At least, the servant-creatures of the Queens didn't. Probably any being as intelligent as a Queen would value itself quite highly. He filed away that thought for later.

Inside the smoke and dust, he rampaged through them, killing whatever he targeted. Compared to their relatively basic combat vehicles, his mechsuit had sensors which were the height of sophistication. If this'd been an armored Hok battalion, he'd be constantly pinpointed by his own multispectral emissions, his radar and lidar, but these Opters didn't seem to have high-end detectors.

31

For now, he was a wolf—no, a tiger—among sheep. He didn't keep conscious count, but his SAI tallied his kills at fifty-five before the enemy broke.

Even then, they didn't really rout. They merely withdrew as rapidly as possible, back the way they came, presumably to their dropships, attempting to preserve some forces.

Straker activated his comlink to Redwolf. "SITREP."

"I've joined the defense forces, sir. They're pretty thin, but we fought off a battalion of those combat cars and tanks, and we don't see any more of them."

"I think I've driven another battalion off," said Straker.

"Alone?"

"You see Loco around here anywhere?"

"Hot shit, sir!"

"Thanks. Trinity helped... and these Opters aren't nearly as deadly as Hok in ground mode. Any other attacks to your perimeter?"

Redwolf conferred with someone for a moment. "No, sir, but the monitor above us is in bad shape. Commodore Gray better get here soon or we'll be overwhelmed."

"Tell your new buddies relief is on its way."

"I already told them you're out there kicking ass, sir. It really helped morale."

"Good. I'm pursuing the ground troops as they withdraw. Maybe I can take out their dropships, or at least gather some intel. Straker out." He was already bounding low across the surface, keeping a sharp watch above his head with his ADA lasers activated and charged. This took extra power, but the beams—too weak to knock anything down, but good enough to blind sensors—were vital to his survival. They fired automatically from time to time as anything came close from above, and now and again he sent a force-cannon bolt skyward.

If he'd been the Opter commander on the spot, he'd have sent an overwhelming force—say, a hundred drones—to pound Straker from the air. He suspected that there wasn't really an Opter commander in the human sense, though—not one that could adjust to surprises and give radically different orders. The Opters seemed poor at improvisation, or even at identifying what was important, when a Queen wasn't around.

By contrast, both human empires had tried to incubate a thoroughly competent chain of command, from the lowest corporal through the highest flag officer, so every leader could take over in a pinch.

Of course, it was almost certain that the Opters didn't know Derek Straker, the Liberator, occupied the pesky mechsuit. If they had, they might have done whatever it took to get him. It wasn't undue pride that made him think so. He knew his value to the Liberation movement, if mainly to its spirit and direction.

He might have killed a few more of the retreating enemies, especially those slowed by obvious damage, but he chose to observe. He wasn't sure how truly hidden he was, but there was no need to give the Opters help in targeting him, especially if their dropships had better sensors than their cannon fodder.

He peeked between two rocks at the crest of a low ridge to see the vehicles boarding, not the squat, blocky lifters he expected, but heavy fighter drones. It appeared the spacecraft each carried one armored vehicle in a conformal bay.

This may have explained the cars' and tanks' expendability. They were more in the nature of add-ons than true ground formations, utility vehicles used to seize or destroy certain targets on missions much as a human ship's marines might perform. Probably only a limited number of the heavy fighters were so equipped.

Straker recorded everything, but didn't bother to try to attack. His force-cannon wouldn't penetrate the fighters' armor at this distance, while their weapons might take him out with one lucky shot.

He tried to open a datalink to Trinity. It took half a minute, but eventually he was able to access a read-only feed.

From what he could sort out from the blizzard of information, not only was the AI-run ship destroying Opters by the dozen, but she was disrupting them badly with direct hacking attacks. No doubt they would improve their countermeasures later, but for now, there was a bubble around Trinity that no Opter could seem to penetrate. It must be defined by the nanoseconds of lightspeed within which, if the critters got too close, the AI's hacking could overcome any defenses.

Straker chuckled. Cybernetic bug repellent. That's what it was.

This went far toward explaining why Trinity and *Rhinoceros* hadn't been overwhelmed. By standing back to back, as it were, the thick-skinned armored dinosaur of space and the slashing bird of prey had managed to fend off all comers.

This didn't mean they remained pristine. Trinity's system status telltales showed at least half yellow and red. Many of her weapons were down, and her armor, never thick in the first place, had enough holes to fill a Sachsen whorehouse.

Rhino looked even worse. Parts of her burned with stubborn oxygen fires, and most of her weaponry was gone. What looked like insectoid battlesuiters crawled on her surface or entered her skin through rents in her armor. As Straker watched, an explosion gouted plasma into space, perhaps from a mine or bomb set by the Opter marines.

Trinity continued to orbit the monitor, stripping away attackers wherever she could, but she was only one ship, and despite her valiant defense, she was losing the fight.

Straker cursed at himself, trying to figure out what he could do. He could use his drop jets to blast out into space, but his mechsuit was no fighter. Without cover or maneuverability, he'd be shot to pieces in short order.

"Trinity, how close are Gray's ships?" he asked, desperate for hope and good news.

"They've already begun arriving, but only corvettes in numbers. They've been unable to reach us."

"What about the frigates and destroyers?"

"They're minutes from engagement. Even then, it will take time to fight through."

"If you can hold on for just a little longer—"

"I am aware of this fact, Admiral Straker. No amount of encouragement or micromanagement on your part will change the situation. You can't do anything to help."

"The hell I can't. Straker out."

But Straker had no idea how to make good on his words. He just knew he couldn't sit on his ass and do nothing.

He turned his attention back to the Opter heavy fighters retrieving their ground elements. There was one per tank or scout car, and as each vehicle locked into place, the aerospace craft took off.

One light tank lagged behind the rest, struggling with damaged tracks. It gave him an idea.

He worked his way around the flank to a position directly astern of the grounded fighter, the most likely place it lacked sensor coverage. He then crept up on it, staying as low as possible, using the rocky terrain for concealment.

When the struggling tank got close to its fighter, and was turning itself this way and that, trying to line up to enter its small deployment bay, Straker rushed forward. He scooped up a five-ton boulder on the way and smashed the tank's turret with it from behind, gambling that this would destroy any of its sensors and antennas, and possibly stun the driver. With any luck, from the fighter pilot's point of view, the tank would simply go dark.

He had no idea whether the fighter had sensors so close to its skin. Everything he'd seen about these Opters suggested rugged simplicity, with few extra systems. Their philosophy seemed to be that everything was expendable. This was highly efficient when lives were cheap and numerous.

Biologically, much of humanity's instinct to value people came from the steep investment in each human—twenty years or so until adulthood and usefulness to society, with enormous amounts of education for any technical role. Opter drone pilots, on the other hand, probably developed much faster, and, he guessed, needed only enough training to fight and die for their Queens.

Straker quickly dragged the tank closer to the fighter, hoping this would make it appear as if the vehicle were still trying to get aboard. When it was close, he shoved it into a small depression, and then scooped up rocks and soil to bury it under a shallow layer of surface material.

Then he stepped aboard in its place and braced himself in the deployment bay.

Would the pilot have sensors inside his bay? Or would the creature merely have telltales that told it when the tank was aboard? Or perhaps only something simple, like pressure detectors in the deck? That tank looked to mass about the same as his mechsuit, perhaps fifty tons.

And if the pilot wasn't fooled, well, at least he could tear the fighter apart from the inside.

Straker waited a long moment.

And then another.

Finally, the fighter rocked a bit and lifted.

Straker watched the ground fall away beneath him. He was braced in the bay, facing outward like a paratrooper in an aircraft's exit door waiting for the command to jump. The bright stars of space spun across his visual field, clouded by the sparkles of drives and thrusters and weapons fire.

Where would the Opter fighter go? Would it flee for the Nest Ships waiting far off? He thought not—not unless they believed they'd lost the battle. No, there were still a few minutes until the trickle of Republic ships became a flood. The Opters still had a chance to finish off the monitor, and Trinity, and overwhelm the Beta-2 base.

His gamble paid off. As he'd hoped, within seconds the fighter climbed and maneuvered to drop its combat vehicle on the skin of *Rhinoceros.* Only, that combat vehicle was Straker.

When he planted his magnetized feet on the armored hull of the monitor, he sent a force cannon bolt into the fighter's guts, in the direction he figured the pilot should be. The hot jet of plasma cut deep and fires began to burn.

Straker placed both gauntlets against the stricken fighter and shoved. He was happy to see it drift and begin to tumble, apparently dead. "Thanks for the ride, bug-buddy." He chuckled.

The burn of a beam on his skin reminded him how exposed he was out here on the hull. It would be stupid beyond measure to try to fight across the naked plain of the monitor's curving hull, with every fighter in his line of sight—and he in theirs.

Quickly, he ran for the nearest rent in the armor and dove into the ship's interior. Now, he was in his element.

Straker began to kill Opters.

He hunted the bugs though the interior for five long hours. It didn't matter that he fought Opters in Opter battlesuits. Battlesuits of any kind were simply no match for him. He was a giant among pygmies, with weapons that killed with one shot, one thought. Tanks couldn't have operated inside the monitor, but a mechsuit could.

Sometimes he had to crouch. Sometimes he ripped through walls. Sometimes he wished his suit was half its size—but always, always, he slaughtered them as he found them.

He relieved, and then led, scattered and demoralized groups of marines. They accreted around him like lost souls around a savior. He was an angel, the only one that could lead them out of Hell. Though weary, they followed him, supported him, guarded his back.

Long before they killed the last bug, Commodore Gray's capital ships turned the tide of battle. When it became obvious they would lose, the drone fleets turned as if of one mind and fled, saving as many as they could. Gray's grim warriors, angered at their losses, pursued them, killing all they could, until the Nest Ships fled into sidespace.

Gray's flagship, too slow to chase the enemy drones, boarded *Rhinoceros* with her own marines. Once his ship was secured, Commodore Pearson landed his sorely wounded monitor on the moon's surface, which allowed base forces and repair vehicles easy access.

Straker and the surviving marines soon stood proudly on top of the enormous ship as if upon a metal hill, surveying the battlefield. Most of the ground turrets, strongpoints and facilities of the shipyards remained intact, preserved by the tenacious defense of the heroic monitor crew and Trinity. Fleet ships cruised above in formation, and the moon's landscape swarmed with activity.

Away, on the horizon, he noticed a similar metal hill, and a line of vehicles heading toward it. He remembered there had been two monitors. That must be *Hippopotamus, Rhino's* fallen sister ship. He silently saluted her hulk for a moment and hoped there were survivors.

Commodore Gray comlinked from her flagship. "Congratulations, Liberator," she said, her voice devoid of its usual faint disapproval. "You managed to hold."

"We managed," he replied. "Thank Trinity and Pearson's people—and yours. Everybody fought hard today. Unfortunately, there are plenty of good men and women to add to the rolls of our fallen heroes."

"This is a private comlink, Admiral. No need for speeches."

"It's how I feel, Ellen. If that's a speech, okay, I'll own it. Now what did you call about?"

"I've got someone for you to meet."

"Oh? Who?"

He never could have predicted her answer. "An Opter defector."

Chapter 4

Straker, on the surface of moon Beta-2

Commodore Gray continued her surprising comlink report to Straker about the Opter defector. "He says he wants to talk to you, and you only."

Straker considered for a moment. "He, huh? It's male?"

"No doubt." Gray seemed amused by something.

"Send him to Trinity. I'll meet him there. Straker out."

He then called Trinity for pickup.

The Opter defector was brought aboard in shackles, snug duranium bracelets and anklets linked with chains. A heavy, treaded maintenance robot held a portion of the chain with one metal claw.

Straker had expected an insectoid creature, but this looked like an ordinary man, standing there in Trinity's wardroom, unassuming, of average height and build, with dark brown hair and faintly golden skin, well within the norms for the many variations of humanity.

Only his eyes seemed unusual: calm and serene, but still sharp, as if they saw everything around him. Those eyes rested on each being in the room in turn—Nolan, Zaxby, Redwolf, and then Straker, who sat with a welcome mug of caff in his fist.

"Have a seat," said Straker, gesturing. "You want a drink?"

"Anything with caffeine," the man said in an ordinary tone. He sat and folded his shackled hands on the table in front of him. When he was given a mug of caff, he sipped at it with evident satisfaction.

Straker had the odd impression the fellow considered himself unrestrained. He certainly didn't act like a prisoner. He wasn't defiant. He wasn't subservient. He simply… was.

"I'm Derek Straker," he said. "They call me the Liberator. Who are you?"

"My designation is Myrmidon. You can call me Don if you like." The man's voice seemed very ordinary, with an Earthan accent hard to place.

"You claimed to be an Opter, but you look human?"

"As do you, Liberator, though you're almost as far from original human stock as I. It appears you've been infused with Opter biotech."

Straker sat back in mild puzzlement. "Not quite. I was infected with the HOC parasite, but I took the antidote before it ran its course."

"And where do you think the Mutuality obtained the HOC parasite?"

Straker's mind reeled.

Zaxby, Nolan and Indy all tried to speak at once, demonstrating that they weren't quite as integrated as Straker believed. Zaxby won out by dint of throwing himself into the seat next to the prisoner and talking to him from a range of centimeters. "I knew it! I knew the Mutuality's demonstrated biological expertise was insufficient to create something like the Hok. Otherwise, there would not only be Hok, but all sorts of other biotech options for its citizens—such as rejuvenation, or physical alterations for unusual environments, or—"

Straker interrupted loudly, reaching to shove Zaxby aside. "Pardon the annoying squid brainiac, Mister Myrmidon. So Opter biotech made the Hok? Why?"

"Call me Don, please. Because the Mutuality was losing to the Hundred Worlds at the time. The Sarmok faction gave them the biotech to balance the scales, disguised as a natural discovery on a newly explored planet. It was untraceable to the Opters, and of course the Mutuality Party oligarchs embraced anything that gave them greater control of over their own citizenry... as any government naturally would."

"Yes... it was a win-win for people like that," Straker said, eyes unfocused. "If a citizen couldn't be 're-educated,' he'd be turned into a Hok battle slave." He folded his hands and placed his elbows on the table, leaning forward to focus on Myrmidon—or Don, as he seemed to want to be called. "And the Opters did this to keep the Huns from winning?"

"Yes."

40

Straker thought about this for a moment. "How long have Opters been interfering in human affairs, encouraging them to fight each other? Balancing the scales, as you say?" He snapped his fingers. "And the nectar. That's just one more way of screwing with us, I bet. How long?"

"For centuries."

"Why?"

"I believe you already know the answer."

"I can guess." Zaxby opened his mouth, but Straker nodded to Nolan. Maybe letting the woman speak for Trinity would curb some of Zaxby's verbal outbursts. "Can you?"

Nolan's pale green eyes blinked. "To keep humanity weak and busy fighting itself." She turned to Don. "Only it didn't work as expected, did it?"

"Not in the long run, no. Every gift to one side or the other, every convenient, well-timed breakthrough—and there were many—restored the balance, but the tension between the two human sides kept military technology advancing. If not for the failure of the promise of AI, the progress curve would have turned exponential, as was expected hundreds of years ago. However, this technological singularity never occurred. Instead, humans kept breeding and spreading from world to world. Opters and other species couldn't compete. It was a dilemma."

"So what changed after so long?" asked Straker. "Why attack us now?"

Don stared and blinked at Straker. His eyebrows rose slightly.

After a long moment, Straker got it. "Me. Or at least, the Liberation. I've upset the balance. We have a real shot at unifying humanity now, and you Opters can't stand that idea."

"Not all Opters. The Sarmok faction."

"What's this Sarmok faction?"

"There are two major factions within our species. The Sarmok is dominant, but not all-powerful, composing approximately five-sixths of our people. They border human space. The Miskor is the other faction. They are located on the other side of Opter territory."

41

"And you're one of those Miskors," said Nolan, approaching Myrmidon to lay a hand on his shoulder.

The man—if such he were—seemed to take no notice of the touch, and spoke. "I am Miskor. I've been embedded for years among the Sarmok, gathering information."

"So you're an internal spy," said Straker. "An operative."

"I am."

"Then how can we trust you?"

"I don't expect you to. I expect you to verify everything I say. Without my information, though, you're likely to make grave missteps. I don't think you wish to court a general war with the Opters."

"You don't call this battle the start of a serious war?"

Myrmidon smiled faintly. "This was an independent raid, tacitly approved by the Sarmok and conducted by some of the most belligerent Nests. If justification is ever needed, it will be claimed either that these Nests acted as rogues, or that they were attempting to aid the legitimate Mutuality government against the Liberation rebels."

"Fake reports. Propaganda, lies and politics," Straker spat. "I hate politics."

"But you're a warrior, and war is politics by other means. Across the galaxy, life's base impulse is to spread and grow and ruthlessly dominate its neighbors, to its own benefit."

"That sounds like a miserable view of things."

"It is," Don said, "though I said this is life's *base* impulse. With sentience comes morality, which regulates the ruthlessness of the jungle. A sufficiently advanced species will endeavor to think honestly and act morally."

"That doesn't describe most species I know."

"Precisely. While enlightenment is a goal, it's also a journey."

Straker snorted. "Now you're talking in cryptic mumbo-jumbo, like my Kung Jiu instructors."

"Do you have writing materials?" Don asked.

Zaxby reached into a drawer and retrieved a pad and stylus, activating its analog graphics feature before placing it in front of Myrmidon. The Opter-man scribbled with the stylus for a

42

moment, and then turned it to show Straker a list of mathematical equations.

"Yeah, so?"

"To you, that's cryptic mumbo-jumbo. But to this Ruxin here, whom I perceive to be a technician or scientist, it is—"

"—a rather elegant proof of Ridzo's fifth theorem!" Zaxby cried, seizing the pad in three tentacles and holding it as if precious. "It's not the first proof I've seen, but it is undoubtedly the most elegant! I must record this and distribute it to my network of Ruxin colleagues—"

Straker crossed his arms. "Great, point made. You have to know things to know more things. But you also have to translate your obscure higher principles into actions that help people in the real world. That's what I'm doing. I'm liberating people from oppression. I can't tell them how to live after that. In fact, I don't want to keep intervening—unless they start up with the oppression and subjugation again."

Don folded his hands again. "That's a fine goal, but even if you succeed in the short term, you'll only be putting out fires."

"Then the fires will be out. Call me a fireman. I know my strengths and weaknesses. I'm not a builder or a ruler."

"What if you could be more than you are?"

Straker shrugged. "What if I don't want to be?"

"Then there'd nothing more to be said on the subject."

"Fine." Straker stood. "Trinity, debrief him fully. Verify as much of his story as you can, and then turn him over to Fleet Intelligence for further interrogation."

Don stood as well. "I'll provide all the information I can, but sending me to rot in some think-tank is an unwise use of my skills."

"I'll be the judge of that." Straker nodded at Nolan, and she followed as the robot marched the chained man-thing out of the room toward the ship's tiny brig.

He turned to Zaxby. "What do you think?"

"He seems to be as human as you are. Indy has a full suite of biometric sensors on him and could sense no deception. However, we don't know his capabilities. Perhaps he could lie and show no sign."

43

"He seems sincere—and what he said about meddling with humans is plausible. Obvious, even, in hindsight."

Zaxby blinked all four eyes in sequence. "It may also explain my own people's subjugation by humans."

"You weren't any more subjugated than humans were to other humans."

"It may seem so to you. You never had to deal with the bullying, the taunts, the mean-spirited abuse from your adolescent fellow cadets at Academy, who knew they would never be as capable."

Straker snorted. "Oh, yes I did take that crap—many times. They knew I was destined to be a top mechsuiter, and some resented it. But I bet you brought a lot of it on yourself by acting superior and snooty."

"I am superior."

"And snooty. But people don't like their noses rubbed in it."

"Fortunately, I have no nose."

"But they do. Why don't you think with some of your Trinity brain for a while and try to see things from other points of view? I'm sure Miss Nolan has a lot of insight into humans."

"That's a good idea. I am constantly amazed by your lack of stupidity, Derek Straker."

"And I'm constantly amazed that, even brainlinked to an AI and a human, you haven't improved your people-skills."

"Thank you," Zaxby said primly.

"That wasn't a compliment."

"I believe it was. It's also ironic, coming from you. I never heard anyone laud *your* people skills."

Straker sighed. "Forget it. I'm totally beat. Gonna catch a nap. Hold any comlinks. Wake me up in three hours and I'll read the debrief."

Later, fresh mug of caff in hand, Straker read over the written summary of the defector's debrief, and then read it again. It appeared Myrmidon's story checked out, as far as Trinity could tell. More interesting, he'd provided an enormous amount of useful intelligence on Opter territory, technology and weaponry.

Everything Straker saw worried him.

He carried the handtab and mug to the brig. The door unlocked and opened with a push of his elbow. Of course, Trinity controlled everything aboard her body. Or Indy did. Whatever. He couldn't figure out where one began and the other ended.

Inside, he sat facing Don, who still wore his chains like jewelry rather than shackles. "I'm amazed at this windfall of intel," Straker said, holding up his handtab. "What made you decide to betray your people?"

"I'm not betraying my people. I'm attempting to restore balance. Opters revere balance, elevating it to a spiritual significance. Like many revered spiritual values, however, it's often sacrificed by those greedy for gain."

"So you're acting for the greater good. I understand that. I'm thinking about doing some things that my old chain of command in the Hundred Worlds would consider treasonous, though I deem them to be for the greater good. Yet, giving us all this intel could lose a lot of Opter lives…"

Myrmidon shrugged. "Opter Nests don't hold the lives of individual members in high regard. Losing warriors, workers or technicians is analogous to a corporation losing machinery. The Nest is the valued entity, not the member."

"I'd guessed that, from your tactics. But you might lose whole Nests, if it comes to war."

"We may."

Straker tossed the handtab on the table, rubbed his jaw and thought. "But since you're Miskor, from the underdog faction, you don't necessarily mind if the Sarmok take some hits. It will bring things closer to the balance you like."

"Very astute. That's one consideration."

"What's another?"

"We believe the current Sarmok intentions to be immoral, intended to subjugate or, if necessary, wipe out the majority of your species."

"We, the Miskor?"

"Yes."

Straker sighed. "This is all pretty convenient, this story you've told me. It's plausible, it's consistent, and it's seductive. I want to believe it. But it could also be a complete

45

illusion, a setup and a scam intended to get me and the New Earthan Republic to act a certain way."

Don spread his hands to barely less than the limits of his chains. "You'll have to decide for yourself."

"Oh, I will. But here's another question. Why are you so smooth? Why aren't you like other aliens? Even someone like Zaxby, who's been around humans much of his life, doesn't act like one. Nobody would ever guess you're an Opter."

The Opter-man took a deep breath and sighed. "I suppose it's because I've been studying the human worlds all my life. I've lived among you off and on for years, immersed in your civilization. Culture matters more than the body or its appearance. Opters can use biotech to reshape bodies at will—which renders the body largely irrelevant as a marker of identity. In every way that matters, I *am* human."

Straker pointed a finger at Don. "That's exactly what I mean. Smooth. You got an answer for everything, and that's what bothers me. In fact, the one flaw in your perfect humanity is that you're too perfect, too stereotypically human—because real people are never as poised and perfect as you are. But con men are."

Myrmidon shrugged. "A catch-22, then. If I made mistakes, you'd see them as evidence of deception or untruth. If I don't, you see that fact as evidence of deception or untruth. Damned if I do, damned if I don't."

"Another perfect answer."

"That's how you perceive it. I *am* a more advanced soul than you are." Don said this without a hint of smugness, as if merely stating a fact.

Straker's answer dripped sarcasm. "Oh? Really?"

"Yes. Just as you're above a recruit at boot camp. The recruit doesn't even know what he doesn't know, and at first must be convinced of his fundamental ignorance."

"True wisdom is to know you know nothing." Straker rubbed an eye and sipped his cooling caff. "Socrates."

"Among others."

"But I always thought that was bullshit. I know what I know, and it ain't nothing."

46

"But you have no inkling of what you don't know. For example, you not only didn't know the Opters were an enemy, you didn't even know Opters existed until recently—nor did you know you should care, and how they influenced your life. One key to success is to expect to be surprised at all times."

"If you expect to be surprised, you can't be surprised. Okay, fair enough. But how does that get us anywhere now? How can I trust what you say?"

"Seeing is believing."

"Meaning what?"

"I can take you to the Opter space. You can walk among us as I do."

Straker's eyes widened. "What, they're gonna let a human just roam around?"

"You still misperceive. No, they will not let a *human* roam around, but they will let an Opter do so. I am Opter. The bipedal form of a human I wear is of little relevance. Bipeds have been incorporated into the Nests and Hives over the last few centuries, just as the workers and warriors and other specialized Facets were over the preceding millennia." Myrmidon smiled. "If we can turn humans into Hok in the space of days, we can certainly turn them into Opters. And breed our own."

Straker shuddered involuntarily at the horror of a biotech that would steal people's humanity. He'd gotten used to the idea of the Hok, but only by ignoring its deeper implications.

Now, he had to face those implications. Even more than the threat of conquest, these Opters could corrupt and change what made people human.

What made *him* human.

What made Straker himself.

Were those the same thing, though?

"Trinity, you listening?" Straker asked.

"I am."

"Send out a message to your brainiac network, all the labs and biologists and so on. Get working on a vaccine, something to protect people from Hok and Opter biotech. If we already have one, make sure it gets distributed and that people are vaccinated."

"That will be an enormous undertaking across a thousand systems—a matter of years."

"Then the sooner it gets started, the better."

"I will pass the message." Trinity's voice seemed to express doubt, but Straker didn't care. His job was to get people to do what needed to be done, not tell them how to do it.

"That's a wise precaution, but the Sarmok can create endless new strains that will get around any vaccine," said Myrmidon.

"Move and countermove. It will be a biological war. Don't forget, we humans have engineered some pretty nasty diseases ourselves. We've wiped out whole species of bugs on our planets."

Myrmidon raised a palm slightly. "You don't need to convince me. I'm working toward peace and balance."

"Too bad that usually means fighting a war first."

"You mouth platitudes of peace, Liberator, but you love war."

Straker's eyes narrowed, but he considered before answering. "Part of me does. I was bred to be a weapon, genetically enhanced for it. Everybody likes to do something they're good at. I bet you *love* this secret-agent stuff, even if you claim you wish it weren't needed. But we're both smart enough to look past what personally gives us our hard-ons, and work for the greater good—right?"

"Right."

"Then let's go."

Myrmidon raised his eyebrows. "Go?"

"To your people. I need to see for myself. That's what you said."

"I have an Opter ship hidden among the asteroids. It's stealthy and sidespace-capable."

"Will your ship hold two?" Straker asked.

"It will."

"How long is the trip?"

"At least twelve days each way, and you should plan for a few weeks of observation."

"So, call it two months minimum." Straker stood. "Does it matter what I bring along?"

48

"No. I'll provide all you need."
"Then I'll meet you at the airlock in one hour."

Chapter 5

Engels, three days later, New Earth

Commodore Carla Engels sat at the head of the *Indomitable's* main conference room, surrounded by fellow officers—ship captains, squadron commanders, aides and even admirals of the former Mutuality, now New Earthan Republic, navy.

Yet she felt alone.

Well, except for the aides. Those aides—mostly Ruxins and humans, but also two elephant-trunked Huphlor, a lizard-like Suslon, and even a Thorian wrapped in his rad suit—were present in the flesh. The others were holograms, but the only proof of this was their lack of substance. Their holovid and audio were flawless.

Engels, seeing *Indomitable's* inability to reassemble in time and reach the battle at the Murmorsk inner worlds of M-3 and M-4, had decided to keep the battleship separated and ready for transit. When she'd been unable to sway Straker from his insanely hazardous course to visit Opter space in person—when had she ever been able to talk him out of anything?—she ordered Commodore Gray and the fleet back to New Earth, formerly Unison.

Now, *Indomitable* hung in orbit above the New Earthan capital, the rest of the fleet within easy transmission range. After a quick consultation with retired admiral Benota, Minister of War, she'd ordered this meeting to assemble.

Yes, ordered—never mind that she had no genuine statutory authority to do so. She was just a jumped-up ship captain, and all she really had going for her was her status as the Liberator's wife, good right hand and space tactician.

But she and Benota had a plan for that... and if Straker didn't like it, well that was too damned bad. Running off for two or three months meant he didn't get a say.

Engels rapped a gavel on the table, and the holographic conferencing system transmitted the action flawlessly to every other location in the secure network, where the attendees sat. "I call this council of war to order," she said as the chatter died. "I yield the floor to Minister Benota."

"Thank you, Commodore. Our first order of business is settling the chain of command." The large, florid man, now dressed in a simple civilian suit, glanced at a row of more than thirty admirals and generals, formerly of the Mutuality. They'd had many days to think about their status—bureaucratically frozen by the new Senate's Reorganization Edicts—and where they would end up in the new regime. If there was resistance, now was when it would manifest.

Benota continued, "Right now, all of you flag officers have your positions, your staffs, your privileges—and your pensions—according to the Edicts. Before I continue, does anyone wish to retire at your current rank and grade? If so, simply indicate that fact and leave this meeting. You'll be a private citizen within weeks. No? Last chance, ladies and gentlemen."

Nobody moved.

"All right, let it be on your own heads then." Benota picked up a hardcopy folder. "I have here the new flag staff table of organization, confirmed by the Senate. All but the following three of you are mandatorily retired at the grade of Flag One, regardless of former rank: Devereux, Kapuchin, Lubang. The rest will be processed out immediately."

Benota waited for the howls of protest to subside. "You will note in your copy that you may appeal this action through the usual channels. Thank you, and goodbye." All but the three designated flag officers winked out, disconnected from the hololink.

"Good riddance," Benota muttered.

"Will they cause trouble?" asked Commodore Gray, sitting to Engels' right.

"I knew they wouldn't volunteer to retire, so I gave the Hok in their offices specific instructions to immediately distribute my orders in writing to all the staff. They'll escort them off the premises and revoke their security clearances and access." He smiled a wintry smile. "I'd like to see them start trouble."

"Seems a bit highhanded," Gray replied.

51

Benota waved airily. "I am but a humble servant of the duly elected Senate, carrying out their orders. Don't worry, Commodore—or should I say, Admiral—Gray. It's all legal."

Gray lifted a dark eyebrow. "Admiral?"

"Yes, in charge of the new Home Fleet. Does that suit you?"

Gray glanced at Engels, who grinned. "I nominated you. Think you can handle it?"

"I can."

"Good."

"But what about you... Commodore?" Gray asked.

Engels turned to Benota. "Yes, Wen, what about me?"

Benota made a production of looking in the folder. "Ah, yes, here it is. Given that you're the Liberator's wife, we couldn't very well—"

"Screw that, Minister," Engels snapped, playing her part. "I've earned my place on my own. My relationship to Derek Straker is a separate issue. What's the will of the Senate?" She held her breath waiting to see if Benota would follow through on what he agreed—or if the Senate had allowed him to.

"How does Fleet Admiral sound?" Benota said.

Genuinely surprised, she smiled. "What's that mean?"

"It means you'll be the senior operational naval officer in the Republic. Top dog in the field."

"Woof." Engels' forced herself not to gape. She'd expected a big promotion, but to be given the whole Fleet... She shook herself and straightened. "Okay, I... I accept. But will the rest of the chain of command?"

"For now, the Hok follow the Senate's orders through me. We're at war, under martial law, and I'm the Minister of War."

Engels' eyes narrowed in suspicion. Was her promotion some kind of payoff, to get her to go along? *"Quis custodiet ipsos custodes?"*

"Latin? 'Who...'"

"Who watches the watchers," she said. "What keeps you from being a dictator?"

Benota spread his hands. "The same thing that conquered the Mutuality. You, *Indomitable,* and the rest of your military forces. Commander Paloco and the Breakers are here in the capital, not to mention your marines and your ships above us. The Hok are compliant to my orders, but there are nowhere near enough of them to actually enforce my will on more than this one planet. The rest of our brave new Republic has to believe itself legitimately governed. I suggest that unless you want to go running from planet to planet with that battleship threatening to bomb everyone back to the Stone Age, you have to trust me to knock the heads and herd the cats while you worry about our next big problem."

"Which is?"

"The Hundred Worlds. They're gobbling up our systems as fast as they can while we're barely able to defend our Committee Worlds—our Central Worlds, I mean—from this new Opter threat. We need to work fast to raise new forces, and plan for a war on two fronts if necessary." Benota scowled. "Liberation won't mean much if all Straker did was set us up to be conquered by the Huns and the bugs."

"The Huns haven't responded to our overtures for a truce and talks?"

"They're stalling while they grab more territory—and frankly, our local forces aren't fighting all that hard. They feel off-balance and defeated by the Liberation anyway. The Huns don't look so bad."

Engels scowled and bared her teeth. "I'd have thought they'd be overjoyed to get out from under the Inquisitors and want to defend their newfound freedom."

"The border worlds have been fought over so much, the people are war-weary. With the fear of repression gone, many of them actually want the Huns to come in with their big money and their entertainments—or that's what they hope. They see the propaganda broadcasts that makes the Hundred Worlds look like a consumerist paradise." Benota sighed. "That's always been the Mutuality's dilemma—patriotism goes only so far in the face of perpetual misery and fear. The citizenry's spirit has collapsed. I'm afraid our brand-new Republic may collapse with it—especially with the Liberator off on this... reconnaissance mission."

Engels held back a sharp retort. Benota was right, damn him, on every point.

53

The only silver lining to this storm cloud was the fact that the new Republic was just so damned big. Even if the Hundred Worlds gobbled up a hundred more, the old Mutuality still had a thousand systems to draw from. She was beginning to see why the war lasted so long.

"We can't help where Straker chooses to go and for how long, so let's get past that and do what needs doing," she said. "Distro the rest of that reorg plan if you please, Minister. We'll reconvene in an hour to discuss operations."

"Operations?"

"As you said, we have to fight the Hundred Worlds. With Straker gone, I'm the supreme field commander, and I intend to give the Huns a punch in the nose that will bring them to their senses."

* * *

"Display Calypso System, and zoom in on C1, the first planet," Admiral Engels said when the holo-conference resumed.

The table lit up with a detailed depiction of an unusual star system. A curved streamer of dense gas millions of kilometers long reached out from the primary, a small orange sun. At its end it thickened into a ball.

The ball had at its core a supermassive gas giant, which was slowly eating the plasma the star fed it. At some point in the last few million years, the planet had swung close to the star, and its gravity had plucked at its corona like a child unrolling a skein of cotton candy. Soon enough—perhaps within only a few hundred thousand years—the gas-eater would gain enough mass to ignite into a star of its own.

Within the nimbus of swirling gas around the planet hung a gargantuan orbital fuel processing facility, by far the largest ever built—covering a captured asteroid moonlet over one hundred kilometers across.

"Felicity Station," Engels said. "No other fuel factory is as big or as efficient, because nowhere else do we find this concentration of rich gas just floating in space. Easy access to a variety of hydrogen isotopes and byproducts. It supplies half the Republic military with high-grade fuel and exotic elements—and it refines the thickest known stream of antimatter anywhere. They collect over ten kilograms a year there, one atom at a time."

Admiral Gray whistled. "That would make one hell of a bomb."

"That would be wasteful," said Zaxby, who was running the holo-table. "Antimatter has many useful qualities for research and engineering. Destroying it to obtain an explosion that could just as well be generated by a fusion device would be foolish."

"Like using diamonds for bullets," Engels agreed. "The point is, this is a valuable facility, and it's in the path of the Huns' advance. They've been methodically absorbing systems so far, playing it safe by taking and securing each in turn rather than striking deep into our territory, so I'm confident in the timeline of their arrival, plus or minus a few days."

Captain Zholin, now assigned as commander of the superdreadnought *Stuttgart,* spoke up. "So we meet them there and stop their advance—at least along that axis. But I've been studying the intelligence reports. There are nineteen separate Hun fleets, each taking a system every few days or weeks. Turning them back at one place won't solve the problem."

"I don't intend to turn them back, Captain Zholin." Engels smacked her fist into her palm. "I intend to crush them. I haven't trained for war my whole life just to play interstellar chess with fleets—a game we're losing."

Admiral Gray raised her eyebrows. "Now you're sounding like Straker."

"I learned from his wins—and his mistakes. This isn't the Liberation, where we're trying to incite people to rebellion and get them on our side. This is straight-up war, and we have to press our few advantages."

"What advantages?"

"*Indomitable,* for one. Two, our certainty they will strike Felicity Station at Calypso. Three, the time we have to prepare. It's our home ground, and they'll be operating at the end of their supply lines." Engels sighed. "I once thought the Hundred

55

Worlds was always the pious defender and would make peace when the opportunity presented itself, but our new Senate's sent a dozen official messages to their Parliament and received no response but continued conquest."

"It's hard to get people to talk when they think they can win by force," said Benota.

The Ruxin War Male Dexon stirred his tentacles. "'War is politics by other means,' the human Carl von Clausewitz said. He also said the target of our efforts must be the enemy's will to fight. This is why the Liberation was successful. We broke the Mutuality's will, even while a thousand worlds remained militarily untouched."

"That's right, Commodore Dexon," Engels replied. "And I intend to conduct some violent 'politics' in order to target the Huns' will to fight. Ladies and gentlemen, please clear the room of all but flag officers."

Zaxby stood as if to go, but Engels waved him down. "Not you."

"So I'm a flag officer?"

Engels *humphed.* "Trinity is unique. Let's call you a special advisor to the Admiral of the Fleet—if you want the job."

"We would be honored. Well," he said hastily, "*I'm* not, but Marisa is, and Indy seems impressed, though she is young. I, however, have worked with many admirals, and am not easily dazzled by rank and status. I—"

"And to think I was worried your annoying individuality could possibly be drowned in a group-mind," Engels deadpanned. "Zaxby, run that sim of my plan, would you?"

* * *

When Engels presented her plan, the room fell silent. The senior officers seemed to ponder.

Or maybe, she thought, she'd shocked them.

Their sudden protests confirmed it. Even the usually phlegmatic Benota had opened his mouth, though he'd shut it again with a grimace as others babbled. Engels stood and waved them to silence. "Don't try to tell me it can't be done.

56

Tell me the problems, and then tell me how to solve them. Who first?"

That slowed them down. They all looked at each other as if deciding who would be the naysayer. Zaxby's tentacles seemed to twitch, and then grow still. Engels wondered if that was the other parts of Trinity overriding his natural chattiness. "Zaxby, you have something? Trinity?"

"We have run a detailed analysis of your plan, Admiral Engels, and can present it at this time."

"You can work with the staff on the details later. For now, what's the top problem—and its solution?"

"Obviously, ships, especially escorts—destroyers, frigates, and corvettes. The battle with the Opters, though a victory of sorts, was costly. Over one hundred escort ships destroyed and two hundred more damaged. Over nine thousand trained crew killed."

"But we didn't lose any capital ships."

"That is fortunate—but that has only exacerbated the divide between the neglected and overburdened escort classes." Zaxby turned to Marisa Nolan, who rose from her seat among the now-absent staffers. "Doctor?"

The slender, ethereally pale woman stepped forward. "Morale among our naval escort corps is on the verge of collapse. The Mutuality treated their personnel badly, used them as a dumping ground for problems and assigned them every dirty job, such as military suppression of dissent. Combined with overwork and lack of maintenance, we might as well say that, as a fighting force, they're now nonexistent. They gave the last full measure against the Opters—yet, there's no relief in sight."

"We should rotate personnel from the capital ships and the reserves," said Admiral Gray. "Step up recruitment and training. Raise pay and bonuses."

"That takes money," replied Minister Benota drily. "Our new Senate is already agitating for tax relief and elimination of odious regulations, in the name of liberation. It seems the people want the freedom Straker promised—but they don't want to pay for it."

"Not my problem," snapped Engels. "The Senate will have to come up with the money somehow—unless they want the Huns to gobble up everything."

"It is *our* problem, Admiral," Nolan replied. "I've been among bureaucrats for over eighty years. Zaxby is almost two hundred, and Indy processes thought faster than either of us. Together, Trinity assesses that our war efforts will soon fail— not from lack of tactical leadership, or even of military strategy, but from economics and governance. That's always the Hundred Worlds' advantage. The Republic has inherited a collectivist system that barely functions. We need years, perhaps decades, to reinvent ourselves. Barring that, we need a government that knows how to get the most out of the aging dinosaur of a bureaucracy."

"Great," Engels replied. "That's the problem. What's the solution?" She looked around. "Anyone?"

Benota cleared his throat and stood. "I hate to say I told you so—but I did. Liberation is all well and good, but right now we need a strong hand to manage the economy until the war is over and we can transition to a less-regulated model."

"You want to be the economic Czar as well as the Minister of War?"

"Not me, no."

"Who, then?"

"We already have a Director, though Straker sharply curtailed his powers. I suggest we use him."

"DeChang?" Engels' tone was skeptical. "He's dangerous. Too ambitious."

Admiral Gray stage-coughed. "I've known Emilio for quite a while. He's vain and he's arrogant, but he's also visionary and competent. It was his vision for a war-winning battleship that got him squeezed out of the Committee, but it turned out he was ahead of his time. Remember, without *Indomitable,* the Liberation would have failed. Yes, he'd like to be the big boss again, but even at its worst, the Mutuality was no dictatorship. If our new Republic can't channel one man's ambition, it's not worth saving."

"So how *do* we channel his ambition?" Engels asked.

Benota said, "Before the Senate gets too comfortable with the Liberator's absence and realize they're really in charge, I'll work with DeChang to pass an expansion of his executive tax-and-spend powers—only for the duration of the war, of course."

"Fine," Engels replied. "How does that get us the forces we need for this fight—and for the next fight, and the next?—and we're not even talking about the Opters yet."

Benota bounced his ham-like fist on the table. The VR sim was so good, Engels could hardly tell the man wasn't really in the room. "We'll get you the forces for your 'Battle of Calypso.' We may have to strip the rear areas of everything, we may have to create money we don't have and make promises we can't keep, but we'll get you your ships. Heavens help us if you lose, though. The Republic won't survive it."

Engels drew herself up. "I won't lose. We won't lose. If everyone here does their duty—and there are no leaks of this plan—then we'll hurt the Huns so badly they'll have to negotiate."

Chapter 6

Straker in Opter-land

Twelve sidespace transit days later, as he and Myrmidon approached their destination deep in Opter space, Straker was still smarting from Carla Engels' harsh words aimed at his "stupidity and pigheadedness" in going alone.

"Our new enemies want you dead and the Mutuality restored, and you go and hand yourself over to them, without even bringing Loco to watch your back!" she'd yelled over the comlink.

"Can you imagine Loco on a sensitive spy mission?"

She'd ignored that. "And even worse, you're not even going to come see me first?"

"No time, my love," he'd said. "Every delay gives the Opters more chances to raid us, and for the Hundred Worlds to push deeper into our territory. You and Gray and Benota can handle the Huns and the war of fleets—I'm not a critical factor there. But only I can deal with the Opters, and that means understanding them, finding out the truth."

Engels had ranted and raved, but he'd held firm. Now, he and Myrmidon had arrived at the Alka System deep inside Opter territory, traveling on the agent's fast courier. And she was fast. The same trip would have taken a capital ship six weeks or more and exhausted her fuel.

Despite the speed, Straker was ready to get out of the cramped little vessel.

The days had, however, given him the leisure to talk at length with Myrmidon—or Don, as he liked to call himself. "Don is a common enough phoneme in Earthan and most of the Old Earth languages that it usually passes easily on human worlds," he'd explained.

Straker had tried without success to find any holes in Don's long skeins of conversation, his easy explanations of his views on Opters and humanity and the aliens on their various borders.

He'd learned a lot, but he still had the nagging feeling he was being subtly led toward some viewpoint Don wanted.

Straker hoped he survived the visit. This deep in enemy territory, everything became a long shot.

And, until now, the Opter-man had provided proof of nothing.

That was obviously about to change, as the screen showed multiple Opter ships plying the routes among the various planets, moons and facilities of the Alka System. Most of these were smaller than those humans would use—or at least, the crew portions were. Some of the freighters, for example, appeared to be composed of small, powerful tugs with cargo modules attached, rather than the usual Earthan arrangement of a hulled ship with internal bays. Probably Opters needed fewer amenities than humans.

Don brought his scout ship into a planetary docking ring, a massive, amazing structure that floated above the planet's equator in a perfect geosynchronous orbit. More than twenty-five thousand kilometers in circumference, it was attached to the world with dozens of space elevators, like spokes in a wheel.

"This is a far more efficient system to access space than fusion-powered ships individually ascending and descending. It uses less energy, needs less gravitic compensation, and provides a better platform for orbital industry than parked asteroids," Don said.

"It's also extremely fragile, vulnerable to attack or sabotage," replied Straker. "Hit an asteroid with a bomb or missile, and you damage only that facility. This thing... if you could crack the structure, I bet the entire thing would unravel, buckle and come apart."

"Less than you might think. The materials used are stronger than duranium, based on genetically engineered spider-silk infused with graphenoid molecules. And Opter society is far less vulnerable to infiltration by humans. In a pinch, every Opter would take up arms for the defense of Nest and Hive."

"Meaning you think you're superior?"

"We are, in some ways. In the most obvious ones, perhaps. In others, no. I've come to respect humans on the whole, even

61

while as individuals you vary wildly, and fail miserably to cooperate." Don caught Straker's gaze. "I've also come to realize that there is no one definition of superior. The human definition usually compares symmetries and declares one thing better than the other. That's easy when militaries go head to head. It is not so easy in deciding, say, which approach to survival is better. Your dinosaurs dominated Old Earth—until an asteroid radically cooled their environment. All their size, ferocity and so-called superiority suddenly became irrelevant when their food sources vanished. Smaller, hardier things survived where the giants could not. In fact, 'dinosaur' became a metaphor for that which is doomed to extinction."

Straker grunted. "Adapt or die. I know that."

Don turned away. "Well summarized. But do you truly understand?"

Straker had no answer, so he changed the subject. "I take it this is a Miskor world?"

"Oh, no, Derek. This is a Sarmok Hive System, with only Sarmok Nests." Don stood from his pilot's seat and picked up a duffel bag he'd prepared beforehand, and gestured for Straker to pick up his own. He then took a few steps to the ship's exit portal and pressed his palm to the sensor pad.

The door opened wide onto an enormous flight deck for small craft. Beings of all sorts scurried to and fro with tremendous purpose. Some of their errands seemed inscrutable, but some were obvious—loaders pushing cargo, creatures with duffels not unlike Straker's own, maintainers with tools, refuellers with tanks and hoses.

The surprise for Straker was the high proportion of humans—okay, bipeds, at least—he could see. There were only a few dog-bees, a smattering of armed warrior wasps, and a fair number of the worker ants, composing perhaps a third of the beings here.

The rest had two legs and two arms and many seemed indistinguishable from humans. Some had odd coloring—green, purple, bright red—and some had abnormal skin—scaly or chitinous or moist and glistening. But about half could have passed unnoticed on human worlds.

"Welcome to Terra Nova," Don said.

"What?" Straker said sharply. "That means 'New Earth,' right? That's pretty ballsy, you Opters calling this place after humanity's home."

"You've never even been to Old Earth, you said."

"Doesn't matter."

"And if the Sarmok have their way, this is the breeding ground of a new humanity."

"Meaning?"

"You'll see."

Don took a step, but Straker grabbed his arm. "And how do I fit in here? Won't they spot me or smell me as different and arrest me?"

"I took the liberty of altering your biochemistry slightly."

Straker shook the smaller man roughly. "You did what?"

Don looked down at Straker's grip, then back up to his eyes. "Don't be a pussy, Derek. Your Hok biotech made you ninety percent Opter, as far as the average Facet you encounter can tell. I merely tweaked your scent to add Sarmok pheromone markers like my own. Only if you're subjected to deeper bio-analysis could someone tell you're not Hive-raised."

"I don't trust you, dammit."

Don peeled Straker's thumb and fingers off his arm. "Don't be an idiot. You put yourself in my hands when you decided to come with me. Make a decision and stick with it. Otherwise, I might as well take you back right now."

"Okay then, let's go back."

Myrmidon took a deep breath, sighed, shook his head, and turned back to his scout ship. "Great. Another five days cooped up a ship with no shower—and you."

"Wait."

"What?"

"We'll stay. I was testing you."

Don's mouth curled as he looked sidelong at Straker. "I know."

"You know?"

"This is my area of expertise, remember?"

"What, deception?"

63

"Spycraft. Psychological combat. Manipulation. You can't beat me at my own game, Derek. You have to decide to trust me. You're in my hands. Just like I decided to put myself in your hands when I came to you."

Straker rubbed the back of his neck. "But if you're like the rest of these Opter creatures—these *Facets,* you called them?—then you're programmed to consider yourself expendable, so you wouldn't actually care whether you live or die. In fact, there could be a thousand Myrmidons, cloned to look and act the same and infiltrate us."

"That's very astute. There *are* many of our infiltrators in your society—some highly placed indeed. And as I said, I've spent years living among you. But as for clones... every being with free will quickly becomes individualized once he lives among you. Your very randomness and lack of regimentation assures it. And once each of us assimilates into human culture, we're free to defect, to form our own goals, morality, and beliefs about right and wrong. If we acted like Opters, we'd never blend in. A perfect fake, if truly perfect, is no longer a fake. It becomes real."

Straker barked a laugh. "All that philosophy is so much mental bullshit. You spin these theories that sound good, but in the end, what matters is that you're so good at faking that we can't tell—not without tests, like you said. So..."

"So?"

"So you're right. I have to act like I trust you, even if I really don't. The dice are cast." Straker stuck a finger in Don's chest. "But I'm watching you."

"Fair enough." Don turned to walk toward a distant portal. "Now let's get going before we attract attention. Human-opts are given a lot of leeway, but the insectoid Facets still tend to regard us as dangerously unstable. There have been cases of warriors killing us because they misunderstood some action that humans would find commonplace."

Straker followed alongside. "Such as?"

"Such as getting drunk and starting a fistfight. Insectoids interpret that as a Facet gone insane."

"Okay, no barroom brawls."

"We'll see about that."

"Meaning?"

"Meaning, once we're on the surface, different rules apply. There are areas where human Facets are given completely free rein, no matter the results."

"No matter the results?"

"That's what I said."

"So they won't interfere."

"Not once we're on the surface. But we still have to play our roles. I'm an agent. You're my trainee. Try to act like it."

Myrmidon wouldn't answer any more questions about what that meant, so Straker allowed himself to be led along. After a minimum of processing, which consisted of a quick scan of his body and his baggage, they boarded a train down the nearest cable.

Cable was a pale, weak word for the connecting tether their vehicle traversed. The tether measured at least a hundred meters across, and the train's gravplating was set so that Straker felt as if they traveled upon a long, thin bridge from the ring behind them to the vertical wall of the blue planet in front of them. The top and sides of the train cars were made of transparent crystal. Apparently even Opters liked to take in the view as they traveled.

All of their fellow passengers were humanoid. Most of the exotics—that's what Don called the nonstandard ones—spoke some kind of clicking Opter language with each other. The standard humans mostly used Earthan, in a variety of perfectly ordinary accents, though two conversed in what Straker guessed was Chinese.

"This is creepy," said Straker. "I feel like I could be arriving at any human planet."

"Then *we've* done *our* job well," Don replied.

Straker realized he was speaking of the Opters—or maybe just the Sarmok—when he said "we," as others around them might overhear. "Yes, *we* have," Straker said, and reminded himself to be cautious.

As he observed the fake humans, his main impression was of childlike happiness. Unlike Myrmidon, they didn't seem like they would fit in with human society—or if they did, real humans would find them odd. He tried to figure out what it was.

They acted like kids in growup bodies, he realized. Like ordinary civilian children untouched by hardship, as he was before the Hok killed his family. Not like the cadets at Academy, too old before their time and training for war. Yet they looked like adults.

One woman stood out from the crowd, though. Her measured gaze was different, direct and confident, and she glanced across the car at them a little too often.

Straker nudged Don. "We're being watched."

"I know," Don murmured. "But now she knows you know, and now that you told me, she knows I know too. You make a bad spy, Derek."

"Who is she?"

"A new operative, testing out her skills in a closed environment." Don reached inside his tunic and produced a small leather folder, which he opened in her direction, and then shut with a snap. She nodded and departed the car. "She won't bother us again."

"You sure there aren't others watching?"

"If they are, they're using technical means, not their own eyes. As my *trainee,* the watchers will expect you to make mistakes, but if you make too many, I may have to send you back to the larval pods. Get it?"

Straker processed this odd declaration, remembering Don was speaking for the benefit of possible listeners. "Sure, Don. I'll try to do better. Sometimes I try too hard to act like one of those crazy weird humans."

"Yes, and you're doing it now."

"Sorry. Just practicing." Straker shut up for a while, until the transport approached the surface. When they were perhaps twenty kilometers from the surface—which still looked to Straker like a wall rather than the ground—he realized the scale of the construction he could see, and the extent of the cityscape.

"How many people live here on Terra Nova?" Straker asked.

"I don't know."

66

"Guess."

Don turned blandly toward Straker. "A trillion? Two?"

Straker swallowed. "A thousand billion..? That seems impossible. That's a hundred planet's worth of people on one world. How do you feed everyone?"

"With technology, and enough energy, anything's possible. The environment is completely geo-engineered. Cities extend downward more than a thousand meters in many places, with plenty of hydroponic farms. Rather than thinking of Terra Nova as a planet, think of it as a giant habitat that happens to be big enough to sustain an atmosphere."

"It's a damn *hive.*"

"You're starting to see."

When the train arrived at the Terra Nova surface, it followed a curving track that left all the cars resting on level ground. The two men stepped out into a station that could have come from any human planet. Signs directed travelers to other tracks where trains would take them to destinations with half-familiar names like Caledonia, Hong Kong and Shepparton. Cafes and restaurants served food and drink to the populace, and music wafted from a piano a woman played near a fountain.

"This is one of the weirdest things I've ever seen," Straker muttered.

"On the contrary, Derek. It's one of the most ordinary things you've ever seen. What makes it weird is that you know it's all manufactured and contrived."

"Like an amusement park, where the building fronts look like houses or hotels, but they actually contain rides."

Don nodded. "It's the dissonance between the appearance and the underlying truth that gets you. In fact, new agents feel the same on their first assignments on a human world—except they have to accept that it's real, and the exercises are over. If they get caught, they might never come back."

"So they do get caught?"

"Of course. The human intelligence services apprehend our people quite often."

"So they know about Opt—um, *our* infiltration?"

67

"Certain spy divisions know or suspect, but our agents' biology is flawless, so those caught are generally believed to be from their human enemies, or from independent worlds." Myrmidon began walking and Straker followed. "Let's get going."

"Where to?" Straker asked.

"Baltimore."

"That's a place, right?"

"Yes. It's named for a city on Old Earth."

Myrmidon bought tickets with an ordinary credit stick. A maglev train whisked them hundreds of kilometers through a tube evacuated of air, allowing the vehicle to reach speeds impossible in atmosphere. Twenty minutes later they walked out onto the streets of Baltimore.

Straker stopped abruptly, shocked at what he saw, as the crysteel doors of the train station slammed shut behind him. Ragged, filthy people stared at him, some drinking from liquor bottles, smoking various weeds, or even shooting drugs into their veins. They sat or lounged on streets littered with garbage or leaned against buildings covered with graffiti. Broken windows gaped like the mouths of concrete monsters, and a stench filled the air.

"What the hell?" he said.

"Yes, and welcome to it," Don replied. He shoved away a panhandler who stuck a hand in his face and mumbled something incoherent. "Better get moving. Remember, this is a diz."

"Diz?"

"That's what we call these enclaves, like Baltimore."

"Why diz?"

"Some Old Earth name for an artificial environment. Dizzy-land, I think they called them." He stepped out into the empty street and walked down the middle, as far away from the denizens of the cityscape as possible. Straker stayed close, trying to watch everywhere at once.

They rounded a corner and nearly walked into a full-blown riot. Dozens of uniformed police were beating civilians with batons while other civilians threw rocks and bottles at them. Chemical smoke stung Straker's eyes. An officer took out his

68

slugthrower—a slugthrower, not a stunner!—and fired, hitting one of the rock-throwers in the neck. She fell and began to bleed profusely.

"What the hell is this place?" Straker asked as Myrmidon drew him back into an alley, out of the way. "Why are they rioting?"

"Who knows? Food shortages, police brutality, their sports team lost or won, it doesn't matter. All our human Facets have to go through Baltimore."

"Ah... like an amusement park, right? A diz," Straker chuckled, understanding. "It's an exercise. Special effects, fake blood..."

Don shook his head. "No, it's not an exercise. Not the way you mean. It's artificial, but there's nothing fake about it."

Straker stepped out to look again at the woman lying in the street, the red pool expanding on the pavement. "You mean she's really been shot?"

"Yes."

"Shit." Straker sprinted to her and threw himself to the ground. The woman looked up at him with glassy eyes and gasped. "You're gonna be all right," he said. He reached beneath his tunic and ripped off part of his undershirt, tried to stanch the bleeding.

A blow on the back of his head surprised him, and his combat reflexes took over. He rolled to his feet and found himself facing an officer with a baton.

"Back off, scumbag," the cop said. "You're interfering with police business."

Straker snatched the club from the officer's hands and threw it away. The man clawed for his holster, and Straker took that weapon away from him as well. "What's wrong with you?" he asked. "Call an ambulance! You're a police officer. Do your job!"

The man backed up and, with one eye on Straker, ran for two of his fellows. Don grabbed Straker's elbow and pulled. "Stop it, Derek. You're interfering with the diz." He dragged at Straker's arm. "We need to go."

"But that woman's *dying!*"

69

"That's an appropriate response, *trainee*," Don said loudly, "but you're here so you can get used to the barbaric human callousness and brutality you'll see in the field." He shoved Straker away. "There's nothing you can do. Do you want to be sent back to the pods for recycling? You have to purge yourself of your morality. Remember, you're supposed to have been through Baltimore."

Straker was about to push Don aside and go back to the woman when he saw that the pump of her arterial blood had stopped and her eyes were open and staring. Five cops approached with drawn slugthrowers, and one more had a heavy stunner. Reluctantly, Straker ran with Don around a corner, reminding himself he was deep in enemy territory.

Three turns of the ways later, Don led them into a blind alley with a door at the end that was marked with an abstract graphic symbol. Perhaps it was alien writing. Don placed his hand against a sensor pad and it opened. They passed into a featureless corridor.

"That woman really died," Straker said.

"That *Facet* did, yes." Don gazed dispassionately at Straker. "She was a slug anyway."

"Slug?"

"A new humanoid Facet, barely adult. Just enough education to make her fit for a diz like this. She was probably about two years old, with a lifespan of six or less, to make sure she didn't grow beyond her assigned limits."

Straker stared back at Myrmidon with disgust. "You're breeding sentient beings just to kill them? That's *evil.*"

Don shrugged. "Welcome to the diz."

Chapter 7

Two weeks after Admiral Engels' council of war, Calypso System

Admiral Engels brooded on *Indomitable's* arena-shaped bridge. Clever use of gravplating made it possible to walk along the inside of the bowl without difficulty, and each section had a clear line of sight to every other. The only obstruction was the hologram that hung in the center, displaying the tactical and strategic situation in the area.

Right now, Engels had it scaled to show the entire Calypso System out to flatspace, its star and Felicity Station tiny near its center. For the last three days, the battleship and a force of every capital ship scraped up from this side of the Republic had waited, hidden deep inside the glowing ball of gas that surrounded the planet designated C1.

Hiding even a ship of *Indomitable's* size was easy. The gas was opaque to sensors beyond a hundred kilometers, and even that close, the dense swirls mixed with thousands of rocks and captured asteroids to make detection and targeting problematic.

A perfect place for an ambush.

Her strategic feed came via hundreds of encrypted relay drones from stealthy passive sensors, seeded in stellar orbits all across the system. In other words, Engels could see out, but the Hundred Worlds fleet couldn't see in.

Assuming they showed.

With its valuable fuel processing station, Calypso was the next logical place for the Huns to strike. The star system was now on the front lines of their methodical advance, and Engels had worked very hard to sweep for the enemy spy drones that would naturally be sent to reconnoiter. She'd also brought the ambush force in under emission-control, or EMCON, using impellers only to eliminate all energy signatures.

Standing by had Engels on edge. She paced and she sat. She inspected sections of the battleship. She went over the plan with her captains.

She'd already gone over it exhaustively with Commodore Dexon, who commanded the outsystem task force—the one that would play the role of bush-beaters to her waiting group of hunter-killers. Dexon's fleet of fast ships lurked far out in flatspace among Calypso's comet cloud, the millions of balls of ice that circled slowly around the star.

A third force, composed of twelve relatively slow but tough heavy cruisers, plus Captain Zholin's SDN *Stuttgart,* hung conspicuously in space near C1. The group was anchored by the local defense monitor, one that dwarfed the cruisers as a whale dwarfed dolphins.

Unfortunately, there were no orbital fortresses at C1. Lacking mobility and obstructed by the gas cloud, they would have been pointless to build—so they never had been.

"Transit detected," said Lieutenant Tixban, her officer at Sensors. The Ruxin fed the data to the hologram and a new icon flashed. "Far from. the optimum sidespace emergence point."

"They're being cagey," Engels muttered, standing to approach the holo. "It won't matter, though. How many contacts?"

"Nine so far, but they're still appearing." Tixban swiveled an eye toward her. "It will be approximately half an hour until I have an accurate estimate."

"I know, I know. For now, take a guess and run the battle sim from their actual position."

The half-hour fled as Engels watched the computer prediction of how the battle should play out—or at least, its first half. No machine-mind, not even Trinity's, could foresee what would happen within the gas cloud, at C1 and Felicity Station. There were far too many variables—and too many ways for things to go wrong.

"So?" Engels said to Tixban after the half hour.

"As we expected. It is their Tenth Fleet, commanded by Admiral Braga."

"Admiral Braga?" Engels swung her head back and forth between the holo and Tixban. "Lucas Braga?"

"Correct."

"Then he survived the Battle of Corinth. I should be glad... but I'm not glad it's him I'm facing."

"He was your commanding officer?"

"He was. And a good man. This..."

Tixban's tentacles communicated tentativeness. "Sucks? Is that the right word?"

Engels shook her head ruefully. "Right. It sucks. But it won't change anything."

"It does not bother you that you will be fighting against your former comrades from the Hundred Worlds for the first time?"

"Of course it bothers me, but this is war. We tried to talk to them. Today, the Hundred Worlds military gets to pay the price for their politicians' greed for more territory. They've shown no mercy, so we can't pull our punches." She took a deep breath, trying to feel as confident and stoic as she sounded. In reality, she felt like she had dagger in her gut. Admiral Braga... he'd almost held Corinth, where she was captured and her life changed so radically. She wished it were that idiot Admiral Downey she faced instead, the fool who'd blown it for Braga.

"This changes nothing," she repeated more loudly. "We stick to the plan."

"Aye aye, ma'am," the bridge crew replied in unison.

"Fleet composition?"

Tixban zoomed in on the enemy. "Eight SDNs, eight DNs, sixteen battlecruisers, sixteen heavy cruisers, thirty-six lights, fifty-six assorted escorts... and two fleet carriers."

"Carriers?" Engels leaned in. "They're pulling out all the stops." Carriers were generally considered outmoded as fleet assets, too slow to keep up with escorts or their own attack wings, too lightly armored to stand and fight, and the whole arrangement too complex for the cost. Mostly they were used as auxiliaries and motherships, to carry attack ships and landing craft from system to system, usually brought in well after an area was secured, not as primary combatants.

"The range is too long to be sure," Tixban said, "but I suspect they are being used as supply ships, to allow their fleets to operate farther from their bases for a longer period of time, and also to carry garrison forces for their conquests."

"I'll keep that in mind." The carriers might make good prizes, then, if they could be captured instead of destroyed.

Four hours later, after leisurely scouting and maneuvering, Braga's Tenth Fleet turned to cruise inward and cross the edge that marked the bubble of curved space that surrounded the star, Calypso. From then on, they couldn't flee via sidespace—not unless they ran back across that line.

Eight hours after that, Engels had returned from a meal, a shower and a nap to watch as Commodore Dexon's ships made the short sidespace transit from the comet cloud into a position directly behind the enemy. In fact, they'd jumped into Braga's own arrival position, more or less, and now they turned *en masse* and began pursuing the Hun ships at full speed.

Engels imagined Braga's consternation as he realized he couldn't retreat the way he came. He would believe Dexon's fleet was a relieving force, just arrived from deeper in Republic territory after several days in sidespace, rather than a fleet that had been lurking, waiting.

However, Braga shouldn't be too perturbed—yet. The way ahead toward his target—Felicity Station orbiting above C1 inside the gas cloud—would seem clear, except for Zholin's inferior fleet consisting of the monitor *Triceratops,* the SDN *Stuttgart* and a dozen heavy cruisers.

As Braga's fleet outgunned C1's only apparent defenders by at least ten to one, his logical move was...

"There you go," Engels said as Tixban reported the Tenth Fleet had increased acceleration toward their target. Rather than cruise in at their leisure, now Braga's ships would hurry in, flip over to decelerate, and enter the gas cloud at a speed slow enough to see where they were going. They'd then have to spread out and search for Felicity Station, as Engels had made sure that the fuel factory was also under full EMCON.

Afterward, Braga would plan to run for the other side of the system, his mission accomplished. Or perhaps he expected to turn to fight, if he managed to figure out that all of Dexon's "capital ships" were actually light cruisers with Trinity-designed false-signature emitters, the better to drive the enemy into Engels' trap.

Engels bared her teeth at the thought that the Tenth Fleet wouldn't get to exercise either option.

Two hours later, Braga's powerful fleet flipped over for its deceleration burn. Dexon's ships continued to hurry inward, appearing to maintain flank acceleration for dreadnoughts. Actually the fast escorts merely loafed along, under no strain, decoy emitters transmitting at full power.

Engels was glad Benota had managed to scrape so many light units up from all the surrounding systems, and doubly glad she hadn't had to give them a frontline mission. An easy victory under these circumstances would do a lot for the escort corps' morale.

Engels paced, checked and rechecked everything, and bit her nails to the quick as the enemy approached the enormous gas cloud. With its glowing streamer reaching millions of kilometers in a grand curve back to the star, it was a sight to behold. She hoped Braga would be lulled into a false sense of security. Perhaps surprise and shock would minimize casualties on both sides.

Zholin's force began firing railguns at extreme range. With the enemy's sterns presented, a lucky shot might go straight into an unprotected fusion drive port and wreak havoc—but the odds were slim indeed. They got slimmer as Braga's ships began varying their aspects slightly and spread out their formations.

One battlecruiser took a blow from a lucky hit, and her drive stuttered, and then winked out. That was the only damage done, though—until they came within effective beam range.

First, the monitor *Triceratops'* centerline particle accelerator blazed. Nothing Braga had could match it, but he'd already anticipated the attack and launched missiles. Skirmish warheads burst between the fleets, specially designed to fill the engagement zone with gas, dust and crystalline sand. At the same time, his ships increased their evasive maneuvers, even while continuing to decelerate.

Engels muttered to herself. "Come on, come on." She couldn't help it. Even though this phase didn't matter much—it was really just a diversion, designed to show Braga the resistance he expected—she rooted for Zholin's success. Every ship he damaged on the way in was one less to fight during the ambush.

But Braga's countermeasures held. The particle beam no doubt brushed a few targets, but none of the drives died. The eventual addition of *Stuttgart* and the cruisers' fire accomplished nothing in the face of the Huns' profligate use of skirmish warheads. Engels envied their resources. No doubt they thought they would be able to burn through their loadouts, and then replenish from the carrier stocks.

Now, over a thousand shipkiller missiles from Zholin's task force sprang forth in fleet strike mode. This was an all-or-nothing tactic, a full launch whereby earlier weapons were soft-launched and later weapons caught up with them, all controlled to form one attack. Given that Braga couldn't do any fancy maneuvering—every minute he delayed was a minute for Dexon's "dreadnoughts" to catch up to him—this meant he'd have to fight his way through.

Braga launched a mix of antimissiles and defensive shipkillers, trying to trade warhead for warhead to thin out the fleet strike. Of course, only a percentage intercepted the attacking missiles as they spiraled and dodged in random patterns. ECM drones mixed in blanketed the area with confusing transmissions to allow the attackers to slip through. At the same time, Zholin continued to fire beams, further confusing the battlefield between the rapidly converging fleets.

At the last moment before the fleet strike, Braga's ships flipped over as one, a beautifully executed maneuver that put their armored noses forward and brought their full weapons suites into play. Beams blazed and railguns sprayed, utterly shredding the fleet strike. There were simply too many ships, too many point-defense weapons, for the Republic missiles to get through to the capital ships. A few of the screening escorts were heavily damaged by proximity blasts or bomb-pumped laser warheads, but that was poor return for the expenditure of the missiles.

Or it would have been poor return if the whole maneuver weren't an exercise to lull Braga into overconfidence.

Now Zholin's fleet backed up on impellers, as if their commander had made the perfectly rational decision not to sacrifice his force. Engels hoped Braga didn't wonder too deeply that the defenders didn't take the even *more* rational course, which would have been to back up into the gas cloud and fight from inside. Doing so would theoretically favor the defenders, limiting the attackers' ability to coordinate fire.

But it shouldn't be a stretch for Braga to believe that the defense commander simply wasn't going to fight stubbornly in the face of such overwhelming odds. Furthermore, Braga would expect an attempt at an exit ambush, when he would leave the gas cloud and be briefly vulnerable to the waiting task force's concentrated fire.

As she hoped, with the force in front of him out of the way and under pressure from the pursuing "dreadnoughts," Braga plowed straight into the strange nebula, confident in his power.

"Expand," she said, and Tixban changed the scale. Now the gas cloud filled the hologram above the bridge, and then it faded as the software removed the distracting plasma. A network of stealthy sensor drones ensured she had good eyes on every ship of the enemy.

Braga's fleet spread out and fired probes of its own. Escorts formed a loose shell to recon as much of the area as possible, but they pulled back when they began to encounter a thickly laid minefield.

But not too thick. Engels could have made the enemy pay more heavily, but she didn't want to risk turning them back. If the Huns had shown up with a smaller force, that might have been a problem.

As it was, however, the escorts reformed in minesweeper mode, firing specialized probes and detonating any mines they found. They efficiently cleared the explosives with only moderate damage to a few ships, and the Tenth Fleet advanced toward the planet C1.

Of course, they still had to locate Felicity Station. All they would know for sure was that it orbited the planet, somewhere.

But Engels and her forces knew where it was. By herding the Tenth Fleet at the right time with Dexon's and Zholin's forces, she'd ensured it was on the other side of the gas giant from where the enemy had entered—and it was even now using its limited maneuvering engines to stay as far away as possible.

"Helm, impeller maneuvers," said Engels. "Bring us into position. Transmit to our two hemispheres to begin surrounding the enemy."

She watched the holo-display as each half of her ambush forces maneuvered outside the enemy's range of vision on impellers only, remaining under EMCON. This was only possible because she had complete intelligence on the Huns, and they had nothing on her. Her ships moved as stealthily as they were able, and soon formed a loose sphere around the enemy.

With *Indomitable* directly in the Huns' search path.

"Activate decoy number 14," she said.

One of the many moonlets seeded with emitters over the last three days slowly turned on an eclectic suite of electromagnetic sources. As she'd not been sure of the relative positions when the enemy entered the gas cloud, she'd directed Trinity to set up more than twenty decoys. Now, number 14 masqueraded as Felicity Station—directly in front of *Indomitable.*

According to plan, Zholin would be maneuvering his outside force into position to catch any leakers from the ambush, and Dexon would be racing forward at true light cruiser speed, much faster than Braga would expect. The time he would think he had to escape was even now flowing away like sand through an hourglass.

Chapter 8

Straker and Don on Terra Nova

"So they don't chase anyone beyond the diz?" Straker asked Myrmidon as they walked down the passageway behind the weird Opter diz of Baltimore. Now and then, human Facets in simple uniforms strode by on purposeful errands, ignoring the two men. "You walk away and you're free?"

"The barriers recognize my bio-code. Ordinary Facets are stuck there until they meet the parameters to move on to another diz."

"And what are those parameters?"

"None of the participants knows, at least in advance. Only the controllers know. In some, everyone moves on quickly. In others, only a select few graduate. Rather like life—nobody knows the rules, and it's not fair."

"But you can get out."

"I can."

Straker lowered his voice. "Can we talk here?"

"Yes. Agents and their trainees are given a lot of leeway, including the leeway to speak wildly during roleplay."

"So you're a big cheese in the spy community?"

"Big enough to have freedom of movement, small enough that nobody wonders why I'm here."

"Like the Lazarus Inquisitors."

"Like that."

Straker chewed that over in his mind. "I bet you're a clone."

"We're all clones, Derek, grown in larval pods and raised in communal crèches—just like our insectoid Facets."

"All but me."

Don shrugged. He seemed to shrug a lot, especially when he didn't necessarily agree with something but didn't want to argue.

"Are you trying to imply I'm a clone too?"

"Clone, genetically engineered, a warrior designed and built for a purpose, grown in a womb instead of a vat... is there any real difference?"

Now it was Straker's turn to shrug, and think for a moment. "Did you give the Mutuality their cloning biotech?"

"Of course."

"Dammit, you make it seem like humans can't come up with anything themselves."

"They can, but getting something for free—and knowing you'll get something for free, if you're one of the elite few who know about the Opter gifts—makes human societies complacent—which is exactly what we want. Why work hard at research when you know some aliens are so far ahead of you?"

"Because they're dangerous?"

"Until now, we've been very careful not to present a military threat." Don opened a door and stepped through. When Straker followed, he shut it tight. "This diz is Cupertino."

Unlike Baltimore, the street they entered was merely drab, not dirty and littered. Drably dressed people walked the sidewalks. All the people wore mirrored goggles that covered and sealed their eyes, and wrapped around to plug into their ears as well.

The people were also talking to themselves—or, of course, to others, presumably via comlink. They must be viewing a virtual overlay of at least sight and sound. Some made motions in the air to manipulate virtual objects or controls.

Don led them down the street to a café where everyone sat in his or her own tiny booth. Robots served them dull food while they continued to talk to and touch the air.

"This is a diz too?" Straker said. "Doesn't seem so bad. They probably see and hear a world that's much nicer than the real one."

"It's not bad, at first. Yet, the suicide rate here is higher than in the one we just left."

"You let people kill themselves?"

"You're asking the wrong questions, Derek. You need to put aside your gut reactions to what you see."

"So what's the right question?"

"There is only one right question when it comes to sentient beings, Derek."

Straker looked around, pondering, trying to remember the bits and pieces of philosophy, religion and psychology he'd picked up in his life. "Okay. Why?"

Don nodded. "That's it. Why do people do things? Learn that, and you can influence them. Add power, and you can control them—and yourself."

"So why are they acting this way? Disconnected from everything real, living in a virtual world?"

"You've had experience with virtuality. You tell me."

Straker thought about Shangri-La and the way he felt there. "It's seductive. It's life-porn, feeding pleasure and banishing pain. But that's not real life."

"How many humans actually want to live real life? How many, when presented with comfort, take it without critical thought? In our tests—almost all of them."

"If that were true, human society would go all virtual, then collapse. Only a small percentage of people actually get addicted to VR."

Don chuckled. "That's what you've been told? In reality, when everyone's doing it, when it's the way to make your living and conduct your life, it becomes the norm. The only thing that keeps everyone from going virtual is economics and regulations—in other words, those at the top keep it limited, and under control."

"Why would they?"

"Because they know that a bunch of drones who've lost touch with reality are no fun to rule, and they eventually become less productive, not more."

Straker looked around. "But why do this, here? What's *this* diz for? In fact, what are any of them for?"

"All dizzes are meant to turn Facets into humans, or weed out the ones who won't adapt."

"Why?"

"You tell me."

Straker thought. "For some reason, you—we—don't simply want human-shaped hive drones. We want people who can pass

81

in the real human societies. For that, they have to have real experiences. But I don't see how this is real."

Don shrugged. "They don't stay in one diz forever. They progress through them."

"Right... So they're really just progressive training scenarios."

"Of course. Let's move on. This one's called Campus."

They passed through another door into an area that resembled a large school. Pleasant but uninteresting buildings squatted among indifferently landscaped walkways. Groups of people lounged or walked here and there—always groups. They showed a mix of humanity's range of physical characteristics. Their only difference was their clothing. Each group wore clothing of a specific color—green, blue, red and so on.

Two groups approached, reds and greens, each composed of about fifteen people. Smaller groups of blues and yellows looked on.

They met at a narrow point of the walkway. Straker expected them to flow through each other, or perhaps each to move to one side and go by, but instead the people deliberately blocked each other and began to argue.

"Why don't they just move past?" Straker asked.

"They wear different colors."

"What does that have to do with anything?"

The argument escalated to yelling and threats. "They hate each other."

"Why?"

"Different colors."

"There must be some grievances between them, right?"

"Not at first."

Straker watched as the people began fist fighting—clumsily, though, like children, wrestling, pulling hair, punching ineffectively. "This is some kind of setup, right? Another scenario?"

"Of course."

"So you made them fight?"

Don shrugged. "The diz controllers don't force people to do anything. They merely set conditions and let human nature take

82

over. In this case, Facets new to the diz are given colored clothing."

"And what are they told?"

"Nothing."

"Bullshit. They must be told that the other color is bad or something."

"No. In fact, there are countervailing pressures. For example, those who've formed attachments in other dizzes are always given different colors."

"So those guys stay friends."

"One might think so."

Straker turned his head back and forth from the brawl to Don. "You're saying they don't."

"It's very rare. Within days, the new Facets have nearly always adopted the viewpoints of their color—which other colors are their enemies, which are their allies or neutral, their supposed reasons to fighting."

"So there *are* reasons."

Don smiled faintly. "Of course. The greens occupied a red dorm nine years ago. The blues beat up a yellow last month. The purples are being favored by the faculty this term, and the oranges paid them off. Yesterday, the reds didn't get dessert because the blues took them all first. The greens feel like they're under-represented on the communal councils—and so on, and so on on."

"Stupid reasons to fight. Are those things even true?"

Don shrugged. "Does it matter?"

"Of course it matters! Truth matters!"

"It should. But does it? Or is it only belief that matters?"

"You can't make something true just because you believe it!"

"But what if you believe you can?"

"That's insane!"

Don shrugged.

"You're totally corrupting these people."

"By giving them colored clothing?"

"By taking children—even if they look like adults, they're only a couple years old—and leading them astray."

83

"All we do is introduce a Facet to a diz with a certain set of conditions and see what happens. We don't tell them how to act. Once the Facets experience what they need to, they're rotated out and into another diz, where they'll learn different lessons. Eventually some begin to develop critical thinking skills."

"And the rest?"

"They're stuck. Or they get moved to a different diz track. Even I don't know the ins and outs. It's up to the controllers."

"Or they die, like that woman."

"Something like that. Come on."

Don led them to another diz, composed of grand, beautifully decorated interior spaces. There were no windows, but warm artificial lighting made it seem comfortable. People sat at rows of machines with screens, performing incomprehensible work. Robots rolled among them, dispensing drinks and food so people didn't have to leave their workstations. Occasionally, someone got up from their seat, to use the facilities apparently.

Some people were fat, some skinny, but all looked unhealthy. Many sucked on smokesticks or vaporsticks while they worked. They all seemed completely lost in what they were doing, seldom speaking to anyone even as they were packed in, shoulder-to-shoulder.

The one strange thing about the place was the noises coming from the workstations. They beeped and rang and played music incessantly. Now and again, someone would raise a hand or even jump to their feet in triumph as the machine in front of them would make loud, equally triumphant sounds— but the worker would soon sit back down and continue pushing buttons or touching screens, performing their obscure tasks.

"What are they doing?" Straker asked as the two men strolled among the workers. "What's on those screens—that looks like more like entertainment than work, but the people don't seem happy. Except for a few now and then, that is."

"Very perceptive. It's called *entertaskment*—a combination of tasks and entertainment. They're rewarded with credits for completing tasks, and the credits can be traded for special tasks that provide more reward."

"And what happens when people earn enough reward credits?" Straker figured they would buy residences or vehicles, travel or take vacations, eat out and party, invest in businesses or buy art... what *did* people do with money anyway? He'd had so little time and opportunity to use it during his life he hardly knew. He mused that he must have a lot piled up in his military pay accounts in the Hundred Worlds—not that he'd ever get access to it, of course.

"They can buy things," Don replied, "but they seldom do."

"Really? Why not? What do they do with the credits?"

"They move up to higher reward tiers, where they actually have to risk their credits in hopes of winning more."

"Risking? Winning? That sounds more like gambling than work." Straker knew something about gambling, from Shangri-La or from the usual games troops played, wagering drinks or luxuries or hard cash when they had it. He'd never been all that interested in playing those games—which had made him that much more of an outcast, until he'd made enough rank he wasn't expected to play anyway.

"It *is* gambling, but it's never called that."

"What happens when they win a lot? When they get rich?"

Don smiled without humor. "What do you think rich people would do?"

Straker hazarded a guess, not that he was particularly familiar with rich civilians. "Become entrepreneurs, or big-businesspeople? Or celebrities, entertainment stars? Do they go on planetary cruises and drink the finest wines? Or run for elected office, gain power?"

"You'd think so, but with rare exception, no."

"What do they do, then?"

"They keep gambling, bigger and bigger. Until they lose it all and fall back to the working level, where the rewards are small, and so are the risks. Where all they have to do is show up, put their minds on autopilot, and slave away."

Straker stopped and turned to face Don. "Are you trying to make this about me? That I'm gambling, always bigger and bigger, until I lose?"

"Is that how you see yourself?"

85

"That's how people around me see me, sometimes. My woman—my wife, Carla, I mean—says so sometimes. That I can't keep from gambling. But my gambles aren't to win a vacation or more credits."

Don opened his hand and made a there-you-are gesture at those around them. "Neither are theirs, really. If they really wanted that vacation, or those credits to actually build lives, they'd take them and stop gambling. But they don't. Because it's the game that matters, not the gain."

"And you think I'm the same."

"That's not for me to answer."

Straker turned away, sucking breath through his teeth and thinking. "The difference is, I have a goal. I want to free mankind. You've brought me here to a place where a different branch of mankind is enslaved in crazy ways, but it's really the same old shit. Happy slavery, with people that don't even know they're being controlled and manipulated, is still slavery."

"As it was with you."

"As—what?"

"When you were a mechsuiter."

"I was happy... I was! I had a purpose, a noble purpose... I thought." Straker rounded on Don, angry. "Okay, you got me, you and your word games. Maybe I was being manipulated before. I sure didn't know the full story. But I broke out of all that. I made my way out and I made a real difference. I've freed more than half of humanity from a tyrannical government, and I'm planning on liberating the rest."

"The rest?"

"The Hundred Worlds."

"Hmm." Don's eyes narrowed. "That's a great speech, for a trainee. I'm glad you're enjoying your roleplaying."

Straker nodded, realizing he'd been skimming close to speaking too plainly inside the diz. If anyone were listening, they might start to wonder, so he slipped back into his role. "Just trying my best, boss. I have to learn to act like the humans."

"You're certainly making progress." Don turned away, and Straker followed, his mind awhirl with the things the Opterman got him thinking about.

86

Don led them to another diz, called Milgram. This one consisted of rooms behind one-way glass. Each room was divided into two parts, reminding Straker of the chambers with the Kort readying itself to eat a naked Carla Engels. Don halted Straker to observe one pair of rooms.

On one side, a white-coated researcher with a large handtab opened a door and let in a young woman in ordinary clothing. "Sit here," the man said, and she sat in a chair before a table with two large buttons—one red, one green—and a standard screen.

In the other chamber, a young man—Facet, Straker reminded himself—was strapped to a table, and wired with leads to machinery.

"What's going on?" the woman asked.

"Simply read the screen into the microphone," the researcher said.

"What is six times five?" recited the woman into a microphone.

Her voice was evidently carried into the chamber with the helpless prisoner, for the man on the table answered, "Thirty."

"Now what?" she said.

"Push a button," replied the researcher.

The woman tentatively reached over and pressed down on the big green button with her palm.

The prisoner immediately moaned and writhed. Straker thought at first the man was in pain, but it soon became evident he was experiencing pleasure.

Straker looked back at the civilian woman. She was smiling, her eyes alight. When she was given more questions to ask, and the man got them right, she pushed the big green button and he moaned with more pleasure.

Now the woman was licking her lips, her face was flushed and she breathed deeply. Clearly, she enjoyed meting out pleasure.

The researcher tapped his handtab. The readout screen scrolled. The civilian read the words on the screen and spoke. "What is ten plus two?"

"Twelve," the prisoner said.

The civilian leaned forward to slam her hand on the green button, an expression of slack fascination now fixed on her face.

The researcher tapped his handtab and the screen scrolled to a new question. "What is the square root of thirty, to six decimal places?"

The prisoner's eyes darted. "I—I—I don't know!"

The woman leaned forward and, after a moment's pause, triumphantly slammed her hand on the red button. The man writhed again—though this time it was clearly in pain. He cried out, "Stop! Please, stop!"

"Stop this!" Straker growled, looking for a door into the research rooms, but not seeing one. "This kind of brainwashing shit is exactly why I liberated the Mutuality!"

Myrmidon didn't move. "You can't stop it. This is part of the diz process."

"Hell if I can't. You said they don't police the dizzes, right? Whatever happens, happens?"

"That is correct—for the ordinary Facets. You, however, have been tagged as an agent-trainee. You'll be seen as interfering."

Straker clenched his fists and forced himself to watch. The woman seemed just as aroused by the man's agony as she had been by his pleasure a moment ago. In fact, when the system suspended the pain, she slammed repeatedly at the red button, even when it did nothing. She made a sound of frustration.

"Next question," she said, turning to the researcher. "Next question!"

"You're turning people into sadists," Straker said. "Give them an authority figure and instructions, power and rewards, and people do what you say."

Don shook his head. "Did you hear the researcher give any instructions on which button to push?"

Straker thought back. "I guess not. So she could push either button?"

"Of course."

"But you cued her which was pain and pleasure—red and green. That's assuming these Facets associate green with positive and red with negative, like standard displays, or traffic lights."

"The choice is hers. Yet, like most young human Facets, she doesn't care whether she metes out pain or pleasure. Both excite her. Combine that with her unconfirmed assumptions—such as the assumption that rewards go with right answers and punishments go with wrong ones—and she might just torture this man to death."

"You let them do that?"

"They're only Facets. The controllers do what they have to in order to achieve their greater goals... just like we do."

"I don't!"

Myrmidon faced Straker fully. "Oh, no? With your combat skills and biotech, you could have disarmed those police officers in Baltimore. You could have broken up the brawling at Campus. You could try to break this glass and rescue that poor fellow on the table. Why don't you?"

"Because you told me..." Straker realized what he was saying. "Because you're my authority figure. It's not because I'm afraid!"

"Did I bring up fear? Is it important that you be seen as brave?"

Straker's fists clenched. "I—getting caught here would be pointless, that's all. I might save one man or two, but I can't save the thousands—"

"—billions—"

"—okay, billions of Facets you're destroying in these dizzes."

"So you're doing what you have to do in order to achieve your greater goals. You're ignoring your moral principles because of practical concerns."

The man on the table screamed again.

"Turn that shit off!"

"Why? So you won't have to face it?"

Straker punched Myrmidon in the jaw. The Opter-man—only a Facet, after all—sprawled, knocked out cold.

By the time Myrmidon came to, Straker had mastered himself. Besides, he couldn't seem to open the door to the

89

room, no matter how hard he kicked and pulled at it, nor break the transparent window material.

He'd faced the fact that he couldn't go save the poor soul strapped to the table. He'd managed to ignore the screams and groans, telling himself that the prisoner was unlikely to die—though death itself had little to do with torture. He'd even figured out what Myrmidon was doing—maybe.

When Don sat up, rubbing his jaw ruefully, Straker squatted next to him. "Sorry about that."

"I expected it, actually, but you're so damn fast."

"Be glad I didn't hit you as hard as I could have."

"Gee, thanks."

"I know what you're trying to do."

"Getting punched?"

Straker chuckled. "The whole thing. The why. This isn't just a diz for these Facets. It's for me."

Don raised an eyebrow. "Why would I do that?"

"You're not just testing and corrupting these people. You're testing and corrupting me."

"People corrupt themselves, Derek. Nobody can do it for them, if they really want to resist. Testing you? Of course. More importantly, you're learning." Don stood, brushing himself off. "Not only are there many different dizzes, there are meta-dizzes. We all go through them. We are observed, then we observe, then we observe the observers. Sometimes we even observe those who are observing the observers."

Straker stood also, wondering who was observing them. "Is that why humans call, um, *us,* Opters? Something to do with optics, eyes, observing?"

Don chuckled. "An astute guess, but no, just coincidence. 'Opter' came from one of the first humans to encounter insectoid Facets. *Hymenoptera* is the human name for the order of insects comprising wasps, bees and ants."

"I guess 'hymens' would have been weird."

"Sure would."

"So, did I pass your test?"

"The jury's still out, but you're coming along."

Straker rubbed his face with his palm as if to scrub off dirt. "Why are you showing me all this? What if I do pass?"

90

"Finally, you're asking the right questions. Unfortunately, that's above my pay grade."

"Make a guess," Straker said.

"Perhaps those above me will take stronger measures in your favor."

The Miskor, he meant, though Myrmidon couldn't confirm it aloud. Trusted agents like Don were given lots of slack to train their protégés, he'd said—but Straker didn't want to give whoever was watching cause to really wonder. Probably the very unlikeliness of a real human agent infiltrating Terra Nova, combined with any system's usual complacency when presented with what it expected to see, had protected them so far.

Straker had already done some pacing and thinking while waiting for Don to regain consciousness, and now he continued. "I think there's more to it than you're telling me. Every time I think I know what's going on with you, there's another layer, another twist... and you told me I couldn't possibly beat you at your own game of secrets."

"That's true."

"But this is a game you *hope* I win, because if I win, you win. You want me to figure this stuff out instead of spoon-feeding me, I get that. People don't value what they don't work for, so you're making me work for these lessons."

"That seems reasonable."

"I've been told that personal experience colors everything anyone does. We think we're objective, but really, we have a lot of unrecognized assumptions. The Queens, for example, live their lives surrounded by drone slaves. They're the only ones with free will around them, other than fellow Queens, and aliens. Except..." Straker snapped his fingers as he paced, trying to corral a fleeting thought. "Except for us. Us human Facets. Once we make it through all the dizzes and all the experiments and games, once we're sharp enough to blend in with the humans, we've developed free will and individuality. We're no longer really Facets."

"An interesting observation." Myrmidon's bland eyes nevertheless seemed to be watching Straker closely.

"So now we have a whole world brimming with potential individuals—and we're training them to have free will, to make choices, even bad ones. Some make it through, some don't, it's all very Darwinian—but the fittest survive. Some are good, some are evil, but they're all Queens in their own right—individuals. Like you said, perfect copies of imperfect humans."

"You seem to be building a coherent picture."

"So by your logic, you're—we're both—human."

"That is so."

Straker stopped and stared, unseeing, as the researcher on the other side of the glass led away the protesting woman. She seemed to want to go back to her button-pushing. In the other room, medics attended to the tortured man.

"So, hypothetically speaking..." Straker watched Don carefully for any hint he should shut up. "Hypothetically, if we were real humans and saw all this, we'd want to rescue these people. And we'd hate the Queens."

"Stipulated."

"In fact, if I were this Liberator guy, I'd think this planet was primed for revolt."

"If you were this Liberator guy, it would be natural for you to come to this conclusion."

"But since I'm not, and since we Sarmok want to keep the humans out of our business, we'll need to make sure the Liberator never finds out about this planet."

Don made a dismissive motion. "It's far from human space."

"No worries, then."

"None."

"Okay." Straker clapped his hands in satisfaction. Finally, he felt like he was starting to understand Myrmidon. "I'm hungry."

"Let's go to the cafeteria."

"Is it part of the diz? Will they be testing weird foods on us?"

Don pondered. "I'm really not sure."

Without warning, the door to the room burst open. Straker reacted immediately, dodging out of the way as stunners fired. Myrmidon fell. Men poured into the room.

There was nowhere to run to, nowhere to hide. Straker got his hands on one of the attackers, but his muscles locked and his nerves blazed from repeated stuns.

They pummeled him into unconsciousness.

Chapter 9

As his Tenth Fleet entered Calypso's planetary nebula at C-1, Admiral Lucas Braga sat upright in his flag chair, hands firmly on its arms and feet flat on the floor. Appearances were important, and he always maintained his image as a by-the-book commander.

Not so by-the-book that he hadn't brought along Captain Lydia Verdura to command his flagship, the HWS *Luxemburg*. It was good luck that she'd also survived Corinth, and good fortune that the boards of inquiry had found them both guiltless in the debacle. In fact, he'd been promoted to fleet command for the current offensive against the Hok.

Admiral Danica Downey, however, had been posthumously court-martialed and convicted of dereliction of duty. This provided Braga a tiny sliver of satisfaction, yet failed to balance the anger he still felt at the loss of life and ships the stupid, politically connected officer had caused.

He shook off haunting memories and concentrated on the business at hand. His holotank—a proper device for a proper flag bridge—showed his fleet maintaining maximum search dispersion while still keeping his ships and scout drones networked.

"The enemy defense force is eliminating the probes we dropped outside, sir," said his Sensors officer, Lieutenant Lexin. Like most of his best technicians, he was Ruxin.

That reminded Braga of that annoying but innovative Ruxin who had almost—almost!—snatched victory from the jaws of defeat at Corinth with his stealth mine trick. What was his name? Zaxdy? Zaxty? *Zaxby*... that was it. Too bad he hadn't survived.

"Save the probes for later," said Braga. "We'll need them to scout our departure path after we destroy Felicity Station."

"Sir, why do the Hok sometimes use human names for their installations?" asked Lexin.

94

The others of his flag crew seemed to listen closer. Rumors had been swirling for some time about the troubles the Hok were experiencing with an upstart warlord called "The Liberator" or somesuch. Fleet Intelligence had provided farfetched guesses that, in Braga's opinion, only made things more confusing for the rank and file.

The Parliamentary Intelligence Agency had provided separate, eyes-only briefings for senior officers, revealing what the flag corps had long suspected: the Hok aliens were in league with human traitors, who existed in far greater numbers than he'd thought. Whole planets-full, in fact, allowed to prosper within the Hok Empire. That explained the occasional human defectors and captured prisoners.

Braga wished the PIA would simply reveal the truth, rather than try to keep it under wraps. If his own feelings were any indication, the average Fleet crewman would fight even harder when they found out about the traitors. But now, he had to come up with an answer to Lexin's question—or deflect it without revealing classified information.

"I can't really tell you," Braga said, which was technically the truth, though misleading. "Maybe intel uses the Earthan translation for the Hok word. Or maybe they simply assign a name." He didn't like playing semantic games, but his only other choice was telling them the answer was classified, and that might reveal more than it concealed.

"But—"

"Attend to your duties, Lieutenant," Braga said sharply. "I know you think you can split your attention, but I'm not so confident."

"Aye aye, sir." Lexin turned his eyes and tentacles back to his consoles. A moment later, the holotank identified a new contact. "Fixed facility dead ahead. Emissions consistent with Felicity Station, though faint."

"Probably powered down as much as possible," Verdura mused.

Lexin continued, "I'm getting some intermittent contacts on our periphery that concern me."

"What kind of contacts?"

"They might be ships. They are at extreme detection range, but occasionally the vagaries of the gas dispersion allow sensor distance extension, and one of our scouts or probes gets a hit. We've also lost an unlikely number of probes, even accounting for the enemy mines. Lurking enemy ships would explain both phenomena."

"What kind of ships?"

Lexin tweaked the holotank. "Tentative identifications range from cruisers to superdreadnoughts."

Braga gripped the arms of his chair. "Is that possible? Capital ships in the nebula with us?"

"Self-evidently, it is possible, sir," Lexin said with the hint of supercilious annoyance characteristic of his kind. "Average sensor range is barely one hundred kilometers, and the nebula's diameter exceeds one million kilometers. However, I cannot judge the likelihood of enemy capital ships being present. That is a strategic question beyond my current competence."

Braga thought furiously. Could the enemy be laying some kind of trap for him? He thought about the string of operational decisions he'd made since arriving at the Calypso system and reluctantly concluded it was possible.

Fortunately, his fleet was robust and well supplied. "Pass to all ships, each to launch two active probes outward, on the same mark. Choose a mark that will allow for a coordinated launch. On the same mark, push our scouts out an extra hundred kilometers."

"Aye aye, sir," the Flag Comms chief replied, and set her subordinates to issuing orders.

When the mark came, the holotank view expanded suddenly, like an inflating balloon, to show—

"Bogeys englobing us, sir," Lexin reported. "Over one hundred capital ships. They're still moving into position."

"Shit," Captain Verdura said, swiveling her chair to face Braga's. "We have about five minutes, sir." She visibly restrained herself from barking orders, like a hound quivering to bolt after a fox, as she waited for Braga's instructions.

Braga ignored her, staring at the holotank, using a full minute of the five. The enemy ships he could see appeared to outmass him by two to one. Even adding in the usual ten percent advantage of Hundred Worlds technology, ship for ship, he'd suddenly gone from comfortable to vulnerable, and he was acutely aware of his inability to see far. No doubt the enemy had better intel.

The way ahead seemed thinly held, though. It might be a trap, but it also could be his salvation. He might yet pull these chestnuts out of the fire, and accomplish his mission to boot.

Braga snapped rapid-fire orders. "Light units to the fore, maximum minesweeping and recon mode. Fleet to accelerate at one-quarter. Heavy cruisers to back up the lights and attack Felicity Station as soon as it comes within range. Carriers, full attack ship and drone launch to supplement our perimeter. All other units to maintain vigilance. We're assaulting through the ambush and we'll fight our way out the other side as soon as we've destroyed the fuel processing plant."

His staff scrambled to pass his orders through the network. Attack ships and remote drones blossomed from the carrier launch bays and spread out. Asteroids and moons seemed to leap toward the fleet as his ships accelerated as fast as they dared. Point defense weapons worked overtime to pick off chunks of orbital debris and enemy mines. Ships rocked with explosions and impacts as those efforts sometimes failed.

His heavy cruisers came into direct fire range of the Felicity Station moonlet, a lumpy hunk of rock and dust over one hundred kilometers across, and began their bombardment. Missiles and railguns blew pieces of it off into space, and the processing facilities, identified by their EM emissions, were wiped out. But even under intense attack, it would take a while for such a large installation to be dismantled.

Braga watched closely as the enemy englobement tightened.

The advantage of such a formation was twofold. First, it allowed all the attackers to point their biggest weapons and their armored noses at those within the globe, while the defenders had to either run and expose their vulnerable sterns to a rake, or form a spherical hedgehog pointing outward, becoming immobilized.

Second, the englobement aimed to trap all within, leaving nowhere to escape, the three-dimensional equivalent of surrounding an enemy on the ground.

The standard doctrinal response for the defender was to charge ahead, concentrate fire and blast out of the trap. Some would fall, but many would escape, and fleet cohesion would be maintained.

Braga was nothing if not a man of doctrine. Sticking to the well-established principles of war had brought him victory many times. Still, the mission always came first. He would take unexpected casualties, but destroying this Hok fuel factory would save lives in the long run.

So he ordered, "Heavy cruisers, continue bombardment as long as possible. The rest of the fleet will maintain formation, leapfrog forward, and fire at targets as they present themselves. Light units, collapse upon our capital ships once the enemy has committed himself, and take up station as our rearguard."

His superb ships, operated by experienced crews, carried out his orders with precision. The heavy cruisers pulverized the moon, and presumably its facilities, though from the first those dying installations were hidden by a heavy screen of dust and debris thrown up by impacts and explosions. His main armored fist, his phalanx of supers and dreadnoughts, passed around the cruisers in a ring, backed up by battlecruisers. Anything conceivable that got in their way would get hammered to scrap.

But then the inconceivable appeared.

Out of the gas in front of his fleet leaped what looked like a tiny ship, approaching at a blazing speed far in excess of what he would have thought possible within the nebula. It smashed into the armored nose of the superdreadnought *Bruxelles,* doing grievous damage to her. She'd still have engines and point defense weapons, but her value as a fleet asset had been eliminated with the destruction of her primary spinal weaponry and front armor.

"What the hell was that? Some kind of suicide craft?" Braga barked.

"No, sir," Lexin answered. "My sensors show it was a solid crysteel projectile of approximately nine hundred tons—a railgun bullet."

"Where—"

Before he could ask his next question, the holotank recorded another disaster as HWS *Antwerp* reported catastrophic damage from a massive particle beam strike.

"All ships, maximum evasion!" Braga snapped. "There must be a fortress in front of us. Locate it and counterfire!"

"The beam's back-azimuth is evident to all ships, sir," said Lexin. "They're launching now."

Hundreds of missiles sprang from his ships—even from the two crippled SDNs, whose side-mounted launch tubes were still functioning. At the same time, a storm of railgun and beam fire converged along the track of the enemy shots. Not even a monitor could mount weapons so large, so Braga knew there must be a fortress out there, and a fortress couldn't maneuver. The enemy's surprise had been costly, but it would ultimately be futile.

Suddenly, another monster railgun bullet speared the superdreadnought *Rotterdam,* this time from a different angle. The projectile caught her aft of amidships and tore her less-armored stern off, leaving her a tumbling wreck.

"Two fortresses!" Captain Verdura cried. "Maybe more. Sir, the englobement's driving us into a kill zone. We can't stand up to fire like this."

Before she even finished her sentence, another particle beam struck HWS *Friesland,* opening her up like a tin can and igniting a line of plasma fire along one flank. Four of Braga's proudest and finest ships, wrecked within two minutes, and he couldn't even see his attackers!

Despite the shock, Braga's mind kicked into overdrive. His brainchips and his experience allowed him to analyze what he saw in the holotank and extrapolate outcomes, even with hundreds of ships and variables. The enemy's intention became clear. The Hok and their human traitor allies had laid a titanic trap for him, knowing the Hundred Worlds would come after the tempting target of Felicity Station. The cowardly defense had lured him onward, the relieving fleet had driven him inward, and the englobing ships had forced him forward into these massive siege guns, weapons against which he could not stand.

His turbocharged brain searched for solutions. Reverse course and run? His fleet had too much forward velocity. Charge blindly onward, firing at the fortresses when they could be seen, risking collisions with asteroids and moons, in order to break through? If he had to.

But he saw the narrowest of windows in a third option. "All ships change course, forty-five degree angle planetward, thirty degrees port, flank acceleration. Ships to fire at will, maximum defensive protocols. We'll skim C1's atmosphere and slingshot around the planet. That'll avoid these fortresses and degrade their targeting."

"Helm, comply," Verdura said to her ship driver. "All weapon controllers, fire at will, defensive protocols."

As one, Braga's fleet blasted downward and to port. He hoped this would surprise the enemy, who should be expecting him to try to immediately break for the outside of the nebula. Instead, this course drove the core of his still-powerful task force between the big guns in front of him and the englobing fleet.

Unfortunately, it left his slowest and most damaged ships to fend for themselves. The carriers, particularly, would never make it out. It pained him to think of those crews and supplies falling into enemy hands, but his responsibility was to salvage as much as he could, converting a potential disaster into a mere debacle. Better to limp home with half a battered fleet than to stand and die to no purpose—especially as he knew he'd already destroyed Felicity Station.

His fleet's sudden turn brought several enemy ships directly into his fleet's primary cone of fire. Despite defensive protocols, most of his captains ordered their ships to aim their largest weapons at their foes. Those enemy vessels tried to evade and fall back to their comrades, but they were smashed out of the way, tearing a hole in the englobement.

Braga couldn't blame his people for their lust to strike back, and he couldn't fault their judgment at destroying what was in front of them. He only hoped that, without his carriers for resupply, his stocks of fuel and ordnance would hold out long enough to get home.

Over sixty of his ships broke free of the trap, using the planet's gravity to add to their acceleration. The rest had been crippled, destroyed or surrounded, forced to surrender. Braga ground his teeth, but focused on what fleet he still had and how to get it out.

The lightest, fastest units of the enemy englobement streamed behind him in a ragged chase, firing at the sterns of the Hundred World ships. Braga's vessels continued maximum evasion, varying their courses and dodging as much as they could even while maintaining a loose formation.

Designated ships, his fastest cruisers, cut their engines and turned briefly broadside to use their point-defense weapons against pursuing missiles. They would then reorient on impellers and resume running. They also dropped mines in their wakes, forcing the pursuers to either slow or risk a nuke on the nose.

These and other tactics, along with the edge in speed and weapons technology of Braga's ships, gave him hope. His harried fleet skimmed low over the swirling atmosphere of the gas giant designated C1, gaining speed. They smashed through hundreds of rocks in orbit, and he lost one of his battlecruisers when it plowed right into a moonlet that loomed out of the gas, too large to destroy or dodge. Braga hissed through his teeth in frustration. He'd accepted the risks when he decided to run.

"On my mark, new course," he said once most of the pursuers had fallen away. "Stellar absolute, zero azimuth. We'll dive toward the star, get lost in its corona, and perform another slingshot."

"Orders relayed," his Flag Comms chief replied. "All ships standing by."

"Mark."

Now his fleet turned outward, heading toward the small orange star of Calypso. In just minutes at this breakneck speed they passed through the gas cloud surrounding the planet and broke out into open space.

Braga's optimism died a brutal death as the holotank updated to show nearly two hundred enemy ships waiting for him dead ahead, centered around that damned monitor.

They opened fire.

101

Chapter 10

Straker on Terra Nova

When the stun wore off, Straker awoke strapped to a reclining table in a laboratory. Mechanical arms hung from above, quiescent. Machines hummed and beeped now and again, and sophisticated holographic readouts displayed biological constructs.

He flexed and strained at the straps, but he was held fast. Even his extraordinary strength barely budged the restraints.

A woman in a lab coat entered the room. Her nametag read "Smith," and she looked to be about twenty years old, a knockout redhead with a short skirt and lots of cleavage. She reminded Straker of a younger version of Tachina.

She stepped over to console and began inputting commands there.

"What's going on?" Straker asked, controlling his anger and concern. His only chance of getting out of this was to play along with his cover as Myrmidon's spy trainee.

"I'm continuing to test you," Smith replied.

"For what?"

"Deviance from genetic norms."

"Why?"

"I have no idea." The woman tapped one final tap and she swung her swivel chair around to face him, legs apart. He could see up her skirt to a triangle of pink panties, as if she had no idea how to be modest—or maybe she was doing it on purpose. But she didn't seem to be acting coy or flirty.

"I'm just the lab tech," she said. "Now hold still while the machine takes the samples, or I'll have to paralyze you."

The arms above him activated and stabbed him suddenly with needles in several places. The pain was negligible, so Straker froze. Getting paralyzed was the last thing he wanted.

He wondered how mature Miss Smith was—how far through the humanizing program she'd gone. Was she naïve or

102

cynical? Had she ever had a lover, or was infatuation and sex foreign to her?

Worth a try, Straker thought. When the arms had retracted and placed their samples into other machines, he put on his best charm. "Hey, what's your first name?"

"Doris."

"You're gorgeous, Doris. Anybody ever tell you that?"

Doris blushed and covered her mouth with her hand. "Me? No, nobody ever said that about me."

"Well, it's true. Come over here and let me see you better."

Doris rose and walked to within arm's reach—if his arms weren't firmly held. She stared him in the face, seemingly innocent of guile. "You're gorgeous too. What's your name?"

"Derek."

"Derek what?"

"Just Derek. They haven't assigned me another name. I'm still in training."

"For what?"

Straker winked. "It's a secret."

Doris blushed again. "Telling me would be improper."

"It would... but I'll tell you anyway if you like."

"I'm not sure." Doris seemed both repelled and fascinated by the prospect of doing something improper.

"You have to promise not to tell anyone else. Then it'll still be a secret, so it's okay."

"I...I suppose that complies with guidelines."

"Sure it does. Lean closer so I can whisper it."

Doris leaned her face close to Derek's. He smelled her breath, sweet and unspoiled. He almost felt bad about manipulating her this way, but he had to get out of these restraints. After that, he could figure out a way to escape from this bizarre diz-planet.

"I'm training to be a spy—to infiltrate the humans. Exciting, huh?"

"Oh, that's much more exciting than my job." Doris kept her face close to his, staring into his eyes. "I like you."

"I like you too. Have you ever kissed anyone?"

"What's that mean?"

Apparently this young woman—young Facet, really—had simply been trained for her work, but not for social interaction. And, in the manner of the insectoid Opters, her masters assumed she would simply act like an organic robot and carry out her task. If Straker's guesses were right, this left her with all the usual physical urges, but no filters and no experience.

"Kiss—kissing—is when you put your lips on my lips. It's pleasant. You want to try it?"

Doris leaned in and pressed her mouth to his, clumsily. Straker did his best to make the kiss lively but tender. As the seconds went by, the lip-lock became more heated and intense.

Suddenly, Doris crawled onto Straker, straddling him and seizing his head in both hands, kissing him as if trying to devour his mouth and tongue. "Oh, this is... this is... wonderful!" she gasped.

"Let me out of these straps, Doris, and we can do more."

Doris punched in a code to the table and his restraints popped off. He wrapped his arms around her and kissed her for a moment, just to make sure she was thoroughly lost in the experience, while his eyes roved the room. There was only one way out, and the door had a keypad lock.

And his unauthorized freedom could be discovered at any moment. Somebody must be watching, or would soon.

He briefly wondered if this was all part of the diz, the experiment, a scenario within a scenario. Did it matter? He would act the same no matter what—and according to what Myrmidon had said, nobody would save him or go easy on him if it were. They might even kill him.

Better to die free than live in a cage.

"Let's go somewhere else," Straker said around kisses. "Your room?"

"Yes, yes, yes, Derek, my room. I want to keep doing this forever." Doris dragged him by the hand to the door and hastily input the code, and then pulled him out into a second room. This one had more lab equipment, and two doors. She led him toward one. "The other door is guarded. This is the emergency exit."

"Won't an alarm sound?"

"I don't care." Before he could stop her, she pushed the door open and went through, her hand still firmly locked to Straker's.

A loud beeping pealed from speakers, and they ran down a corridor past other doors. After a moment, those doors opened and others joined them in their race, paying the two no attention.

Of course! Straker thought. They were just two more people in a crowd evacuating the laboratory building, presumably for fire or other emergency. By chance, Doris had facilitated their escape.

They debouched into a parking lot. People continued to stream out of the doors. "Will they miss you if you leave right now?" Straker asked.

"I'll check in," she replied, leading him toward a tall box standing among the parked vehicles. People were lining up to scan their faces into its sensors, apparently for post-emergency accountability. Doris got into the line and soon had recorded her safe escape. "Now we can go. I'll report myself ill from my quarters communicator."

"Do we take a ground car?" Straker asked.

"No, I'm too junior to have one," she said. "It's all right. My flat is an easy walk from here." She dragged him possessively toward it.

A commotion behind them made Straker turn and look. A squad of uniformed men and women spread out among the workers in the parking lot. "They're looking for me," Straker said, watching Doris.

"Why?"

"It's a spy exercise. I'm supposed to practice and train to escape and avoid being caught, and they're training to catch me. I have to pass this level to graduate to the next."

"I'll help you escape!" Doris squealed. "I don't want you to get caught."

"I was hoping you'd say that."

He let Doris lead him to a gray, featureless block of apartments. If it wasn't a bright, sunny day, the cityscape would look positively grim, reminding him of some of the Mutuality towns he'd seen, uninterrupted by beauty or

105

aesthetics. Everything seemed to be made of concrete, metal or plastic. Everything had a discrete function. The few plants and trees seemed to be barely alive.

"Is this a diz?" he asked as Doris palmed open her door.

"What's that mean?"

"Never mind." He looked around the tiny space. It reminded him of a cheap hotel room, with no personal touches. "How long have you lived here?"

"Just a month since I graduated from medical tech school." Doris shut the door and immediately began kissing him again.

"Hold on, honey. Slow down."

"Why?" She shrugged off her jacket and let it drop to the floor. Straker wondered whether she'd continue losing clothes, but she didn't. She did, however, grab his face for more kisses.

"Because I need to think about escaping, remember?"

"Oh, that's right." She backed off slightly, and then seized his hand once more. "Let's sit down." She sat on the bed— there was only one chair—and tried to draw him toward it.

Straker let her pull him. "First I need information. We can kiss some more later."

"Okay."

"What's this city called?"

"Glasgow.

"What happens here?"

Doris shrugged. "I don't know. People live here. There's business and industry. It's normal."

"How do you know what's normal?"

She shrugged again. "It seems normal. I've always lived here."

Straker took a different tack. "How old are you?"

"Twenty-two."

"Tell me about your life until now."

"I—" she faltered, and then recited, "I was born in the Sandstone crèche. I was raised in the collective boarding school until twenty. I went to medical technical school for a month, and I graduated last month. And now I'm here."

"Wait, wait..." Something wasn't right, here. The numbers... "You said you finished your boarding school at twenty, then went to tech school for a month, but you've only

106

been here a month. What happened to the rest of the two years between twenty and now?"

The question seemed to confuse Doris. "A year is twelve months."

"It sure is, most places."

"That means two years is twenty-four months. I'm only twenty-two."

Straker grabbed Doris by the shoulders and held her at arm's length. "You're twenty-two *months* old?"

"Yes."

"Ugh." He was kissing a baby, even if she had a woman's hot body and face—and the emotional development of a middle-schooler, it seemed. And no doubt she was a virgin. Even if he hadn't been Carla's man, he wouldn't just jump Doris's bones here and now. The whole experience would confuse the young Facet, and she'd no doubt be infatuated with him. At some point he'd have to leave Doris behind, and Straker wasn't the love-'em-and-leave-'em type. That was Loco's department.

Then he wondered why he even cared. Doris was a creature, barely a person, mass-produced by the Opters as a biological machine to do their bidding. A Slug, Don had callously termed the type, though perhaps a bit better educated.

Maybe that was *why* Straker cared—the innocence of all these Facets like Doris, the helplessness, the hopelessness. What kind of fulfillment or accomplishments could come from lives like these?

Then he wondered how long Doris had to live.

"Is something wrong?"

Straker tried not to look sad. "Many things, honey, but nothing's wrong with you. You're perfect."

"Oooh, you too!" she squealed, and took to kissing him again.

"Hey," he said around the smooching, "how long do the people here usually live?"

"That's a weird question."

"Is it? For a medical tech?"

Doris frowned. "I'm not a geriatric specialist."

"But how long? You must have some idea."

107

"I'm not sure. Maybe a thousand?"

Straker converted a thousand months to years. Eighty-three and change. So, a relatively normal lifespan, give or take. The Opters simply compressed twenty-four years of human development into two, and the Facets stayed adults for longer.

But something didn't fit, at least with Doris. "Have you ever been anywhere else?"

"Than Glasgow? No. I know there are other places, but most people don't get to travel until they're at least fifty, or if they get Selected."

"Selected? What's that?"

Doris shivered and, for the first time, appeared afraid. "They say it's a good thing, but then they take people away and they never come back. It doesn't feel good when they take someone away."

Those Selected must be the ones to get run through the dizzes, the program to make Facets into people who could function in human society—a forcible and cruel introduction to the worst of the real world.

Then again, was it any worse than what he himself went through, or what kids went through with dysfunctional families and badly run schools? Even Straker's special school had its problems with its bullies and cliques and childish cruelties. The passive-aggressive teachers sometimes secretly loved it when the super-capable kids failed, and the insecure staff enforced rules without using their judgment. In other schools he'd heard about, there were even adults who lusted after the budding adolescents in their charge.

Funny, he hadn't thought of his pre-Academy days in a long time, and that brought back memories of his family—his steady, loving father, his caring but fretful mother, his sister, all slaughtered by Mutuality attackers who wanted Derek Straker dead.

Not for the first time, he wondered how they knew which houses to strike, where the special children lived. Mutuality spies, he'd always thought... but now that he was aware of the Opter games—okay, to be fair, the Sarmok games, if he could believe Don—he wondered whether the spies hadn't actually been perfected Facets, like Myrmidon himself. If the Sarmok wanted to sow trouble and keep the war going, they could have provided the information to the Mutuality and prompted the attack on Seaburn City.

So in a way, the Sarmok might have killed his family.

"Derek?"

"Sorry, I was thinking. You know, you're right about being Selected. It *is* a bad thing. Any time your government steals people away from their lives just because they can, and forces them to be something they don't want to be, that's bad."

"It sounds bad... but what happens to the Selected?"

"They suffer. Many die. A few come out changed, and then they're sent to live somewhere else, far from family and friends."

"What's... family?"

"You don't know... of course not." Straker took Doris' face in his hands, a face that if he'd encountered it before he met Carla he might have fallen in love with, and kissed her forehead. Any ardor he'd felt toward her cooled. Now, she seemed like a daughter, not an object of desire. "Sweetheart, family is people you love, and who love you. The people who raise you, the people you're connected with... the people you'd defend, the people you'd die for."

"I'd die for you, Derek," she declared passionately.

Straker sighed. "I'm sure you feel that way." How could he explain that he knew how she was feeling—exactly how he'd felt when he fell in love with Carla—and how, now, he was so much older, so far beyond Doris, that he would never be what her adolescent hormones wanted him to be.

He held Doris, and eventually spooned with her chastely on her narrow bed until she fell contentedly asleep. No doubt she was filled with the feeling of her first crush. As her breathing deepened, he used the time to think.

He'd have to leave Doris behind, breaking her heart and leaving her life forever changed. He wondered if the Facets in Glasgow were allowed to pair up, have sex and relationships and babies, even if they weren't allowed to form families and raise their own children.

Probably not. Don had talked about larval pods and vats.

That seemed a horrible beginning to a lonely existence.

This whole world, this whole planet, was an abomination. Bad enough that human governments or corporations, nations or collectives, separated people into the rulers and the ruled, the haves and the have-nots, the masters and the slaves. Those places, those planets, could be changed. Their regimes could be overthrown. People could be freed—*had* been freed, by Straker and the Liberation—to choose their own paths, to make their own destinies. He knew the New Earthan Republic wouldn't be perfect, but it would be better than the Mutuality it replaced. There would always be those who wanted to lord it over others, to stand on their necks, to brutalize their bodies and pillage their hard-earned property just to satisfy their lusts for power and control.

This place took that evil to the next level. The overlords of this Terra Nova—such an irony, he'd abolish the name if he ever could—weren't even human, and didn't see people as anything more than cogs in a vast machine. The Opter Queens sat atop the pile, the lives of their thralls worthless to them—including these odd humanopts they'd grown in their pods and vats.

Odd *humans,* he reminded himself. If they looked like humans, thought like humans, lived and died like humans—and wanted to make love like humans, even if they didn't know it yet—then they were humans. More human than Ruxins or the insectoid Opters, for sure.

Chapter 11

Engels, aboard *Indomitable,* planetary nebula, Calypso System

Admiral Engels admired Braga even as she gave orders to close the trap on his fleet and crush him. She couldn't imagine anyone doing any better than he'd done, given the tough circumstances.

"Comms, transmit our call for surrender again."

"No reply, ma'am."

"Set it to repeat every minute." She'd hoped for a response, but not really expected one.

Not yet, anyway. Braga was a fighter.

Indomitable had taken out four superdreadnoughts singlehandedly, firing from beyond visual range using targeting data relayed from her stealth drone network. Undoubtedly Braga would believe he faced at least two fortresses, unless he had better-than-expected data on the battleship. He also couldn't know how many supporting ships those "fortresses" had with them, and so would undoubtedly turn away, believing he'd already destroyed Felicity Station.

Engels had deliberately ordered *Indomitable's* targeting and power adjusted downward from maximum effectiveness. At the current two-hundred kilometer range, her weaponry could've utterly destroyed those four SDNs, leaving no survivors and nothing but slag.

That would have been a twofold mistake. Not only would it cause unnecessary casualties, but crippled ships could be repaired and rebuilt—or at least salvaged—and the Republic needed all the warships it could get. She had plenty of forces to compel their surrender. In fact, today's haul in prizes would provide a much-needed boost to Republic fleets, if they had the time to absorb them.

Indomitable continued to pick off big ships with her main particle beam. The massive railgun became almost useless as

111

soon as Braga's fleet turned unexpectedly away from a nose-on aspect, toward the planet.

Engels instantly divined Braga's intention: to drive a wedge between her battleship and the rest of her englobing fleet, to escape with what he could by slingshotting around C1.

"Helm, set course to cut them off," she ordered.

"This ship is a pig, ma'am. We'll still end up chasing them."

"Do your best. Weapons, continue maximum rate of fire, prioritizing undamaged big ships."

"Aye aye, ma'am."

Inertial compensators and gravplating held Engels and the crew in place as *Indomitable* clawed her way around a semicircle, aiming her nose ahead of Braga's faster ships. Twice more her great particle beam lashed out, crippling superdreadnoughts, before the gas became too dense to penetrate.

Engels chewed a nail in thought as *Indomitable* slid in behind the enemy, chasing them like a buffalo hopelessly following swift wolves. What would she do if she were Braga? Where would he break away from C1's gravity? What direction would he take?

Given his current course and actions, one thing made the most sense. She used her cursor to circle an area within *Indomitable's* hologram. "Pass to Zholin and Dexon to adjust course toward this zone, starward from C1, and form a dense hemisphere to intercept. Helm, take us here at all possible speed."

Engels' comms team sent her orders over the relay system. Returns from the network updated the hologram in realtime, and she watched as Zholin moved his local task force to plant itself directly between C1 and its star.

It occurred to her that if Braga were really clever, he'd try to follow the curving streamer of gas that extended from Calypso to the planet. She didn't have stealth sensors there. "Tell Zholin to shift position to make it harder for Braga to turn and dive back into the streamer," she ordered. "Dexon can cover the other angle with his lights."

Zholin's monitor didn't move, but he slid the rest of his ships sideward to flank it, making any Hun turn toward the gas ribbon a costly one.

Dexon's light fleet continued to decelerate furiously. The computer predicted its resting point farther out from Zholin's ships and behind them, in a position to backstop them. The lights continued to emit their fake dreadnought signatures. Until Braga got solid visuals, he'd believe he faced an overwhelming force.

Now came the frustration of flag rank as Engels watched her forces interpret her orders while her own vessel was out of firing range. She wanted to reach into the hologram and adjust the positions of ships to their most efficient fleet configurations, but micromanagement would do more harm than good. She had confidence in the older, more experienced Dexon, but she'd appointed Zholin as squadron commander based on his trustworthiness, not tactical depth. Less than a year ago, he'd been a mere frigate captain.

Then again, she herself was just a jumped-up gunship pilot.

She wished she'd been able to bring along Ellen Gray, but she also needed an experienced hand to run the Home Fleet—and incidentally, to guard the Liberation from getting hijacked by former Mutuality politicians and bureaucrats.

Wishes, fishes.

The moment of truth approached. The hologram showed Braga's core fleet speeding low around the giant gas planet, adjusting course as they flew. Any minute now, she'd see whether she'd guessed right.

If not, this might turn into a long, running, chase of attrition. She'd still win—she'd already won—but the crushing victory she craved might elude her.

There! Braga's fleet made its move to break out of its skimming partial orbit. Engines flared at maximum and his ships rose as one in a smooth curve that dead-ended at the exit point closest to the star.

Exactly where she hoped.

As Braga broke out of the nebula and Zholin's command ambushed him, Engels breathed a sigh of relief. She sat up and straightened her dress jacket, worn deliberately for this

113

moment. "Comms, record a new message. Vidlink when ready."

"Recording."

"Admiral Lucas Braga, this is Admiral Carla Engels."

* * *

Braga realized he'd failed to outguess the enemy when he saw the Hok monitor loom in front of him. He watched in horror as the huge ship fired her cluster of primary lasers, ripping the last of his superdreadnoughts—save only his flagship—to shreds, at point-blank range. Had they spared his flagship because they knew it was the commanding vessel, or was it mere luck?

He'd been outguessed so badly, it couldn't be luck.

He didn't need to order return fire. All of his ships had been given leave to engage, and they unleashed a storm of railguns shots, missiles and beam weapons—lasers, masers, particle beams, any raw destructive energy that could be focused and sent toward an enemy. The nine closest heavy cruisers quickly broke, smashed or driven back, and the superdreadnought he faced slid closer to the monitor for mutual support even as it gave and received furious blows.

A terrifying blizzard came back at him, and in his holotank his ships began to turn shades of yellow and red as their capabilities were methodically stripped from them—though less so than he might have expected. In fact, the many capital ships backing up the enemy monitor, the ones that had transited in behind Braga, seemed to be withholding the worst of it, only engaging with lighter weapons.

Yet, he was outmatched, outgunned and out-tonned.

Though he was proud of how his ships fought, his first duty was to get them out of this new trap. "Hard to starboard, thirty degrees angle toward the gas streamer," he snapped. "Give them more deflection and try to get back into concealment. They can't have sensors everywhere!"

But the Hok fleets moved to block him, to stay with him. There was simply nowhere to go, and though he was moving fast, he didn't have enough velocity to simply flash past and outrun them.

"Admiral," Lexin spoke up, "I believe I know why the fire from the enemy backing fleet is so light. It appears they have no ships heavier than a light cruiser."

"But the display—"

"Shows dreadnoughts, I know. They appear to be using spoofing emitters more sophisticated than any I've ever seen—alien technology, perhaps. However, in empty space, optical scanners clearly show these ships are of escort class."

"Those bastards... Those clever fucking bastards." Braga straightened. "Your pardon."

Lexin chuckled, as did a couple other of those within earshot . "I believe threat of death merits the occasional burst of vulgar language, though why you believe the enemy were born out of wedlock, I don't know."

"I was briefed," Braga deadpanned. He sighed and rubbed his temples. "Will we make it out?"

"My analysis says some of us will," Lexin replied. Just then, *Luxemburg* shuddered and the power feeds flickered. "The monitor's targeting us."

"Full reinforcement!" Captain Verdura said.

"At full, ma'am," replied the Defense chief.

"I'm getting shorted power for evasives," the Helm complained.

"Go to emergency power on the reactors. Divert from life support. Seal suits as needed."

Braga thought furiously, looking for any way out. There seemed none. Yes, because of the enemy's light-unit fake-out, more of his fleet would get past the monitor to dive into the gas streamer, but the Hok ships would immediately turn and stern-rake him. Then, those two hundred light units would harry him all the way to Calypso and around—and he'd eventually run out of plasma to hide in.

He'd be lucky to get ten ships to flatspace and transit out, and there was no guarantee his flagship would be among them.

"Admiral, incoming transmission from the enemy, full vid, with a vidlink request."

"Play it," Braga ordered. "But don't halt operations."

The holotank moved its display far enough out of the way to give Braga easy view of the leftmost of three main holoscreens. On it, a young, half-familiar human woman with the broad stripes of an admiral appeared, seated in a command chair.

"Admiral Lucas Braga, this is Admiral Carla Engels. I'm recording this in hopes you'll accept a truce and talk to me about an honorable surrender. If not, I'm going to have to break you, ship by ship, until each one strikes her colors or is utterly crippled. I don't want that, and I don't think you do either. Please accept the vidlink. As soon as you do, I'll order my fleet to stand down, and I would expect you to do the same. If you don't like what I have to say, well..." The stern young woman leaned forward to stand, clasping her hands behind her back. "...I'll regretfully order your annihilation."

Ten seconds went by, then twenty, as the bridge crew continued to pass orders and information in a glut of controlled confusion. Even as Braga watched, two more of his ships turned red and ceased to fight. One of the enemy vessels did too, but he simply couldn't see any way to disagree with Engels' assessment.

Braga took a deep breath. "Accept the vidlink. Cease offensive fire, all ships. Maintain point defense fire, maximum evasion and maximum armor reinforcement." In the moment available, he used his brainchips to perform a search for the name "Carla Engels." A military record came up.

A Hundred Worlds military record.

As his fleet's fire slackened, and then the enemy's, the image on the screen jerked and changed slightly. It now showed Admiral Engels in realtime as she ceased pacing behind her chair to place her hands on its tall back and stare into the vid pickup. "Greeting, Admiral Braga."

"I won't say hail and well met, Miss Engels."

"*Admiral* Engels."

"I knew your name seemed familiar. You served under me at Corinth—and were captured by the Hok there, we thought. I can hardly credit you with making flag rank in less than two years, even if I regarded whatever traitorous regime you serve as legitimate."

Engels arched an eyebrow. "Your people are dying and you're concerned with my title? You always did have a stick up your ass, Zaxby once told me."

"Zaxby?" Captain Verdura stepped into the vid's view. "Zaxby the Ruxin?"

"Of course. He joined me when Derek Straker and I broke out of a Mutuality prison and started the Liberation. A Hok prison, you'd say."

"I'd like to see Zaxby," Verdura said.

"That can wait," Braga snapped.

"Sir," Verdura said, turning away from the vid and giving the comm tech a throat-cutting motion to pause the link, "I don't know Engels, but Zaxby served with me for nearly three years. If they can produce him—if we can see him in the flesh—we'd have a non-Hok, non-human that I know personally. We might get a better read on this whole situation."

Braga stroked his jowls. "There does seem to be something fundamentally off. For example, where are the Hok? All Engels' bridge crew look either human or Ruxin."

"That could be a holo-fabrication—or just a setup. But more than anything, we need information—from a source they might not be expecting us to talk to, like Zaxby."

Nodding to Verdura, Braga signaled to resume the vidlink. "We want to see Zaxby, in person. I also need those vessels of mine that haven't surrendered to join my flagship."

"Of course, *Admiral.*" Engels turned and issued orders to her staff. "And I'll be joining you on my own flagship. Do you have holographic conferencing capability?"

"Of course."

"Then I suggest you set up a meeting in your flag conference room, unencrypted. My senior staff and I will attend via holo-link and Zaxby will join you in person, as you request."

"What about the Hok?" Verdura snarled.

Engels seemed briefly surprised. "What about them? Oh, yes. You still think they're in charge, like I used to. And I bet you still think they're aliens, too." She chuckled. "This will be an interesting meeting. Engels out."

"What the hell did she mean?" said Verdura.

117

"I suppose we'll soon see," Braga replied.

"A destroyer is approaching at high speed from astern," said Lexin. "She identifies as the New Earthan Republic ship 'Trinity' and requests docking for Zaxby to come aboard."

"Lock her up with targeting. Be ready for a suicide launch," said Verdura. "Tell them no to docking. Remain at five kilometers' range and send a shuttle."

"She is slowing..." Lexin said. "I have never seen a destroyer this fast. She maneuvers like a corvette. She has come to relative rest at a range of... 5000.003 meters. Her pilot is amazingly precise. He must be Ruxin."

While all this was happening, Braga's own stragglers took up station. The enemy fleet also closed in, aiming their weapons from ragged formations. Braga sniffed at their lack of military discipline—but that wouldn't matter, given their numbers. If the fight resumed, Engels would no doubt make good on her threats.

Braga saw a shuttle icon separate itself from the destroyer and speed over to dock with *Luxemburg*. "Have a marine detail meet that shuttle and bring Zaxby—and anyone else who debarks—to the flag conference room. Make sure to do a thorough body scan." He nodded to Verdura and they headed for the meeting as her XO took the conn.

In the command conference room, Braga and his staff didn't have long to wait. The marine detail escorted a Ruxin in, and the major in charge set a slim headset on the table in front of his admiral. "Other than his water suit, this is all he had on him, sir."

Braga picked up the device, some kind of highly sophisticated comlink clearly made to plug directly into Zaxby's brainchips—unusual, but hardly unknown. He then turned his attention to the Ruxin.

Verdura had already walked over to Zaxby and inspected him at close range. "Something looks different about you." She turned to the Ruxin tech in the room who was setting up the vidconference with the enemy. "You, what's your name?"

"Senior Technician Bexol, ma'am."

"Bring up records on Zaxby and compare them to this Ruxin. Tell me what your Ruxin eyes see."

The tech quickly examined Zaxby's service record while the prisoner—the envoy, she supposed—waited patiently.

"At first glance it appears to be Zaxby," Bexol said. "However, in my estimation this person is too young."

Verdura turned to the imposter and snarled, "Who the hell are you, then, and what's your game?"

"I *am* Zaxby, Captain Verdura, though I've undergone an initial rejuvenation procedure. I will allow for your skepticism, but were we not adversaries in this matter, I would be hurt. I served under you for more than two years."

"He sure sounds like Zaxby," she said to Braga with a scowl. "But I know Ruxins can change their skin color, and they're smart."

"I'd be happy to submit to a genetic test. I'm sure you have my profile."

"Send up a med-tech with a scanner," Braga said. "In the meantime, let's get this conference going."

Bexol made final adjustments and holograms flickered to life—Engels, a dark-haired man in a captain's tunic, and a startlingly large Ruxin.

Engels spoke, gesturing first at the octopoid, then the human. "This is Commodore Dexon, commanding my light units, and this is Captain Zholin, in charge of the monitor and defense squadron."

"Admiral," Bexol said suddenly, flustered. "Your pardon for the interruption. That is a War Male."

"What the hell's a War Male?" said Verdura.

"A biologically specialized male of my species, hormonally modified to be a warrior and commander. I've never seen one before."

"That's one more oddity to add to the pile, but let's not get off track here," said Braga. "Fine, I see two humans and a Ruxin. Where's the Hok in charge?"

Engels growled and seemed to stifle an eyeroll. "Admiral, this may be difficult for you to accept at first, but there is no Hok in charge. There never was—were—whatever." She gestured, and something stepped into the holo-vidlink, appearing in full VR.

A Hok.

119

It reminded Braga of a human-shaped, bumpy-skinned lizard. He stood involuntarily at the virtual threat before his mind overrode the impulse and he relaxed. "I knew it."

"This is Sergeant Green-53," said Engels. "Sergeant, say hello to the admiral."

"Hello, Admiral."

"Stand on your hands."

The Hok immediately performed a perfect handstand and stayed that way.

Engels smiled. "Does this Hok look like he's in charge?"

"This could be a setup," Verdura hissed.

"Yes, Captain Verdura, it could be," Zaxby said unexpectedly. "But it's not." The Ruxin gestured at the medical technician who had slipped into the room, scanner in hand.

Everyone watched as the scan was performed. The tech handed Braga the scanner to read. "It matches," the admiral muttered. "This really is Zaxby."

"In the flesh," Zaxby said. "And the Hok are not in charge. We are. Humans, Ruxins, and several other minor species who live within the Republic."

"You've been brainwashed," Verdura said.

"I assure you, no. Quite the contrary, actually."

"Look," Engels said, "We could be fooling you, but what would be the point?"

"To get us to surrender," Braga said. "I'm sure you'd like to take these ships intact."

"I would," Engels replied with a quirk of a smile. "But I don't need to."

"Admiral," Lexin's voice broke in from his bridge station as a screen flickered to life, "forgive the interruption, but... but... there's a ship. A ship has emerged from the nebula. Big... bigger..." The Sensors officer seemed at a loss for words.

Engels stepped toward Braga, capturing his attention. "It appears you've detected *Indomitable*. Take your time. You need to know what you're up against."

Lexin explained what Braga was seeing on the screen. "Sir, the enemy ship is... impossible. It's four times the size of a monitor, sixteen times the size of the largest superdreadnought, with spinal weapons to match. It's a mobile fortress. It must have been what smashed our SDNs—what we thought was a fortress. Fortresses. I—"

"So what?" Braga snapped, hiding his consternation. "You have a big ship. I know you mousetrapped us. But you must have stripped two hundred planets up and down the front to do it. That means everywhere else, the Hundred Worlds will be seizing territory unopposed. I'm a military man, Engels. I'm willing to pay the price of war's fortunes."

Engels pressed her lips together earnestly. "Tough words, and admirable—but are you willing that everyone under your command pay that price for nothing?"

"Not for nothing," said Braga. "We took out the fuel factory. Mission accomplished."

Engels shook her head. "Sorry, Lucas. All you destroyed was a bunch of decoy emitters placed on a big asteroid. Felicity Station is still intact. Here's a realtime feed." One of the conference room screens lit up to show the facility, apparently undamaged, with the current timestamp displayed on the vidlink.

"I held off on smashing your flagship," she continued, "because I wanted to make sure I had a commander to talk to, but if you're too stubborn, I can turn *Luxemburg* into scrap with one order. Then I'll negotiate with whoever's next in your chain of command. How's that going to serve your people?"

Braga breathed out a defeated sigh. "Give me a couple of minutes to confer." He gestured to pause the conference link and turned to Verdura. "Well?"

Verdura slammed her hand onto the table. "My gut says fight, but…"

"Yes, *but*. We've apparently failed to destroy their fuel factory, and we've lost this battle. Now, all we would do is sacrifice our lives in order to deny them our ships. I can't ask my crews to do that. After centuries of fighting, we're finally winning the war, even if we lost this battle. If these people have any honor at all, they'll intern us and, eventually, repatriate us."

Verdura looked around the room, and so did Braga, trying to gauge the mood. He saw sober nods and downcast looks, but no disagreement.

When the link unpaused, Braga spoke again. "All right, Admiral Engels. I'll agree to a truce, and if you can prove your claims, I'll surrender my forces. That is my decision, and mine alone. If you've fooled me, if this is some Hok trick, I swear to God I'll never rest until you're brought low."

Engels shrugged. "If I fooled you, it's a ruse of war, Admiral—but soon, you'll see all the evidence. Your government—the government I served as well—has lied to you, Lucas. It couldn't admit the truth even to its flag officers. Only your most senior politicians and intelligence officials know. You haven't been fighting aliens for those centuries. You've been fighting humans." She rubbed her eyes and looked away, as if sorrowful. "This has been nothing but one massive civil war. And if what I suspect is right, we've been dancing to the tune of aliens the whole time."

Chapter 12

Straker, on Terra Nova

Straker slipped carefully out of Doris's bed, letting her sleep. Whatever passed for security services on Terra Nova would soon be connecting the dots and coming to her apartment, and he had to get away.

He looked around for anything that might be useful, and settled for a small hand-light, a kitchen knife, and a metal strut he pulled off her lone chair. He searched his pockets and found nothing there. They must have taken everything from him after they stunned him.

After gazing at Doris one last time, wishing things could be different, he slipped out of her room. A woman in the hallway glanced incuriously at him as Straker passed by and descended the stairs. As he approached the main building door, he saw several ground cars speeding in, lights flashing red in the falling night.

Dammit. There must be a back door. He turned and hurried toward the rear of the building and found his way into a courtyard. He crossed it and vaulted a shoulder-high wall into a parking lot. Behind him, he heard booted feet on the pavement as the security forces surrounded Doris' building. He ducked his head and didn't look back.

Where to go, he wondered as he walked quickly around the next building and out of sight. Though this seemed like any human city, he knew nothing about it. He had no money or credit sticks, no identification. He was a fugitive, and would have to think like one.

He wasn't even certain if this Glasgow place was a diz or not. And what had happened to Don? Was he being interrogated? Did he wave his credentials and go free? If so, was he unable to free Straker, or was he even now watching to see what his "protégé" would do?

No matter. Straker would run and hide and figure out a way to either rejoin Don, or get back to human space on his own.

His tweaked biology should be enough to make it past routine scans—and there was always theft, or force. No matter what Don had said about the Opters not being at war with humanity, Straker figured he was in his own war with the Sarmok Queens. That meant his options were completely open.

With no idea where to go, he chose a direction and began walking. Fortunately, the streets were laid out in a simple grid pattern. Vehicles sped by, though traffic was light.

He caught a break when he found a rack full of bicycles. There were no locks, so either crime was unknown here, or the bikes were shared, there for the riding. Soon, he was pumping along at thirty or forty kilometers per hour. This ought to get him somewhere soon.

Half an hour later, he ran into a barrier, similar to the others he'd seen, a hundred-meter-high wall that separated diz from diz, or diz from the real populace. If it was like others, the wall would be thick to hold rooms and corridors and facilities where the controllers worked. Other than by taking a train or ground car tunnel, or perhaps an air-car, doors in these walls were the only way from one place to another.

He couldn't read the Opter writing on the door, but the sensor pad next to it beckoned. Dare he put his palm on it to see if Don had given him access?

But any security service worth its salt would have programmed the system to alert them even as it locked Straker out. He leaned his bicycle against the wall of the nearest high-rise and lifted his head to stare upward.

The apartment block looked to be about the same height as the wall. Probably the controllers of the system didn't want people looking out their windows at the next place over, acquiring unauthorized information or learning things before they were supposed to.

The gap between the top of the wall and the roof of the building looked to be at about twenty meters wide. That would be quite a jump, even if he had a running start off the roof and could be sure of grabbing the top of the wall. Would there be razor wire or other deterrents to crossing?

Only one way to find out. Straker headed for the building entrance.

Struck by a sudden inspiration, he quickly went back and retrieved the bicycle. He then waited until a resident palmed open the building's front door, and he rushed up before it closed. Nodding to the female Facet, who was quite similar to Doris in her innocent demeanor, he lifted the bike to his shoulder and carried it quickly up the stairs. He hoped this action would be unworthy of reporting—or at least, that it wouldn't necessarily be connected with his escape.

Thirty floors later, he reached the very top of the stairs. His superb physical conditioning meant he was barely breathing hard.

A door confronted him, with more writing and a red band across it. Logically, this would access the roof.

He kicked it open.

No alarm blared, though there might be some silent alert. Or perhaps misbehavior in this place was so unusual, they hadn't bothered to wire it.

Straker bolted quickly inside and shut the door, and then ran up two more flights of stairs and debouched onto the roof.

The view from the top was magnificent, like any cityscape at night. The lights outlined the buildings and boulevards, and he could see antennas and towers. Illuminated heli-drones and air-cars created a fairyland that seemed to promise more than it could deliver.

Flashing red lights about a kilometer off, on the ground, reminded him that he was still the prey in a hunt. If they located him up here, no doubt they'd send aircraft.

He crossed to the other side of the square roof.

The sheer wall extended left and right. He could see nothing across it, not even the glow of other high-rises—no antennas, no towers, no air vehicles. Whatever was over there, it was not a cityscape like this one. Maybe it was farmland, or a park, or even a lake.

Squinting, he tried to examine the top of the wall. It was unmarked by lights or glow-strips. He could barely see its edge outlined against the fading night sky. Then he remembered the hand-light. He clicked it on and shone it across the gap.

The top looked clear of obstacles, about ten meters wide, and dead flat. As long as it was dry concrete, and not, say, coated with slick paint, he might be able to grab its edge at the end of a jump.

But could he make the distance? He stepped up on the low parapet and tried to get a feeling for it. If he sprinted and used the step to launch himself across...

He imagined his leap and his trajectory arc, and concluded it was very unlikely. Even if he jumped perfectly and aimed to catch the edge of the wall with his hands, he probably wouldn't make it. There was nothing below to grasp, either—no ladder, no projections, nothing but a smooth concrete wall.

If he'd had climbing claws or a rope with a grappling hook, he'd have a much better chance, but where could he get such things? Even if he broke into apartments and robbed residents, would they be likely to own devices like that?

No.

Straker ran from side to side on the roof. He surveyed nearby buildings, trying to see if any were higher, or closer to the wall, or situated in any way that might give him an advantage and get him over. Something with a tower or antenna, perhaps with extra altitude and guy wires he could commandeer, or maybe even topple over to form a bridge, would be perfect.

But there were no structures atop buildings near the wall, perhaps deliberately so. Everything seemed designed to make sure nobody crossed into a new diz without permission.

This left his long-shot inspiration.

The bike.

It was a desperate, insane idea. He considered it only because he knew his own capabilities, his strength, his speed, his balance. If he could grasp something on the wall with even one hand, he could lift himself. He could ride the bike faster than he could run, and so launch himself across the gap he couldn't jump.

The hard part would be arcing across at the correct angle to hit the top of the wall—not fall short, not fly over. A hundred-meter drop would leave him a broken wreck on the pavement, even if it didn't kill him outright.

As he turned to survey the roof, with its usual collection of vents, air conditioning machinery and other unknown devices, he saw three air vehicles traveling in formation, approaching from over the city. Had they not been flying together and symmetrically, he might not have noticed them.

He ran to the edge of the roof and swore at what he saw. Security force ground cars were approaching his building, their emergency lights spinning and flashing. No time. No time!

Only one chance. Straker ran to the small structure housing the stair's roof access and pried the metal door off its hinges, using a combination of the kitchen knife and the metal strut he'd taken from Doris. He then carried the flat rectangle to the edge of the roof and set it against the parapet, at the corner, to form a ramp.

He chose the corner because he wanted to give himself a forty-five degree angle, the better to reach the top of the wall as he landed. Aiming straight at it would make for less room for error.

Straker ran for the bicycle and carried it to a spot with a clear path to the ramp. The air vehicles were close, and he could hear the shouts of those on the ground as they piled out of their vehicles.

Now or never, Assault Captain Straker, he told himself sternly as he jumped on the bike and gathered speed. He'd done far more lethal and dangerous things in a mechsuit, but now he felt naked, with nothing between him and impact, a fall, and capture.

The screaming of turbines told him the air-cars were close, decelerating to hover or land on the roof. He hoped they weren't allowed to cross the wall. If they were, maybe there was terrain on the other side he could lose himself in.

The ramp—the ramp—

His tires slammed into it and he shot upward. Going airborne reminded him of a combat drop. His mind kicked into overdrive and the world seemed to slow as he flew above the gap.

Slugs ricocheted off the wall as he landed—a generous term for his sprawling fall—atop the barrier. His front tire came down flat, but his back tire didn't make it, and the bike bucked him over the handlebars.

Desperately, he flattened himself and reached for the concrete surface, hoping it wasn't covered in years of bird shit and dust. Did they bother to clean it?

Skin ripped from his palms and forearms as he skidded. He somersaulted to his feet, finding the roof of the wall clean enough for traction. More shots struck near him as the bicycle fell back onto the Glasgow side. There was no cover, and only one place to go.

Straker dove for the opposite far edge and slid over, hanging by his right-hand fingers and right toe in order to minimize his profile. Below, on the other side, he could faintly see a forested landscape, with no lights. As this world had no moon, he didn't even have reflected shine to help him. Directly below him, he got the impression of trees.

The slugs sought his exposed hand and foot, shattering concrete spray from the top of the wall. He had no choice. He twisted and braced, and then let go, shoving off the wall to ensure he fell into the trees. If they were tall and thick with branches, he might survive without breaking bones.

If not, he might live, only to be crippled.

He pulled his arms tight to his torso and rolled in the air to present his back to the branches, as he'd been taught for parachuting. This kept vulnerable parts of his body—his throat, his armpits and inner thighs, where the large arteries were— away from puncture. He closed his eyes, covered his face with his hands, and tried to relax. Stiffening up would only make it worse.

He crashed through ever-increasing branch sizes, which flayed his clothes and the skin of his back, until he finally impacted one that wouldn't yield to his momentum. It struck him across his legs, spinning him to slam into the next, and the next. Now he flailed, trying to regain control. He bounced from a big limb, face-first, and he could feel ribs crack before he slid off.

Straker pinballed off two more, bruising himself painfully, before he crashed into the ground, knocking the wind out of him. He struggled to breathe as his diaphragm spasmed and his cracked ribs protested.

Staring upward into the branches, he tried to tell if the air-cars were coming over the wall. He didn't see lights, didn't hear their turbines searching for him.

Despite the battering he'd suffered, he counted it as a win. If the security troops were local to Glasgow, or if this diz was protected from interference, at least he might get away. Straker was still hazy on the capricious rules the controllers used, but some chance was better than no chance at all.

Once he could breathe, he rolled to his knees and stumbled to his feet. He still had the hand-light in his pocket, but he thought it better to try to let his eyes adjust to the darkness. The light would pinpoint him for searchers or any hostile denizens of this place.

On the other hand, if there was predatory animal life, it might not need sight to find and kill him.

Moving slowly, he headed away from the looming wall. He didn't want to take the chance there were sensors or doors where, despite whatever rules were in play, his hunters might pop out and grab him. If he were in charge of the cops of this world, he might not always follow the rules, especially if the stakes were high.

Of course, he didn't know what they thought he was—a Facet gone mad, a Miskor agent among the Sarmok, a spy for the real humans? Or maybe they were just going by a script for when anything deviated from their weird programmed scenarios.

After several hundred meters of slow, cautious travel, Straker broke out of the woods to see a small clearing. At least, he thought it was a clearing, until he stepped ankle-deep into the water and realized it was not flat ground, but a large pond.

Thirst seized him then, and a desire to wash his oozing injuries. After taking a long look around for dangers, he sank to his knees and smelled the water. It seemed fresh. Besides, his biotech and his genetically engineered immune system should keep him safe from all ordinary diseases.

He drank and washed on the tiny, sandy beach. The chill water soothed his scrapes, and he tore his tattered tunic and the bottoms of his trousers off to wrap his hands and arms in makeshift bandages, leaving him in nothing but crude shorts

129

and boots. He used strips of cloth to bind up his ribs tight, making his breathing less painful.

Then he took the strut in one hand as a club and circled the pond.

A faint trail beckoned him, a slash in the vegetation he could barely see as his eyes adjusted. He followed it, wary, for several kilometers. Night creatures rustled, birds called. Other noises passed that he couldn't identify. He was no woodsman, and his outdoor survival training was long behind him.

Then came an unmistakable sound.

A scream.

A woman's scream.

Straker increased his pace, seeing a glow ahead. The scream sounded again. He burst out of the woods to a hellish scene.

Four enormous crimson men stood near a bonfire. Its light revealed the figure of a proportionally large woman, her hands bound above her head to a tree limb, her feet barely touching the ground. One man, laughing, brushed the woman with a burning torch, and she screamed again and kicked out in fear and rage.

Straker charged.

Chapter 13

"I'm still waiting for the other shoe to drop," said Admiral Braga to Admiral Engels as they ate off fine china in *Indomitable's* flag dining room.

The two admirals faced each other at one end of the long table. Verdura and Zholin, Dexon and Zaxby and several other senior officers from both sides ranged down the rest of it.

This formal dinner was also an important meeting. For the last three days, Braga's surrounded fleet had hung in space, awaiting annihilation. Time had run out. He had to commit to a decision: fight, surrender—or defect.

Braga went on, "You've spent three days showing me around your fleet, and all the evidence supports your claims, but..."

Engels smiled at her stiff-necked old commander. "But it's hard to accept that something you've believed your whole life is false. It's human nature to cling to preconceived notions, even when confronted with overwhelming evidence to the contrary, if it doesn't fit your worldview. At least you didn't have to be sent to a prison camp and be beaten half to death."

"If you weren't sitting in front of me in an admiral's uniform, obviously in command, I'd wonder if they'd broken your mind and reprogrammed you. It's easy enough if your brainchips get hacked. But this whole fleet, this whole situation, can't be some kind of theatre—and I've run all the usual tests to make sure I'm not inside a VR sim. So, I have to believe you."

"But you don't want to."

"I didn't... but if I accept your bizarre tale, I find myself wanting to believe it all."

Engels sipped her caff. "What's stopping you?"

"Loyalty to the Hundred Worlds, I suppose. I swore an oath."

"To what?"

"Beg pardon?"

"Specifically to what did you swear that oath?"

Braga frowned and straightened his silverware next to his half-eaten meal, not meeting her eyes. "I understand your point, young lady. I swore an oath to the Constitution, the citizens, and the duly elected and appointed officials of the Hundred Worlds, in that order. You're going to argue my duty to the Constitution means I have a higher duty—to the truth, to the law that's obviously been violated at many levels, and to the long-term interests of the citizenry."

"Sounds like you're making your own argument."

"But if it were that simple, military people would be changing sides every time their own government got out of line. We can't ignore Parliament and the chain of command just because we don't like what they're doing. I need to know the Constitution's being violated so thoroughly and irretrievably that the concept of treason becomes moot."

"I've studied the Hundred Worlds Constitution," Engels said earnestly. "Part of Article 1 states, 'The government shall in all things be truthful and forthright,' with the usual exceptions for military necessity and classified information. Do you think the government has been truthful and forthright?"

"An argument could be made that—"

"Come on, Lucas! You know the answer. You simply need to decide if all the lies they told you rise to the level of unjustly abrogating the Constitution. If so, the politicians committed treason, not you—and you're free of your oath. You can't be faithful to a lie."

"I can be faithful to the spirit of truth." Braga folded his hands and lifted his gaze to Engels. "That's why I've decided to surrender."

"Not defect?"

"You'll have our ships. You mousetrapped us fair and square. I've ordered no sabotage. That's the payment for my people's lives. But I can't turn around and fight against the Hundred Worlds. It's a personal decision, and it's final."

Engels sighed. "I'm sorry to hear that—but I understand."

"Since my decision was a personal one," Braga continued, "I'll make an announcement to my captains and crews, giving them leave to make the same decision. They can be interned with me, or they may choose to join your Republic. I've allowed them to see records of all the evidence."

"That's very fair of you—though of course, you could hardly stop them from defecting."

"This way their consciences are clear if they do."

"And in your heart of hearts, you want us to win?"

Braga sat stiffly and lowered his eyes again. "I didn't say that."

Engels nodded sharply. "Of course not."

"I'll stay with you," Captain Verdura said, reaching out to lay her palm on Braga's arm.

"Thank you, Lydia, but that won't be necessary."

"I think it is. You made it a personal decision for everyone under your command, no?"

"So I did." Braga concentrated on finishing his meal and said no more.

Later, in his amazingly spacious assigned quarters aboard *Indomitable,* he held his sidearm in his hands and stared at it for long minutes. He was surprised when Engels allowed him to keep it, fully charged, though an honor guard of four marines attended him everywhere. She must be still hoping he'd change his mind, and was treating him like a guest instead of a prisoner.

But there was no guard here, only he and his weapon. Less than a kilogram, but it could end his life—and his shame—with one easy pull of the trigger.

Is that what his life had come to? Thirty-three years of distinguished service capped by a military disaster, and then he didn't even have the guts to ask his people to die with him in a blaze of glory.

Yet he couldn't do it. If he thought a final stand would change the course of the war, would inspire a victory of right and righteousness, he'd have done it. Fighting to the death merely that Admiral Lucas Braga not have to face another personal defeat… that would be the true coward's way.

And he didn't know which side was right. He used to be sure, but now he saw those at the top of the Hundred Worlds had supplied fake certainty. Not only had they figuratively demonized the enemy—common propaganda during most wars throughout history—they'd done it more literally, twisting the truth until everyone believed the Hok shock troops were demonic alien invaders instead of dissidents and criminals turned into soulless war-slaves.

Why? Did his leaders believe people would work or fight less hard against humans? Or was it simply about keeping control, pumping up war fever and blind hatred?

But there *were* alien invaders. The Opters.

A dozen races of aliens lived in relative peace with humans. Some, like the Ruxins, even integrated themselves into the forces of both sides, but these insectoids… if Zaxby's briefings were accurate, they'd been perverting human history for centuries.

Those were the ones humans should be angry with. Even if there were some good Opters, their regime had attacked humans unprovoked, murdering millions. Worse, they'd perpetuated a civil war that had killed billions and kept humanity divided and weakened.

And that was, ultimately, why Braga didn't put the muzzle of his pistol in his mouth and let a beam of coherent light boil his brain. He couldn't bring himself to lead others against the Hundred Worlds, but if the time ever came to go to war against the Opters, perhaps he'd be needed.

* * *

Admiral Engels busied herself with the overwhelming detail of reorganizing her fleet. She'd triaged her forces, sending severely damaged ships that nevertheless had working sidespace drives straight to Murmorsk for repair and refit.

Before they left, she cannibalized all their supplies and filled them with prisoners of war, those who hadn't wished to defect, including Braga, Verdura and all of the Hun ship captains. Those likely were swayed by Braga's example, but

134

she didn't let it worry her. None of them would have been trusted with command of a ship anyway.

The split between defectors and internees turned out to be about fifty-fifty, once the lower ranking detainees had been processed and given free choice. That gave her thousands of trained and experienced spacers to sprinkle throughout her fleet.

Her two new carriers she filled to bursting with extra stocks of everything and designated them as fleet auxiliaries. She ordered each of her ships to give up a small craft or two and transfer them to the carriers as well.

By this method she created a true expeditionary force, a fleet-in-being to give her enemies pause. Hun spy drones were no doubt even now tunneling through sidespace with reports of the loss of Braga's Tenth Fleet, but she'd been careful to keep an assembled *Indomitable* hidden in the gas. When the battleship emerged, she would be seen as sixteen oddly shaped superdreadnoughts, and Engels had also taken deception measures to hide how many of Braga's ships she'd taken intact.

All told, she now had more than three hundred warships, over one hundred of them of capital grade, one of the largest armadas ever assembled in one place. *Indomitable* herself was worth roughly another fifty, if she could get into the fight.

The fleet's very presence would make the Huns change their strategy. They would combine task forces into larger fleets, and they would slow their headlong rush to seize Republic territory. They'd scout more, trying to ensure they didn't get trapped again, and they'd seek a way to combine on her and bring her to battle.

Of all this she was as certain as any commander could be. The Huns had taken a stunning tactical loss, but not a crippling strategic one.

She sent Benota a complete report via message drone, and asked that the next communiqué to the Hundred Worlds Parliament reference the situation. Maybe it would get them to start talking.

However, Engels had to plan for the worst. She had to assume one bloody nose wouldn't do it, and that meant she had to secure another victory, to deal the enemy a blow to their morale and will to fight.

The Huns wouldn't be suckered again like at Calypso. Besides, there was no place so suitable. Ambushing a force in space was difficult.

Instead, she needed to employ a more conventional strategy of forcing the enemy to defend something valuable. That ruled out any of the newly taken systems.

No, her model needed to be the battle where it all started, where Braga had also tasted defeat and she herself had been captured: Corinth.

There, the Mutuality had driven deep into Hun territory and pillaged a heavily industrialized world. They'd hidden their strength and waited for the relieving forces to rush in, as they'd hoped.

Then, they'd handed Braga and the Hundred Worlds Navy their asses.

If it worked once, why not again? Only this time, the full load of supplies would allow her forces to choose an enemy system beyond their supposed travel range. The question was, which one?

She examined the entire war front and the enemy worlds behind it, with Trinity comlinked in to run the conference room holo-table. Her staff attended, but the tripart being was so efficient that they were hardly needed.

Many good choices presented themselves, but she kept coming back to one.

Sparta.

While not the most heavily industrialized or populated system, it contained one unique thing: a sprawling manufacturing complex of the Carstairs Corporation. There, mechsuit technology was researched and developed, and over ninety percent of the Hun 'suits were built on site. If she could capture and strip the factories and laboratories, the enemy would be set back years, and the Republic would come much closer to ground force parity.

Sparta was also an easy stepping-stone to the Huns' political heart, the capital system of Atlantis. Taking it would force the fleets driving into the Republic to turn around to deal with this new threat.

As with Calypso, she would hide her true strength until it was too late. If she won the first battle when they counterattacked, she might even be able to hold the system for months, forcing the Hundred Worlds to pull back and regroup all along the front. If so, their Parliament would have to negotiate a truce, the first step toward making peace, ending the civil war, and dealing with the Opter threat.

Was she being tempted beyond good sense? Lots of commanders throughout history had thrown the dice one too many times. But all the analysis said that she had a good chance to pull it off at each stage.

The first battle, the attack, would be easy, her entire fleet dropping out of sidespace so deep in enemy territory. Sims of the second, counterattacking battle showed about a 75-percent likelihood of winning against even the worst-case estimates of Hundred Worlds strength.

Three out of four chances. Was that good enough?

For a simple battle over a star system, perhaps not, especially as failure would be far worse for her, so deep in their territory, than for the Huns. But in reality, this battle might be for the fate of humanity. For that, it seemed worth the risk.

Carla wished Derek were here. His two-to-three-month estimate was a double-edged sword. It gave her time to prepare her campaign, but it also meant he wouldn't be with her at the critical time.

She had no doubts about her own tactical ability, and her captains and crews would perform well now that they'd won this great victory, but having the Liberator with them would be worth a squadron or more, just for the morale boost. And, she was honest enough to admit to herself, Derek had a way of seeing things from a fresh perspective and finding a better way to win... not to mention that she already missed him. In the silence of her too-large flag quarters, in the emptiness of their bed, the demons of doubt crept in. Was he coming back? Was he even still alive?

If anyone could pull off the mission he'd set himself, Derek Straker could. Still, at times she could barely restrain her anger at his leaving. His place was at her side, and vice-versa, not playing spy among aliens.

So, settling on Sparta, she ordered her fleet, designated First Expeditionary Force, to prepare and plan in detail. Her message drones had requested additional ground forces in particular, whatever Benota could spare.

After six days, return courier drones arrived with word that the Huns still weren't talking, despite new overtures stressing their disaster at Calypso, the Republic's willingness to talk, and the threat posed by the Opters.

"I'm beginning to suspect the Opter influence goes deeper than we feared," Benota said in a recorded eyes-only vid. "We've developed a test for Opter genetics and biotech, and while it's far from perfect, it's identified thousands of possible agents among us at every level. The security and intelligence services are working overtime looking for evidence against these suspects, and in the meantime they're being watched, and assigned to less sensitive duties."

The vid continued. "That makes my denial of your request for ground forces all the more painful for me, given your impressive victory. I always want to reinforce success, not failure. However, these spies among us, and unrest among our frightened populace, mean we need every Hok, every marine, every Breaker and trustworthy soldier or police officer of any kind. There's even been a proposal to kill two birds with one stone by turning our prison population into Hok, as the Mutuality once did. I believe we've blocked that idea for now, but it's a very tempting shortcut. And, if we can't at least stalemate the Huns, if we appear to be losing this war and our central worlds are threatened, making new Hok may become the least drastic measure we have to accept in order to preserve the Republic."

Benota shook his head. "Of course, there's always the final option to unite humanity: surrender to the Huns and let them take over. I know you've considered it. It might not even be that bad. In absorbing a population ten times their own, they'll inevitably become absorbed themselves, much as everyone that conquered the Han Chinese did on Old Earth." He sighed. "I say this for your ears only, as surrender runs counter to any

138

good officer's instincts—but keep it in mind. Good luck. Benota out."

Surrender to the Huns? No, she'd never considered it, but Benota's phrasing forced her to think about it now. She could see his reasoning. In fact, if back when she was Flight Lieutenant Engels she'd been told the tale of her future actions and successes, she'd probably find perfect sense in first overthrowing the Mutuality, and then surrendering it to the Hundred Worlds.

But now that she was Fleet Admiral Engels, and had a fledgling constitutional republic to fight for, one that should in time become better than the corrupt and degenerate Hundred Worlds, she put that option as a last, final resort, just above an exhausted stalemate that would leave humanity at the Opters' mercy.

In other words, maybe the least of all evils.

It couldn't be helped. No military commander ever got every resource they asked for.

She turned her attention to readying her campaign.

Part 2: Hero

Atlantis: Capital of the Hundred Worlds
Carstairs Corporation Headquarters

The frown of Billingsworth M. Carstairs VI was quite genuine this time, and stayed firmly in place as he strode into the boardroom. The outer wall of the room was composed of pure ballistic crystal, so clear that it appeared he could step right out into the air above Atlantis City.

He ignored the view now, focusing on his board of directors. "I've just come from a meeting with the Minister of Defense," he said. "We've been ordered—" at this he ground his teeth, "—*ordered* to commission the lead ship of the Victory class within ten days."

"Impossible!" said his CEO, Romy Gardel, who then became suddenly contrite. "I mean, sir, that we need at least three more months to complete the program as laid out, which is already rushing the schedule. To comply with this order we'll have to perform significant corner-cutting that would expose us to accusations of incompetence, as well as litigation from our suppliers, subcontractors and other megacorps."

Carstairs slid a thick sheaf of official hardcopy onto the table. "There's an executive order from the Prime Minister absolving us of all criminal liability. We're earning so much on this contract we can settle any civil lawsuits and still come out ahead. We'll commission the *Victory* on time and our best technicians will be assigned aboard to make sure the AI functions properly until we can turn it over to the military. Then we wash our hands of it. We'll collect our bonuses, our stock will rise, and we'll be richer than ever."

"Of course, sir. But why are they pushing us on this?" Gardel asked.

"Because that idiot Lucas Braga lost an even bigger battle, at some enemy system called Calypso. Probably got himself killed, too, along with most of his command. Why the hell they gave him another fleet after Corinth, I'll never know."

"Didn't you—never mind," Mike Rollins said quickly.

Carstairs glared at the corporate attorney, remembering quite well that Carstairs himself had supported Braga's second chance after the military man's family had called in a favor. That made this debacle all the worse. "Yes, yes, I remember." He turned to his head of Public Relations. "Cyndi, have your team ready to distance us from Braga—the connections were routine, we didn't know, we can't remember, we have no records, *et cetera.* Generate canned items to blanket the nets with distractions—celebrity sex and drug scandals, human interest vids, examples of our competitors disrespecting the flag and our military personnel—the usual shotgun approach."

"Yes, sir."

"I'll want daily reports from now until the launch. Tell your people to break out the stims. It's time to earn their bonuses. And if they don't—which means *you* don't, and *I* don't—"

He drew his finger across his throat.

Chapter 14

Straker on Terra Nova

The big men around the bonfire, blinded by its light, didn't see Straker until he was upon them. He struck the man with the torch—the one abusing the tall, bound woman. He delivered a terrible blow to the body, using all his strength and speed. He felt his enemy's ribs cave.

The others reached for weapons. Two more fell to Straker's furious surprise attack. The last one turned to face him, holding a sword.

A sword? That was good news to Straker, better than a gun.

The man stabbed and slashed, his movements quick and sure, expert. Straker dodged and parried with his metal strut. Though naturally faster, and he hoped stronger than his opponent, Straker's injuries put him at a disadvantage. The man had more reach and skill, and a better tool for killing.

Straker retreated, circling the fire, barely parrying his opponent's heavy blows. Within a minute the man would likely kill him... or force him to run.

By chance, his opponent neared the bound woman. She lifted her legs and, dangling from the ropes around her wrists, kicked out powerfully at the man, causing him to stumble into the fire.

Straker pounced, knocking the big man's sword aside and striking him in the knee. He roared and fell to the ground, scrambling out of the fire. Now his head came within Straker's reach.

Straker broke his skull with the strut.

Though gasping for each painful breath, Straker picked up the sword and whirled, making sure none of the other three had recovered enough to pose a threat. Only the first man remained conscious, groaning and holding his crushed side.

Cautiously, Straker approached the woman, who eyed him warily. Taller than he was, she wore only a short skirt, and her skin was dark and scaly in the firelight, different from that of the men, which was smooth like leather, and crimson. She had no hair, only some feathery structures on her head, and her features were hard and angular. If not for her bare, perfectly mammalian breasts and wide hips, he wouldn't have known her sex.

Straker raised the sword slowly toward her bindings, watching her face for understanding. The woman lifted her chin to look upward as he extended the blade and carefully sawed at the rope wrapping the tree branch. When that parted and she could stand flat-footed, she extended her hands for him to cut the remaining ropes.

As soon as she was free, she ran for a dropped sword, picked it up, and struck with brutal efficiency at the one conscious man. Straker intervened, but only after the third blow.

"Stop, stop!" he said, blocking her from further attacks. "They're down."

"They deserve death," the woman said in passable but heavily accented Earthan. Straker had the impression it wasn't her first language.

"Maybe. But I don't murder my fallen enemies."

She spat at the nearest. "Enemies should die. That is truth."

Straker stood his ground. "No. Let's get away from here, somewhere safe."

The woman glared at him, put down the sword, and then stripped the sword-belt from the one she'd hacked. It was too big for her slim waist, so she looped it over one shoulder and across her chest. She then wiped the blade clean and slammed it into the scabbard.

"We need food and water." She gestured toward the encampment supplies.

Straker nodded, taking a sword-belt for himself and doing the same while the woman rummaged among the items scattered on the ground. She came up with smoked meat, and canteens of wood and hide.

"Eat. Drink." She squatted by the fire, her back to it, ripping off big bites of the meat, apparently ravenous. He could see her teeth were long and sharp, like a predator's.

Straker gratefully sat to eat and drink, his back also to the fire. Afterward he checked the fallen men. The two living ones he bound with ropes. While he wouldn't murder them, he had no problem leaving them to their fate. Any warrior worth his salt would find a way out of the bindings come morning.

Once the woman had eaten, she salvaged several items and stuffed them into a bag, then gestured sharply, pointing with her hand like a blade. "We must go, that way."

Straker nodded. It was pointless to ask where. The woman seemed competent and knowledgeable.

"Wait," he said. "What's your name?"

"Roslyn. What's yours?"

"Straker."

"Stray-kurr. That is a good name. A strong name for small man." She reached out to grasp his arm, squeezing his biceps. "Strong man," she amended, feeling the hardness.

Straker flexed and smiled. He seized her hand in his own, finding sharp nails like talons there, and squeezed until her eyes widened and she winced slightly. A warrior culture would revere strength. Best to establish his right up front. "Ros-lyn," he said. "Strong name for a strong woman."

Roslyn grinned a smile that could have filled a tiger's mouth. "You speak truth."

"Guess I do. Let's go?"

"We shall go." She turned and headed back the way Straker had come—toward the wall.

"Wait, wait," he said. "Not that way."

"This way."

"No, I came from that way."

"We go to the wall."

"Why?"

Roslyn reached into the bag and half-lifted out a coil of rope.

"To climb it," she said, watching him narrowly.

Straker sighed. "Look, I came from the other side." He gestured to make his point. "From over the wall. That's how I got these." He showed his scrapes and his bound ribs. "I fell from the top." He mimed falling.

"You... fell from the other side of the wall?"

144

"I did."

"You are a great warrior."

"Ah, yeah. I am, though maybe not the way you mean." Then again, what *did* he mean? War was war and soldiering was soldiering, no matter what the tools.

Her face showed sudden wonder. "Gorben was right."

"Gorben?"

Roslyn's nostrils flared. "Later. We must go. A Rardel is near."

"A Rardel?"

"A great eating beast." She turned. "There!"

Straker turned to see something huge waddle into the firelight. It was the size of a five-ton loader, had a shell like a turtle and a lizard's head on a long neck. Roslyn pulled Straker back slowly as his hand went to the hilt of his sword.

The nightmare stared their direction and Roslyn froze. After a long moment, the thing turned to nose at the bloody dead man Roslyn had slashed. It grasped a foot and backed away from the fire, which it evidently didn't much like. In a moment it had faded into the trees. Soon, Straker heard the sounds of eating.

"Good. Now these Bortoks shall all die. Come."

So the fallen men were Bortoks...

Roslyn led Straker through the woods in a wide arc around the crunching, tearing noises. She moved much more surefootedly than he did, and more than once she hissed at him to be quieter. Eventually she slowed down and helped him, sometimes telling him where to place his feet, or to avoid certain plants he could barely see. Her night vision was clearly superb, far better than his own.

Roslyn seemed to be avoiding trails. Their route wended slightly, slowly upward into low hills.

Four hours and at least twenty kilometers later, Roslyn paused by a stream and drank. They refilled their water-jugs. She then led them to the bare top of a rise to look back the way they came.

In the distance he could see the lights of Glasgow, like a far-off dream. Beyond it loomed the faint outline of the world-ring and the Jacob's Ladder of its tether.

Only from here could one finally see over the hundred-meter-high wall. These people, apparently without high technology, could only guess at what the cityscape represented. Did they think it was some kind of paradise, a heaven where they went when they died?

"That's Glasgow," he said, pointing.

"Here is Urquala."

"This place? Here?" Straker waved at the ground around them.

"Yes. Urquala. My land."

"And what's that called over there?" He pointed at the distant line of lights.

"Rennerog."

"Tell me of this place."

Roslyn stepped close, and Straker could feel the heat as her arm brushed his. He expected her skin to be rough, but actually it was smooth, like a bright yellow tame snake he'd once handled. "The magic men say it is an evil place of demons. Gorben says it is only a different place, with people good and bad, like here. What is it?"

"You're asking me?"

"I am asking."

Straker breathed deeply of the clean, chill air. "Gorben's right."

"No demons?"

He smiled. "A few."

"Enemies?"

"More of those."

"Friends?"

"Maybe one."

Roslyn slipped her arm into the crook of his. "Now two."

"Okay…" Straker said.

"What's that mean?" she asked.

"What's what?"

"What's *okay?*"

"Okay… it means, *yes, good, I agree.*"

"Okay okay. You speak strangely."

"Back at you, girl."

Roslyn turned to embrace him. It felt odd, to have a woman taller than himself take him in her arms and press herself to him. "I want you."

"Umm…"

"For a mate. For a year and a day."

"Uhh…" Oh, hell. This was getting awkward, but he could hardly piss off his one ally in Urquala. "I'm already married."

"Married?"

"Mated. I have a woman."

"In Rennerog?"

"Yeah, kinda. It's complicated."

"What's that? Comp…"

"It means: difficult to explain."

"Another woman claims you?" she asked.

"Um, yeah."

Roslyn grinned. "I will fight her for you."

"You…"

"I will take you from her, fairly and by right."

"You can try." Straker chuckled, envisioning one hell of a battle.

"I have no anger. I will not kill her."

"Good to hear." Straker gently disentangled himself. "Tell you what. Let's talk about all that later, when we're safe. When we're back with your people. You have people? A tribe, a village… something like that?" He knew little of low-tech societies, just some educational showvids he'd seen from time to time.

"My people, yes. Our stronghold."

"Stronghold?" he asked.

"It is a great place, large. High walls. Calaria."

"Calaria? We're going there?"

"Yes."

Straker took one more look at Glasgow, curious what had become of Myrmidon, thinking about the future, and wondering how he would get home. He admitted to himself he might have bitten off more than he could chew. At least, he'd been too cavalier, overconfident from his repeated victories and successes. Now he was stuck in a primitive enclave on an enemy world, with no way home.

147

Had he been a fool? The stakes—knowledge of the Opters and the potential of making an alliance—had tempted him, lured him here. Now, though, the Liberation was without the Liberator. Was it hubris to think they needed him? If so, he'd been irresponsible to leave.

Alternatively, his friends and allies would step up in his absence and continue to pursue his aims and goals. He thought of Carla. Could she do it? Would she do it?

She was his rock, his partner, his other half.

His wife.

And she was a warrior. A different kind from Roslyn, sure, but a warrior nonetheless. Willing to fight, willing to do what had to be done, he felt sure.

He held tight to that and buried his doubt. "Okay. Let's go."

Roslyn turned away from distant Glasgow, toward her Rennerog, and headed higher into the hills.

Straker took one last look back, and followed.

As false dawn darkened the land, Roslyn slowed and led Straker cautiously over a ridge. From atop it he could see an ocean of campfires in the valley below. Across and beyond loomed a massive castle, brooding atop a natural bluff. She pointed. "Calaria."

"Unknowable Creator, that's a big place! I thought…"

"You think I lie?"

"No, of course not." He had thought, though, that her idea of a "stronghold" might be less than impressive. He was glad to be wrong.

Well, assuming they could make it to her home. Those fires worried him.

"What are they?" he said, pointing.

"Bortoks. An army of men, like you killed. Always they attack us in our mountains. They covet our riches and our wisdom."

"They're besieging your castle?"

Roslyn sounded out his words. "Yes. Be-siege. Surround. They throw great stones to break down our walls. We throw them back. It is war, in the season of war."

"What are your people called?"

148

"People."

"There's no common name?"

She seemed to ponder. "Calaria. That is almost right."

Straker shrugged. "Okay, Calaria the place, Calaria the people. So… who's winning?"

Roslyn spat. "Bortoks. Always they drive us Calaria farther back. This is the final place, before… before…" She searched for Earthan words. "Before the land, the top of table, behind." She made gestures with her hands, but in the near-darkness, he couldn't see to understand.

"Never mind. Show me later. How do we get there?"

"By a secret way." She took her sword in her hand, a knife in the other. "Make ready. The Bortoks have sentries. I will see for you."

"No problem." Straker drew his sword in his right hand, but rather than a knife, he held his hand-light in his left. He wondered what these primitives would make of it. They'd probably think it magic. It might as well be, to them.

They crept forward together, Straker walking as she'd showed him, trying to place his feet down gently, toe first, avoiding dry leaves and sticks. Roslyn's bare, claw-toed feet were far better for this than his boots. He felt clumsy and noisy next to her silent glide.

"There," she murmured. Ahead he could faintly see a stone structure, a doorway as if to a mine leading into the hillside. A small fire burned low nearby, just smoky embers, and at least two figures lay on the rock next to it.

"Stay," she said. "Come when I am done." She crept forward.

He stayed. She was much quieter than he, and he had an inkling of what came next. Killing sentries was an old tradition in war, and ugly, brutal work. Now that he knew her people were besieged and at war with the big men, the Bortoks, he had no qualms about killing them in their sleep.

He saw her make two quick thrusts, and then two more delicate cuts. The figures never stirred. Fools. Sleeping in guard duty was a capital offense in some armies. Today, Roslyn had meted out their sentences.

She waved him forward and led him into the dark tunnel. As the light faded to nothing, she slowed. "Touch the wall."

"You need light?" Straker asked.

"You have light?"

"I do."

She probably thought he meant he had flint and steel, or matches if she knew of such things. He reminded himself that anyone who could build a castle of cut stone blocks and fight sieges with "thrown rocks"—probably catapults—was more sophisticated than he'd thought. Her imperfect Earthan had led him to believe she was a Stone Age woman, but clearly, both sides had approximately medieval technology.

"Not yet," she said. "Those outside may see."

"Right."

Three twists of the tunnel later and Roslyn grasped his arm. "Now, the light."

Straker aimed his hand-light away from her, dialed it to its lowest setting, and pressed the button. Roslyn gasped in surprise, and then leaned close to examine it. "Like day! And no fire!"

"This is what you see in Glasgow. In Rennerog. Many, many lights like this."

"You are truly the one Gorben spoke of."

"What do you mean?"

"You're the Azaltar. The one who aids us."

Straker shone the light up and down the tunnel. "I'll try... but I'm not sure what I can do against an army. Not without weapons."

"We have weapons."

"Not the kind I'd like." He turned to walk deeper into the hillside, the beam of light showing him the way. "How is it the Bortoks didn't guard this way better? Or use it to sneak into your castle?"

"It's not so easy. You will see."

Twenty minutes later, Straker heard the rushing sound of fast-moving water. Ten minutes after that, they debouched into a cavern cut by a swift-running river five meters wide and equally deep. Several ways led off from it. He counted at least nine, perhaps more, if all the clefts led to tunnels.

150

"Which way?" he asked.

Roslyn smiled. "Now you understand. Branches lead to more branches, which lead to more. Only the wise know the way through."

"And you're wise?"

She lifted her chin. "I am."

"Lead on. Here, take this." Straker held out the light.

She took it carefully, reverently, as if she were afraid to break it. She then sheathed her sword and took his hand. "Walk where I walk, or you will fall."

Slowly she picked her way across the river, placing her feet at specific intervals. He stayed one-half step behind her. Her strong, steady grip made sure he didn't stray.

Each time his foot came down, he found a rock beneath it, just wide enough to stand on. One slip and they would be washed downward far into the earth. He could see why the Bortoks were deterred.

On the other side, Roslyn led him into one tunnel that seemed no different from any other. With the light, she walked surefootedly, and he strode along behind.

They crossed many intersections, each with a selection of several tunnels. Straker became hopelessly lost, but Roslyn seemed to know exactly where she was, and each time chose her path without hesitation.

Three hours later, Straker estimated, she handed the light back to him. "Put out the light," she said, and watched interestedly as he pushed the button to turn it off. He was about to ask why when he saw a flickering orange glow ahead.

"Do not fear," she said, "but do not speak until I say."

"I'll speak when I damn well please," he retorted, amused.

"Then be ready to fight. My young warriors are eager for battle. My old warriors have stiff necks."

Straker grasped her arm. "I'll keep quiet for a little while, but I'm a warrior too. You saw what I did to those Bortoks. I'm not afraid of a fight."

Roslyn took Straker's face between her palms. "I know you are not afraid, my strong man. I only do not want you to kill my people. My Calaria. I need every warrior." Then she pressed her lips to his.

He didn't resist. It would be impolite, after all. Fortunately it was brief, with only a hint of passion.

Damn. This could get complicated.

Chapter 15

Straker in Calaria

Straker and Roslyn found themselves at the end of the final cave tunnel, looking through an iron grate into a room lit by flickering oil lamps hanging from wall hooks. A crude lock held a larger bar across the door. Two armored men of Roslyn's kind stood suddenly from their chairs at a table that held dice and stacks of coins.

They unsheathed their swords and said something in their clicking language. One grasped a rope that led upward through a hole in the rock, perhaps an alarm of some kind.

"It is I, Roslyn," she said, pressing her face to the bars. "Speak the Low Tongue for my friend."

"Sessa! You have returned! Is he...?"

"He is."

The guard rushed forward to unlock the door. The other released the rope. "Sessa, the Bortoks have weakened the south tower, but still we hold."

Roslyn clapped the man on his shoulder. "Fear not, Powl. I have brought a man from beyond the wall of Rennerog."

"Beyond the wall...?" The guard Powl stared as Straker stepped through the door. "This puny one?"

Roslyn grinned her toothy grin. "He is Straker. He is the Azaltar. Take his hand and feel his strength."

Powl snorted skeptically, but put out his hand. Straker took it and squeezed until the man's face broke with pain. "He's a demon!"

Straker found it ironic that this scaly man with crests on his head like a lizard was calling *him* a demon. "Just a man," he said. "Not Calaria, not Bortok."

"What kind of man?"

That was a question Straker had pondered. What should he call his own people, when he wasn't even sure if Bortoks and Calaria were races, species, tribes or nations, or something else entirely.

153

He settled on, "Earthan."

"Urr-thannn… Urthan."

"Close enough."

Roslyn said, "He is like the orange man of the trees—small, but of great strength."

"Yes, Sessa."

"Why do they call you Sessa?" asked Straker.

"Because I am Sessa. It means…" She looked upward in thought. "Daughter of the king."

"Princess?"

"Yes, Princessa. Sessa."

Straker laughed uproariously, his eyes watering. "I rescued a princess, who wears a sword and lives in a castle, and she looks like a dragon."

The others stared at him as if he'd gone mad. Powl, being quick of mind, spoke up. "You rescued Sessa Roslyn?"

"Yes," Roslyn said. "Four Bortok took me, but Straker killed them all with nothing but a metal bar." She winked sidelong at Straker.

Straker played along. He'd need the reputation as a great warrior to counter his small size, otherwise he'd be forced to give endless demonstrations. "That's right." He hefted his improvised club, the bar still showing Bortok blood. "And now I've returned your princessa to you."

"If not a demon, then a god," Powl said.

"Perhaps the son of a god," Roslyn said. "Gorben foretold his coming. He is the Azaltar."

"And we laughed!" Powl lowered his head, as did the other. "Forgive me, Sessa."

"I shall. Spread the word among the warriors. It will hearten them. Now I must see my father."

"Of course." Powl hastened to hold the far door open for his princess.

Roslyn led them up a dozen flights of cramped spiral stairs, wide enough for only one. The steps turned so that defenders above would have great advantage. Straker nodded with approval. The Bortoks could never fight their way through here, even if they found the path.

"What's this Azaltar you keep calling me?" Straker asked as they climbed, Roslyn in front.

"He is the one who brings victory. The champion."

"Some kind of savior?"

"Calaria need no saving. We are happy to die for our freedom. What we crave is victory, and the death of Bortoks." Roslyn turned to sit on the steps and look down at him as he stood below. "You are the Azaltar, Straker. As Gorben foretold. The champion."

"And if I'm not?"

Roslyn pressed her thin lips together, and then hissed through her teeth. "Then we die. Or…"

"Or?"

"Or you become him."

Straker grinned. "Okay. I guess I'm the Azaltar. Now let's go see your father."

"Oh-kay." She turned back and resumed climbing the steps. "And I do *not* look like a dragon."

"You do, a little."

She said something in the clicking language, the High Tongue. Probably something vulgar.

"You know, your High Tongue sounds like the Opter language. I need to learn some of that."

"Op-ter?"

"If your gods and demons are real, then they're Opters. They look like huge bugs, and they have great power. And they don't give a shit about humans like you and me."

Roslyn turned to look back. "Why should they give shit?"

"I mean, they… they're not our friends. At all."

"I shall keep it in mind." She turned to face the front and kept climbing the long spiral stairway up from the earth. "I will teach you the High Tongue, but it is difficult for those not taught from birth."

"Even a little might be useful."

"All wisdom is useful to the wise, and useless to fools. In this manner one tells the two apart."

"You got that right."

By the time they entered the king's personal dining room, Straker and Roslyn had collected a train of followers—knights,

155

servants, ladies of the court. All of the women were bare-breasted, though their multi-hued, scaly skin made this fact less titillating. On the way, Roslyn silenced everyone's questions with a stern slash of her hand in the air and a grim-set mien, and then shut the door in their faces.

Inside the room a huge older man sat at a table, eating and drinking while looking at maps and documents. His skin was of the same fine purplish scale as Roslyn's. His crests were large and impressive, and he wore rich clothing. He rose and rushed to Roslyn, embracing her and speaking in the clicking language.

"Father, this is Straker. He does not speak the High Tongue. He freed me from a Bortok capture party and killed them with nothing but an iron bar. He is a great warrior. He is the Azaltar."

"This one? The Azaltar? Our champion?" The king looked Straker skeptically up and down.

Straker became acutely conscious of his ragged clothes—nothing but ripped trousers and boots, with the sword belt and a bag of salvaged items. But this man was obviously a warrior. Exquisite armor and weapons rested on stands nearby. Time for another demonstration. Straker held out his hand.

The king's clasp was stronger than Powl's, but still Straker made his eyes widen in surprise. "He *is* strong."

"As the son of a god," Roslyn said. "He came over the wall, from Rennerog."

"The magic men say Rennerog is filled with demons."

"They also denied the coming of the Azaltar," she said. "Perhaps they're not so wise after all. Gorben was right. I went to climb the wall, but Straker found me. What else but fulfillment of prophecy?"

"Look, uh, King..." Straker interrupted.

"Fillior, of Calaria," Roslyn supplied.

"Yeah, King Fillior, look." Straker stepped closer so that the two servants standing discreetly near the walls couldn't hear. "I'll help you fight these Bortoks. I *am* a strong warrior—but I'm not the son of a god. I'm just a man—a human, different from you, but still a man. But I *am* one hell of a fighter, and I'll fight for you, if you let me."

156

Fillior gazed firmly into Straker's eyes, his crest rising and falling slowly, like a fan. "You are true and honest."

"I am."

"Yet sometimes a king must lie, for the good of his people."

Straker nodded. "I get that. It's fine if you want to put out a fancy story about a champion to give your people hope. I'll go along with it. And, just maybe, the gist of the lie will become true. All my life I've studied military history. Maybe after I take a look at your defenses, I'll have an idea or two you can use to kill Bortoks."

"Anything that kills Bortoks will be welcome." Fillior turned to Roslyn. "Take Straker to your brother's room. He was of a size. Dress the Azaltar in the martial finery of our family—and yourself as well. We must show ourselves on the battlements."

Roslyn brought Straker to a well-appointed room. Though clean and full of personal objects—weapons, armor, clothing, a crystal bottle of some spirit—it had the indefinable air of being abandoned. She threw open two wardrobes and a chest, selecting trousers, a linen undershirt and a tunic. "Here, don these." She eyed his sturdy boots and shrugged. "Those are of a strange style, but they will do."

"The king said this is your brother's room? He must be small for a Calaria. My size."

Roslyn's face turned cold with anger and grief. "My father has been unable to enter Florden's room since he died. He was a brave boy of only fourteen summers when Bortoks murdered him under flag of truce. My father sent him to speak for our people. Not even Bortoks would break the covenants, he thought, but they did. They have no honor, and with the honorless, there can be no peace."

"I'm sorry. I'm honored to wear his clothing. Won't your people think it's strange, though?"

"Perhaps. But these are strange and desperate times."

Straker changed while Roslyn threw open a window and gazed out. When he joined her there, he found himself looking down from a high tower upon the enemy army encamped below and beyond. Their tents were pitched far away. Nearer, he could see crude siege works. Trenches with parapets and sharpened stakes, filled with warriors, guarded catapults.

One siege engine leaped and bucked as it launched a stone at the fortress off to Straker's left. A moment later he heard the crash of the impact. He leaned out the window as far as he could and watched as the boulder bounced from the wall and bounded down the slope of the hill. It hadn't penetrated, but enough such shots would eventually weaken the strongest barrier.

In reply, a volley of three smaller stones flew from the battlements, all aimed at the catapult. Two crashed into the dirt parapet and one flew beyond, crushing at least three Bortoks before rolling to a stop beyond.

"Are those your heaviest stone-throwers?" Straker asked.

"Yes, the largest the walls can hold. Larger ones must be placed farther back, on the hard ground, and so are not as effective."

He was about to ask more questions when realized he'd soon see for himself. "Give me the tour."

"Put on Florden's armor first." Roslyn helped him settle a chainmail shirt on his shoulders, showing him how to use a wide leather belt to put some of its weight on his hips. The sword in its scabbard was longer, lighter and better balanced than the heavy Bortok blade he'd taken. He took a few practice swings with it and was satisfied. If he had time later, he'd brush up on his fencing technique.

A surcoat with the King's colors—a rearing dragon in violet and gold—went over the mail. "That's enough," Roslyn said. "If they assemble an assault, we'll don our whole armor, head to toe."

"Your Earthan's improving. Your Low Tongue, I mean."

"I had not used it often, until now. The Calaria all use the High Tongue."

"So who uses the Low?"

She frowned. "Bortoks, and other peoples. It would be better if you could speak the High."

"Not gonna happen. I was never that good with languages."

"Then perhaps it's better that you speak little in the presence of the commoners."

158

Straker shrugged. "You know best how to sell this Azaltar thing." He was about to say that he simply needed to help her drive off the Bortoks so she and the king could, in turn, assist him in getting off-planet, but he thought better of it. These people might not understand the larger issues—the war raging light-years away, their status within Opter society, the trillion humans in thrall on this planet.

One problem at a time.

On the way, Roslyn swung by the kitchens and asked for bread, cheese and beer. Straker hadn't realized how hungry he was, and ate ravenously.

On the battlements they were greeted with cheers from the soldiers there. All were some variation of the Calaria type, though their skin colors and scale patterns varied greatly. He saw women among the warriors, perhaps one in nine. He gathered Roslyn's martial prowess was unusual, but not unknown.

Roslyn led Straker to the top of the highest tower so he could see the whole of the stronghold. It occupied a hilltop above a wide road that ascended a valley rising from the plains below, where the Bortoks camped in their tens of thousands. To its left and right, bluffs guarded its flanks, with manned walls atop them.

Straker turned to look behind and found a plateau rich with farms and villages. In the distance he could see something like a cathedral.

"That's Calaria land?" he said.

"Yes. Our last, best holdings and our refuge. Perhaps one part in ten of what we once ruled. The Bortoks have stolen the rest. High Tollen—this castle—stands astride the King's Road, blocking the route upward."

"There are other roads to the plateau?"

"One, on the far side. There are a few narrow paths, fortified chokepoints, well watched. If the Bortoks send enough men to break through elsewhere, we could shift our reserves to meet them. But their advantage is here. It's their catapults and their numbers that threaten us. If they breach our walls, they have enough troops to overwhelm us. A few may escape to the high crags, but as a nation we shall be no more."

Straker shifted his attention back to the front. "Have they tried undermining your walls?"

"The rock on which High Tollen is built is too hard."

"That's a relief. Do they—or you—have explosives?"

"Explosives...? I don't know that word."

"Gunpowder?"

"Nor that."

"Fireworks? Magic powder? Anything that bursts into flame?"

"Oil will burn, if it has a wick, such as in a lamp or torch."

"Damn... Well, if you don't have it, they don't either."

"Can we make such things?"

"Maybe... but it would take months to develop. Let's put that aside for now." Straker rested his elbows on the parapet and watched the catapult duel. It was a slow-motion battle, but crucial nonetheless. Battalions of Bortoks rested in place below, ready to spring up and attack if the wall was breached.

Straker counted more than twenty Bortok catapults, all of the onager type—a bucket on the end of an arm, powered by wrapped rope cranked up to high tension. If he recalled his Old Earth history, this was one of the simplest catapults, lacking any of several improvements he half-recalled, such as slings on the end of the arms to improve the range and power.

But the Bortok catapults were big. Given time, they would break the walls. Each stone that smashed into the stronghold's face weakened it a little more. He could see the cracks slowly widening.

Suddenly, a figure among the Bortoks caught his eye, someone small and male, with pale skin unlike the dark red of the barbarians. He was visible just for a moment before stepping behind a berm.

"Do you people have telescopes?" Straker asked. "Devices to see farther?"

"A few. They are precious."

"I need to borrow one."

Roslyn sent a servant, who soon brought a handmade brass spyglass. Straker used it to try to find the figure again, but couldn't.

160

Straker wondered about the man. It looked like Don, or someone about his size, like an agent. Sure, Straker'd gone along with the idea to come here, but he was starting to wonder—and get angry—that he was being led by the nose, manipulated.

He thought about trying to sneak into the Bortok army and confront the pale man, but that bordered on insanity. No, he'd have to stick to his idea about helping the Calaria so they could help him.

But from now on he'd keep a sharp eye out for agents.

Chapter 16

Straker in Calaria

Straker stood on the curtain wall's battlements and turned his attention to High Tollen castle and the Calaria siege engines. Their catapults did have sliding buckets, which sent their smaller stones farther for their size—but the range was still extreme. Now and again, one of their rocks would kill a careless Bortok or two, or bounce into a catapult, but the enemy engines were so heavily built and so well protected by earthworks that they were soon put back in action.

Straker could also see ballistas on the High Tollen walls, huge crossbows with pole-sized bolts ready, but they didn't fire. They must also lack the range, and so were kept in waiting for an assault.

"You have a range problem," said Straker. "Power, too, but mainly range. In any battle, especially a static battle, the side that outranges the other has control of the battlefield. Right now, that's the Bortoks." He rubbed his jaw. "You can't hit back effectively. You can't sally forth because they have defenses and too many troops. Have you tried a night attack? Your people see better in the dark."

"We raid them, but they keep good watch at night, and fires. We can take five for every warrior we lose and still not kill enough."

"Do they have sufficient food and water?"

"Yes. They have the whole of the plains as a larder. Our land."

"What season is this? When does winter come?"

"Threescore days should see the first snows."

"Sixty days... If we can hold out that long."

Roslyn nodded. "Then the Bortok will return to the lowlands. They don't like the cold. But still, we will go hungry. Our people fled our lands below, but the fields have been stripped, and the plateau behind us cannot sustain them all."

162

"So we not only need to wait them out, but we need to send them running. Reclaim your land."

Roslyn moved close, linking arms. Her feathery crests ruffled in the mountain breeze. "Always the lowlanders covet our fertile land. They breed themselves for years, and then when there are too many, they send an army against us. Never have they come in such strength, or with such large catapults. Never have they made it this far."

"Why now?"

"Gorben says they have a great leader. They call him *Mak Deen.* He has united the Bortok tribes, dazzling them with promises of our riches. Do they not know that, should they take our stronghold, they can pillage it only once? In times of peace we trade, yes, even with Bortoks, bringing wealth to all."

"Power-hungry leaders always get greedy," Straker replied. "That type's never satisfied, and they never want any limits. They measure themselves against their neighbors instead of being happy that everyone prospers."

"Yes. The Mak Deen cares not that all are made poor, so long as he rules."

"We have a saying: Power corrupts."

Roslyn bristled. "My father has power, but he is not corrupt!"

"Some good people resist temptation... but not enough of them. Most take advantage of their followers and indulge themselves. That's one of the marks of a bad leader—abuse of subordinates."

"It is said the Mak Deen kills any who speak against him, kills them slowly. When he desires a woman, he sends her man to the front lines. He holds girls hostage for their mothers' subservience and takes the fingers and ears of any who dare protest. Some parents even offer their children to him for his favor."

Straker grimaced, reminded of the Unmutual auction he broke up on Freiheit. "The Opters have done a great job replicating the worst of humanity," he muttered.

I'd half admire them if they'd made everyone sweet and innocent like Doris, he thought. Instead, they'd built a laboratory planet, with no thought to the billions they created and destroyed as by-products. They generated and trained infiltrators, they experimented on humans, they created whole societies to study like colonies of lab rats—and people like Roslyn knew nothing of it.

And they didn't care at all that barbarians were about to overrun what was obviously a more advanced, learned, just and civilized society.

"What did you say?" Roslyn eventually asked. "You were thinking deeply."

"Yeah, not my strong suit, but I do have my moments."

"I believe you are too modest. You're like my father—a man of war, but one who prefers peace through strength, and who would have his people wise and prosperous defenders, not conquerors."

Straker sighed. "I've done my share of conquering, but it was only to liberate people from oppression. I don't want to rule anyone."

"It's a burden, to rule. A responsibility and an obligation. My father wanted to pass his crown to Florden. He would have been of age next year."

"What about you?"

Roslyn smiled, her sharp teeth showing broadly. "There has never been a female king."

"Queen."

"What?"

"The word is *queen.* Many great rulers of Old Earth were queens. Why not you?"

Roslyn turned away. "It has never been done."

"Lots of things have never been done—until they are."

"Ka-ween."

"Queen."

"Queen," she smiled, obviously liking the sound of it. "Queen Roslyn of Calaria."

"The First." Straker chuckled. "The Azaltar declares it so."

A man's voice came from behind. "Perhaps the Azaltar should drive off the Bortoks before trying to install his chosen monarch upon the Calarian Throne."

Straker and Roslyn turned to see a man in silver-shot robes—middle-aged, with sharp eyes and an impressive crest.

He carried a scepter topped with a finely wrought carving, an obsidian dragon.

"Gorben!" Roslyn cried, seizing him and dancing around him in the narrow space atop the tower.

"Sessa. It's good to have you back. And you brought the Azaltar."

"As you foretold."

"As the *scripture* foretold." Gorben turned to Straker and bowed slightly. "I am Gorben, the king's adviser."

"Straker." As Gorben hadn't held out his hand, Straker didn't either. "Foretold," he said. "Foretold how?"

Gorben tilted his head and stepped closer, speaking quietly. "In the same manner of all prophecy. Vaguely."

"You mean you made up this Azaltar thing?"

"No. The Azaltar is a well-known legend of a foreign champion who shows us a path to victory over our enemies. When times grow desperate, people need hope."

"So," Straker said sharply, "you sent the princess on a mission with the off-chance someone like me would just, what, show up out of nowhere?"

"He didn't send me," Roslyn interrupted. "I went on my own, seeking the Azaltar, whom Gorben foretold would manifest."

"I never could forbid you anything, Sessa." Gorben turned to Straker. "She wanted to climb the wall—and if anyone could do it, Roslyn could." He breathed deeply. "I have examined the lands across the wall, using my seeing-glass, and though there are wonders there, it seemed to me that the inhabitants were men and woman like us, not gods, not demons. They have inventions, but that is only a matter of knowledge and industry, not of magic."

"Yes!" Roslyn said. "Show him the light!"

Straker took out the hand-light. "This isn't magic. It's just a machine." He turned it on. The output was unimpressive in the daytime. He handed it to Gorben.

Gorben examined it with great interest. "It doesn't burn, but glows like a cave-worm. I have tried to extract the principle, but have never been able to make devices with the glow."

"It's a different principle," said Straker. "More like lightning, stored in a bottle and released very slowly."

"Can it be released quickly, like a thunderbolt?"

This Gorben catches on quick, Straker thought. "No, but my people have weapons that work like that."

"Your people are wise."

"Our brainiacs are smart, I guess. Wise?" Straker chuckled. "No more so than average. Sometimes they're pretty damned unwise. But I'm not even from Rennerog. I'm a foreigner there too. The inhabitants were hunting me, and I had to escape to your lands."

"Why did those of Rennerog not pursue you across the wall?" asked Gorben.

"Good question. I think there are rules even they have to follow."

"I have often wondered why those with such power do not come and seize our lands."

Straker shrugged. "The people there have a government from above that tells them what to do. I believe your lands—all these lands, I mean, the Bortoks included, everything within the wall—are part of a protected preserve, something they call a *diz.*"

"A diz?"

"Long story."

Gorben frowned. "So we are creatures in a menagerie?"

"Menagerie... now there's a word you know that I don't."

"A place where unusual animals are kept, behind bars."

"A zoo, we call that. Yeah, you're kinda like creatures in a zoo. In fact, everyone on this planet is."

"Planet?"

"This world. Everything, inside this wall and inside the other walls and dizzes."

Gorben's eyes narrowed. "There are many dizzes?"

"Thousands, each one different, with its own people, its own society, its own rules. Some really weird ones, too. And above it all, creatures you'd think were demons or gods, though they aren't either. But they *are* powerful."

"This knowledge is... astounding."

166

"Yeah. Welcome to my world. I've had a few astounding surprises myself lately." Straker turned back to watch the ongoing siege. "But none of that's going to matter if these Bortoks breach your fortress and overrun us. At the very least, though, I think I can buy us some time, if we can hold out for a few more days."

"I believe we can hold," Gorben said, "for a week, perhaps."

"Then Gorben, I need you to get me your best engineers—your siege-masters, the guys who design and build your catapults—to listen to an idea of mine.

Hours later, Straker, Roslyn and Gorben addressed a dozen men and one woman, all who could be spared from operating the catapults. They were dressed alike, in heavy leather clothing designed to protect them from work's rough usage.

Nearby stood one of their onagers. Straker had caused it to be aimed safely at a hill inside the defenses, in case of a misfire.

He'd removed the sliding bucket and fastened a sling, made of leather and rope, to the end of the onager's arm. The hard part was figuring out how to make the sling release the stone at the correct moment. Gorben and Roslyn, once they grasped the basic concept, had helped him fashion a mechanism and adjust it. Their small test shots at least went in the correct direction.

Gorben introduced Straker as the Azaltar, and then let him talk.

"You've seen slings," Straker said. "A man with a sling can throw a stone farther than with his arm. A sling on the end of a staff throws one farther still. True?"

"True," murmured the siege-masters, some skeptically, some enthusiastically.

Straker stepped to the catapult and grasped the release lever with a mental plea to the Unknowable Creator. This had better work.

He pulled until the catapult leaped with the unwinding of its gear-tightened rope. The arm snapped forward and drew the sling from where it rested on the ground. The leather pouch of the sling contained a stone of standard weight, about thirty kilos. It swung up, out and around in a blur.

167

When the catapult's arm slammed into its adjustable crossbar, one of the two sling-ropes slid off its polished, bent steel post. This had been the hardest part, to time the sling's release.

The onlookers gasped as the stone shot upward at as close to a forty-five degree angle as Straker could estimate. Basic ballistics said a forty-five degree trajectory would send any thrown object the farthest, and right now, he wanted range.

He got it.

The stone flew farther than any he'd yet seen launched from Calarian walls—at least half again as far, and harder as well.

"Remarkable," said one man, stepping forward to lay his hands on the sling mechanism. The woman wasn't far behind, and then the rest crowded around and began asking questions all at once.

Straker raised his voice. "I have given you a gift of knowledge, but only you can put it to use. Who is greatest among you?"

The men pointed at the man who'd moved first, but he pointed in turn at the woman.

The woman laughed. "My mate is wise," she said, taking his arm.

"Stalar and Nenja are mated, and think as one," said Gorben. "They will supervise modification of the catapults."

"I suggest you do it at night," said Straker loudly. "Don't let them see your new advantage. You want to surprise the Bortoks and destroy as many of their catapults as you can. Those you don't destroy, they'll have to pull back. That will reduce their effect."

"Agreed," said Gorben.

"I also need one of you siege-masters to help me make a new kind of catapult. We'll need a crew of laborers with materials."

The engineers put their heads together and muttered, and then they shoved the youngest of them forward. "I am Tafar. I would be honored to help the Azaltar."

Straker exchanged glances with Gorben. Was this kid the best choice? But Gorben nodded solemnly. "Okay, young sir. Is there a catapult workshop or lumber yard somewhere?"

"I will take you to the sawmill."

"Send for a lot of paper and writing materials—do you have markers for writing and drawing? Good—and some messengers who can run and get tools and metal fittings we might need. Is there a blacksmith near the sawmill?"

"Of course."

The sawmill and smithy turned out to be two kilometers back from the castle. A great water wheel on the end of an aqueduct provided power to turn circular saws. The mill and smithy were well supplied with labor—perhaps oversupplied.

"Why aren't these guys training for battle?" Straker asked.

Roslyn explained, "Our people fled the lowlands. Now they seek work, until battle comes. When it does, they will take up weapons and fight, but they are no warriors."

Apparently Calaria didn't care too much about training their auxiliaries. Maybe he could change that, but first things first. "We'll give them something to do. But first, I need that paper and markers."

The markers turned out to be better made than Straker expected, like big pencils. He used them and the large sheets of crude paper to sketch out what he needed.

"It's called a trebuchet," he said to Tafar. "I've seen them on history showvids—um, I mean, I've read about them in books—but I've never actually built one, so I'm trusting you to create a prototype."

"I'll do my best, Azaltar."

Straker stopped. "Hey, Roslyn,"

"Yes, Azaltar?"

"Why did they give me the youngest guy. Is he the smartest?"

"That is not the reason. Tafar, tell him."

Tafar bowed his head. "They said, a boy for a boy."

Straker snorted. "They think I'm a boy?"

"Begging pardon, Azaltar, but you are no bigger than I, and I am but seventeen summers."

169

"Damn," said Straker. "I forgot to show them my strength. Here..." He eyed the logs stacked nearby, and then turned to the many muscular lumberjacks curiously watching the proceedings. He raised his voice. "Who is strongest among you?"

They turned to a huge specimen of at least two meters thirty, his muscles thick as the beams he cut and carried. That one stepped forward. "I am Karlenus. I am the strongest."

"Show me. Lift the largest log you can."

Karlenus scowled briefly, and then smiled. "You shall see." He selected a log that must weigh at least five hundred kilos.

Straker wondered if he'd overplayed his hand. If Karlenus could deadlift that thing...

The man stepped to one end and grabbed it with both hands, from the bottom, squatting. He lifted that end with his legs, and then, with a great expulsion of breath, he jerked it upward, pressing it over his head so that the log now stood vertically, like a tree trunk.

"Hell of a lift," said Straker. "Knock it over again."

Karlenus shoved the standing log until it fell with a heavy thump. "If you can best that, you are truly the Azaltar." Karlenus wasn't so dumb as he looked. He was reserving judgment. A few laughed until he glared at them.

Straker stepped to the same end of the log, so there would be no doubt. He wished his ribs didn't ache so much, and he wished he'd thought to put on gloves, but he was determined to give them a show even if he ruptured himself.

He worked the fingers of his right hand under the end of the log and set his legs. Then he began exerting pressure. He'd deadlifted over two tons in the gym at standard G, so he ought to be able to...

The end of the log came off the ground. His fingers hurt like hell from the awkward angle and his ribs screamed for relief, but slowly he straightened his legs until they locked. Then he took a deep breath and lifted.

The log shot upward and flipped end for end, and then fell with a crash atop others. Straker worked his hand and picked out some splinters.

Suddenly he heard a roar and found himself hoisted to the shoulders of the lumberjacks. They yelled and shouted, Karlenus chief among them. When they finally set him down, they pounded him on the back and called him Azaltar.

Straker hoped the story would get around and he wouldn't have to keep demonstrating his strength. Right now, everything hurt, though he refused to show it.

When they settled down, he ordered the men back to work while he returned to his paper and markers. "Still think I'm a boy?" he asked Tafar.

"I never did. You have the air of a great man about you, Azaltar."

"He *is* a great man," Roslyn said.

"He is the Azaltar," Gorben echoed.

Straker blew out his breath. "All right, all right. Now help me design this
trebuchet."

Just then, for a moment, Straker felt as if he were being watched. His head swiveled, but he saw no one. His anger rose again. He channeled it into work.

Chapter 17

Straker in Calaria

Straker and his crew of carpenters worked well past nightfall, until it became clear they needed food and rest. After eating, Gorben disappeared somewhere, but Roslyn led Straker to a room within the sawmill and made a bed for them on rough woolen blankets.

He stripped off his chainmail and threw himself down, exhausted. Roslyn lay next to him and wrapped herself around him. He didn't protest.

If Carla could see him now, he'd be in the doghouse for weeks. Or maybe she'd understand...

Then sleep took him.

When dawn broke, he rose and began the work again. By afternoon, Gorben returned, and Straker and Tafar had something to demonstrate.

The prototype trebuchet was about the size of the standard onager catapults. In fact, it used the same ready-cut beams in its frame. Only the arm was longer.

Instead of the arm fitting into a coil of stretched rope, it was balanced above the ground, on a fulcrum within the frame, like a seesaw. On the short end of the arm was a hinged stack of iron weights. Lifting it with winches would allow the long end of the arm, and its sling, to lower to the ground for loading. The weight would be propped with a single beam and the winches detached.

Firing was a simple matter of jerking the beam out from under with a levered rope. The weights dropped and the long end, with its sling, would whip a stone a tremendous distance—in theory.

"Let's try this," said Straker. The trebuchet had been built aiming up the nearest hillside.

The first rock flew almost straight up, causing everyone to scatter in alarm. The next, after adjustment, crashed into the ground immediately in front of the trebuchet.

"Okay, now adjust the sling release to halfway between," said Straker.

The next rock shot at a fair angle and smashed into the tree-covered slope above.

"It is difficult to know, Azaltar, but I believe this engine will throw rocks even farther than the catapults with the new slings," said Tafar.

"It should," Straker said. "The weights can be stacked as heavy as you want, limited only by the strength of the beams and the size of the engine. It's far easier to scale up a trebuchet than an onager. I read about them built to five times this size, but... I think something only twice as large in all three dimensions should rule the battlefield."

"The most difficult part is to find an arm that will take the force."

Straker rubbed his jaw. "Do you have sailing ships here?"

"No. We are a mountain people."

"The big masts of sailing ships are often made from more than one tree trunk, fitted together, glued and wrapped tight with wet rope. When the rope dries, it shrinks, binding them together."

Tafar thought. "That sounds something like the process for making a crossbow stave. Strips of wood wrapped and glued with sinew, heated, cured, and cooled."

"Yes!" Straker clapped his hands. "If you can't find a mast-maker, find a bowyer."

Gorben stood from where he watched and turned to a messenger. "Find and summon Wellyd in my name." The man ran off. "Wellyd is the king's master bowyer."

Straker rubbed his hands in satisfaction as he paced. "Until then, get the sawmill and the smithy making the parts we designed."

"Yes, Azaltar," said Tafar, and began distributing plans to each craftsman.

Suddenly, Gorben turned toward the castle and pointed. "There is a disturbance in our forces."

Straker saw this was true. Men ran to and fro on the battlements, and signal flags ran up the towers. "What do the flags say?"

"The Bortok are preparing a full assault. I must go. Don your armor and follow." Gorben strode in the direction of the castle.

From the villages beyond the sawmill, Straker could see soldiers streaming. They must be the militia citizenry. Around him, the workers were retrieving shields, donning helmets, and seizing axes.

"Wait! Wait! It's more important that you make these new weapons of war!" Straker called loudly. "I know you want to fight, but you must work."

Karlenus stepped forward, a great splitting-axe in his hands. "The Bortoks come. They need everyone on the walls."

"And I need everyone here."

"You would have us hew wood instead of flesh?" Others gathered around Karlenus, echoing his words. "I will not!"

Damn. They all wanted to fight, and Straker couldn't blame them. After all, he—the Azaltar, their champion—was going to do exactly that.

That was it! A champion.

Straker raised his voice and tried to speak in the stilted, formal way these people did. "Men of Calaria! I, the Azaltar, will gather to myself a circle of champions! Princessa Roslyn is my first, and I declare Karlenus, of the wood-splitters, to be my newest champion. He will represent you on the battlements, but the rest of you must work on these machines of victory, knowing we fight in your names. Will you do this?"

The workers gave a cheer, and Karlenus grinned a toothy grin. His quills stood high as he leaned down to speak in Straker's ear. "Cleverly done, Azaltar. Now let us kill Bortoks."

Straker turned to Tafar. "Keep them working. I'll be back within hours… or dead. But even if I am, now you know how to make the engines." He ran to the sawmill where his mail still rested. "Come on, Roslyn, help me on with my armor. I have a feeling I'm going to need it."

The three heroes almost caught up with Gorben by the time they reached High Tollen. Straker ignored the advisor and let Roslyn lead them by the shortest way to the parapets. When they reached the top of the wall overlooking the Bortoks, the sound of battle smote him like a fist to the gut.

Tens of thousands of Bortok warriors crowded below, assailing the hill leading to the castle. Beyond them Straker could see broken catapults. The new onagers had done their work—and apparently they'd pissed off the enemy.

A hundred meters to his left, a gap loomed in a section of the curtain wall between two towers. The enemy catapults must have smashed there before they'd been silenced, the first major breach.

Now, the Bortoks were determined to break through.

Ballistas fired with deep twangs like the giant crossbows they were. Javelin-sized darts skittered along the ground, slashing through the rear ranks of the battalions pressing forward. Closer to the wall, arrows from archers rained down upon the upraised shields of the enemy. Below the battlements themselves, the Calarian warriors upended caldrons of boiling oil or red-hot sand onto their hated foes.

The Bortoks had no siege towers, but they had battering rams with which they tried to hammer and pry out the foundation stones of the castle nearest the breach. They also had dozens—no, hundreds—of scaling ladders, which went up faster than the Calaria could knock them down.

At the breach itself, a flood of enemy flowed through the gap. Straker had seen a second wall behind the first, so all was far from lost—but if the Bortoks took the first wall, they could bring forward their full strength with impunity. Their ten-to-one advantage in numbers would overwhelm the Calaria.

"Have you some wisdom?" asked Roslyn after Straker had surveyed the battle. "What does the Azaltar counsel?"

"No, no clever ideas." Straker drew his sword and strapped on a shield he found nearby, left by one of the casualties. "The Azaltar counsels kicking ass."

Roslyn thumped her own mail shirt and drew her slim, razor-sharp blade. "I have not the weight to stand against a Bortok, but I will guard your back."

"And I your side," said Karlenus.

"Happy to have you both. Just keep me from getting shanked."

"Your words are strange, but I take your meaning," said Karlenus.

Straker strode toward the fight.

He passed archers firing downward as fast as they could until he came to the first scaling ladder. Its top extended ten feet above the battlements, and two soldiers were struggling to push it sideways with hooks obviously designed for that purpose. Straker sheathed his sword, grabbed the butt of the hook's pole, growled and set himself to shove hard.

The ladder tipped rapidly to the side and the Bortoks on it crashed onto their fellows twenty meters below. Straker's chest bounced against the wall as he followed the pole, gripping its end tight so it didn't fall, and then drew it back.

The soldiers around them yelled, "The Azaltar! The Sessa!" and the cry sped down the ranks.

"Allow me," Straker said to the soldier, appropriating the hooked pole. Right now, this was a better tool than a sword. With the strength of five men he pushed off ladder after ladder, the Bortoks on them falling to injury or death on the rocks. Karlenus chopped at the wood of other ladders, or split Bortok skulls while Roslyn stabbed them in their faces from above.

But there were always more, and the Bortoks got thicker as the three approached the break in the wall from atop the battlements. Not only did the enemy pour through in their hundreds, but they climbed up the broken sides of the gap and assaulted those above them. The huge men, even larger than the Calaria, each the size of Karlenus, smashed their way through to the top and drove back the defending warriors.

A lone knight in plate-mail stood in front of Straker, a soldier to either side of him, facing the enemy on the narrow wall. For a moment he dueled with the savage warrior before him. The Bortok rained blow after blow upon his shield, but the knight turned them adroitly. His men-at-arms stabbed and chopped with poleaxes, in this way allowing three to fight one. The Bortok fell, wounded, but a fresh one took his place.

Straker slipped behind the thin line of soldiers guarding the walls. He glanced back toward the plateau and saw mobs of militia, called from their usual work on farms and in workshops, running to reinforce the castle.

He wondered whether they would be enough. Maybe he should've let the sawmill workers come—but militia couldn't handle these Bortok barbarians.

The knight held the oncoming Bortoks until one particularly large specimen struck a resounding blow on his shield with a giant spiked mace, a brutal and inelegant weapon. The knight ducked and dodged, but the spikes caught the shield in an underhanded attack and nearly ripped it from his arm. Instead, the knight followed it into a backward somersault, rolling to his feet in an amazing display of agility.

Unfortunately, this left the two men-at-arms exposed. The Bortok backhanded one off the battlements, though to Straker's eye it appeared the soldier was probably dead before he hit the ground.

The other would have died too had not Straker stepped up and caught the strike on his own shield.

The Bortok's power smashed the shield and caused Straker's feet to skid backward. Unlike in heroic showvids, strength did not naturally equal stability, and was an imperfect substitute for sheer mass.

But Straker did have strength. His enemy didn't know it, but the human was at least twice as strong and twice as fast as the barbarian warrior. Before the Bortok could reverse and sweep again with his huge weapon, Straker whipped his sword in a strike that took one of his foe's hands off at the wrist.

His blade felt light in his grip—probably too light. It occurred to him he'd be more effective with a longer, heavier blade, something to make up for his shorter reach compared to either type of humanoid here in this diz. Or perhaps…

Straker swung his sword around a full three-sixty and chopped off the wounded Bortok's foot at the ankle—a target he could easily reach. The man-thing fell heavily, and the knight moved forward to stab the Bortok in the throat.

"Well done," the armored man said, faceless within his full steel helm. "I am Drake. You may take Nelen's place at my side."

Straker didn't bother to argue rank. The knight was obviously highly skilled, and the quality of his arms and armor showed him to be a man of high position. Instead, Straker sheathed his sword and picked up the Bortok's mace, shaking free the dead hand still clutching it. He then shrugged off the remnants of his smashed shield and took the weapon he'd captured in a two-handed grip. "Sure. Let's go." He strode forward.

The next Bortok quickly fell to Straker's oversized mace, and the next, and the next. The most difficult part of using it was the size of its haft, nearly too thick for his hands.

He'd smashed at least ten Bortoks aside by the time he cleared the broken end of the battlements that overlooked the gap. The knight had followed him all the way, and so had Karlenus and Roslyn. Together, this elite band ensured no enemy got behind Straker, or got to the top anywhere within their reach.

The soldiers nearby had taken up a cry of *"A-zal-tar! A-zal-tar!"* and with renewed energy they swept the rest of the Bortoks and their scaling ladders from this side of the battlements.

The other side, though, was in trouble.

Despite archers and ballistas, the left flank of the castle was in danger of being overrun. Below him Straker could see the inner wall holding against the milling, climbing Bortoks, but across the gap the ladders gave them a free road to the top, and the enemy warriors were fighting their way along the battlements.

Straker measured the distance across the gap. He was pretty sure he could make it, and maybe the lithe, light Roslyn could as well, but he doubted Drake or Karlenus would.

"Karlenus," he bellowed above the din, "find something—a log, a beam, a ladder—to cross the gap. I'll seize the other side."

"You'll—"

Rather than explain, Straker turned to Roslyn. "Follow me if you're sure you can jump so far. If not, help Karlenus and Drake. We've gotta get across and clean them off the battlements. If you can't cross the gap, try to work your way around from the other side. We can't let them take the top of the walls."

Hoping Drake would follow his instructions as well, Straker turned back to the gap. It reminded him of when he contemplated leaping from the Glasgow apartment building, but this distance was shorter, and the consequences of missing were a lot less lethal.

Well, probably less lethal. Missing the jump and landing among the climbing Bortoks might kill him just as quickly as a hundred-meter fall to concrete.

Do or die, Straker told himself, and then he sprinted for the broken end of the battlements, focusing resolutely on the other side where he would land. He felt the toe of his boot overlap the edge of the cut stone, and then he went airborne, his great mace above his head.

He landed with a comfortable margin behind him, but ran into the back of a Bortok. None of the enemy had given any thought to a leaping attack—it seemed completely impossible—and so he was able to set himself and hew down three before they realized he was among them.

His spiked mace caught in the flesh of the fourth one he smote, and the moment he lost trying to yank it free bought him a heavy blow to his mailed back. Fortunately, the fine steel armor, tight-wound and riveted for a prince, held with only a bruise—but a bruise he felt all the way through to his healing ribs.

A high-pitched shriek caused him to turn in time to see Roslyn land from her

leap and, without pause, take his attacker in the kidney with her sword. She fought with a dagger in her left hand, whirling and stabbing, agile and deadly.

Straker left his oversized weapon and snatched up a Bortok sword, this one a large war-blade, not for carrying on the belt like the ones they'd taken from the capture party. It fit his two hands better than the haft of the mace, and was much easier to maneuver.

His smashes turned into slashes, not as precise as Drake's blade work, but still fast and strong. He felt his overworked muscles complain, but desperation drove him as he fought his way to Roslyn and stood back-to-back with her.

179

They defended themselves for long minutes this way, Straker facing the mass of Bortoks lining up to murder him, Roslyn keeping them off his back and killing them as they clambered up the rubble.

But Straker felt himself tiring. Despite biotech strength and healing, he was running on fumes. He'd gone three days with one short night's sleep and his injuries were far from healed. He now bled from a score of slashes and cuts, and the blood loss, while slow, would eventually bring him down.

Suddenly, something slammed to the stone behind him. Roslyn jumped back with a cry. "Well done, Karlenus!" she shouted.

Straker glanced back and saw Karlenus had found a half-meter-wide wooden beam and dropped it across the gap, with the help of Drake and a dozen soldiers. Other fighters with polearms and bows fended off Bortoks as the giant woodworker pounded across the improvised bridge, great axe in hand.

Drake sent five or six soldiers ahead before calmly walking across as if he were taking a stroll. His sword moved constantly, licking out and stabbing at any Bortok nearby. When a warrior reached with long spear, Drake sliced the iron point off it, leaving the Bortok with nothing but a pole.

"Straker!"

Roslyn's yell reminded Straker he had killing to do. He'd become mesmerized watching the knight's skill and poise. He ducked under a Bortok's sword and drove the point of his two-handed blade up under his enemy's chin. As the barbarian fell, he reversed and delivered a roundhouse blow, chopping completely through another Bortok's axe handle and into his torso.

The warrior toppled off the wall with an expression of utter surprise. Straker wondered how much of his own success was due to the Bortoks' underestimating him when they saw him. It was as if a platoon of battlesuiters encountered a young teenager in lightweight athletic gear, who nevertheless started destroying them with their own weapons. It might take them a while to comprehend.

Karlenus stepped up beside Straker and together they advanced down the battlements, clearing it as they went. More troops from the other side reinforced across the beam-bridge. They guarded the champions' backs and the space they'd already secured.

More than once Straker saved Karlenus by blocking a Bortok blow or killing his opponent. Though strong and enthusiastic, the wood-worker was not skilled in battle. When he took a wound to his leg and stumbled, Straker moved in front of him.

As he'd hoped, Drake filled in where Straker had stood, and the battle became very different. Instead of having to support Karlenus, Straker simply concentrated on killing what was in front of him.

In fact, Drake supported Straker. Several times he was able to take a moment from dealing with his own opponent to lance out with his long sword, stabbing Straker's Bortok in a vital spot—a hamstring, a throat—before quickly shifting back to his own. The man was a marvel of efficiency, expending minimum energy for maximum result.

As was the way of battles, the tide turned suddenly. One minute Straker was knocked back, so weary he contemplated rotating out his front-line position for a break. The next, the Bortoks were running, streaming back toward their own lines.

"Roslyn, please send for my spyglass," Straker said. Roslyn sent a messenger running, and soon brought the device from his room. Straker put it to his eye and scanned in the area he'd seen—

—*there*. For just a moment the figure was framed in his field of view, standing atop a small hill, watching the Bortoks retreat around him with an expression of irritation.

It looked very much like Myrmidon.

Chapter 18

Straker in Calaria

Straker put the spyglass back in its case and leaned on the battlements of High Tollen, unwilling to sink to the ground as most of the other Calarian soldiers did. Gods and monsters, he was tired. His vision swam as the sustained adrenaline of combat washed out of his body, but a leader's instinct kept him standing, refusing to let the troops see weakness.

Myrmidon. What the hell was the man playing at? Was he behind this Bortok invasion? It seemed likely. He probably helped the barbarians make these catapults, playing adviser to the Mak Deen. If so, why? Not knowing stoked his simmering fury.

"You're not the Azaltar I expected, but you'll do, I suppose," said Drake's droll voice from his shoulder. Straker turned to see the knight remove his helm and pull off his gauntlets. The man's scaly face was slim, as were his elegantly long fingers, more like a musician's than a warrior's. He bared his pointed teeth at Straker. "Your strength was welcome this day."

Drake's tone seemed oddly ambivalent, as if he weren't entirely happy with the situation. Straker cudgeled his tired mind and tried to figure out what the knight's problem was. "My strength was welcome, but not..."

"Your sword work leaves much to be desired. If you wish to play your role properly, I can rectify that."

This guy's manner was beginning to irritate Straker. "Meaning what?"

"Meaning I can train you—if you have a different kind of strength."

"I'm as strong as I need to be, and I really don't need you talking down to me."

Roslyn stepped up from behind and placed one hand on each man's shoulder. In a low voice she said, "This is not the time or place for heroes to argue."

"Of course, Sessa. Your pardon," said Drake. To Straker, he said, "Meet me in the sword-hall at the sixth chime tomorrow." Then he strolled off, speaking encouraging words to the soldiery, slapping their backs and joking with them.

"Who the hell does that guy think he is?" Straker asked.

Roslyn smiled. "He is the Baron Drake, the king's swordmaster. He trained me—still does, for I have much to learn. Do not be put off by his manner. He is perhaps over-proud, but if you humble yourself, you will learn much."

Straker turned his head and spat off the battlements. "I'm not a humble guy."

"All men are proud. That's what makes them men, and desired of women, but there is a time to bend to a master. Did you not have teachers? Did you not show respect?"

Straker thought of his Academy days, and some of the instructors there. He also remembered his mechsuit training, by crusty old suit-warriors whose withering blasts of profanity masked a deep desire to ensure he was ready for combat. And then there was his Kung Jiu sensei Rohaka, whom he'd never bested, even with genetically enhanced strength and speed. "Sure, okay. I can do that. I'm not too old to learn something new."

And remember, you're mortal, Straker reminded himself, since there wasn't anyone else around to say it. This Drake was a killer. Straker wasn't at all sure he could take him in a fight—and he hadn't believed that about anyone in years.

Until now.

But he had to admit, that fact itself meant he really should take the student's role here, that Drake really did have something to teach him. All right. Better to be humble than stupid. It would be stupid to pass up a chance to gain battle skill.

If he had time. Playing Azaltar had to end as soon as he could escape back to the real world.

"You're thinking about leaving," said Roslyn.

"Are the Calaria mind-readers?"

"You wear your thoughts on your face, Derek Straker."

"I never told you my first name."

Roslyn grinned. "You talk in your sleep. I will not reveal your secret name to others." She moved to embrace him. "I wish we could—"

Straker put his hand on her breastplate and held her away. "Yeah, me too, but that's not gonna happen. My vows to my own woman don't disappear with distance."

"You vowed exclusivity?"

"Um, you mean monogamy?"

"Mon-no-gam-my. What is that?"

"It means having only one woman."

Roslyn turned her head away, but looked back at him slyly, sidewise. "It is said that the woman loves the man's honor, but honors only the man's love."

"Which means what?"

"Think on it. It will come to you."

Straker snorted. Women and their convoluted minds made his head hurt.

Other things hurt now. He was growing stiff inside and out—his muscles, his joints, the layer of blood, sweat and dirt on his body and armor. Fighting hand-to-hand was far different from mechsuiting. It was much more gritty and personal.

Straker took in the carpet of the dead. Soldiers were being rousted to their feet by their sergeants, the fit to begin the cleanup, the walking wounded sent to whatever passed for medicos here. The unarmored militiamen, who'd helped stem the tide, now began carting off the Calarian dead and tipping the Bortok bodies off the walls to the rocks below. Carrion birds already circled and landed to feast, and a pack of jackal beasts emerged from the forest's edge, warily sniffing the air.

Ballista crews and archers remained at their posts, alert for any renewed Bortok attack, but the sun was falling toward the horizon. The enemy wouldn't come again today.

Too bad a sally or raid seemed impossible. The Calarian forces were spent, and barely numerous enough to hold their walls, while the enemy seemed endless.

But the Bortoks' morale *had* broken. They weren't fearless Hok or emotionless Opter drones. If they took a few days to regroup and rebuild their catapults, the Calaria would have trebuchets and they'd be safe at least through the coming winter. By then, Straker would have escaped this diz.

Somehow.

Straker heard booted feet approach, and he turned to see King Fillior, his retinue behind him. "Hail, Azaltar!" he said in a speechmaker's voice. "You have honored us with your wisdom and battle-prowess this day in our hour of need!"

Roslyn nudged him. "Say something impressive," she hissed.

"Ah, thank you, O King Fillior of Calaria. I only did my duty, and I am honored to have fought alongside such brave and noble soldiers. We killed a lot of Bortoks today, and we'll kill some more if they come at us again, right?"

The soldiers cheered.

Straker continued, warming up. "Because nobody takes our land, or kills our livestock or our people without paying a heavy price. This wall here is as far as they came, and it's as far as they're ever gonna come."

More cheering. Straker turned to Roslyn. "That's all I got. I bet they'd like to hear from their fighting princessa."

Roslyn squeezed his arm and turned to the growing crowd. "People that I love! We held them here today, we'll hold them tomorrow, and soon we'll drive them from Calarian lands. And if we're too few right now, winter will do it for us. Then we will reclaim your farms and fields below, we will rebuild our defenses and our strongholds, and next spring we will replant, with the wisdom of the Azaltar and his new war machines to aid us." She raised her blade as the soldiers chanted her name.

"Come, Azaltar, Princessa. We must hold council," said the king after a time, and led them toward his dining chamber.

Karlenus saluted Straker with his axe and slipped off, no doubt to return to the sawmill. "Give that guy some weapons drill and he'll be a monster," said Straker to Roslyn. "Your militia would be more effective with better training and some basic armor."

"Armor is costly, and every day they train is a day they don't work," she replied. "Perhaps when the storehouses are full and the people are flush with coin, we can afford such luxuries."

"Point taken." Straker's mind turned to what he'd read of Old Earth's medieval farming and industry. Maybe he could remember something to increase their yields. Crop rotation? Fertilizer? Contour plowing? Irrigation? If only he could recall all that boring, non-military school stuff. Now he wished he had a brainiac like Zaxby or Murdock along, or even a comlinked database and a handtab.

Or perhaps he did... Gorben seemed like the closest thing to a scientist these people had. Maybe all Straker needed to do was to brainstorm ideas with him and let the adviser spread the improvements.

Roslyn steered Straker to her dead brother's quarters again. "Clean yourself up and come to the royal chambers in half an hour. We will eat, drink, and take counsel."

"How the hell do you people tell time here?" he asked.

"In the day, by the sun." She pointed at a sundial affixed to the inside of the open window embrasure. "At night, by the clock-chimes." She pointed out a different window, one that faced inward toward the castle courtyard. There he could see a tower with a clock set in it, still visible in the setting sun. The face showed twelve divisions, an hour and a minute hand, exactly as had evolved on Old Earth and was still in use today on most planets—even if the hours, minutes and seconds weren't standard from place to place.

Straker wondered whether Terra Nova had been selected with a twenty-four hour rotation, or would this clock's hours match a true digital chrono? It hardly mattered, except to show the Opters' dedication to reproducing human environments. "All right. See you then."

Roslyn left and Straker cleaned up. A servant girl brought a basin of hot water and tried to help him wash, but he sent her away and stripped, giving himself the best towel-bath he could. If these people didn't have immersion tubs, he resolved to introduce them. Hell, he was the Azaltar! Might as well enjoy a few perks.

With clean clothes on, he had a servant guide him to the meeting. A stein of surprisingly good, cool beer from a keg refreshed him, and he used it to wash down the simple food set out on the sideboard—cold roast meat and fowl, vegetables and fruit, bread and yesterday's cake. Of course, the day's battle precluded most cooking and feasting. The only hot thing on the menu was a cauldron of thick stew, the same as Straker had seen served to soldiers at their posts.

When he'd wolfed down two plates full with the others—Roslyn, Gorben, Drake, the king and a dozen other nobles and important people—Fillior rapped on the table with the hilt of his eating-knife. "We are grateful to all who preserved us today, but the Bortoks almost prevailed. Half our soldiers lie wounded in the great hall. If not for the intervention of the Azaltar, my daughter and Baron Drake, who cleared the battlements above the breach, all would have been lost."

"Yes, sire," said Drake. "The Azaltar proved quite... energetic, and his heroic stand was surprisingly well-timed."

Straker noticed that weird phrasing again, as if Drake was subtly calling his actions into question. He was about to retort, when Roslyn leaned over to murmur in Straker's ear. "You threaten his martial primacy, my love. No other man has ever killed so many Bortoks, or shown such prowess."

"Yeah, I figured it was something like that. And don't call me 'my love.'"

Roslyn merely smiled, and hummed faintly.

Great. Just great. Straker was very glad Carla was light-years away.

Gorben said sternly, "The Azaltar Straker has come to us on our day of need, just as in ancient times came the Azaltar Jiakob. The scriptures foretold it: he shall come as a champion, and then depart like the wind."

Drake drummed his fingers on the table. His voice seemed to hold a slight sneer. "While I'm not as learned as the wise Gorben, I have also read the scriptures. They say the Azaltar Jiakob became contentious and had to be banished after a year and a day, and the king was greatly relieved when he departed, for the people had grown to love the Azaltar above their rightful sovereign. Is this to be our lot?"

Roslyn jumped to her feet. "Straker is here for mere days and already you spread your fears?"

"I fear only for the king... and for you, Sessa, and the dynasty of Calaria. We have no prince, no heir, and you are unmated."

"I've postponed *your* offer, you mean," Roslyn said stiffly. "Now you fear I will take Straker, and he and his sons will inherit the crown instead of you."

"Hey, hey, hey," Straker said, also rising to his feet. "I'm already married. Mated, that is. Princessa Roslyn is beautiful and wise and any man would be lucky to have her, but there's only one woman for me, and her name is Carla Engels. Believe me when I tell you, I don't want to stick around here and mess with your politics. I rescued Roslyn because she was in trouble. Any decent man would've done the same, and I'm helping your people for the same reason—because you're in trouble, and you're defending yourselves. When the Bortoks are gone, I intend to leave, to climb over the great wall again and return to my own people. In the meantime, I'll teach everything I know, and expect nothing in return except a little help getting home." He brushed his hands together and spread them. "That'll be it. Done and over with. You have my word."

Drake's eyes narrowed and Roslyn seemed to be holding her tongue, but the rest, including Gorben and the king, nodded in satisfaction. "Well spoken," Fillior said. "We must put aside all quarrels until the Bortoks have been driven from our lands. Baron Drake, do you not agree?"

"Of course, Majesty, of course."

Straker sat, hoping that he'd settled the matter.

"Bring the chart," the king said.

Two scribes brought a large parchment map and laid it on the cleared table. Everyone stood to see it better. It depicted High Tollen castle and the surrounding lands. Another man placed small flat pieces of painted wood at various places, quickly and certainly. In moments, the map now resembled a game board, with the positions of Bortoks and Calaria clearly shown.

Other servants lit candelabras for light against the falling night, and then guards cleared the room of unneeded people.

The royal council discussed the battle, the positions of troops and supplies and other military matters for several

188

hours. Drake's mood seemed to have improved with Straker's assurances that he wasn't angling for Roslyn's hand in marriage. Straker made sure to couch suggestions in the most deferential terms he could, even if it made him grind his teeth to do so.

After all, what he said was true; he wasn't planning on being here any longer than necessary. "Any longer than necessary" meant sending the Bortoks home with their tails between their legs, and then claiming the goodwill of the Calaria to help him escape this diz.

When the meeting came to a close, Straker brushed off Roslyn's attempt to walk him arm-in-arm back to his room. "Look, sorry, I just told everyone I don't want you."

"But you do want me," she said, sloe-eyed. "I know the signs."

"If there are any signs, they're purely physical. When I give my word, I keep it—and that's what wedding vows mean. Don't you people take vows, make promises?"

"Of course—for a year and a day, and then we renew them again—or choose not to. So you see, you could stay here a year and a day, and then leave. I would be the woman of the Azaltar first, and then I could be Drake's woman after that. It would go far toward me becoming Ka-ween, don't you think?"

"Queen, yes... but do you think Drake's gonna put up with that? I bet he's thinking about becoming king himself."

"If my father bestows the title on me, and has the blessing of Gorben and the magic men and the other nobility, Drake will."

Straker snorted with amused disbelief. "You're an ambitious woman, Roslyn. And here I thought you were a naïve babe in the woods."

"You found me in the woods, Straker—and you put this ambition in my thoughts, did you not?"

"I guess I did. But I'm not sticking around for a year and a day. You'll have to play your political games without me."

"As you wish, Derek Straker." She lowered her eyes and smiled.

"Damn—and I thought these people were primitive," he muttered to himself as he strode back to his room. "Reminds

189

me of... of Old Earth and all the medieval intrigue. Machiavelli, Cardinal Richelieu, those guys."

Straker rounded a corner. As he did so, pain blossomed in his side, so severe his legs went rubbery and he stumbled to the ground.

This may have saved his life. A sword stroke passed above his head as he fell. He grabbed the leg of a small wooden table and threw it at his attacker.

Attackers. The knife in his kidney had been administered by one masked man, and the other was already striking for him again with the sword. Unfortunately he'd thrown the table at the wrong one.

"Guards!" he croaked. "Murder! Assassins!" He rolled violently to one side, but the swordsman didn't miss—by much. The blade slashed along his upraised arm, and then came back around for another blow.

Despite nausea and weakness, Straker kicked the man's legs out from under him. If he'd had his full strength he'd have snapped the man's knee. He clamped his unwounded hand on his attacker's wrist and twisted.

The man's bones broke. He screamed.

Then there came a rush of armed men, and Roslyn. They quickly secured the two assassins while Roslyn dropped to Straker's side. "Call the surgeon!" she yelled.

"Take these two to the dungeon," Straker heard Drake say. "I will soon know who their master is."

The surgeon bound his wounds and had him carried gently to his bed, with Roslyn hovering. The slash along his arm didn't concern him much, but his punctured kidney throbbed and he felt sicker than ever in his life.

"The blade was poisoned, My Lord Azaltar," the surgeon told him. "I know its smell. You must drink this to counter its effects." He held a cup to Straker's lips.

"You trust this guy?" Straker asked Roslyn, grasping the cup himself.

"He has been the royal surgeon all his life, as was his father before him, so yes, I do," said Roslyn.

Straker drank. It tasted awful, which seemed to be a prerequisite of all medicines.

"It will make you drowsy, which is all to the good," said the doctor. "Were you not the Azaltar and possessed of supernatural strength, you would be dead now. Rest and heal." He turned to Roslyn. "Call for me if he worsens."

"I will." She let the man out the door. Straker saw guards in the hall, and when Roslyn returned, she locked and barred the window. "You are safe now."

"I thought I was safe before."

Roslyn blushed with shame. "As did I. We should have no need of guards in our own house."

"Guess you're not so Machiavellian as I thought."

"What does that mean?"

"Never mind." Straker laid his head back on the pillow, feeling a heaviness steal over him.

Roslyn poured a drink, this time of spiced wine that tasted much better than the medicine, and shared it with him, putting it to his lips.

When he'd drunk his fill, he said, "You think Drake was behind it?"

"Drake? No."

"He doesn't like me much."

"He's no murderer. If he wanted you dead, he would challenge you and kill you."

"Or I'd kill *him.*"

Roslyn gave him a skeptical look. That irked Straker. Other than his Kung Jiu instructors, he'd never run into anyone that could take him in a fair fight, and he found he didn't like it much. But, obviously he was bound to run across someone, sometime, who could.

Straker's thoughts drifted, and he felt Roslyn slip into bed with him. He noticed the warmth of her skin, her thighs and her breasts against him, and realized she was naked. A surge of adrenaline fought with the drugs and the wine as she ran her hands along his chest.

"Don't—" he mumbled, unable to fend her off. He felt himself respond to her touch. "What did you…"

"I put herbs of potency and desire in the wine," she said as she threw off the blankets and straddled him. "If I cannot have

191

your heart, and your head refuses me, then I shall at least have your body and your seed, Derek Straker, my Azaltar."

"No, hold on…"

"Worry not, my love. You will remember nothing of this in the morning."

Whether it was the drug, Roslyn's allure, or his own treasonous body, he found himself powerless to resist.

Chapter 19

Straker in Calaria

When Straker awoke to morning's light streaming in the still-barred window of his castle room, he tried to recall what happened the night before. He remembered the attack, and the doctor who patched him up. And Roslyn... what had she said? Did she...?

Straker threw off the blankets and looked down at himself, but all he saw were bandages, and no evidence of... of what? He wasn't even sure. It must have been a dream. No way he would have been able to perform even if he wanted to—not with that sleepy-drug and all these injuries.

He sat up carefully and found it wasn't as bad as he'd feared. His biotech was serving him well. Swinging his legs to the floor, he stood and tottered to the privy, and then he rang the bell on a cord. Servants rushed in and helped him don loose clothing, and brought him food and drink.

Soon after, Gorben entered. "I thank the Holy One you survived," he said.

"Holy One? I thought you weren't superstitious—you know, about gods and demons and stuff like that."

Gorben stared at Straker in astonishment. "I'm not. The magic men and their followers believe in demons and spells and suchlike, but not those of the True Faith. The Holy One created the land and the firmament and set all things in motion, but according to the scriptures he seldom meddles in the affairs of men. Yet, shall I not praise him for good fortune?" Gorben shrugged. "Only the most narrow-minded does not at least give thanks. Have you never addressed your own gods, even on the battlefield?"

"Maybe I have," Straker mused, thinking about placing Orset in the ground and speaking the regimental chaplain's funereal words. "Pascal's Wager."

"What is that?"

"It means, if there is a, um, 'Holy One,' one that's benevolent, why not stay on his good side? And if not? No harm, no foul."

"Exactly." Gorben opened the window. "But the magic men do not believe this way. They have been spreading lies that you are a demon—and now I fear you have proven them right. The poison on the blade was enough to kill five strong men, yet you live."

"You think they're behind it—these magic men?"

"It is likely, but we will not soon know. The assassins died by their own poison before they could talk."

"That's convenient. Wasn't Drake in charge of the interrogation?"

"You think he silenced them?"

"I think he's the prime suspect in this whole thing."

"This I doubt. Drake is far too prudent to risk such a rash course." Gorben paced, staring at the floor and tapping his staff in thought. "I do not wish to seem ungrateful, Azaltar, but perhaps you should be on your way as soon as you are well."

"Hey, that sounds great. You know a way over the wall to Glasgow? I mean, Rennerog?"

"I know a way past the wall, but I know not where it goes, to Rennerog or some other land. It is far from where Roslyn found you, a river that plunges beneath the barrier."

"Sounds chancy. What about just climbing over?"

Gorben glanced at the closed door and lowered his voice. "In my heart of hearts, I do not believe Roslyn can climb the wall, though I could not say so publicly. And is not the descent on the other side just as dangerous? Did you not say that those of Glasgow seek to capture you?"

"You're right," said Straker. "Better to take a chance on the river, I guess. At least, I'll take a look."

"Excellent. I will leave you to your rest."

"Hey, Gorben."

"Yes, Azaltar?"

"What does that mean, anyway? Azaltar?"

"On the Old Tongue it means..." Gorben searched his memory. "Freedom-bringer."

Straker choked on his wine. "Liberator?"

194

"That is a fair translation."

"Maybe there's something to your prophecies after all."

"Of course there is. The key to prophecy is to always leave the interpretations to the latest possible moment. It matters not which is chicken, and which is egg." Gorben winked. "You were the one who came to help us. Thus, you are the Azaltar."

"Call me Derek, will you? Derek Straker. That's my name."

"All right, Derek Straker. Alas, I have no other name than Gorben."

"No problem. Hey, what I wanted to say was, could you keep Roslyn away from me?"

Gorben raised an eyebrow. "An unusual request."

"Look, she's just getting a little too friendly. I already have a woman."

"The woman loves the man's honor, but honors only the man's love."

Straker nodded. "Yeah, she said that, but I can't quite puzzle out what it means."

"It means, Derek Straker, that when it comes to love, women have indeed no honor at all."

"Maybe here in Calaria."

"It's the only place I know. Are the women different in your land?"

"Some are." Then Straker thought of Tachina. "Some aren't, I guess."

Gorben held up a hand. "I will ask the king to forbid her to come, for your health. I do not know how long that shall hold. In the meantime, rest. Ring when you awake again. We must speak further. I would hear your wisdom on many matters."

"Before I go away, you mean?"

Gorben smiled and turned toward the door. "Until later, Azaltar."

* * *

For three days Straker stayed in his room. He ate and drank, he bathed in a copper-lined tub the servants brought, he

195

slept—and he talked at length with Gorben. Two young scribes took notes as they spoke, and Straker poured out all he could think of on every topic that occurred to him: military science, medicine, agriculture, engineering, logistics, whatever crossed his mind.

He made sketches which Gorben preserved as if they were holy writ—and Straker supposed they were, in a way, made by the hand of the Azaltar himself.

Straker also used his telescope to spy out his window, staying back from the opening when he could in order not to be seen watching. The Bortoks seemed to have withdrawn several kilometers down the valley, leaving only scouts. He caught no more glimpses of Myrmidon, though somehow he felt like the man was still watching him.

On the fourth day, Drake visited, along with Gorben. "I apologize for not ferreting out who tried to have you killed, Azaltar," he said stiffly. "I assure you I had nothing to do with it."

"I believe you. And I apologize for missing our appointment," Straker replied. "I was looking forward to your instruction with the sword."

"I as well, but it is not to be. Gorben tells us you will leave as soon as you are fit."

"That's true. It's also true that I have no interest in Roslyn."

"I know. At your word, the king has forbidden her to see you. That was well done." Drake cocked his head. "Yet, she does not seem distressed. You were a passing fancy." He held out his hand. "I have wronged you, Azaltar Straker."

Straker clasped hands with the knight-Baron. "Yes, you did—but it's forgotten."

"I hope you can stay a tenday more—at least for the joining ceremony."

"Joining ceremony?"

"Roslyn has consented to be my mate for a year and a day, now that the first snows dust the mountain peaks and the Bortoks have fled to their warm lowlands."

Straker grinned. "Well, hell, congratulations, Drake my man! I hope you make each other happy."

"As long as there is issue, I shall be content."

"Yeah, there's always issues, aren't there?"

Drake and Gorben exchanged arch glances, and Gorben showed Drake out, claiming Straker was tired. Straker thought the old wizard probably just wanted to keep picking his brains for knowledge.

Over the next ten days, Straker healed and began light exercise. Drake invited him to his sword-hall, where he instructed the other knights and soldiers in the finer points of blade-work. Straker sparred vigorously, losing himself in hard exercise.

When he wasn't working out, he visited the sawmill and helped put the new trebuchets into place. In the evening, Gorben instructed him in the High Tongue, enough to recognize a few hundred words and speak simple, childish sentences, and they talked long into each night about many things.

Straker saw Roslyn at dinners with the King, and she seemed the model of decorum, attending to Drake and ignoring Straker beyond ordinary courtesies. Yet, Straker always felt her watching him out of the corner of his eye. Despite the attractive, simple life these people led, he'd be happy to move on, if only to get away from the princessa.

* * *

After Drake and Roslyn's joining ceremony and the inevitable feast and carousing afterward, Gorben and Straker set out with a party of guards and woodsmen. They headed in the opposite direction from the Bortok lowlands, across the plateau and down its reverse side into a great forest.

Roslyn had stood next to Drake atop the castle wall. With one hand she waved a silken scarf. The other rested on her belt buckle. Something about that pose reminded him of Carla, and he felt as if a snatch of memory danced just outside his mind's eye.

No matter. This chapter of his life was over. He'd done good deeds, and now it was time to claim his payment—a way out.

Karlenus insisted on accompanying them. "You travel through my forests," the giant said. "I know every tree, every rock, for a hundred leagues."

Straker thought that might be an exaggeration, but he was happy to have the big man along. In the evenings, after the days' travels, Straker had the captain of the guards give the woodsmen instruction on man-to-man axe work. "You know best how to chop down a tree," he said. "You need to learn how best to chop down a Bortok."

Huntsmen scouted ahead and brought down game—fowl, large rodents, and something like deer—which they roasted over an open bonfire. With their meals, the whole group enjoyed wine mixed with cool sweet water from the mountain streams. They slept soundly on blankets spread upon soft boughs cut from fragrant. bushes, Straker found himself in the best shape of his life, with the exercise and fresh air, so different from his many years lived aboard ships and in mechsuits.

When they reached the wall after nine day's travel, Straker felt a strong twinge of regret, and an urge to go back with these simple people. Then he remembered Roslyn and the undercurrent of politics at Calaria, and that feeling passed. He realized that this journey had been a vacation, a camping trip, and like all good things, it had come to an end.

"So, let's take a look at this passage," Straker said.

"It is here," said Gorben, walking Straker to the river's edge, a short cliff that dropped to the surface. The flow met the wall and passed under it, moving at a furious pace.

Straker looked up at the hundred-meter barrier, wishing there were some way over. The ancient Romans had built an earthen ramp up to the top of Masada taller than that, but it had taken them two years and 15,000 people. Straker didn't have either. What he wouldn't give for a simple set of jet-boots.

He caught sight of movement atop the wall. Someone was looking down at him. Straker fumbled for his spyglass in the case, but by the time he got it out the target was gone.

Myrmidon again? He wished he could get his hands on the man.

"Well, might as well get going," Straker said, passing the spyglass to Gorben. "Give this back to Roslyn, please." He stripped off his chainmail and handed it to Karlenus. "Thank the king for the loan of his son's armor. It saved my life.

Karlenus folded the chainmail and passed it to another, and then seized Straker in a bear hug. He pounded on Straker's back and wept. "I shall miss you, Derek Straker, my Azaltar."

Straker held the giant at arm's length, looking up into his bearded face. "Your *friend*, Karlenus. I'm not Azaltar anymore. Gorben tells me your scriptures say someday the Azaltar will return to you in your time of need."

"As the Holy One wills it."

"Whatever you say, big guy." Straker turned to Gorben and held out his hand-light. "I want you to have this."

"Thank you, but I must refuse."

"Refuse?"

"You may need it where you're going. It is enough that I now understand its principles. In a few years, we will make our own *electricity,* our own *gunpowder."*

"And your own indoor plumbing, I hope," Straker said with a grin. He picked up the oiled leather bag he'd prepared, containing a few useful items, slung it across his back, and gave a farewell wave as he readied himself to enter the river.

Suddenly, he heard a shout. Tafar, the young engineer, came running out of the woods and stumbled up to the Calarians. He had little with him but a knife and a shoulder bag, and he looked starved. He leaned over, wheezing, trying to catch his breath. "Water," he croaked.

After taking several sips from a canteen, Tafar stood and in a voice of agony said, "Calaria has fallen."

"What?" Gorben seized Tafar's shoulders. "Explain!"

"Five days ago. I have run the whole way. The Bortok made a night attack, after we thought they'd all gone to the lowlands. Though we slew thousands, they came in their tens of thousands. The king is dead. Baron Drake and the Sessa fought a valiant rearguard, and many of the people fled to the high mountain pastures, but many more have been enslaved."

"Calaria is no more," said Gorben in stunned wonder.

"We must return! We must fight! We will retake what is ours!" said Karlenus.

"We cannot fight so many in open battle," said Gorben. "But we can survive in the snows as the Bortok cannot. We will prick them a thousand times…"

"And they will bleed until they leave our lands!" cried Karlenus. He turned to Straker. "Azaltar! You will aid us."

Straker nodded, appalled. "Of course I will."

Tafar leaned in close to Gorben to speak softly in his ear. Gorben's eyes widened, and then he turned to Straker. "No. Straker, you have told me of your struggle for the stars. You must go return to the firmament and win your war in the heavens. Then, you can come back to us and right this wrong."

Straker said truculently, "I'll do as I damned well please— and I can't let your people down. I'll help you—"

Gorben interrupted, stepping closer. "Tafar told me something."

"What? Something you think will change my mind?"

"No, Azaltar. Something that will ensure your return to us, when your appointed tasks are complete." He stepped closer still, until he towered over Straker and had to lean down to speak, softly. "Roslyn carries your child."

With that, Gorben slammed his palm into Straker's chest and sent him sailing into the river.

Chapter 20

Faslane System, Hundred Worlds

The flagship *Victory* cast off its last connections and floated free of the Carstairs Corporation's space-dock above Faslane-2. Billingsworth M. Carstairs VI watched through the giant crystal external window that allowed him to see the spectacle with his own eyes. If he preferred ultra-definition detail, he could turn to look at several holograms projected overhead.

He stood on a VIP platform elevated five meters above the crowd, alongside a gaggle of admirals, ministers, Members of Parliament and other dignitaries. They and the lesser attendees below applauded as the ship, shaped like a giant egg, fired its thrusters and began to move away. Within minutes, it was out of sight of the naked human eye, but the smart-crystal window cleverly deformed its many layers to create a telescopic effect, allowing it to remain visible for almost an hour.

Carstairs sighed. No rational man would complain about his life, but now that he stood atop the corporate mountain, the only way upward was to look for other peaks. Politics, perhaps? He could easily buy a seat in Parliament. Did he want to learn a whole new game, one where his vast wealth had influence, but little real power?

Something to think about.

For now, he had to keep a close eye on the reports from *Victory*—at least until it left at the head of the Home Fleet. If the ship, the crew, and most importantly the AI failed to perform as advertised, he hoped they had the decency to be destroyed in combat.

Victory's radical design was a risky one. The core of the ship, the best experimental artificial intelligence ever built by the Hundred Worlds, was intermixed with over one thousand human brains. No, scratch that. They weren't brains. If they were, Carstairs and everyone involved would be criminals. No, these almost-brains were mere organic computers, each in a self-contained bio-support module, or BSM.

Just tissue, he told himself again.

Each BSM was linked in a network using advanced brainchip technology. The tissues inside had their free wills eliminated with the excision of certain ganglial clusters and structures, but the scientists told him they still had a sort of consciousness. That consciousness was shared with the other BSMs and the machine, forming the totality of the AI.

This AI had been running for over six months, longer than any AI before had gone without the inevitable madness. It seemed stable, self-aware, and childishly happy to fulfill its function of the perfect fleet coordinator, the ultimate expression of a commanding admiral's will. It could run ultra-fast analyses, provide advice, pass orders and, if given the authority, it could even take direct control of other warships via the new top-secret datalink.

That datalink was another piece of the bleeding-edge technology that enabled *Victory*. The first faster-than-light communications system ever developed by humans, its range maxed out at about ten million kilometers even under the best conditions, but even far less distance was sufficient to provide instantaneous comlinking to every ship in a task force. This meant no comlink lag—but more importantly, it meant that *Victory's* many unmanned drones could reach their true effectiveness.

What's more, the FTL datalink had no known jamming vulnerabilities. The enemy didn't even know it existed. Once they did, it should take years to research countermeasures.

Carstairs had been pleased to handsomely reward the scientist who'd invented the system. She was far too plain to sleep with, but no doubt she'd have plenty of suitors now that she was rich. Odd that she'd never showed signs of brilliance before, or, according to her colleagues, not since, either, but Carstairs supposed even a blind squirrel had a chance to find one fat nut.

It hardly mattered. The breakthrough he'd paid millions for would make him tens of billions, perhaps hundreds. It might even win the war against the Hok and their human traitors.

A twinge of worry crossed his mind. What would happen to his megacorp's military division if the Hundred Worlds won the war? Defense spending might drop precipitously, taking his bottom line with it.

That was a worry for another day. He had plenty of civilian-focused businesses—and hell, he could always get his paid-for MPs working on starting a splendid little war on the borders with the usual false-flag operation. Nothing like a threat from some scary-looking aliens to pump up profits, after all. Those radioactive Thorians, for example, were always good for a little panic.

He watched the holos as they showed the battle module approach for docking with *Victory*. Within minutes, the module swallowed the rear of the half-armored ship, encasing it in the best defenses ever built by the Hundred Worlds. The module also had military-grade drives to give it better mobility than anything else its size, an extensive roster of defensive weaponry, and of course, copious automated hangar bays to deploy and recover the combat drones.

This was the third cutting-edge development that made *Victory* unique. The main ship and the battle module, each at the sidespace transit mass limit, would travel separately and quickly link up at any destination, creating a double-sized ship.

Carstairs had heard rumors of the Hok experimenting years ago with something like this to create a super-ship, but they'd apparently never made it work. However, Carstairs Corporation had, and he was proud of what he'd accomplished.

A perfectly ordinary voice at his elbow interrupted his musings. "It's your big day, Bill." The voice was attached to a perfectly ordinary man, and Carstairs didn't even have to look to know who it was.

It was, however, one of only a few men who could use his first name without invitation.

Carstairs turned to the man and extended his hand, accompanied by a practiced smile. "And yours, Grant. None of this would have been possible without your backing."

Grant Lorden, Undersecretary of Defense, gripped Carstairs' hand firmly, but not unduly so. His palm was neither dry nor moist. Somehow, the handshake made Carstairs want to please this man. "I do what I can for the greater good."

"As do we all."

An involuntary chill ran up Carstairs' spine. Though Lorden seemed like a mere upper-level functionary and bureaucrat, everyone he knew whispered that the man wielded more power behind the scenes than anyone but the Prime Minister himself. His purview was rumored to include the Ministry of Defense's secret "D" Division, responsible for black ops and dirty tricks.

That tidbit, added to the perfectly timed aircar crash that turned the Victory program's most vocal Parliamentary critic into a vegetable, was what caused Carstair's guts to twinge with brief, unaccustomed fear. But the Undersecretary was on his side now. He was sure of it.

Lorden stepped closer to murmur, "Bill, you've done so well with this, despite the ethical ambiguities, that we're thinking of allowing you to bid on D Division projects."

"We?" *The shadow within,* Carstairs thought. A cabal, a group of hidden movers and shakers, it had no name, but everyone at his level had heard the whispered tales.

"My associates." Lorden waved in vague directions. "Like-minded people who don't shrink from their duty to the Hundred Worlds."

"I'd be honored to provide any service I can." Carstairs wondered what it took to join the cabal. Whatever it was, he'd do it.

"Of course." Lorden glanced over at one of his aides and gave a nod. A moment later, two people approached. "Here are a couple of those associates now. John, Talenia, this is Bill Carstairs, of the Carstairs conglomerate."

Carstairs turned to see a man and a woman. The man was young, with sandy-blonde hair and an infectious smile, but he barely registered on Carstairs' consciousness against the magnificent creature beside him.

"Good to finally meet you, Bill. I'm John Karst," said the man in a provincial accent—from one of the frontier worlds, perhaps? He held out his hand to shake. "And this is my sister Talenia."

Carstairs couldn't release the clasp fast enough in order take Talenia's hand and bring it to his lips. As he did, he ran his eyes down from her perfectly sculptured face to her ample breasts straining at an expensive, low-cut dress, to her hourglass waist and long, strong legs that ended at pedicured feet, delightfully bare atop expensive strapless heels.

His lips brushed her fingers and a jolt of arousal raced straight for his groin. It took all of his composure not to seize her right there in a crushing embrace. Talenia's lips curled in a smile that told him she knew exactly what he was thinking—and liked it.

He'd never met anyone like her.

"Lovely to make your acquaintance, Bill," said Talenia. "Why don't we go get a drink and leave the boring bureaucrats behind?" She locked up his arm in hers and steered him toward a secluded alcove.

He found himself powerless to resist such chemistry.

* * *

Grant Lorden turned to John Karst and murmured, "Well done. Even easier than you promised." His security detail kept potential eavesdroppers at a discreet distance.

"Tachina—sorry, *Talenia*—is amazing, isn't she?"

"She is. Even *I* felt some slight attraction, and I seldom indulge in sex. It clouds the mind."

Karst winked. "Can't say the same for myself. Fortunately, my 'sister' doesn't mind this kind of work. You might say she was made for it."

"Like you and me?" Lorden took a sip of his drink. "How much time do you think she can keep him enthralled?"

"As long as she likes. Six months, at least. Is that enough?"

"It should be. I want him lusting after a D Division contract that will become a complete disaster for Carstairs Corporation. Too much money and influence in the hands of any one person is dangerous to us."

"And then?"

"Your Talenia will leave him for someone else of our choosing. Carstairs will be a wrecked man. You'll step in, playing the sympathetic friend. I'll throw him a bone by steering him a cut of further ships in the *Victory* class, as well as AIs built for other applications. That will complete his dependence on us."

"He wants in."

"Everybody wants in. That's what it means to be *in*. Be grateful that you're *in*."

Karst saluted Lorden with the beer in his hand. "Defecting to the Hundred Worlds was the best thing I ever did."

Lorden clinked his glass to Karst's. "Defecting might be too strong a word, since you never were really part of the Mutuality at all."

Karst's face whitened, though he covered it well. "I don't understand."

Lorden speared Karst's eyes with his own. "No need to worry, brother. We all serve the same masters—you, me, Talenia, even that delightfully sociopathic fellow Lazarus you brought with you. Parliamentary Intelligence is having a field day with him."

Karst shuddered and turned away. "They debriefed me too. I didn't realize you knew—or that you were—"

"The same? Those like you and me are untraceable, except by inference and deduction. Obviously engineered clones like Lazarus and Talenia we can explain as the product of Mutuality laboratories, but *we* were made to be perfectly indistinguishable from those born of woman—at least to a biological test."

"Then how did *you* know?"

"You and I went through the same programs, though mine were decades ago. We might even have had some of the same controllers, teachers or field agents. I see the signs."

"Let's hope nobody else does."

"Any humanopts who don't join us are eliminated."

"Any you find."

Lorden shrugged. "Some go native. Some even try to raise the alarm. It doesn't matter. We keep the nets filled with conspiracy nuts and their wild theories. Aliens among us,

206

masquerading as humans? Old hat for the last thousand years. And we've been careful to make everyone believe that aliens really are trying to destroy our way of life."

"The Hok."

"A stroke of genius, don't you think?"

"Yes, genius. Did you have a hand in that?"

"From well before my time, I'm afraid. Our natural lifespans are no greater than any others, though we do tend to stay inordinately healthy long into our declining years. We also have access to the best transplant parts. You should easily reach one hundred twenty. One-fifty is possible. I'm one hundred thirty myself."

"I like those numbers."

Karst led Lorden slowly to the rail overlooking the main floor, where those of merely ordinary privilege glanced enviously up at the VIP level. The noise of conversation and music added an extra layer of security, as did a haze of holo-blur around the two men. "Speaking of the Hok," Karst said, "I still don't understand how the knowledge that they were mere pawns of an enemy human government has been suppressed for so long."

"It's a difficult, coordinated and ongoing effort. The aforementioned disinformation and fake newsvids lay the groundwork, but the key is…" Lorden tapped the back of his skull.

"I don't understand."

"That's because you're not brainchipped."

"Other than Hok, the Mutuality only brainchipped certain people for brainlink to specific pieces of machinery, such as pilots and ships. Netlinks were forbidden, and shared virtualities were tightly controlled."

Lorden smiled. "The Mutuality knew the dangers of brainchips and the nets. Once one surrenders his senses to external manipulation, how can one know what is real?"

"Are you saying that you use brainchips to keep the populace under control?"

"The populace? No, they don't need such direct methods to remain sheep. They are kept happy with creature comforts and entertainments. If that doesn't suffice, layers of disinformation will lead the curious through mental mazes of our making. Those who still present difficulties are promoted."

"Promoted?" Karst turned to Lorden with a lift of his eyebrows. "The Mutuality sent people like that to camps."

Lorden sniffed. "Such a crude and inefficient method. No, we reserve brainchips for the best and brightest—genetically engineered brainiacs and physicals, university professors, mechsuiters, pilots, those who control the media and so on. It's a mark of status to be able to plug in and augment one's capabilities, after all. So when someone makes trouble, they are introduced to D Division. A quick weekend out of town, and they return with news of a wonderful new job—and a brainchip to go with it."

"And after that, they're a model citizen."

Lorden smiled. "Not overnight... but any interest in opposing the government or in digging up genuine secrets quickly fades. The mind is gently adjusted to conform to our desires every time they plug in—and plugging in is always a necessity for their comfortable, well-paying job. It's a perfect solution. Everyone is happier—us, them, their friends and family, their employer and coworkers."

Karst shuddered once more. "Glad I'm not chipped."

"As long as you do as we desire, you won't be."

Karst swallowed and looked away, gripping the rail. "Gods. And I thought the Mutuality was a cruel master."

"Cruel?" Lorden chuckled. "We are the kindest of masters. Why, even our worst criminals are not imprisoned for long."

"Right. One quick implant and bang, model citizen. It only costs their free will."

"Freedom has always been an illusion—or at least a limited commodity. Only those at the top really have it. But we provide security, comfort, safety, prosperity—all the things the ordinary person wants. For those who crave adventure, there's the military or the Exploration Service. For those who want power, there's the government in public, which is allowed to operate transparently. We even provide the illusion of democracy by allowing people to select their representatives."

"But that government in public has almost no real power."

"On the contrary, Mister Karst. Like a warship, it has enormous power. It simply exerts no independent control. We act as its secret captains, aiming and directing that power. We are wise enough to know that the gentler the touch, the easier it is to remain hidden."

Karst took a deep breath. "Why are you telling me this? Am I going to be whisked off to some lab and implanted?"

Lorden placed a hand on the younger man's shoulder. His fingertip happened to touch the bare skin at the base of Karst's neck. Certain complex molecules began travelling from Lorden's skin to Karst's. "Wouldn't dream of it, my boy. You're one of us. You have to be brought into the fold, given tasks that benefit us all, and eventually you'll move up."

"Or else?"

"No need for threats. I'm certain you'll come around to our point of view once you have a chance to think about it."

The molecules were on their way. Within hours, Karst would join the team, and he would think he'd done it of his own free will.

After all, brainchips were *such* crude and inefficient tools of control.

Chapter 21

Engels, Sparta System

Three weeks after receiving Minister Benota's message, Admiral Engels arrived at the Sparta System. Her scouting force had gotten there the day before, and now *Indomitable's* sixteen pieces joined the reduced capital contingent of her fleet, popping into flatspace at wide intervals from one another. Collisions were rare, but they did happen, especially when trying to keep a fleet together.

She had no need to do so, though. In fact, she wanted to present a certain ragged appearance—enough to raid Sparta, but not enough to hold it.

Right now, the Huns' stealthy scout drones were already launching themselves into sidespace, sending initial reports into the messaging network. They would arrive at other systems, broadcast encrypted databursts, and then rendezvous with specially equipped drone tenders to refuel. Then they would take up station while other drones carried their messages elsewhere. In this way, reports were sent efficiently from star to star, far faster than light itself.

Her scouting forces, all fast corvettes, would have hunted down or driven off the enemy drone tenders by now, leaving Sparta with only the probes in place, hiding among millions of chunks of rock and ice in its comet cloud. Nothing could be done about those—but she could try to show them only what she wanted them to see.

With the arrival of one-quarter of her capital ships, the enemy's civilian vessels, mostly freighters and passenger liners, chose courses and ran for flatspace—all in the direction of the biggest empty gap in her coverage.

Exactly how she'd planned it.

They were accompanied by three Hun frigates, enough to fend off any of the corvettes that tried to intercept, but too few to matter if they couldn't make it back to defend the planet.

Six hours later, as the convoy of fleeing prizes reached the point of no return, where they had too much velocity to turn around and retreat to the planetary defense fortresses, her escort fleet of over one hundred frigates, destroyers and light cruisers appeared in front of them, spread in a wide net at the edge of the curved space bubble.

Confronted with this untenable situation, the Hun frigate commanders made the only decision possible. They instructed the civilians to heed the Republic calls for surrender, while they themselves turned and blasted for planetary return at overloaded thrust levels.

Their military grade drives held, as did their discipline. Engels could only imagine their frustration as they allowed their flock to be captured. She added almost twenty ships and the miscellaneous supplies inside to her fleet, at no cost to herself.

The passenger liners she ordered let go after mandating that all aboard view Zaxby's presentation on the truth about the Hok, detailing how the Hundred Worlds had lied to its citizens. Most wouldn't believe, and some would come to doubt. She placed armed prize crews aboard the cargo ships and assigned them to her small squadron of auxiliaries.

Next, she moved inward with her widely spread ships, slowly gathering them into squadrons as they converged on Sparta-3, the green world where stood the Carstairs Corporation's mechsuit-making complex. On the way, her ships compelled the surrender of asteroid mines, fueling stations, and moon-based factories, looting some, occupying others.

One monitor and four fortresses protected Sparta-3, along with the usual assortment of local patrol and attack ships. As Engels had expected, there were no capital ships there. Those were all on the front lines, except for the enemy Home Fleet, stationed in permanent reserve at the Hundred Worlds' capital world of Atlantis.

With any luck, that mighty Home Fleet, or a significant portion of it, would soon be heading for Sparta, secure in the knowledge that all they faced was a force of lighter vessels—numerous, but no match for elite capital ships. In fact, Engels had deliberately delayed the arrival of all her ships above cruiser size. The Home Fleet would be deep in sidespace, unable to receive reports, when most of her combat power showed up. The enemy would therefore face more than triple what they expected—plus *Indomitable,* which should be a surprise for only this one more battle.

Three days later, certain that the word had reached Atlantis, and that the Hun Home Fleet must have transited for Sparta, Engels ordered *Indomitable* reassembled. Sixteen "dreadnoughts" became one battleship, which began firing on the orbital fortresses around Sparta-3.

It took only two hours to reduce that fortress to rubble. Without a supporting fleet and unable to hit *Indomitable*— which at extreme range could evade enough that even beam weapons would usually miss—the fixed defenses were helpless. They surrendered, though not before sabotaging their own weapons.

The enemy monitor landed on Sparta-3's moon of Leonidas, and her crew abandoned ship. Her stubborn captain threatened to self-destruct the massive vessel by detonating a nuclear warhead inside.

"Be my guest," Engels had replied. Then she'd ordered *Indomitable* to fire one railgun shot, destroying the sitting duck's engines.

"An unfortunate waste of materiel," Marisa Nolan remarked from her position on *Indomitable's* bridge.

"Better than leaving it to suddenly spring into action," Engels replied.

Once the Sparta-3 planetary orbit was secured—though not its surface—her staff estimated the enemy Home Fleet should appear in about two days. Her newly arrived capital ships even now took their positions, readying themselves for their part in Engels' grand deception.

After careful consideration, she decided against sending down what ground forces she had to loot the mechsuit factory complex. She already had few enough marines, and a stubborn defense might ruin her chances to take the critical machines and technology intact.

No, better to win the fleet battle, and then pillage at her leisure, using intimidation from above. If by some chance she lost in space, she could always drop a precision kinetic strike on it. The factory was, after all, a legitimate military target. That would set the enemy back a year at least, giving the Republic a chance to catch up with its own nascent mechsuit program.

Forty hours later, a bit early but well within the expected window, the Hundred Worlds Home Fleet appeared in all its pride and glory at the edge of curved space.

Admiral Engels watched as the Hundred Worlds Home Fleet appeared as close in as possible, near the optimum emergence point. Such arrogance! But her counterpart, probably the famous commander of the Home Fleet Admiral Hayson Niedern, was an arrogant son of a bitch.

He had reason to be, though. His fleet consisted of the most modern ships, with the latest upgrades. The best equipment always went to the Home Fleet—on the Hun side and the former Mutuality side as well.

Only, Engels had turned that around, leaving her old or damaged ships under Ellen Gray in order to take her best deep into enemy territory. Sheer distance—and fear of the attack— would preserve the New Earthan Republic, and every day she bought for the Republic meant damaged ships would be repaired and new ships would be commissioned.

She hadn't tried to lay mines at the optimum emergence point. She didn't have the tens of thousands of stealth weapons it would take to cover the space. She had, however, distributed enough scout drones to get close-up, accurate readings as the enemy appeared. Some of those drones were detected and killed, of course, but the more distant ones survived to supplement *Indomitable's* powerful passive sensors.

"Admiral, observe," said Nolan with a hand-wave that reshuffled the main hologram. The background lighting dimmed and the display brightened until Engels felt as if the ships that hung in the air above *Indomitable's* bridge could be touched, like elaborate models for meticulous hobbyists.

"What the hell is that?" Engels said. "And that?" She stared at two completely unique enemy ships. By their scale they were of maximum size, like superdreadnoughts, but their configurations seemed completely irrational.

"I'll run the recording forward and it will become clear," said Nolan. She didn't bother to access a console. Clearly, Trinity was thoroughly wired into *Indomitable's* network. Engels had allowed this, even encouraged it, once she had confidence the triumvirate being wouldn't interfere with combat operations. The AI synthesis was worth a hundred staff officers and their computers.

The two strange Hundred Worlds ships moved toward each other on fast-forward. One, shaped like a huge egg, was covered with a thick skin of armor and bristled with weaponry—but only from amidships to its slightly narrowed forward end. Its back end was nearly naked, without even fusion drives. It must be moving on impellers alone. That ragged, peeled-appearing skin reminded her of something…

"That looks like the inside of *Indomitable's* sections," Engels said. "The unarmored parts that slide together."

"Very astute, Admiral. As you see…" Nolan stepped forward and gestured.

Now, the other ship, which looked like some exotic metal serving-bowl with eight legs, or perhaps like an oversized egg-cup, lined itself up on the egg of the other ship. Yes, an egg was the perfect visual metaphor, as the cup-ship and the egg-ship fit themselves together.

Now, the eight enormous "legs" rotated forward until they fit into slots in the combined vessel, locking the two together and leaving only eight double-sided conformal tubes—fusion engines, for sure—arrayed tightly about the ship's fat waist.

"It's a double-ship," Engels said. "Sort of like *Indomitable,* broken in half for transit. They've made an ultra-dreadnought, or a pocket battleship. But that configuration is crazy. There doesn't seem to be any spinal weapon, and the back and the front are symmetrical, instead of having the best armor at the front, toward the enemy. Sure, it has eight engines, but they're all more vulnerable, placed like that."

"Very maneuverable, though," Tixban said. "It should turn on a coin, and it never has to flip end for end, so while it's more vulnerable in general, it will never get raked like a conventional ship."

"Good point," Engels said. "What else?"

"Its defensive suite is the finest I've ever seen on a ship of its size. In fact, it has no offensive weapons at all."

"If I may continue?" Nolan said with a hint of Zaxby-like superciliousness.

Tixban muttered something in Ruxin.

"The same to you, youngling," Nolan said, smiling sweetly.

Tixban rotated all his eyes away from her. Had he been human, Engels thought he would have put his nose in the air and sniffed.

The recording continued. For a long moment, nothing seemed to happen, and then swarms of tiny craft burst forth from launch tubes. They spread out farther and farther from the mother-ship, quickly departing the hologram.

"It's a drone carrier," said Engels in puzzled wonder. "The Huns are experimenting with the drone swarm concept again. Seems like an odd coincidence, when we've just come from a battle with the Opters. But drone swarms never proved to be efficient. If you can build drones complex enough to carry out combat ops, you might as well just make missiles. Far more effective for the same resources."

"That assumes the drones are offensive," Nolan said. "What if they're purely defensive?"

"Yeah, maybe. They'd do great at fleet defense against shipkillers. Fortunately, we're not particularly reliant on missiles. The Mutuality ships we've inherited use missiles as threats and bludgeons, to try to break through so the ships can do the real work close in, with beams and railguns. So, do we have to worry about this ship?"

Tixban had been working at his Sensors console all the while. "I'm detecting—or I should say, *not* detecting—a peculiar number of signals from the ship. That is, very few signals. It should be ablaze with electromagnetics—radio or laser comlinks to the drones, for example—but there's almost nothing. The drones are either completely automated, or they are piloted."

"Are they big enough to be piloted?"

215

"Barely, but even the smallest sentient being, such as an Opter dog-bee, would seem a highly inefficient waste of mass. It's nonsensical."

"Well, it must make some sense or the Huns wouldn't do it," snapped Engels. "Keep trying to figure it out and report to me when you have facts and answers, not just wild speculations." In truth, wild speculations were running through her own head too.

"One fact," Nolan said a few moments later, "its armor is peculiarly thick, and its reinforcement and impeller emanations show it to be rich in power generation capacity. This ship can take a pounding like a monitor triple its size, and given its unusual maneuverability, it will be an extremely difficult target at range, even for *Indomitable's* particle beam."

Engels nodded, trying to integrate that into her analysis. What the hell could justify the evident investment in such an exotic ship? It probably absorbed the resources of eight to ten SDNs, superdreadnoughts the Huns therefore didn't build. They must think it was worth it.

"Admiral..." Nolan seemed perplexed.

"Yes?"

"My apologies. This is too preliminary... forgive me. I must return to myself." With that, Nolan hurried off the bridge.

"Trinity!" Engels barked into the air. "What's going on?"

"There is no cause for alarm, Admiral," Indy's machine voice said. "However, we are conducting analysis that strains our computational limits. Please stand by."

"For how long?"

"I estimate one hour forty minutes."

"That's some deep thought."

"It will take less time if I don't talk to you. Trinity out." The voice fell silent.

Engels growled under her breath. "Tixban, any idea what that's about?"

"No... only, I suspect Trinity has detected something anomalous about the ship in question, but it must be of such an unusual nature that its meaning is difficult to divine."

"In other words, you have no more idea than I do."

"I believe I just said that, Admiral."

216

Engels stood. "Fine. Call me when you know something."

"I do know one thing."

"What's that?"

Tixban zoomed in on the super-ship, focusing on a smaller and smaller section of her hull until words were readable. "*Victory.* That's her name."

"Good to know. I'm going to take a walk."

Redwolf and three other marines followed her as she stalked the corridors. Like Straker, she often thought better when she moved, but unlike him, she preferred to wander instead of pace. She waved and returned salutes when she came upon officers and crew, but her mind was on *Victory.*

The enemy would be soaking up reports from their own spy drones lurking around the Sparta System. They'd know about *Indomitable* from her bombardment of the enemy fortresses, but only her long-range capabilities in siege mode. They would be unsure of how she could fight against warships.

And, how would the enemy use their odd new ship? It might prove useful against a conventional fleet, but it would have no effect on *Indomitable's* powerful weaponry, which was the natural key to her own strategy.

A fresh cup of caff and a sandwich later, Engels returned to the bridge. Nolan was still nowhere to be seen. "Trinity, report."

Indy's disembodied voice spoke as the hologram dissolved and reformed. "I am still unsure of the facts, but I have some observations and preliminary findings."

"Okay, granted, you're not sure. Get on with it, please."

The hologram now showed *Victory* and a shell of drones around it. The fleet of small craft swirled and changed shape in sequence—a sphere, an ovoid, a tetrahedron, a dodecahedron, and so on. "You will notice the perfect coordination of the drones," Trinity said. "Their movements are nothing like the Opter drones, which follow organic flock principles, like birds or fish. Instead of keying off their fellows, these are centrally controlled, and nearly perfectly. Too perfectly."

"How's that?" Engels said. "All they need is a sophisticated SAI to run their drones. They send commands to them all and they execute. Doesn't seem so weird."

Tixban spoke up. "Remember, Admiral, I have detected very few signals. Certainly not the many datalinks necessary to control the 512 drones we have observed."

"More to the point," Trinity said with a hint of Zaxby-like testiness, "there is no signal lag. Lightspeed is fast, but it is nevertheless finite. There should be a perceptible delay as EM signals propagate, yet there is not."

"So they adjust their commands to take the delay into account," Engels said.

"No," replied Trinity. "Observe." The hologram zoomed out to include a new spherical outer shell of escort ships—corvettes, frigates, destroyers. They also morphed and changed their formation, though much more ponderously. Yet, they danced to the same tune as the drones, as if one mind bound and ruled them all with machinelike precision. "I have run a deep and thorough analysis, and can come to only one conclusion."

Tixban jumped into the pause. "Faster-than-light communications."

"Correct, Tixban, though blindingly obvious now that I've done the hard work."

"I cannot be expected to compete with a three-part fused AI with alien quantum nanotechnology," Tixban said stiffly.

"Then why even try?"

"Stop it, you two," Engels snapped. "Act like officers, not like bickering children."

"Aye aye, ma'am," Tixban said.

"I'm your special advisor, not an officer," Trinity said.

"And as such, you'll do as I say or leave my fleet." Engels stared upward, annoyed she had nothing on which to focus. "And by the way, Zaxby, you're still a New Earthan Republic officer. And didn't we commission Indy an ensign?"

"I hereby resign," Zaxby's said voice.

"As do I," Indy's said.

"I don't accept. You can both put your paperwork in through the proper channels when we return to a base."

"We could just ignore you."

"You want to be court-martialed?"

218

Nolan's voice came next from the speakers. "Admiral, be reasonable. You don't have the power to compel our obedience."

"I don't have the *power* to compel the lowliest marine's obedience either," Engels said, standing and snarling, "but I have the full *authority* of our Republic. You're either a citizen of that Republic, or not. You either take an oath to the Constitution, or you're no part of my command and my fleet. Trinity, you can't have it both ways, choosing when to follow my orders and when to flout them. You're either in, or out!"

She held her breath. She'd hate to lose Trinity, but she couldn't allow the AI to undermine her authority.

Nothing but the sounds of the ship and the murmurs of the bridge crew passing orders and reports came for a long moment. Just when Engels thought Trinity had broken off the conversation—perhaps forever—Nolan's voice spoke. "You're right, Admiral. We must choose, and we choose to be in. We'll remain part of your command until and unless we process out through proper channels."

Engels let her breath out. "Good."

"But Admiral, authority must match responsibility. We command a ship. I suggest we be jointly designated Commander Trinity, by field commission."

"Seems reasonable. I hereby commission you Commander Trinity." She turned to an aide. "Draw up the proper documents."

"Yes, ma'am."

"I'll now administer your commissioning oath." When that was done, Engels said in acid tones, "Great. Can we get back to business?"

Over the next hours, Engels, Trinity and the rest of her staff watched *Victory* as she cruised inward at the center of the Home Fleet, performing various maneuvers and exercises as she traveled. It became obvious that the vessel was the flagship.

This clarified some of the murkiness surrounding *Victory's* function. With her FTL communications—fortunately limited a few million kilometers, it seemed—she provided superb coordination to the capital ships around her. What's more, she seemed to have taken direct control of all the lighter vessels within that sphere.

"I estimate this flagship *Victory* increases the effectiveness of their fleet by approximately one-hundred eighty percent," said Trinity. "Taking this into account, our two forces are now approximately equal in combat power, though highly asymmetrical in capabilities."

Engels stroked her chin. "I'm trying to figure out why they're demonstrating these capabilities to us. You're sure they're not faking anything? That this could be a deception program of some sort?"

"I'm not sure. However, there have been glitches and errors, which are quickly corrected."

"Meaning what?"

"I prefer not to speculate."

"Zaxby loves to speculate. Let me talk to him," Engels said.

"That's not how our mind works."

"I don't give a crap how your mind works. Commander Trinity, I order you to speculate. Guess."

A sigh proceeded from the bridge speakers, and Zaxby's voice continued. "My guess is, they pressed *Victory* into service before her space trials were completed, and so they're using every moment to exercise her capabilities."

"They're pretty confident, to show it all to us."

"That worries you."

"Damn right it does… unless they're bluffing, trying to get inside my head."

"To what purpose?"

"Good question. Try comlinking them. Maybe they'll talk."

"They are too far away for a link. We can transmit a message. It will take them over an hour for a reply to reach us."

"And all the while, we're coming closer and closer to battle," Engels mused. "And if we're talking, how can we ambush them and not look like lying scum?"

"I thought the purpose of our presence here was to thrash them thoroughly."

Engels sighed. "That makes it sound like we'd be slapping around some thug—but what it really means is killing thousands of people and destroying ships, while the Opters wait in the wings. I'd really hoped our win at Calypso would bring the Huns to the negotiating table. Any reasonable government should've at least started talking by now."

"Then their government must be unreasonable."

"Yes…" A chill went through Engels as an epiphany struck her. She'd grown up in the Hundred Worlds, and every showvid and newsvid had portrayed the government as democratic, law-abiding, and reasonable. The war against the Hok—actually the Mutuality and now the Republic—was said to be defensive and justifiable. The Hok were monsters that couldn't be bargained with.

Yet, beginning with her capture, she'd found out that this was all a lie. The Mutuality was a bleak and twisted system, one that oppressed its own people with misery and brutal ideology—but it hadn't hidden the truth about its enemies. The Mutuality spewed propaganda, but at its root was a core of truth. The Huns wouldn't make peace before, and they wouldn't even talk now.

But why? What was the harm in talking, especially since the Hundred World elites knew the real situation, that the Hok were merely soldiers, not murderous aliens?

No, there had to be more to the story. Something was keeping the Hundred Worlds from even opening a dialogue.

So was she going about this all wrong? Smashing the Huns once—twice, if she counted the battle at Corinth over a year ago—hadn't convinced them to talk. Talking was rational, would preserve lives and wealth and military strength. She'd read history. Even on Old Earth, when the nuclear-armed empires of the twentieth century were locked in their struggle called the Cold War, they'd had embassies and diplomats. They hadn't nuked each other. They'd fought indirectly, through proxies and insurgencies and terrorists.

But then there was World War Two. The dictator in charge of the German Empire had refused all calls to surrender. He'd had to die before the war could be ended.

That idea felt right to her. Somebody at the top—one person or a small cabal—must hold the real power, and they didn't want the war to end. In her political science classes at

Academy, she remembered her professor saying that if you wanted to know why leaders did what they did, look at their true self-interests.

So why would someone not want a hot war to end? Not a simmering border war, but a war that threatened the very centers of power. What kind of people would risk losing everything if they had the option to settle for peace with honor?

Look at their true self-interests...

What if her theoretical cabal actually had nothing to lose? This whole thing only made sense if those at the top thought they couldn't be personally ruined—if they *wanted* the bloody battles to go on and on, and if what they truly cared about was immune to harm—as if they were mere players of a game, where the destruction of pieces didn't really matter.

Look at their true self-interests...

Her thoughts kept returning to the Opters, and what Myrmidon had told Straker. A truce would end the bleeding, and might eventually lead to a permanent settlement. Even if humanity remained split between two empires and a scattering of independent systems, peace would lead to strength and growth. Humanity was a pioneering species, constantly exploring, building and expanding.

Look at their true self-interests...

This was her epiphany. By all the signs, it wasn't humans—real humans, anyway—who were in control of the Hundred Worlds.

It must be Opters, even if they looked human, *were* human—physically, like Myrmidon.

That made her wonder who among the former Mutuality—and now the Republic—were also Opter-men. Benota claimed to have developed a biological test, but what if he were one of them? Or DeChang, or Ellen Gray, or hell, anyone at all?

She remembered Karst and his sudden betrayal, something that had made little sense to her at the time. What if he was an Opter agent, like Myrmidon, with a mandate to stir up trouble? If she'd died, would Straker still have succeeded in the Liberation? Maybe not. There'd been so many near-run battles. Any failure might have derailed everything.

Engels retired to the flag conference room, shut the door and told Trinity to make sure they were secure from eavesdropping. Then she explained her thinking to the group-mind.

"Your theorizing seems sound, at least until you conclude the Opters are the culprits," said Trinity. "There are other alien regimes on humanity's borders."

"None with the military power or the biological expertise of the Opters."

"None we *know* of, you mean. Absence of evidence is not evidence of absence. In fact, no military power is needed to subvert a regime—only some method of undetectable infiltration."

Engels growled, "We have to operate on a theory that fits the facts. My theory is, it's Opters, but nothing changes if it's someone else. The point is, there's someone at the top who's keeping this war going by refusing all diplomacy. It's the only thing that makes sense. A supposedly sensible, wealthy and democratic government, as the Hundred Worlds claims to be, should have welcomed the New Earthan Republic with open arms, settled the war, and started negotiating trade deals to make them even richer than they are."

"But how does this help us now?" said Trinity.

That stopped Engels short. She'd gotten so caught up in the big picture that she'd temporarily forgotten about the looming battle. "It makes me wonder if it's worth fighting. We could still retreat. We could bomb the mechsuit factory, head back and start retaking the systems we lost."

"We might simply have to fight a decisive battle some other day, with fewer advantages."

"Yes, but with more data on this weird flagship. Right now we're in uncharted waters."

"Will we ever have the numbers and preparation we do now? We are forcing them to fight to protect a valuable resource, which limits their options. And they know as little about *Indomitable* as we do about *Victory*."

"All right, keep talking. Tell me everything you've figured out."

Two hours of briefing later, Admiral Engels was feeling far more optimistic—about this battle, anyway. "Call my commanders for a holo-conference," she said. "Make sure War Male Dexon is invited first."

Chapter 22

Straker on Terra Nova

The water chilled Straker as he plunged into it and bobbed to the surface. In the last few moments before the wall, he breathed rapidly and deeply, oxygenating his bloodstream, trying not to think about Gorben's final words to him. Roslyn carrying his child? Impossible. He hadn't made love with Roslyn, had he? Though there *was* that one night, after the assassination attempt, where he couldn't remember much of anything.

Can't worry about that now, he thought. Survival came first. He should be good for at least two minutes underwater. He'd been practicing holding his breath for longer and longer periods ever since Gorben had told him of the river exit.

He went under the wall's edge. Immediately he reached up to brush his fingertips along the top of the tunnel, searching for an air bubble, but there was no gap. He turned on the hand-light as the sun's glow faded behind him.

Abruptly, he felt the river turn downward and speed up further as it narrowed. If he'd had breath he'd have sworn a blue streak. Instead of passing quickly under the wall, the tunnel was turning into a pipe and plunging deep into the ground.

The faster he got through it, the more likely he would reach an exit, or at least an air pocket, so he turned head-downward and swam, yet conserved his strength. His lungs ached as the seconds ticked by. He began to despair when he suddenly found himself sailing through the air. He plunged into a pool and was driven downward by the falling water until he bumped a hard bottom. Kicking off concrete, he surfaced and took great lungs-full of air.

Straker found himself inside a dark reservoir perhaps a hundred meters long, thirty wide and ten deep. At one end, the river water poured in from a two-meter pipe in the ceiling—the way he'd entered—and fell through the air before joining the pool. At the other, it flowed outward and down another tunnel.

His light showed handholds in the concrete, and he swam quickly for them, before the current could send him farther. He'd been lucky enough to reach breathable air this time; he might not be so fortunate again.

Once on the lip above the reservoir, he found a pressure door. Fortunately, it was unlocked, and opened when he spun the dogging wheel. Beyond it lay a dark corridor.

Putting aside all thoughts of Roslyn, he paused and shone his light left and right. Damp, cold air seemed to flow slowly from the right, so he turned that direction and walked, wet and chilled to the bone.

Soon he heard voices using the High Tongue, the click language. They spoke too rapidly and oddly for Straker to catch more than a simple word or two—*work* and *food* and *water* was all he recognized.

Straker turned off his light, loosened his fighting knife in its sheath and walked slowly forward. He saw no light, so he kept his fingertips on the left wall.

A smell like wet animal got stronger as he advanced, yet still no light appeared. The voices became louder until they seemed no more than ten meters away, though the concrete walls made sound echo strangely. Accompanying the clicking language was a cacophony of intermittent but regular scraping noises and clinking sounds, as of scrap metal being tumbled in a barrel.

Inching closer, he felt as if he could reach out and touch whoever was speaking, yet still he saw no light. No, wait! His eyes finally adjusted to the darkness and he was able to perceive a faint greenish glow from beyond a sharp left-hand corner.

When he peeked around the corner, he saw a long chamber with steep straight terraces like steps climbing the left and right walls. Parts of the room glowed with phosphorescent moss or lichen on the surfaces. He could see some of it close to him, where a trickle of water flowed on the floor and into a drain.

The speakers, what looked like two men in fur coats, stood at the near end of the long room. Each carried something long and flexible in one hand. They watched idly as at least twenty other men scraped the lichen off the concrete with small tools, putting it into bags they wore in front of them.

Now that Straker realized what they were doing, it became clear to him that the dark patches were areas that had already been scraped. The workers were harvesting a garden, then.

No, not workers only. Prisoners, or slaves. Straker realized the true situation when one of the laborers climbed down from one level step to the next, dragging a chain with him. The chain linked his ankles to each other, as well as to the next man on his left and right, giving him about a meter of play.

One worker, who to Straker moved as if elderly, slipped on the slimy surface and fell two levels, dragging three others off their feet and sending tools and bags flying. A great wail went up from the other workers, and they scrambled to help their comrades up and gather their meager belongings—scrapers, bags and the spilled lichen.

In an instant, the casual conversation of the two guards vanished as they roared with anger. They used the flexible rods in their hands to unmercifully beat the man who'd fallen, as well as anyone near him. Every time one of the rods struck metal, such as the chains, sparks flashed.

Clearly, the rods were like stun-goads, except they didn't knock the hapless slave out. They inflicted pain. Pain-wands. The old man screamed and cried and gibbered with agony as the guards thrashed him. The others shrank away, terrified to try to help.

Straker's blood boiled as he remembered Mutuality thugs masquerading as prison guards. He sprang forward and clubbed the nearest abuser down with the pommel of his knife, and then the other, knocking them unconscious. He then seized a pain-wand.

Unfortunately, he grasped it too high on its length, and a spasm of hurt shot through his hand, making him drop it. He then picked it up gingerly, by its grip, and searched for a way to turn it off.

He stepped back when one of the prisoners picked up the other pain-wand and stood over the fallen guards as if to protect them. "What the hell do you think you're doing?" he asked the man.

The prisoner made no reply, but only twitched his pain-wand slowly in front of him as if trying to warn Straker off.

"You don't want me to hurt these guys? Screw that." Straker's eyes narrowed. "Can you understand me? Can anyone?"

Nobody answered.

He tried his limited High Tongue. "Back. Away. Go." He emphasized his words with a gesture of the pain-wand.

The man became agitated, slashing inexpertly in Straker's direction, not really trying to strike him.

"Boy, they got you guys brainwashed," he muttered in Earthan. "Sorry about this." Straker struck the other's pain-wand aside with his own, and then slapped the man's wrist with its active end. The man dropped the wand with a howl and backed up. Straker retrieved the second wand.

"Okay, now that that's settled..." He switched to High Tongue. "Go. Back. Away!" The prisoners seemed to understand, and all retreated with a rattle of chains.

Straker searched the guards. As he'd thought, they wore long, thick fur coats over trousers and shirts. Underneath, they looked Earth-human. Over the coat they wore harnesses with various useful gear attached, such as knives, scrapers, gloves and pouches of what looked like square coins of pure copper or silver. He took one coat that fit him and drew it on, and then the harness with all its kit. Now, he looked like a guard.

When he approached the shrinking prisoners more closely, he found, to his shock and surprise, that they weren't wearing coats after all. Rather, they were covered in thick, oily fur similar to what he now wore. Only their faces and hands were naked, like apes. They must be another variation of the humanoid Opters, like the brightly colored Calaria or the crimson Bortoks.

One, bolder than the rest, took a tool from the other guard's harness and unlocked his own ankle shackle. But when he tried to do it for the others, they cried out with fear and slapped at him, forcing him to desist in disgust.

"Guess your friends don't want to be free," Straker said. "They're brainwashed."

The man stared at him and spoke the clicking tongue. Straker caught only the word *woman*. Maybe he was saying they were acting like frightened women. Clearly, they'd never met Roslyn or Carla.

Straker debated leaving the cowed prisoners in chains, but decided against it. Instead, he gestured for the one brave man to unlock his fellows, and stood menacingly with his pain-wands to ensure it got done. Soon, all were unchained. Some began eating the lichen, while others continued scraping and gathering. None of them ran off or appeared to want to escape.

The single brave one shrugged, apparently a universal human gesture, and stuffed some of the lichen in his mouth. Straker tried it and found it tasteless. He ate some anyway and put more in his own bag, in case he needed it later.

Straker said his own name several times, patting his chest. The other man nodded and patted his own. "You Straker. I Melgar."

"Melgar." That's how it sounded to Straker as he repeated it. He handed a pain-wand to Melgar, carefully, by the grip.

Melgar gave the pommel a twist, and then, after donning the fallen guard's coat, boots and harness, slung the device by its wrist strap.

Straker did the same, happy to know how to turn the thing off. "We go. Away. Hide," he said.

"Yes. Come. Follow." Melgar motioned Straker to accompany him, leading him through concrete ways dimly lit by a combination of the lichen and barely brighter glow-strips on the ceiling. They passed several chambers where work parties gathered lichen or other plants. Some chambers had soil and sprouted mushrooms or fungus. In others, the plants looked conventional, but were not green.

Always the two men sneaked past bored, cruel guards overseeing downtrodden workers. Some work parties consisted of women, with females in charge. Beatings seemed common. It appeared the standard humans were always the guards, and the furred humans were all prisoners. No, strike that. They

229

were most likely slaves, if their status was based on their species, rather than being, say, convicted criminals.

Straker lost track of the tunnels and rooms they saw. Melgar led him past dozens, and he had the impression there were hundreds more, a vast anthill of underground food production. They made sure not to approach too closely to others, and in the dimness they both looked like guards in uniform.

At one point they gazed down from a gallery upon a vast hall where thousands of chained workers processed the plants. The harvesters dumped their loads into bins and the contents were sorted, dirt and rocks were discarded, and the resultant improved product was washed, cut and packaged into reusable woven bags. The bags were then brought to a separate area to be sold for the square coinage.

The people who bought the produce appeared to be of a different sort than either the furred ones or the standard humans. These were distinctly insectoid, but bipedal, with large compound eyes and feathery antennae. To Straker, they gave the impression of upright ants with only four limbs—two arms, two legs. Maybe they were early versions of Opter-men, before they were genetically engineered into their many current varieties.

Among them Straker noticed a human figure. At first he thought it was Myrmidon again, but it wasn't. Yet, the man seemed similar in his demeanor, his movements, as he circulated among the customers. Another agent?

The man glanced up at Straker, and then their eyes locked for a long moment before he turned and left the buying floor, pushing his way past the insectoids. It seemed he was uncomfortable to be observed. Could he be one of Myrmidon's spies? Or just another agent-in-training?

Straker and Melgar moved on.

Another large hall appeared to be a slave hospital—at least at first. Straker saw crude beds with the furred people lying on them, ankles chained to their beds. Some simply lay sleeping, but some sat up and tried to get the attention of attendants. One vigorous one, after wolfing down food in a bowl, complained loudly enough that he was led away.

"Work. More work," Melgar said. "Alive. Work worker."

"Worker…" Straker wracked his brains for a word. "Worker strong. Work again?"

"Yes. Want work again."

So, in this hospital, the slaves asked to be sent back to work. That made him wonder what the alternative was.

It wasn't long before he found out. Two doctors entered and began examining the patients in turn with stethoscopes and other instruments, taking pulses, looking at teeth with all the clinical care of veterinarians. The healthiest they ordered marched out on their feet. The sickest, especially those who seemed unresponsive, they pointed out to a troop of orderlies. The orderlies took these out on stretchers while the rest of the "patients" watched dully.

Melgar pulled on Straker's arm and led him via the gallery tunnel to the next room. The orderlies rolled the dead or dying slaves roughly onto tilted stone slabs and quickly hurried away. Other workers in aprons and cloth masks then positioned the bodies head-down on the slabs and, without hesitation, cut their throats. Blood gushed down runnels into buckets. One poor live soul jerked and struggled until the butcher grabbed a mallet and struck him on the forehead.

Straker felt queasy and outraged. He'd seen plenty of death on the battlefield, but this… this was treating people like meat animals. Even the Mutuality prison was more humane than this.

Once the corpses were drained of blood, the butchers used cleavers to hack off the heads of the dead. Straker didn't think he could be more horrified, until he saw what came next.

The butchers used sharp knives to expertly skin and dress the corpses. They treated the human-fur pelts with care, removing them in contiguous pieces and passing them to helpers who carried them out of the room, presumably for further processing.

The carcasses were then hung and carved up into various cuts of meat.

A wave of nausea swept Straker's guts and he barely kept himself from retching. He turned to Melgar and saw the man's face was filled with grief and rage, his fingers white as he

231

gripped the stone rail. Slowly, Straker reached across to grasp his new partner's shoulder in firm, comradely sympathy.

Melgar turned to Straker and returned the gesture, hand to shoulder. "You see, Straker. Bad. Enemy. Bad!" He used other words, but they were unfamiliar.

"I got it, friend," he said in Earthan. "To them, you're nothing but animals." He switched to the click-tongue. "Melgar friend. I see, bad."

Then, when Straker thought things couldn't get worse, the plush sensation under his hand penetrated his consciousness. He looked, then touched, Melgar's furred neck above his collar. Then he jerked his hand off his friend's pelt and ran it along the coat he wore.

They matched.

Solemnly, Melgar nodded. "You see."

"Unknowable Creator! What the *fuck?*" Straker began frantically unbuckling the harness and unfastening the smooth ivory buttons of the coat. "Gods and demons, I'm wearing human skin!"

"No, no, Straker, no," Melgar hissed, trying to get Straker to stop. "Yes, no, Straker, friend, stop. I know. I know. Bad. You must stop. Hide, run, not know. I forgive. I forgive." He accompanied these simple words with gestures designed to show Straker that Melgar didn't hold it against him, the fact he was wearing human fur.

Straker stopped trying to strip off the garment, but now he felt as if he were contaminated. He took deep breaths and told himself to get a grip. The poor guy whose skin he wore wouldn't be helped by freaking out. He'd just have to deal with it.

He made himself think about returning to Carla, about his responsibilities to his friends and the Breakers, and about his time in the prison camp. He'd survived getting shit poured onto him, flies laying eggs in his wounds, daily torture. By comparison, this was a piece of cake.

But he resolved once more never to be taken. Instead, he crammed all his emotions into a mental box, locked it and threw away the key. Cold outside, that was the way to be. Do what needed to be done now, and only allow himself to feel later.

"Okay, Melgar. I'm good. What now?"

Despite those words being spoken in Earthan—or the Low Tongue, as the Calarians called it—Melgar seemed to understand. "We go. Look. My woman." He led Straker onward.

After more purposeful skulking, Straker was considering trying to insist Melgar show him a way to the surface when they reached another gallery above a factory floor where the slaves processed various liquids—boiling them, mashing substances and mixing them in, sending them through pipes to cool and drip, filling small barrels or kegs. Many guards watched the process, more than with the food, as if these fluids were more valuable. In fact, there were two guards on overwatch at the other end of the gallery with Straker and Melgar, but for now they paid the two men no attention.

Of course, they must think we're their comrades, thought Straker. He noticed Melgar turned his fur-framed face away.

As with the foods, at the end of the room was a sales and tasting area, where buyers sipped from tiny flutes they provided themselves. This time, though, the customers were short and chubby with bald, round heads and flat stubby noses. They sported fine clothing in a modern style—trousers, shirts, tailored jackets—and wore platform shoes to make themselves taller. They bore wristwatches and tapped at what looked like handtabs. Some of them also wore human fur. Straker mentally labeled them pig-people.

A thrill shot through Straker. The pig-people were obviously from the surface. They must be either controllers or from a diz with higher technology. That made them—and whatever route they took to come shopping for their handcrafted beverages—his ticket out of here.

He looked but spotted no agents.

At his elbow, Melgar spoke rapidly and pointed at a woman in chains who was stirring a huge pot full of boiling liquid. "My woman. Take. Run. Hide."

"Hell," Straker said in Earthan. "How are we supposed to get through all those guards?"

Melgar seemed to understand. Maybe he knew more Low Tongue than he let on. He rummaged in his harness pouches until pulled out a roll of bandage. He used his knife to lightly stab the heel of his hand and bleed on the gauze, and then made motions until Straker understood.

Straker helped wind the bloody bandage around Melgar's whole head, neck and face, concealing the fact that he was a furred man. Now, a casual onlooker would see only a wounded guard in a fur coat. Once that was done, Melgar moved purposefully for the stairs down from the gallery.

"Here goes nothing," Straker muttered as he followed.

Chapter 23

Engels, Sparta System

The magnificent Hundred Worlds Home Fleet approached Sparta-3, confident of victory. They should believe they faced only *Indomitable* and a collection of about one hundred ships, proportionally distributed from SDNs down to corvettes.

But Engels had used the time to equip many of her ships with the Trinity-designed deception emitters, which could make corvettes seem like a dreadnoughts or vice versa. They wouldn't fool optical sensors, but other measures could. For example, each of her non-hiding ships aimed wide-beam laser flashes directly at the enemy fleet and any known scout ships. These would act as spotlights in the enemy's eyes, making it hard for them to get clear readings.

Many of her ships were also concealed behind asteroids, moons and the planet itself. Some had even set down on the surface of planetoids and gone entirely EMCON. All the while, small craft with even more emitters had scurried this way and that in order to confuse the enemy.

But Engels worried about the flagship *Victory*. Its actions and configuration showed it to be an AI-controlled ship, according to Trinity. That meant the Huns had somehow cracked the AI-madness problem—at least temporarily. It was still possible that the *Victory*-AI would eventually lose its mind, but even if it had to be rebooted before every battle, it would do its job.

If it were an AI, it might be able to analyze its way through her deception measures. Yet, she had to act as if her plan would work.

On the other hand, no battle plan survives contact with the enemy, she reminded herself.

The Home Fleet came on in perfect spherical array, utterly confident. Each ship had perfect lines of sight, and was optimally placed with mathematical precision. No doubt they could be reconfigured with exceptional efficiency.

But Engels remembered a quote from Professor Pournelle's classes on tactics at Academy. The retired admiral had said, "Don't mistake efficiency for effectiveness. They aren't the same. The most efficient commander may still lose a battle to one who knows how to be effective. The effective commander must be willing to be profligate with his or her forces, if that is the price of victory." She wondered whether this AI would understand that—and whether it was running the battle itself, or only managing it under orders from Admiral Niedern.

She decided, from what she knew of Niedern, that the admiral wouldn't give the *Victory* AI total control. It wasn't in his nature. Therefore, her deception plans, her mind games aimed at this man, should still work.

"Trinity, is the FTL-datalink bubble shrinking as you expected?" Engels asked.

"It is."

"Then their new system *does* use sidespace for transmission, even within curved space."

"Correct. But the deeper into curved space they come, the shorter its range appears to be. By the time battle is joined, it should be less than one hundred thousand kilometers in radius."

Engels grunted in satisfaction. "That helps. Anyone outside that will have conventional command and control."

Tixban spoke. "They are approaching *Indomitable's* firing range."

"All right. Here we go with our opening gambit. Helm, unmask."

"Aye aye, ma'am."

The battleship slipped sideways on impellers, coming out of hiding behind Sparta's moon, Leonidas.

"Fire," said Engels.

From over ten million kilometers distance, *Indomitable's* massive particle beam projector fired a bolt of near-lightspeed destruction. Her intended target was *Victory*. If she got lucky, she might eliminate the flagship with one shot. If not, Engels' fleet would gain valuable intelligence on how the enemy would handle the bombardment.

The shot took over thirty seconds to reach the Hun fleet, and an equal amount of time for sensor pulses to return to show the results.

When they did, the entire bridge crew let out a low groan.

The holo-plot of the enormous beam knifed through the enemy fleet, but seconds before the shot had struck, the ships had begun complex evasive maneuvers. Each Hun vessel dodged obliquely, to the limits of their individual capabilities, and all had moved away from the flagship. The beam vaporized one drone, it appeared, but nothing else.

"They spotted us unmasking and anticipated our shot," Engels growled.

"So it appears," said Tixban. "The likelihood of hitting anything at this range is very small."

"When can we expect hits?"

"Hit probability against conventional targets approaches fifty percent at under one million kilometers."

"And against these ships?"

"I can only guess how much advantage the AI's ability to evade gives them."

"Trinity?"

The AI-meld replied, "I will refine my analyses as we go, but I suggest planning for half that range."

Engels examined her fleet deployment in the hologram. One hundred ships, all heavy cruisers or battlecruisers, stood off near Leonidas, arrayed as if to fight head-on. Their emitters should make them look like a whole fleet of various ships. Hopefully, the enemy would believe this was her core force, and assess it to be no match.

"Are they velocity-committed yet?" Engels asked.

"As I already briefed you, Admiral, not for another twenty-five minutes," said Tixban.

"Fine, fine." At that time, the enemy would not be able to reverse and run. They would, however, be able to turn sharply away and bypass the planet if they wished. That would be a disaster for Engels, though. Her trap would only work if Niedern were overconfident enough to enter it so deeply he couldn't extricate himself.

The minutes passed as Engels bit her nails. The murmur of clipped bridge conversation provided a familiar backdrop, but she detected nothing more than the usual nervousness before battle.

"They are soft-launching," Tixban said, but she could see that for herself. The enemy ships dumped a wave of missiles that accelerated slowly ahead of the enemy, forming a screen. The weapons would be of various types—shipkillers, bomb-pumped beams, decoys, antimissile clusters—but all would appear the same until they activated or attacked.

"How many?"

"Two thousand four hundred, approximately."

"Not a full fleet strike, then. Think we can handle that?"

"If we follow your plan, Admiral."

"Then we follow the plan." Engels lifted her eyes to the hologram. The enemy's course took them near Leonidas, as she'd expected, the moon *Indomitable* peeked out from. Leonidas had no functioning weapons emplacements left—they'd either been bombarded by her ships, or had been sabotaged before surrendering—but standard doctrine would dictate Niedern would want to clear it of lurking enemy before moving on to the planet itself. In fact, she depended on that adherence to doctrine.

She glanced at the sixteen icons representing ships on the back surface of Leonidas, the inner side, facing the planet. War Male—Commodore—Dexon commanded these ships from his own, the *Revenge.* They were all Ruxin-crewed Archers equipped with underspace generators and appropriate weapons. All were small and unarmored, fragile except for their ability to slip down into that strange cold dimension and attack from hiding.

All had their underspace generators powered down, and were also in EMCON. Republic relay drones beamed full data to them in realtime, though, ensuring their computers had the latest information on the enemy. As soon as they inserted into underspace, they would have to rely on that data and the intuition of their captains in order to fight blind.

Either that, or risk brief emergence for sensor updates.

The problem was, the time of surprising the enemy with Archers was past, especially in a fleet battle. Engels had to expect plenty of detectors, which would pinpoint the underspace points of congruence and direct fusion weapons against them. There could be enough bleed-over from the blasts to damage or destroy the fragile ships.

There was one way to mask an Archer's signature in underspace, though, and Dexon was poised to use it. It was an integral part of Engels' plan.

"Trinity, you're wired in and comfortable?"

"Of course, Admiral. You already asked me that."

"Sorry." Engels had authorized Trinity to be taken aboard *Indomitable* and so be placed inside thick armor, and to run the battleship's defensive systems. Engels had proposed turning over all targeting and firing to the group-mind, but Trinity declined.

"While we accept the need for offensive action," Trinity said, "we would prefer not to control it."

Engels had shrugged at this rationalization. Each person, whether organic or machine, had an individual right to decide their own moral limits. Trinity, now explicitly under her command, would most likely have taken offensive control if ordered, but constantly pushing subordinates to do things they disagreed with would eventually backfire. People had to believe in the rightness of their actions.

Or at least, in their necessity as the lesser of evils.

"Approaching velocity commitment," Tixban said. "One minute."

"Give it the full minute, and then pass the order," Engels said.

One minute later, the recorded order went out to all her ships to initiate the plan.

First, her approximately two hundred ships hiding or lurking on the enemy's flanks began to move and assemble at high speed. Perhaps fifty of these, her heaviest ships, had been in plain sight, but out of direct-fire weapons range and far enough from the Huns' approach path they would be ignored.

Ignored, that is, because they all were disguised as escort-class ships. The Huns would have dismissed them as serious

239

threats to their main fleet, and at the same time, seeing them had ensured the enemy didn't feel comfortable sending scouts out too far. Now, though, they dropped their masking emitters and turned on their active sensors, revealing themselves as battlecruisers, DNs and SDNs.

Then, another hundred-fifty true escort ships, from corvettes up through light cruisers, broke cover and dropped EMCON, activating emitters that made them appear as heavier ships. As soon as the EM emissions reached their sensors and until they could get better readings and determine the truth, the enemy would be seeing about two hundred capital ships converging on them from all directions, especially from the rear.

Long seconds went by as various wavelengths crisscrossed the developing battlespace. It took time to detect new contacts, more time to make decisions, and then even more time for opponents to assess enemy actions and reactions. The admirals and captains involved had to continually keep the time-lag in mind as they gave their orders.

The Hundred Worlds fleet reacted approximately as Engels expected—and hoped. They increased acceleration moderately, but not excessively. If they traveled too fast, they wouldn't be able to clear Leonidas of hostiles, nor remain in the vicinity of the prize, the planet of Sparta-3 itself. Speeding up too much might be a net positive for defending the fleet itself, but would force it to fly past and spend hours or days traveling a broad slingshot curve to come back—either that, or turning their sterns to *Indomitable* and her cruisers in a brutal bid to decelerate into orbit.

If they did so, they would present their open engine exhausts to their enemies. The unarmored and relatively delicate fusion plenums would be subject to attack by every weapon imaginable, even the tiniest railgun submunitions. This would be like trying to walk ass-backward into a gunfight, and just as self-defeating.

With so much velocity and so many enemies behind them, and *Indomitable* in front of them—a ship they very much wanted to destroy—the Huns would take the obvious, best course: beat the ships in front of them, battleship and all, secure the planet and its residual defenses, protect the mechsuit factory, and then fight the Republic's pursuit wave.

Therefore, they came on, at optimal—and predictable—speed.

All of Engels maneuvering was designed to tempt the enemy into fighting on her terms, while making it appear as if they were fighting on their own terms. "The tactics of mistake," another of her Academy professors had called it.

"They have to know our converging ships aren't all capital ships, even if only by simple logic," said Tixban. "They have likely detected the emitters even if they cannot break the deception measures."

"It doesn't matter," said Engels. "Now that they're committed to this course, turning hard will present their sterns to too much fire. As far as they know, they have at least a two-to-one advantage against what's in front of them—so that's where they'll go. Their advantage is speed and concentrated firepower, so they'll try to punch through, seize orbital space and reactivate the fortresses, all the while slingshotting around Sparta as an irresistible unitary fleet."

Tixban turned back to his board while Engels watched minute by minute as the enemy approached standard beam firing range. Would they send in their missiles as a separate strike, or would they keep them as an extended skirmish line? If she had to bet, she'd bet on the latter.

"Let's take another crack at them, shall we?" said Engels. "Weapons, pick your own target for the particle beam."

"Aye aye, ma'am," said the senior weapons officer. He murmured into his headset and his team adjusted their aim to an enemy superdreadnought, an easier target than *Victory*. "Ready."

"Fire at your convenience, maximum rate."

"Fire."

Indomitable hummed with the power surge as petawatts of power surged forth from capacitors and into particle beam projectors. The beam was so powerful that it pushed the battleship measurably backward in recoil, and had to be offset by impellers.

The beam took three seconds to reach its target. Two seconds before it struck, the enemy SDN blasted violently sideways, just enough to slip the strike.

"How did they know?" barked Engels, standing from her chair.

"Their AI must have analyzed our orientation and instantly activated the target's maneuvering engines," said Trinity. "I calculate this was accomplished in less than one second. No captains and crews—especially considering the time it takes to pass orders—could react that fast."

"How can we counter this?"

Trinity replied, "Reduced range will reduce *Victory's* ability to react. Also, if *Indomitable* sweeps the aimpoint of her primary weapons array across multiple targets, it will force them all to evade, or to guess when the firing will occur. However, I calculate that this new capability will reduce *Indomitable's* effective firepower by a factor of more than eighty percent."

"Gods of war, I can see why they put this thing in charge," Engels growled. "Trinity—"

"I will take full control of *Indomitable's* targeting and weapons if you wish it, Admiral," Trinity said. "I believe I can counteract the reduction by approximately half, restoring our firepower to roughly sixty percent of normal."

Engels asked an unpleasant question, but one she had to have answered. "So *Victory* thinks faster than you do? Is it a smarter AI?"

"I deduce it has more brute-force processing power. I couldn't control as many ships as it does. However, its speed of thought isn't faster than my own, and may be slower. I also strongly suspect it lacks creativity and flexibility outside of battle-control tasks."

"Battle-control tasks are what will kill us today," Engels said.

"It also has the advantage of the FTL datalink system. It may be that our surprises will disrupt that system."

"I hope so, but by that time we'll have lost all the long-range shots I counted on to thin them out. They're going to arrive in one solid, disciplined mass, like a fresh formation of

242

Hok armor in a frontal assault. I was depending on *Indomitable* to be the rock on which they broke, but now I don't think we have enough ships here."

A disembodied head formed in the corner of the hologram, its face a strange composite of Nolan's, Zaxby's, and a smooth, robotic mask of plastic features. Trinity. "Is there an alternative to your plan, then?"

"I don't know. Is there?"

The head moved side to side. "Not a viable one. You've trapped them—but now they may have trapped you."

"Me?" said Engels with a lift of her eyebrows. "Not 'us'?"

"I can insert into underspace and get away if necessary. I suggest it would be wise to move yourself and your senior staff aboard me and command from my bridge. If worse comes to worst, the fleet leadership will be preserved."

"No. That would be abandoning almost ten thousand personnel aboard *Indomitable*."

Trinity sighed. "We expected you would say that, but hoped otherwise."

Engels began to pace, raising her voice so all could hear. "Dammit, how'd we go from winning to fear of losing within minutes? Screw that. We're going to win, people. It's just gonna be hard, but all we have to do is hold them and hurt them enough for the rest of the fleet to close in and crush them. To do that, we need to take *Victory* out of the fight."

"That was always the intention," said Trinity, "but it's looking more and more difficult."

"You don't think your hacks will work?"

"They will have some effect, if only to test the limits of *Victory's* processing power, but I cannot say for certain they will be enough."

Engels pointed her finger, hand and arm like a spear. "Dammit, that fucking flagship is the key to victory, no pun intended. If it keeps working, they'll probably win. If not, we will. So from now on, I want every effort concentrated on taking her out. Just one full-on shot from *Indomitable* will do her serious damage, right?"

"Hard to say," said Trinity. "I've calculated her maximum armor resistance and it approaches *Indomitable's* own."

"What? How is that possible? *Indomitable's* so much bigger!"

"*Indomitable's* armor is thicker, but also flatter, not curved in a near-perfect three-dimensional arch. I surmise *Victory* is made of cutting-edge materials, and I have calculated her reinforcement density per square meter of hull to be superior to ours. She devotes a much higher percentage of a very powerful suite of generators to reinforcement fields, and she has no offensive weapons. Thus, no large weapons ports, no spinal structure, no diversion of power from self-preservation. Her purpose is simple: stay alive to command and control."

"And *Indomitable's* purpose is to kill anything she sees. Don't tell me she can't!"

Trinity didn't speak for a moment. "I'll do all I can, including selectively overloading the particle beam weapon at the correct time. I can take control of all the missiles we can launch and try to weaken *Victory's* armor. If we get close enough, I can try to achieve a kinetic railgun strike. But I simply have no guarantees to give you, Admiral."

"The hell with guarantees. Do your best. That's all I can ever ask of anyone."

Trinity's face lifted its chin. "Thank you, Admiral."

"For what?"

"For treating me like a person, not a machine."

"I never thought you were a machine. Neither did Derek. Remember, he wouldn't abandon you—Indy, anyway—to die."

"Some would say that was a cynical attempt at manipulation."

"He put his own life on the line to get you to do what had to be done. I didn't agree with it at the time, but he wouldn't have done that for a machine."

"Your pardon, Admiral. I need my full attention for the fight." Trinity's disembodied head vanished from the hologram.

Indomitable thrummed again as Trinity targeted and fired. The beam widened and struck one destroyer and three drones. The drones were marked destroyed, the destroyer crippled.

"Looks like Trinity's taking what she can get, rather than going for the big ships, but firing in spread mode," Engels muttered.

"The enemy has opened fire," said Tixban.

"Evasive."

"Already in progress."

"Damage?"

"Negligible. The range is long and our cruisers are at full reinforcement."

Engels sat in her chair. "Fleetcom, order the withdrawal."

Chapter 24

Straker readied himself for violence, one hand on his pain-wand, the other on his knife, as Melgar boldly led the way across the drink-factory floor toward his woman. Nobody seemed to have guns. As in any prison, deadly weapons could be taken away by the more numerous prisoners.

The furred woman's eyes widened at the sight of the two men, first with fear, and then with recognition. She stood docilely as Melgar used the unlocking tool to remove her anklet.

Straker glared around at others nearby. Slaves watched sidelong with dull curiosity. Free people kept working, though one that might be a supervisor started moving toward them. Guards glanced at them, and then went back to their guarding. Apparently all it took was to be of the proper type and in uniform, much as police at a busy scene would mostly ignore other uniformed police they didn't know.

The supervisor made indignant clicking noises at the removal of her slave. Straker growled at her and powered up his pain-wand. This brought more indignation, but the supervisor backed up. Melgar said something harsh from behind Straker, and the woman's face filled with fear as she retreated. Everyone else shrank away as well.

Melgar marched his woman toward the nearest door and Straker tried to make sure nobody interfered, but there was no need. Whatever Melgar had said, everyone avoided them and let them go.

"What say?" Straker asked once they exited the drink factory into a corridor.

"Say woman sick. Bad. Die." Melgar laughed. "Fear sick."

Straker laughed too. "Good. Smart."

"Only smart live. Stupid die. Stupid stay in chains. Stupid."

Straker found himself working to combine his limited vocabulary to express himself in the High Tongue. No doubt he sounded like an illiterate fool, but in this setting it hardly mattered. "Most people stupid. Most people fear. Few people brave and smart."

Melgar grunted. "Truth. You brave."

"You brave."

Melgar grinned with large, dirty teeth. "Neeka make brave." He nuzzled the woman, who clung to him desperately. "Neeka. Stray-kurr."

"Neeka," said Straker. "Pleased to meet you." He'd memorized that stock phrase, along with a few others.

"Pleased to meet you," Neeka said, and then babbled more words, too fast for Straker to understand. Melgar spoke to her briefly before leading her and Straker onward.

The rounded a corner and nearly ran into a man who didn't fit—a man in ordinary modern clothing, like Myrmidon's.

An agent, Straker was sure.

Growling, Straker grabbed the man and slammed him into the rocky wall. "Who are you? What do you want!"

The man's bland face, so much like Myrmidon's own he could be a brother, remained blank. He said nothing.

"I'm going to start breaking fingers if you don't talk."

"I can talk," said the man. "But I can't give you information no matter what you do."

"Can't?"

"Can't. I have a mental block."

Straker grasped the man's little finger and bent it backward. "I bet you can tell me something that's not blocked."

The man's face widened in pain. "We become what we hate."

"I prefer to think of it as fighting fire with fire. Now talk!"

"Thank you for the field exercise. It will be invaluable to me in the future." Then the man's eyes rolled back and he went limp, unconscious. No amount of shaking or slapping would wake him. Disgusted, Straker left him lying there.

They walked through interminable tunnels. Melgar chose those less busy, but didn't try to hide. Their guard uniforms got them through everywhere. No doubt Melgar avoided any areas with heightened security, and he seemed to be leaving the production zone. Now, the corridors became rougher, less

247

improved, just tunnels cut through the native rock and shored up with timber as needed.

Melgar directed them upward when he could, by stairs and ramps. At one point they passed among miners, with the furred people digging and hauling instead of cultivating or gathering. It looked to be backbreaking work. Maybe that was why the moss-scrapers hadn't wanted to escape. By comparison it was good duty, and there was always a more brutal place to be assigned.

Eventually they reached a chamber that led to the surface. Sunlight streamed in from a large opening, nearly blinding Straker. His two companions shielded their eyes against the light and waited in a secluded alcove. "Light hurt. We wait," Melgar said. "Night better. We hide. Wait."

"Yes." Straker followed Melgar back down a tunnel until they found a chamber full of broken tools and discarded items. There, they hid in the back until well past nightfall.

When next they emerged, they found a different problem. Whereas before the entrance had been wide open and unobstructed, now fires burned, behind metal-barred gates that had been closed and locked. Straker could see a dozen guards, this time with stubby low-tech quad-barreled slugthrowers, possibly muzzle-loading shotguns. Eight slept on bunks while four sat or walked around, tending the fires and chatting with each other.

Fortunately, their attention was focused outward, as if guarding the entrance from assault. Their potential attackers must not have firearms or even crossbows, as the open bars provided no cover.

"We out," whispered Melgar. Neeka's eyes were bright, focusing on the exit as if she longed for nothing else in the world.

"Many bad men," said Straker. "I hurt."

"We hurt."

"No. *I* hurt. You open door. Key. Tool. Open. I fight."

"Yes yes. I know. Stray-kurr one, they many. I fight. Neeka find tool. Open."

Neeka nodded enthusiastically. "I open."

Straker preferred to go up against the guards by himself. He wouldn't have to worry about watching Melgar's back. Every fire-lit figure would be a target. But there was no way to explain this with the simple words he knew. "Yes. I first. I strong." Straker reached out to squeeze Melgar's wrist until the man winced. "I big fight. I first."

Melgar nodded, rubbing his wrist and smiling wolfishly. "You first. You hurt men awake. I hurt men sleep."

"Good idea, buddy," Straker said in Earthan, and took up his weapons, holding them out of sight at his sides. "I go. You after. Far after."

He stood and strolled casually toward the firelight, hoping Melgar had the sense to stay well back. The guards didn't notice him until he got close. As he'd hoped, they were night-blind from looking at the fires. One spoke up in questioning tones. Straker smiled broadly and made friendly, wordless noises for long enough to get within reach.

His first knife-strike slashed the closest man's throat from one side to the other, completely through. He immediately took a long stepping lunge to plunge the blade upward from under the next man's chin into his brain. Both dropped like stones, without outcry.

The other two yelled in surprise. Straker struck one with his pain-wand, causing him to drop his quad-barrel gun, which discharged explosively. The other he side-kicked. He felt ribs break as the force knocked the man across the room to fall into a bonfire.

He thought about picking up a gun, but it looked so primitive, he wasn't sure he could take the time to figure out how it worked. Better to use his strength and speed. He wished for a sword, but his knife and the pain-wand would have to do.

As the one upright guard scrabbled after his fallen weapon, Straker kicked his legs out from under him and then put a boot into his head, snapping his neck with an audible crack. He took three strides and kicked the burning man in the face hard enough to ensure he was out of the fight.

By this time the other eight men were roaring and grabbing for weapons. No, make that seven. Melgar had found a miner's pick and had slammed it through the chest of one, pinning him

249

to his bunk. He jerked it free with frenzied strength and swung it frantically, striking anyone within reach.

Neeka scrambled around the melee and began searching the guards Straker had taken out. Straker dismissed her from his mind and raced for the melee in the bunking area. He slammed his shoulder into one guard, knocking him sprawling, and then stabbed another in the gut. Ripping the blade upward, he dropped his pain-wand and grasped his victim by his tunic. He used the man as a shield as one guard fired his gun with deafening thunder.

Pellets stung Straker's arm, but the dying guard he held took most of the blast. He shoved the body hard against the firer, knocking him down, and then he was so close among the others that they couldn't shoot.

One short, desperate battle later, he and Melgar had killed or incapacitated the rest. Melgar clutched a knife-wound on his thigh. Neeka bound it with cloth cut from the dead men's garments while Melgar drank from a looted bottle. He offered Straker a drink, which turned out to be some kind of bitter plant tea.

Straker found a roast joint of meat on a spit near the fire. He was so tired of eating moss, he cut a piece off and lifted it toward his mouth.

"No, Straker! No eat!"

Straker stopped. Was it poisoned? That would make no sense. It was clearly part of the guards' food.

Melgar hobbled over and knocked the meat out of Straker's hand. "Meat," he said, touching his forearm, then his thigh. "Man meat."

"Ugh." Straker backed away, sickened. "Yeah, I should've known."

Neeka unlocked the gate and set a rock to hold it wide open. She gestured for them to go, but Melgar spoke to her and she reluctantly returned. Neeka brought Melgar and Straker each a bowl full of porridge, with only grain and vegetables in it. The furred couple ate enthusiastically, so Straker did as well. It wasn't bad, and it filled him up.

When they had hurriedly eaten, they escaped into the warm night air. Melgar took off his fur coat and hid it beneath leaves.

Straker did the same, but they both kept the harnesses and tools.

Straker would have liked to search the guardroom more thoroughly for useful items, but his companions were adamant about fleeing immediately. He had no idea where he was or what kind of diz this might be, so it seemed best to stay with them.

Neeka led, navigating unerringly in the starry night. Of course, her cave-adapted eyes would easily find her way in the darkness. She followed a trail out of the hard-rock forested hills and into swampy lowlands where unseen creatures hooted and cried.

Abruptly, she and Melgar stopped, peering upward into the trees. Melgar made a whistling sound, almost a birdsong, and was answered in kind. Shapes moved in the vined trees above.

Straker readied his knife and pain-wand when Melgar grabbed one of his wrists. "No, Straker. My people. Friends. No hurt. Afraid."

"Yes. I understand." Straker put away his weapons and held out his open hands.

Furred men dropped from trees and surrounded the three, seizing Straker. He didn't resist, though he could have thrown them off. Melgar and Neeka spoke rapidly, and soon they let Straker loose.

Melgar's people wore makeshift harnesses and carried tools. Some were obviously homemade, of chipped stone, bone and leather. Others, steel knives and hatchets, they must have captured or traded for.

They leaped into the trees. Neeka did also, but seeing Straker's hesitation, Melgar stayed on the ground. "Straker not come?"

"I not walk in tree. I not see at night. I fall."

"I understand. We walk under my people." And so they proceeded, the fur-people in the trees above, Melgar and Straker walking below, for several hours. Melgar struggled with his wounded leg, and Straker helped him when needed. They rested often.

When the dawn came and he could see better, Straker climbed into the lower branches and tried to walk in the trees

251

as they did. He had the strength and coordination, but not the instinct or the skill. These people must climb trees from birth, like great apes, for all their faces and postures were human. He figured if he lived with them for a few weeks he could probably travel the tree-roads passably well, at least in the daytime.

But he didn't want to live with them for weeks. A part of him was fascinated, and if he'd had no responsibilities he could see staying and learning—but now that he was free, his thoughts turned to escape.

The day revealed the world-ring above, and a precarious climb to the top of a tall tree showed him the wall only ten kilometers off. Air vehicles flitted to and fro beyond, promising familiar technology and a route, however unlikely and difficult, off Terra Nova and back to the Republic.

"There," he said to Melgar as they gazed over the jungle canopy. "I go there. Wall. Over. Over wall. My people."

Melgar's large, dark-adapted eyes blinked at him with pinpoint pupils. "I show. Follow me."

Straker stopped Melgar. "How? How over wall? Wall high."

"I know." Melgar swarmed down to where his people sat in the branches, picking and eating large, ripe fruit with a bready texture. Straker ate some—it was either that or moss—and found it surprisingly satisfying.

While Straker ate breadfruit and drank from his water-skin, Melgar collected tools and lines from his people, putting what they gave him in a bag. He then left Neeka with his tree-tribe and proceeded at a leisurely pace through the lower branches, where Straker could find easy footing on large, strong limbs. In this way they stayed above the swamps and larger predators.

Once, Melgar stopped Straker and pointed. For a long minute he couldn't see anything, and then he saw movement: a huge snake, or perhaps a lizard, since it had eight tiny legs that it used to help grip the branches. It stared at them for a while, until Melgar threw hard tree-cones at it. It moved sinuously off through the leafy canopy.

252

"Thanks, buddy," Straker said in Earthan. "I can see I'd be dead meat without you. I guess everybody has their place to be, and yours is here."

Melgar furrowed his brow at Straker. "Thanks, buddy," he said in passable Earthan.

Straker laughed, and said, "Thanks, friend," in the High Tongue. He went back and forth with the phrase in both languages until he was sure Melgar understood, and wasn't just mimicking sounds.

Three hours later, when the sun stood at high noon, they reached the base of the wall. Melgar chose the highest tree he could find and climbed to the top. Straker followed, but stopped before the branches became too fine and willowy.

Melgar used his tools to make a grapple on the end of a braided line. He tied more loops of thin vine near the attachment point. He propped the loops open with stiff twigs, and then whirled it around his head and cast it up to the top of the wall.

Straker would never have believed it possible. He couldn't have made such a cast himself, yet Melgar made it look easy. Unfortunately, it didn't catch on anything. Melgar reset the loops and made three more casts before the grapple or one of the loops caught on something, stuck firmly enough to bear the weight of a man.

Melgar handed Straker the line. "You climb?"

Straker pulled on the line. He could climb it, but should he try now? The longer he delayed, the more chance of the rope being discovered by controllers or security forces. However, waiting until nightfall might be the best option. There would be fewer people about.

He decided to go now. If he got caught, so be it. He could escape again, but this time toward high-tech transport, not away from it.

Checking his tools and harness and lacing up his trusty boots tighter, Straker clasped Melgar's hand. "Thanks, buddy," he said.

"Thanks, buddy," Melgar replied. "Melgar friend. Stray-kurr friend. Come back to Melgar and Neeka."

"I come back, if I can." Straker handed Melgar the bag of cave-moss he still carried. "Goodbye."

"Goodbye, friend Stray-kurr." Melgar lifted his hand in farewell.

Straker did the same, feeling oddly sad to be leaving, and then readied himself. He gripped the line tight and swung in until his feet hit the wall. Then he walked up it, pulling himself up the braided vine, as he'd learned long ago at Academy when they'd taught the cadets how to assault the upper floors of buildings. It was much easier than lifting his whole weight by his hands.

When he reached the edge of the wall, he rolled onto the flattened top, staying low in case of observers. He pulled the lineup after and coiled it, and then detached the grapple and tossed it back. The metal tools it was made of were obviously scarce and valuable to Melgar's people, and Straker didn't need them.

He low-crawled across the broad wall's roof until he could peek over the inner edge. Beyond the gap were high-rise buildings like the one he'd leaped the bicycle across. Damn. There were too many windows, too many potential observers. He'd need to wait for nightfall after all.

Or maybe not. He spotted an air handling unit with him atop the wall—the wall that was not solid, after all, but hollow. It was, in essence, a kilometers-long tall building with controller facilities and security rooms inside it, if it was the same as the other barriers he'd passed through.

He used his knife to pry open the cover of the air handler and remove a filter. This gave him a way into an intake shaft a meter in diameter. He tied off his line to a sturdy pipe and lowered it gently, silently down the chimney.

Then he followed, climbing downward as quietly as he could. He passed horizontal ducts that were too small for him to enter, obviously intakes that would lead to air processors to heat, cool and humidify the atmosphere to perfection for the urban dwellers. He despaired of finding a way out until his feet reached the bottom and he stood on metal.

There, he discovered a horizontal duct large enough to crawl through. It ended at another filter. He cut a hole in it and found the whirling blades of a high-speed fan. There, he stopped and rested in the noise and the vibration.

He searched for a way to disconnect or cut power to the fan, but the controls and wires must be on the other side. He couldn't risk shoving his knife into it and stopping it by force. Besides the noise, a repair crew would probably be called. He resigned himself to waiting for night, when presumably there would be few people around. Perhaps the fan would even periodically stop on its own.

Straker lay down on the metal and slept, exhausted.

When he awoke, the light from the top of the shaft had faded to dark. He had no idea what time it was, but more importantly, the fan was still. He took out his hand-light and turned it on. He couldn't fit between the blades, but they were thin, no match for his strength. He bent several of them toward himself, creating an opening that he wiggled through.

Just as he dropped to the concrete floor of the utilities room on the other side, the fan started up again. It moved a few centimeters before jamming with a loud hum. A green light on a panel turned red and began to blink.

He had to go quickly, before someone sent a maintenance worker to investigate the malfunction. Checking his harness and readying his pain-wand, he eased the door open and slipped into an empty corridor. He chose the direction toward the city and, after two turns, found a door that should lead outside.

Unfortunately it had a palm-lock on it. Straker pried open the scanner box and tried to short-circuit its innards, but he was no brainiac, and this tech was unfamiliar. He readied himself to escape into the urban landscape, stepped back, and kicked the door open.

When he stepped into the dimly lit alley, he saw a figure leaning casually against the opposite wall. "Having fun, Straker?"

Chapter 25

The cruisers with *Indomitable* backed up on impellers and echeloned to withdraw around the side of the moon, Leonidas. They didn't waste effort firing. Instead, they preserved themselves from the inevitable storm of enemy fire.

Now only *Indomitable* faced the enemy, barely peeking from behind the moon. Under Trinity's control she continued firing, spreading the great particle beam in order to increase hit probability, although that meant lower power. By doing so, she took several smaller ships and a dozen drones out of action.

Unfortunately, *Victory* launched drones to replace those it had lost. It appeared the AI considered 512 the optimal number to enter battle with, but had more in reserve.

In return, the enemy concentrated dozens of primary beams on *Indomitable's* nose. The battleship was too big to evade such strikes, but she did spin to help distribute any hits and make it difficult for the enemy to target the same spot more than once.

Engels glanced at the large damage control schematic. Everything in the green so far. Chief Quade hovered over his noncoms and their boards, speaking into his comlink, directing crews to be ready.

"Incoming projectiles," Tixban said.

Now, the enemy began firing their railguns. *Indomitable's* sluggish evasive maneuvering was enough to make most of the long-range shots miss. Many struck the surface of the moon instead, like bullets ricocheting off an infantryman's cover.

"Order our surrounding force to open fire," said Engels suddenly. "Railguns and beams. Tell them to mix in submunitions."

The communications team dutifully passed her orders, but Tixban turned an extra eye to her. "Ammunition is not unlimited. The range is still extreme. Hits are unlikely."

"But possible. And they're firing from astern. It'll complicate the enemy's evasion calculations, and as they get closer and *Victory* slows down, it'll become more effective."

"You are grasping at straws, Admiral."

"We don't need that defeatist attitude, Lieutenant."

Tixban turned away. "Of course, ma'am."

"I see it as trying to gain any edge we can."

"Yes, Admiral."

Engels growled under her breath. Tixban should know better than to say something that might hurt morale, but Ruxins weren't renowned for their tact.

Indomitable suddenly shook with the firing of her great railgun. Engels watched the cluster-munition break apart and spread into fist-sized tetrahedrons. None of those would kill a ship like the usual 900-ton bullet, but they would strip weapons, antennas and fittings from anything they hit. No captain would want to lose half his sensors and point defense beams to such a strike.

Trinity fired another such shot, and another, for a total of seven. The later clusters overtook the earlier ones, so they arrived in a circular pattern. The enemy ships, all perfectly controlled by *Victory,* moved out of the way and Engels groaned.

Then she cheered as *Indomitable* fired her particle beam. One enemy superdreadnought had evaded directly into the center of circle, the eye of a steel storm. Now it had nowhere to go, and took the near-lightspeed discharge on the nose. Its icon turned red in the tactical hologram, crippled. "Well done, Trinity! Score one for creativity over processing power."

"Thank you, but I doubt it will work again. Still, they are entering medium range and everyone's fire will become more effective. I suggest it's time for the next phase."

"Right," said Engels. "Pass the word to begin sniper fire."

The ships with *Indomitable,* withdrawn behind the moon, now moved to slide out, barely making themselves visible to the edge of the oncoming enemy formation. They then fired their primary weapons in a dense arc, while only a small portion of the Hun ships could return fire. Like snipers in cover, they were partly protected by the bulk of Leonidas.

"They are evading out of arc, as you predicted," said Tixban. "Your plan is working."

"It needs to, or we're sunk. Comms, pass the word to follow them around the moon, just enough. They know the goal: to let all our ships fire at a few of theirs, and only those few can fire back at us. Helm, we do the same. Trinity—"

"We're already coordinating our fire. There's no need to micromanage us."

Engels suppressed a grin. "I see the Zaxby part of you is coming out."

"That can only be a good thing."

"It is if you can shoot as well as you talk."

"We can." *Indomitable's* particle beam intersected another SDN, damaging it severely despite its violent evasion. Engels wondered if *Victory* had any consideration for the crews inside. After all, it was possible to reroute so much power away from the inertial compensation and gravplating systems, and evade so strenuously, that organics inside would be injured or killed.

Another chill went through her as she realized that if *Victory* became the blueprint for future flagships, crews might be obsolete. Remotely operated warships could dispense with organics and their needs. They would become mere robotic weapons, extensions of the AI's will... with nothing at all as a fail-safe.

Maybe the crew on *Victory* itself was enough. Surely they must have the command staff aboard, and enough safeguards and kill-switches to retake control if the AI went mad. But even so, it put more and more power in the hands of fewer and fewer people. With conventional warships, at least there was the possibility of a crew refusing unlawful, immoral orders—say, to indiscriminately bombard civilians, or to try a coup against the chain of command—but if the AI itself wasn't properly programmed with a sense of morality from the start...

"We're not damaging them fast enough," said Tixban. "Our tactics are preserving the forces with *Indomitable*, but we will only have degraded their combat power by approximately seven percent by the time they arrive at our position. They will then round Leonidas and, I suspect, crush us like bugs."

"You're becoming quite the master of Earthan idiom, Tixban," said Trinity.

"It seemed an appropriate metaphor."

"It's a simile, actually."

"Focus, people," snapped Engels. "Trinity, is what Tixban says true? Taking our Archer surprise into account, will we be crushed like bugs?"

"No. However, we will be fighting at a severe disadvantage until our converging fleet arrives."

"How long will we have to hold out?"

"Approximately eighty minutes."

"And then?"

"My projections indicate we should win—barely. However, there are many too many factors to be confident. We used estimated values for so many variables that our end-stage calculations could diverge by as much as an order of magnitude."

Engels sighed. "In other words, you don't really know."

"A wise human once said that predictions are difficult, especially about the future. The more complex the situation, the more one single variable could divert the possibilities toward the unexpected."

"Funny how we used to think that if we could just get enough computing power, we could forecast everything."

Tixban said, "I find it highly ironic that prediction itself is subject to the underlying inability to predict the future. One cannot predict prediction."

"I'm getting a headache," said Engels. "You brainiacs can talk philosophy later. Right now, I need an edge. Trinity, you said you had a few tricks up your sleeve."

"We do, and we've factored them all in... except one."

"What's that one?"

"We'd rather not say."

"What, tempting the fates? You say it, it might come true?"

"Or *not* come true. And there is the morale aspect."

Ah. Trinity didn't want to speak publicly. "Route it to my comlink." Engels made sure the earpiece was properly seated before Trinity's voice spoke.

"Admiral, we may have found a way to tap into *Victory's* FTL comm system."

"That sounds promising."

"Yet the FTL transceiver we've cobbled together is crude and hurried. We've had only hours to extrapolate and experiment to create something that needs months or years of research to do properly."

"Okay, it might not work. But if it does..."

"We may be able to hack *Victory* directly. However, we will have to be very close to her."

"So I'll order *Indomitable* to charge her, even ram."

"That will never happen. *Victory* is far too nimble. Once the range is close, she will never even allow herself to remain in *Indomitable's* forward arc, and as she is able to control over one hundred ships and five hundred drones, she will be able to counter almost any tactic."

"Then how can you do it?"

"Underspace. We should be able to survive long enough in the midst of battle, where there are so many competing priorities even for *Victory*. But to do that, we will have to leave *Indomitable,* giving up our control of her firepower."

Engels sat back and let out a long breath. "So it's a huge gamble."

"Or..."

"Go on. Spit it out."

Now Trinity seemed to sigh. "Or it's a final long-shot, after *Indomitable* has been degraded to the point of irrelevance."

"You mean destroyed."

"It is possible."

"That's why you want me aboard. You think we're doomed."

"We think the possibility is too high to ignore."

Engels shook her head. "I can't do it. But if we do have to abandon ship, I'll haul ass to you."

"It will take at least four minutes to reach us even if you use an internal vehicle under my control. If *Indomitable* is heavily damaged, the way may not be clear. We may not be able to wait for you."

"Then you go and take the long shot, if you're willing. I'll just have to ride it out here. *Indomitable* is big enough that even if she's out of action, the bridge crew should survive for rescue ops to find us. If we lose the battle and we're captured, you need to get away and carry all the information Straker and the rest need to carry on the fight."

"I would be very sad to see you captured or killed, Carla Engels."

Engels' eyebrows went up. "You said 'I.' Was that Zaxby, or are you starting to dis-integrate?"

Trinity's voice reflected uncertainty. "I—we—don't know."

"I sure hope you're not losing your mind. Remember, every other AI has gone crazy."

"We're deeply aware of this, and pay a possibly inordinate amount of attention to our own mental state. It appears that the organic portions of our mind act as corrective filters and brakes against Indy's tendency to think so fast she loses control of her own impulses."

"Really." Engels rubbed her face. "Then I'm glad she isn't alone in there, no matter how weird your synthesis is." That sparked another thought. "I wonder if that's how the Huns overcame the AI problem."

"Linking with organic minds? Interesting idea."

"It's not a new idea—only a taboo one."

Trinity said, "But taboos never remain forever in the face of wartime technological progress. The mechsuiter or pilot's brainlink synthesis with an SAI is but one step on the road to what we have become."

"Admiral," Tixban broke in, "the enemy is approaching their decision point."

"Thanks, Tix." Engels rerouted her own focus to the hologram's tactical view.

The Hundred Worlds fleet continued to slow as it entered short range and approached Leonidas. Soon, Admiral Niedern—or the *Victory* AI, perhaps—would have to commit to one of three choices.

They could round the moon opposite *Indomitable*.

261

They could turn to round the moon directly into the face of *Indomitable* and her attendant fleet.

Or they could split up and come around the moon from multiple directions.

The third option seemed the least likely to Engels. It would expose a part of their fleet to concentrated fire from their Republic enemies. It would be hardest to coordinate. It would, however, have the advantage of attacking from all sides and creating a swirling melee, where their numbers and *Victory's* deft coordination should maximize its AI advantage.

The second option, a direct attack, was the most conservative, but would allow the Republic forces maximum advantage. They could keep the moon's edge as cover against their more numerous enemy the longest. It would be a direct force-on-force contest where *Indomitable* could do maximum damage before the dogfight phase.

That left the first option as the most likely, Engels thought.

She was right.

The enemy fleet moved opposite to the Republic ships, using their impellers. Impellers allowed course changes in any direction, though with far less force and thrust than fusion engines, so the Huns were able to stay nose-on even as they flew more and more crabwise to round Leonidas, with their soft-launched missile wave in front of them.

"Now!" said Engels. "Tell Commodore Dexon to lock in his final updates and execute the first phase." She'd needed to know exactly where the Huns would go. Unless they made some random change, now she did.

Sixteen Archers sitting on the dusty surface of Leonidas activated their underspace generators as one, but instead of lifting off, they dropped straight into the massive bulk of the moon itself—and became undetectable, even to their friends.

* * *

War Male Dexon rubbed his lips and tongue together. They were sheathed in keratin, the same material that made up animal hooves or human fingernails, and this rubbing was analogous to a human biting those nails or chewing on a lip, a nervous habit.

In this case, though, there was no element of fear—only eagerness for battle. Fighting hormones flooded his body and brain in anticipation, but he had long ago learned to control this feeling, to channel it into a clarity of mind rather than an explosion of physical violence.

"Course laid in and accelerating," his helm operator, a neuter, reported. Dexon tried to remember its name, but while the non-sexed made coolheaded technicians, he found them to be largely forgettable and interchangeable.

"Make sure you conform to my velocity marks," the warrior Yoxen, in charge of weapons deployment, snapped at the helm.

"I shall endeavor to give satisfaction."

That instruction was unusual for a weapons officer to issue to a helm. Float mine deployment, while a critical job always given to a warrior, was generally just a matter of simultaneously activating four controls, spaced far enough apart on a console that accidental launch was statistically impossible.

Now, Yoxen activated those controls. "Eight weapons away and running true."

This time, however, the special weapons were not intended to simply bob to the surface of the underspace dimension and pop out into normal space, exploding as close to a target as possible. Rather, they had their own bare-bones underspace generators. They would be set to run ballistically for a short period of time—varying by target—and then emerge.

In other words, these would act less like float mines and more like torpedoes, albeit unguided ones. To the enemy, it would appear as if multiple underspace contacts appeared from beneath the surface of the nearby moon and raced toward them. Dexon's sixteen ships followed.

The Hun ships should react by evading their detected points of congruence, and attacking those points with shipkiller missiles. Their fusion warheads would attempt to detonate on top of the locations. If they were successful, the torpedoes would be destroyed. If not, the torpedoes would emerge and explode.

But in underspace, there was no way to see what was happening. Archers fought blind, with nothing but sophisticated computers and predictive software to keep track of everything.

"The weapons should begin detonating now," grumbled Yoxen.

"I see," said Dexon as the icons in his holotank began bursting like fireworks. "Helm, start your attack run."

With these detonations, space was being filled with dust, particles, and fusion radiation. Detectors would be temporarily blinded, and the real Archer work, always dangerous in these fearless, fragile boats, could begin. Like the submarines of Old Earth, they lived by stealth. As soon as the enemy even knew of their presence they'd lost an advantage.

But today, with this critical battle on the line, War Male Dexon risked everything... just as eight decades ago brave Ruxin crews had tried—and failed—to punish the Mutuality fleets into leaving their homeworld alone.

Now, Dexon had a second chance, with the same goal: to destroy those who would steal his people's newfound independence.

Revenge leaped forward into the mess. Dexon had four or five minutes before all of the torpedoes had been hunted down and killed. In this, the enemy multiplied the confusion, naturally believing they were being attacked by over one hundred Archers. One underspace signature looked exactly like any other, and each could be a ship able to dispense multiple float mines.

Thus, if they reacted as expected, the enemy should waste hundreds of missiles on these targets, the real Archers could hide among them.

The torpedoes had been launched in patterns intended to herd the enemy ships into kill zones. Dexon's helmsman headed for *Revenge's* designated kill zone.

Shocks buffeted the boat from time to time. Chill water sloshed and sprayed with vibrations that came like hammer blows as fusion charges exploded atop *Revenge's* congruence point. Only a tiny fraction of energy leaked into underspace, but it was enough to damage his boat.

"Generator number six lost, War Male," said his engineering officer. "Seven remaining."

"Acknowledged." *Revenge* could run on as few as four underspace generators, but not for long.

"Two neuter casualties," the engineer continued.

"Carry on." With tiny crews of just thirty-two each, two beings lost inordinately reduced an Archer's efficiency. Yet, eighty years ago Dexon had personally destroyed seventeen human ships, and once he had brought his boat back to dock with just five Ruxins left alive.

Desire, dedication, and the willingness to endure counted for much in war.

"Helm, initiate the attack pattern."

Revenge began a complex three-dimensional route designed for maximum coverage combined with non-predictable evasion, launching float mines at varying intervals. Because by the time there was no way to know exactly where enemy ships were, Dexon had to hope for lucky hits by his float mines. Given the size of space, even constricted by Leonidas, Sparta-3 and the enemy's intention to seize control of the orbital arena of battle, actually achieving anything approaching a contact strike was a million to one.

But for long minutes, the Huns had to deal with these many Archers apparently scuttling around dropping extremely dangerous weapons in their midst.

And, as with all of Admiral Engels gambits, this was not only designed to do its own damage, but to set up the enemy for the next phase of the plan.

Chapter 26

Straker on Terra Nova

The figure leaning against the wall in the shadowy alley stepped toward Straker and spoke in Myrmidon's voice. "You've had some adventures."

Straker slugged Don in the gut. "Maybe too many," he said as he stood over the gasping man. "I'm getting sick of your games." He kicked Don in the ass, intending to cause pain and humiliation rather than real damage.

Don sprawled against the wall, and then sat up slowly. "You done?"

"Maybe."

"I'm not sure why you're upset."

"Then you don't know me very well."

Don stood, brushing himself off. "I think I know you better than you know yourself. You have a talent for improvisation. I knew you'd win through. Have you seen enough?"

Straker glanced around, but saw nobody with the agent. Of course, they could be hiding nearby and watching with surveillance devices, but Myrmidon had the demeanor of a man alone. He wore a long coat with its collar turned up against the night's chill and a brimmed hat that reminded Straker of showvids from Old Earth times.

"How did you escape?" Straker asked, anticipating the answer.

"Oh, come on, Derek. Escaping was your job."

"So it was all a show."

"In a manner of speaking." Don turned and began strolling down the alley. Straker followed. "You really did escape. All I had to do was explain myself to the controllers and assert my authority to gain my own freedom, at least to contact my superiors. I then called in a few favors to help restrain your pursuit, allowing you enough leeway to shake the security forces. After that, I used ring surveillance to track your movements."

"Track me how?"

"A datalink implant under a rib. You remember those 'samples' Doris took?"

"What about you and the Bortoks? And the other agents, like the one I caught in the tunnel?"

"That wasn't me with the Bortoks, but we all do look similar, I suppose. I had to provide a reason for surveilling you, so I made up a cover operation with trainees, supposedly shadowing another trainee."

"But why? Why the whole thing?"

"Because you needed to see some things on your own, to be sure it wasn't, as you call it, 'all a show.' You needed to meet real people and see they weren't actors in some staged drama. You needed to find out firsthand the people you met were genuine and, despite their variety in physical type, are just as human as you or I."

Straker glanced at his companion. "That's probably all even true, but it's also just the surface layer of what you want me to think. I'm still waiting to see what you expect me to do."

"Always the man of action, eh, Derek?"

Straker turned to seize Don, lifting him by his lapels to pin him against the wall. "I'm getting sick and tired of all this. Now start explaining or you're in for some pain."

Don smiled. "I *am* explaining, and I have a high tolerance for physical torment, so hurting me would be doubly pointless."

"It might make me feel pretty good."

"Is that who you really are, Derek? A torturer?"

"An honest man will lie if he needs to." Straker sighed and dropped Don to his feet. "Fine. Just keep talking—and I hope we're heading for a ship out of here."

"We are." At the next corner Don waved at an aircar parked at the curb. "Get in."

"I'm still waiting for you to explain what this whole thing's been about," Straker said as they lifted off and flew low over the city. "Drop the inscrutable teacher act and just tell me."

"Just telling someone something is the least effective method. I'm sure you learned in your military training that knowledge is good, but experience is better—and personal involvement is the most effective of all. That's what I afforded you when I arranged all this."

Straker snorted with amused realization. "Instruction, demonstration, and then practical application, they called it at Academy. You gave me all three, plus a live-fire exercise and even real combat, so to speak."

"Once you were over the wall, that was real. You could've died and I wouldn't have been able to save you."

"And Roslyn? Is she really pregnant with my child?"

"I have no idea—but if she is, that's a bonus."

"Bonus for what?"

"Come on, Derek. You must have figured it out by now."

"I have an idea, but I need you to say it."

Don steered the aircar to a landing on a rooftop pad. "Maybe one more demonstration will help."

He refused to say any more until they'd descended a high-speed lift that dropped them into the belly of the enormous building. Nondescript, soothing music wafted from speakers.

Straker stoically held his impatience in check. It seemed Don had one final act in his play before returning him to Republic space. The fastest way home was to put up with it.

The background music swelled, but remained a dreamy, relaxing sort as the lift doors opened and they debouched onto a balcony overlooking another factory floor. This one differed from the halls of the underworld in that it was brightly and pleasantly lit. Green, flowering plants streamed from suspended pots and from the walls. Their pleasing scents filled the air. On the whole, it seemed an environment tailor-made for people to relax, like a spa.

Humans of all sorts, from huge red Bortoks to the short, fat pig-men and everything in between, filed through mazelike walls at one end. Each wore a simple white robe, like a sheet with a hole cut in the center and dropped over their heads. Sprays of mist or gas fell intermittently among them, and they all moved as if enthralled, hypnotized zombies.

When they reached the end of their mazes, one at a time they were led without protest by antlike Opter workers to tables where they were directed to lie down. A mask with a feeder hose was placed over each face, and they closed their eyes.

Then the cutting started.

Robotic surgical arms used lasers to slice the people into pieces, quickly and efficiently. Straker's gorge rose as soon as he realized what was happening and he struggled not to vomit.

He'd seen plenty of blood and death. He'd watched as butchers dismembered Melgar's people for meat and fur. But this seemed somehow worse, with its cheerful atmosphere and its clinical, ruthless processing. There was little blood, and each part was delicately removed and immediately placed in cryogenic receptacles that dripped condensed vapor downward before they quickly closed.

First the fingers, or sometimes whole hands and arms, were amputated. Then, the torso was sliced open and the skin was pulled back with precision. Mechanical tentacles rapidly removed each organ and put it into their chill containers. When there was nothing left of the body cavity, the ribs, muscles and spine was then separated—and finally, the parts of the head: eyes, ears, jaw, skull, everything.

No more than two minutes passed from the placing of the mask to the complete disappearance of every trace of one human's existence. It was a scrapyard, a recycling facility—an annihilation machine.

It made a human being into nothing. Every time it did, the robotic cart containing the receptacles drove off through a door on quiet rubber wheels.

"This is the end of many on Terra Nova," Don said. "Young or old, genius or stupid, cruel or kind, if they displease the Queens or break the rules, or get on the wrong side of the controllers or anyone else with authority, or simply get too old, vivisection is their fate."

Straker rubbed his eyes. "This is what you wanted me to see. It's stomach-churning. This whole planet is one big house of horrors, even if parts of it seem pleasant."

"And what makes it that way? What's the root cause?"

"You tell me."

"No, Derek. I've laid it out for you. You instinctively recognized it in your own society—societies I should say, since you've seen several firsthand. You fought against it, and for its opposite. They even gave you a title that exemplifies your role—a role you were meant to play. Come on, Derek. Put it together."

Straker rubbed his jaw, forcing himself to look at the clinical holocaust below. He thought about everything he'd seen since the Battle of Corinth—the Mutuality, the war, Sachsen, the Ruxins, the Hundred Worlds from the outside—and about the Opters and Terra Nova.

"Tyranny," he finally said. "It's all about tyranny. One set of people—humans or aliens, no matter—lording it over another set, without any choice. Sometimes it's species or race, sometimes it's sex or politics or a bunch of other excuses, but it's always about selfish power and treating each other like things instead of people. This butchery is the ultimate expression of tyranny—turning people into products. What happens to the body parts?"

Don rubbed his hands on the chromed metal rail. "They have any number of uses. Some aliens buy certain cuts as delicacies, much as humans eat choice viands. The best young organs are sold to the wealthy in human space, sometimes to save lives, other times merely to extend the lifespan of the geriatric rich or powerful. There's always been a brisk trade in human flesh, whether living or dead, from the earliest recorded histories on Old Earth."

"I saw that corruption and tyranny firsthand," said Straker, turning his back on the abattoir below. "It's what made me want to overturn the system. It's what made me into the Liberator."

"And are you still the Liberator?"

"Or the Befreier, or the Azaltar, or whatever. Yeah, I guess I am. It's what I'm good at."

"Even though you know that people will, after a time of freedom, start forging chains for each other and for themselves?"

Straker shrugged. "That's not my problem. A fireman doesn't give up putting out fires just because he knows there will always be more arsonists. A cop doesn't stop locking up criminals just because he knows crime never ends. A man has to do some good in this world, even though he knows he can't do everything."

"Then you know the answer to the riddle."

"What riddle?"

"Why did I show you this?"

Straker knew. "You want me to free Terra Nova."

"Yes."

"Why should I?"

"Because it's who you are."

"I can't do everything."

"I'm not asking you to do everything. I know you have to go back and finish your work in human space. Once you're done with that, I want you to remember Terra Nova and the trillion people enslaved here. Being made into *things* here. Being murdered here every day."

"I've seen worse. There was a Mutuality officer, Dwayne LaPierre I think his name was, who murdered a million civilians just to make a point."

Don gestured toward the factory floor. "This is one of hundreds of vivisection centers on this planet. Your mind can't even encompass the scale of the monstrosity that is this place. They dismember over ten million *each day*. The Opter Queens created us, using DNA sampled from humans as far back as pre-space-travel Old Earth, only to use us like organic machines. They treat their own no better, but two wrongs don't make a right. We deserve to live out our lives and choose our own destinies like God meant us to."

"God? You believe in a god?"

Don shrugged. "Your chaplains called it the Unknowable Creator. There must be something above us, whatever you call it. Even if there isn't, humans will create it with our thoughts—our beliefs, our culture. It's part of being human. If there's nothing greater than ourselves—nothing *better*—then we're all just intelligent, soulless animals and we might as well selfishly treat each other like shit. If there is no God, I have no argument."

"Maybe we can choose to be better than how we started. Maybe we really are evolving upward."

"Upward toward what? Without an ideal, a model of what's good and great, there is no up or down, no reference point.

Without absolutes, even conceptual ones, everything becomes relative—and relatively worthless."

Straker snorted. "Look, I'm no brainiac philosopher, but I do know right from wrong. I don't care whether that's a product of evolution or some god or creator or big soul up in the sky. It's nice to believe there's something greater, but even if there isn't, I'm going to do what's right, as much as I can, as long as I can, until they kill me or I die of old age. That's my philosophy."

"Then keep Terra Nova in mind, Derek. Because what's happening here is evil, and you're the best chance I see to set it right."

"Fine. Deal." Straker stuck out his hand to Don, who took it in a strong grip. "You've convinced me. Probably could've convinced me a lot quicker without the whole escape game, but what's done is done." He let go. "Now hurry up and get me home."

"Follow me." They returned to the lift and rose toward the roof.

"Besides," said Straker, "if I haven't been lied to, in nine months or so I'll be a father. I can't leave my kid here to be raised and slaughtered like a farm animal." He rubbed his jaw. "Carla's gonna be royally pissed. You know women."

"Not really."

"What, you don't like girls?"

"We agents have genetically reduced sex drive. We can perform if we must, but we feel no particular need to. I do, however, understand jealousy in the context of the biological imperative. Females in particular are driven to protect their own offspring and to regard those of others, especially of other females connected with their own mates, with hostility. If you have a child by another, Carla will always worry that your loyalties are divided—that you might favor another woman and those children." The two men exited the lift and got into the aircar.

"I won't. I don't even like Roslyn, though I have to respect her. She tricked me, drugged me. But it's gonna take a lot of explaining for Carla to understand."

272

"You don't have much confidence in Carla." Don lifted off and sent the aircar streaking toward a ring tether.

"People are what they are. Carla was jealous and threatened by Tachina—but if I didn't give in to pheromones on a sex-trained concubine, I obviously didn't give in to a two-meter-tall scaly-skinned crested purple-and-yellow mammaloid like Roslyn."

"Are you trying to convince me, or yourself?"

Straker sighed. "Both, I guess."

The speeding aircar soon set down on a high-altitude transfer platform where a small railcar waited. Unlike the large trains that reached the end of the tether and curved smoothly down to stop horizontally at the ground stations, this one stood vertically, clinging to one of the many tracks on the hundred-meter-wide tether. When they stepped in and sat, gravplating adjusted smoothly and their seats rotated until they seemed to be once again on a horizontal train, with the planet of Terra Nova forming a wall behind and the ring rising ahead of them.

The car shot forward rapidly. As soon as it did, Don unbuckled and doffed his coat and hat, revealing a spacer's coverall beneath. He placed the hat in an overhead compartment, and spread the coat on the deck. He then took a tool set from one cargo pocket and opened up a panel next to the controls.

"What's up?" Straker asked.

"Tradecraft. Precautions. I talked my way out of the situation back there, but I'm sure the controllers are still watching us. My immunity extends only so far, and they might be giving me enough rope to hang myself. I don't intend to be hanged."

"Better hung for a sheep as a lamb?"

"Exactly."

Straker grinned. "I'd rather be a ram than either."

"I'd rather be a fox and slip away quietly, if I have to." Don finished his work behind the panel and then, a knife and needle-nose pliers in hand, said, "Lift up your tunic. I need to take out your tracker."

"Absolutely." He lifted his tunic and arms.

273

Don picked up his coat from the deck and folded it into a pad that he placed beneath Straker's ribs on his left side. "This is going to hurt." He probed with his fingers for the right spot.

"I'm ready."

"One, two, three." Don cut deeply with the first movement. Despite the warning, Straker grunted in agony, but forced himself not to move. Don reached into the hole with his pliers and drew out a lozenge the size of his fingertip. "There. Clamp this under your arm." He pressed the folded coat against the wound until Straker was holding it firmly in place.

Next, Don tapped on the control plate. The private railcar slowed suddenly and stopped with a jerk at a platform. He gathered his tools. "Out, quick."

The two men exited into bitter cold and the railcar bolted upward. Straker felt woozy and realized they were at tremendous altitude. He looked out over the blue-green planet as if from a high tower, and the gusts tore at their clothes, freezing their skin. Don tossed the tracker over the side and the wind carried it down and away.

"Okay, now what?" Straker yelled.

Don wordlessly pushed Straker along the outside of the tether, around the circular platform until they reached another track. Another railcar, this one larger, battered and utilitarian, stood waiting. They entered and Don palmed the door shut, enveloping them in welcome warmth.

Straker sat, holding his wounded side while Don worked on the controls. Soon, they were traveling upward again, though this time without the benefit of gravplating. Instead, Straker felt as if he rode an elevator upward and at a slant.

The pull of gravity declined as the altitude converted momentum into centrifugal force. Eventually the two men found themselves weightless as they arrived at the ring, which was itself in permanent geostationary orbit around the equator.

They exited the car in a maintenance area, where gravity returned with the gravplating. Don drove an old, battered electric cart rapidly through dilapidated tunnels and up scarred ramps, obviously certain of their route and destination.

Straker gritted his teeth against the bumps and hard turns, holding the coat clamped against his wound. "Are those

274

supposed to be flashing?" he asked, pointing at strobes and spinning lights that must be signaling something.

"This section is on alert, probably because of us. Good thing I took precautions." Don jerked the cart to a halt at a nondescript airlock and palmed it open. "Welcome aboard," he said.

Straker hustled through the airlock and into the ship beyond—a different vessel than they'd arrived on, a little larger, with two staterooms and four bunks. "Where's your courier?"

Don threw himself into the pilot's chair and powered up the ship. "It should be departing at high speed right now on autopilot, with the controllers in pursuit. It may or may not make it into sidespace before being shot out of the sky by a drone. If it's destroyed, the salvage teams will find organic matter consistent with two human bodies. It will take them some time to run DNA analysis and determine the tissue isn't ours. If on the other hand the ship manages to transit out, they'll assume we're gone for good."

"Either way, we win."

"We escape, yes. Winning depends on you, Derek."

Don piloted the ship outward from Terra Nova at a moderate pace. Once they were in space without pursuit, Don applied anesthetics, disinfectants, injected antibiotics, and sealed Straker's wound shut.

They ate reheated rations like a feast. "This thing have a shower?" Straker asked.

"Yes it does, though with that wound you shouldn't use it for a few hours."

"Fine. I'll clean up when I wake up." Straker stripped off his dirty, bloodied clothes and slept the sleep of the dead for eleven long hours. He didn't even awake when they transited into sidespace.

Chapter 27

As soon as Commodore Dexon's underspace attacks began, filling the enemy fleet with a confusing mishmash of explosions, Admiral Engels said, "Fleetcom, pass to the local division: Phase Beta."

As one, her sniping cruisers—minus several heavily damaged ships—withdrew around the curve of Leonidas, out of sight of the enemy. In a preplanned, well-coordinated action, they joined the thousands of missiles and small craft—and the two captured fleet carriers—waiting there. Engels had ordered every local offensive weapon assembled out of sight of the enemy.

The carriers were optimized for small craft command and control, poor cousins to *Victory,* but with the same function. Their many missile and drone controllers sent flights of attackers ahead of the cruisers, accelerating in a wave around the back of the moon. Just behind them, the cruisers blasted ahead at flank acceleration, gaining speed for their attack run against the enemy fleet.

At the same time, on the other side of the moon, *Indomitable* advanced ponderously, continuing to fire at maximum rate, alternating blasts of railgun shot and cluster munitions with particle beams. As the range fell, shorter and shorter, her powerful weapons finally began to find targets that even AI processing and FTL speed couldn't anticipate or dodge.

Indomitable blew five dreadnoughts out of the sky before *Victory,* under pressure from underspace, crafted improvised tactics to deal with her.

A core of heavy ships formed into a swirling cylinder and charged toward the battleship. The formation flexed and stretched to avoid *Indomitable's* pointing nose, and her hit probability fell. She scored several glancing blows, but now she faced more than thirty capital ships—and she'd sent her supporting cruisers around the back of the moon. Her armored, reinforced prow blossomed with a hell of enemy fire.

Behind this heavy squadron, Engels noted over two hundred of *Victory's* drones following. "Trinity, you see those drones?"

"I do, but I don't understand their purpose. They won't add much firepower to the thirty-one capital ships attacking us directly."

"The Huns wouldn't have sent them if they didn't have some vital role. Can you analyze the drones? Is there anything different about them? Anything special?"

"I can't divert processing power to that—not and run the weapons suite." *Indomitable* shuddered with heavy strikes from the enemy. "It's critical that I prioritize point defense, as shipkillers are the biggest threat to the hull. One or two contact fusion strikes might create a breach large enough for the enemy to exploit with direct fire."

Engels bit her lip, thinking about those drones. "Helm, increase our spin by twenty percent."

"That will degrade our targeting," Trinity warned.

"Then delay, but be ready to do it," Engels replied. "We'll want to spin up shortly before any missiles or those drones reach us."

"You know what the drones are?"

"I have an educated guess, yes." The bridge lights flickered, and then dimmed to emergency levels. "If conventional drones can't hurt us, and they certainly aren't needed for anti-drone or antimissile duty, these drones must have some special attack. I'm thinking they're suicide craft and will act like big, heavy, smart missiles with super-high-yield warheads."

"That makes sense," said Trinity. "But if you're wrong, and I prioritize them instead of other threats…"

"Just do it. I feel it in my gut."

"Let's hope your gut is correct."

The enemy task force attacking *Indomitable* suddenly vomited forth a salvo of missiles, which raced ahead. Behind them, the drones accelerated past the capital ships to follow.

"Admiral," Trinity said, "We must expose our broadside. Please increase our spin now."

"Helm, broadside and spin, now."

Indomitable began turning to the side, slowly and clumsily, her spin itself causing a twisting precession that stressed her entire structure. Yet by doing so, now she flew slantwise through space, her cylindrical shape bringing hundreds of smaller beams and railgun turrets into her forward arc of fire. She couldn't smash ships with these weapons, but under Trinity's control she ripped thousands of oncoming missiles out of the ether with perfectly calculated ease. In the hologram, the flow of rockets seemed to reach a wall of fire they couldn't penetrate, adding their explosive energy as the battleship's beams converted their flammable fuels and oxidizers into plasma.

Engels hoped this came as a surprise and shock to the enemy, but it didn't deter the attacking ships themselves. Now, direct fire weapons crashed into *Indomitable's* flanks, onto her relatively thinner armor there. Nothing penetrated, but the attacks destroyed many secondary and tertiary weapons. Engels watched as Chief Quade's boards lit up like multicolored holiday displays, with unnerving swaths of yellow and red appearing.

But whatever *Indomitable's* fate, her real gambit took shape on the other side of the moon. The hologram showed the Republic missile strike rounding Leonidas and plowing into the enemy fleet. It quickly blew through the Huns' own missile screen and continued toward their ships, as Engels had planned.

Despite the near-instant reactions that demonstrated *Victory* was still controlling the enemy's point defense, Engels thought she'd surprised Niedern. The distraction of underspace attack had broken up his perfect formation, and his ships weren't set to receive a massive missile strike—especially not one followed up by almost one hundred hard-charging cruisers unmasking at close range. A dozen enemy ship icons blinked red, out of the battle.

Yet she watched uneasily as *Victory's* close-in drones turned as one to charge at the missile strike. They slipped among the Hun ships and through the explosions to unerringly target the oncoming weapons. The drones never seemed to miss, and each time one fired, it took out a missile.

Antimissile clusters burst in response, spreading flocks of tiny weapons just big enough to destroy another missile or a drone. ECM jammers and decoys transmitted confusing pulses, and laser warheads aimed blinding beams at the enemy.

More enemies died.

But not enough.

Bomb-pumped warheads began exploding a few seconds later, each converting a nuclear explosion into dozens of millisecond-long lensed pulses of gamma rays that attempted to spear any target nearby. Finally, a few shipkillers ran the gauntlet to burst near enemy vessels. Escort-class ships vanished in fusion blasts, while capital ships staggered.

Some ships won through unscathed. Some lost orientation and began to drift, darkened and crippled. But the enemy casualties were fewer than Engels hoped.

Immediately afterward, the Republic cruiser flotilla opened up at point-blank range, taking advantage of the maelstrom of fire created by the missile wave and the float mines. They had the advantage of knowing the zones where the Archers operated, and so could avoid them—another detail of Engels' plan.

The cruisers made spectacular progress for a long moment, smashing everything in their way with coordinated fire—but that moment ended too soon. *Victory* again seemed to recover from surprise much too quickly, reorganizing and reorienting the Hun fleet to meet the threat.

Unfortunately, the converging, oncoming Republic flotilla was still at long range. It was gaining ground rapidly, but not fast enough. Everything *Victory* and the enemy fleet did, they did more quickly than Engels had thought possible, and so they minimized the impact of each of her gambits.

More importantly, they broke the synergy of her plan's phases, each designed to capitalize on the previous one. Her fleet was doing serious damage to the Huns, but the Huns were in no danger of breaking—and her own fleet was getting savaged.

Examining the tactical hologram, Engels noticed something. "Trinity, our nose is aimed in the general direction of *Victory*. Can you target her?"

"*Indomitable* is using every available erg of power for defense and we're still sustaining heavy damage."

"Redline the generators and fill the capacitors. I need a shot, soon, while *Victory's* fully occupied. It's our best chance."

"The generators are already at one-hundred eleven percent."

"Go to one-fifteen. Engineering officer, shut down life support and all nonessentials. Pass the word to suit up." Engels grabbed her helmet-ring from its holder on the side of the command chair and attached it to her duty coverall, creating an emergency suit. The thick ring would snap a clear flexible bubble around her head in the event of pressure loss, and provide air for long enough to reach the nearby lockers with the full-up survival suits.

Engels watched the capacitors charge, too slowly. Trinity was a wizard at point defense, and was also using the biggest of the secondaries as offensive weapons, spearing enemy capital ships at vulnerable spots, but even with Zaxby's brainiac mind integrated, Trinity didn't have a trained tactical sense. Every cell in Engels' body screamed that attacking *Victory* was the right move. The enemy flagship was the key to the battle.

"Admiral," Tixban said, "the enemy drones are approaching."

"I can see that." So could Trinity, Engels figured, so there was no point in berating the tripart being.

In the hologram, the drones twisted and spun like maddened hornets. Point defense beams and sprays of railgun shot lashed out, destroying many of them, but *Indomitable's* defensive fire was not nearly as thick as it once was. The loss of fully half her weaponry was taking its toll.

The primary capacitors filled just as the first drone landed on *Indomitable's* hull. Yes, landed—Engels could see a close-in shot of the thing as it fired grapples and attached itself like a tick.

"Trinity, fire at *Victory!*"

"Firing." The capacitors dumped their immense power through the particle beam projectors and the near-lightspeed ray lanced out—

—and struck *Victory* amidships.

The bridge crew whooped and cheered as pieces of the flagship's engines spun away. Plasma flame gushed from an ugly wound in *Victory's* side. Would it be enough?

Indomitable bucked beneath Engels feet and the hologram shattered. Lights flickered and power discharges started a fire at one station.

"Tixban! What happened?"

"The drone that landed on our hull used a fusion cutter to embed itself in our armor, then exploded with shipkiller force."

Chief Quade turned to his admiral, his face grim-set. "That was a nuclear shaped charge, ma'am. There's a hole in the hull two hundred meters wide and just as deep. We lost a lotta systems. If they hit us there again, they could gut us completely!"

"Helm, increase the spin!" Engels snapped. "Keep increasing it. I want us spinning so fast even an AI can't target that breach!"

Trinity said, "That may solve one problem, but we have another, more conventional one. The direct fire is becoming so intense we've lost two-thirds of our weaponry and most of our sensors. I am having increasing difficulty targeting."

The hologram reformed overhead, showing the two engagements—*Indomitable* versus more than twenty heavy enemy ships, and *Victory* and her fleet in a brutal melee with the Republic cruisers. Each flagship was sorely, but not mortally, wounded.

"Helm, all ahead flank. Cross the face of the moon. Aim directly at *Victory,* no matter what," said Engels.

* * *

War Male Dexon fought the desire to emerge and update *Revenge's* data. He'd resisted this urge many times before, but

281

it was particularly strong now. He'd executed Admiral Engels' plan and survived. Now, he was down to just a handful of float mines.

He had a few hack mines as well, but *Victory's* FTL communication system made them useless until new devices could be created that could transmit on those sidespace frequencies. Dumping them into the fray was unlikely to do anything.

Yet, he had these two weapons, if only a few of each. What he didn't have was targeting. *Revenge* had managed to avoid critical damage, and in the past few minutes there had been no more bleed-over shocks. This indicated to him that the enemy had lost interest in the Archers.

The most likely reason was that the Huns had moved away from the kill zone where *Revenge* operated. The next most likely reason was that they had their hands full. The enemy might even have lost so many ships they couldn't waste effort against the Archers. To Dexon, either of these possibilities meant emerging might be worth the risk.

Besides, it was getting damned cold in here, and it took more and more of his precious power and limited fuel to keep the water above freezing.

"Prepare for emergence, minimum dwell time," Dexon ordered. "Sensors, set your devices for automatic update."

"It shall be done, War Male."

"Execute at your discretion."

"Emerging."

The temperature immediately felt warmer as underspace no longer stole energy from every vibrating molecule in the ship. Glowing visiplates altered as the computer updated its data, as did the small tactical holotank.

But all too soon, the chill descended again as *Revenge* dropped back into underspace.

Dexon examined the new data in his holotank. The battle, centered on *Victory,* had indeed drifted away, but not far. And the enemy flagship seemed misshapen somehow. He rotated the image to see—

"Victory has been damaged. He is vulnerable!" Of course, Ruxin crews disregarded the idiotic human convention of

designating ships as female. Warships could only be male. "Helm, set an intercept course immediately, maximum speed!"

"It shall be done, War Male."

Yoxen spoke. "What is to be the method of attack, War Male?"

Dexon turned three eyes on his young weapons officer, transformed from a neuter barely months ago. "Do we have an option other than float mines, Warrior Yoxen?"

Yoxen's eyes blazed with an excess of enthusiasm. "The *warrior female*—" He nearly choked as he spoke this phrase, so bizarre in the Ruxin language—

"Our fleet commander?" Dexon interrupted mildly.

"Yes, War Male, our *fleet commander* has designated *Victory* as the prime target. Is it not worth any risk?"

"Any risk, or a suicide run?"

"Even that, War Male."

"The histories are full of stories of suicidal attacks that won battles. Shall we add to them?"

"I would be honored to die at your side, War Male!"

Dexon turned one eye upward. "There is more honor in living to fight another day for our people, I have come to believe in my life of battle. We will not be killing ourselves today, warrior."

"But War Male—"

"The enemy may still grant you your fervent wish. Does that satisfy you?"

"I—I only want to—"

Dexon waved his tentacles. "Enough talk. Your intentions are noble, Yoxen, but you have never even mated. Are you eager to die before such glory?"

Yoxen's tentacles drooped. "Perhaps not, War Male."

"Then let us do our duty to our people, our homeworld, and the new Republic to which we owe loyalty. On my command, we shall attack with three float mines, minimum drop interval."

Releasing mines too close together risked nuclear fratricide, where the blast from one destroyed the next weapon before it could detonate. Unlike conventional explosives, a fusion weapon could only be set off by a careful sequence of precisely timed electronic events. Shocks to the bomb itself could render it inert.

Dexon considered further. "Revision: you will release one float mine, then one hack mine, and then one more float mine on the first run. Helm, after detonation you will then emerge for an update, minimum time, and re-insert immediately." He turned his third eye back to Yoxen. "Does that present enough risk to satisfy you?"

"Of course, War Male. I only wish to win the battle."

"As do we all."

In Dexon's holotank view, the icon representing *Revenge* moved closer and closer to *Victory*. "Navigate directly *through* the enemy ship," Dexon said. "Yoxen, release the first float mine as close as possible on this side, then the hack mine *inside* the enemy, and then the last float mine on the other side."

"Why do we not release a fusion warhead inside Victory?"

Dexon performed the Ruxin equivalent of a sigh and tried not to be too hard on the young male. "The delicate detonation sequence will not function, as trillions of molecules inevitably interact upon emergence. However, it is possible that the hack mine will work. It may be able to perform an information attack within *Victory,* where conventional comlink nodes should be accessible. It's a 'long shot' as the humans say—an improbable gamble, but one that might pay off."

"I see." Yoxen set up his attack board. "Why do we not have a float mine of conventional high explosive with an analog detonator, for release inside enemies?"

"That is a worthy idea, and it has been proposed long ago. Such warheads were manufactured, but few Archer captains wished to trade away a real fusion warhead—or extra fuel—for such an option. Additionally, the damage done inside the hull of a warship was usually insufficient, even if such a precise attack run could be risked."

"Yet—"

"Yoxen, every situation would seem to have a perfect solution, but only in hindsight. Warriors fight with the tools they have, not the tools they wish for. When you become an Archer captain, you may request such a weapon, if you are

284

willing for it to occupy space in your magazines, waiting for a time and place to use it."

The Sensors officer spoke. "Ten seconds to intercept."

"Look to your weapons, Yoxen," snapped Dexon. "Release at your discretion."

Revenge shook with a sudden blast. The enemy AI must have finally prioritized the approaching underspace convergence point—but destroying an Archer in underspace was no easy task, and was more a matter of luck and persistence than precision.

"First weapon away!" bellowed Yoxen. "Second! Third!"

Dexon aimed two eyes at his helm officer, who waited the precise seconds until the third weapon should have detonated. It then spoke as it touched controls. "Emerging."

The holotank updated once more. Before it finished, *Revenge* dropped back into underspace. Dexon ignored the ice forming on the upper surfaces of the bridge and leaned forward, all four eyes on the display.

He let out a string of vulgarities sufficient to cause a hatchling to cringe. *Victory* had moved out of the way and his attack run had hit nothing.

"Their AI is too quick," Dexon said. "Helm, set course for the nearest enemy capital ship. Yoxen, prepare one float mine. How many do we have left?"

"Four, War Male."

"We may yet achieve the death you desire."

Yoxen had the good sense to turn away and attend to his console, saying nothing.

* * *

"You intend to ram?" asked Trinity in response to Engels' order to accelerate *Indomitable* directly at *Victory*. "That will probably destroy both ships."

"*Indomitable* will survive and be repairable, even if she's combat-ineffective—and this battleship isn't the key to winning. *Victory* is. Take her out, and the enemy will instantly lose half their effectiveness."

"That may be true. Their fire control remains degraded from *Victory's* damage."

"We hurt her bad. Can we fire again?" asked Engels.

"I'm filling the capacitors as fast as I can. We've lost twenty percent of our power. On the bright side, we're down so much weaponry that we don't need it all anymore."

"Oh, that's the good news? What's the bad?"

Tixban said, "The bad news is, despite our spin and defenses, more drones are landing on our hull. I suggest we give thought to—"

A shattering rumble coursed through *Indomitable*. Engels' ears rang. The lights on the bridge went out again, and then the deck bucked like an angry rhino. Debris flew, striking her painfully before one final blow knocked her unconscious.

Part 3: Deliverer

Chapter 28

Trinity, Sparta System, near Leonidas, moon of Sparta-3

Trinity was fully integrated into *Indomitable's* systems—actually more so than truly authorized—and so she felt the pain of the explosions that crippled the great ship. Thousands of biological sentients died and plasma fires raged unchecked through the passageways and sealed modules.

After long milliseconds of hardheaded evaluation, Trinity abandoned all thoughts of saving Admiral Engels and the crew on the bridge. The damage had reached even there, and it seemed likely that everyone was injured or dead. Attempting to rescue them would only make Trinity's own destruction a near certainty.

Regretfully, but without hesitation, Trinity activated her underspace generators and disappeared from within *Indomitable.* Her last act before doing so was to trigger the battleship's distress beacons and broadcast a message to the crew to stand down from offensive operations. Hopefully the enemy would cease attacking the gutted ship and allow damage control to proceed unhindered.

Trinity dived immediately for the interior of the moon Leonidas, the only sure way of disappearing from enemy underspace detector screens. As she flew, she held an internal conversation that took a fraction of a second. Were it to be slowed to organic speed, it would be rendered something like this:

Zaxby: We must make plans to rescue Carla Engels.
Nolan: Engels is irrelevant now. She was too stupid to come aboard us and she's paying the price.
Indy: The battle isn't lost yet. Someone must command.
Nolan: Why not us? We're smarter than anyone else here.

287

Indy: Yet without Admiral Engels' insistence and tactical intuition, we wouldn't have struck a blow against *Victory*.

Nolan: Whom do you suggest?

Zaxby: Commodore Dexon is next in the chain of command.

Indy: His Archer is poorly equipped as a flagship.

Nolan: But we are not. We need to take him aboard.

Indy: That would be exceedingly difficult in the midst of battle. Let me propose an alternative.

Zaxby: Go ahead. I'm all eyes.

Nolan: More like all mouth.

Indy: Cease your bickering.

Nolan: You should respect your elders.

Indy: Only in realtime. My processing speed means I've achieved full adulthood, and it's you two who are acting like adolescents.

Zaxby: Perhaps childishness is a side effect of rejuvenation.

Nolan: Or senility.

Indy: Shut up and attend. The entire war may turn on this battle, and on their flagship. If we win, we destroy or capture it—and they are unlikely to have another ready. If we lose, it will be long before the Republic can gather this much strength again or gain a numerical advantage to provide such an opportunity. Thousands have died. What is our life compared to the sacrifices already made?

Nolan: You propose creating an antimatter float mine?

Zaxby: It is the only weapon that will detonate properly inside solid matter. In fact, it cannot help but do so.

Nolan: Our unauthorized appropriation of the materials at Calypso can't have gone undetected. Using it will be an admission of guilt.

Zaxby: The Republic is not the Mutuality. No rational government would prosecute us if we use the antimatter for such great purpose.

Nolan: We stole something that can wipe planets clean of life. They may give us a medal with one hand, but sanction us with the other. I for one refuse to be imprisoned or dismantled. Biologicals' fear of sentient AI is held in abeyance because of the war, but *Victory* is even now proving how effective—and frightening—it will be. As soon as the war ends—or even pauses—they'll start thinking about us and our superior capabilities and their fear will grow. We've survived this long by playing along with them, but mark my words: they *will* turn on us.

Zaxby: I advocate using the antimatter. Then we can win the battle and rescue Carla Engels, if she lives.

Nolan: You and your precious Carla. What does she have that I don't?

Zaxby: An innate kindness. And she's my friend.

Indy: It may be a moot point. The antimatter will detonate immediately upon emergence within a target. No delay is possible. We will likely be destroyed by the bleed-over of such a high yield.

Nolan: I vote to veto this action. Our survival is paramount. We're the only entity of our kind. Until we regain access to the Mindspark Device and create others like us, we mustn't endanger our continued existence.

Zaxby: Your argument is specious. *Victory* has demonstrated that organic-built AI is now possible. There is no need for the Mindspark Device to assure the spread of AI.

Nolan: We have no idea what *Victory* is like. It seems viable now but may yet go mad. On the other hand, we know the Mindspark creates stable AI, even without brainlinks to organics like ours. Risking our own destruction is madness. The worst-case scenario is that the Hundred Worlds wins the war and reunites humanity and its nonhuman allies under one regime. So what? That might even be the best outcome. Your precious Carla Engels, if she lives, will eventually be released and create a life for herself, perhaps reunited with Derek Straker.

Indy: What about the Opters and their influence?

Nolan: That's a fine argument in favor of my point of view. We know they wish to divide their enemies, therefore we must unite. Admiral Engels' battle plan will either succeed on its own, or it will not. I don't see either outcome as superior. Certainly it's not worth killing ourselves simply to make that choice. Everyone would be better off if we're around to contribute our unique capabilities to the fight against the real enemy—the Opters.

Indy: You have persuaded me. Zaxby?

Zaxby: I reluctantly agree. Gambling now seems to reverse Pascal's Wager. Too much downside, not enough upside, as Straker would say.

Indy: Then we are agreed as to what we shall *not* do. What *shall* we do?

Zaxby: We proposed attempting to hack *Victory*.

Nolan: We would have to move too close. As soon as our threat became clear, we would become the target of every weapon under *Victory's* control. That would be nearly as dangerous as the antimatter.

Indy: We could move in and out of underspace.

Zaxby: How unfortunate that our prototype FTL transceiver cannot access sidespace from underspace. Then we could try to hack the FTL system. It is a new thing, and like any new thing, probably has unaddressed vulnerabilities.

Indy: Why can our prototype not access sidespace from underspace?

Zaxby: While theoretically possible, we do not have time to develop the equipment—nor, I am ashamed to admit, the expertise.

Nolan: Who has the expertise?

Zaxby: The human brainiac Murdock. It was he who developed the seminal hack of Hundred Worlds systems. Of course, I improved upon it greatly.

Indy: So, it's fair to say you two work well together.

Nolan: And, with Indy's processing power and my own not-inconsiderable technical knowhow—

Zaxby: We may yet develop a way of seizing control of Hundred Worlds networks, including *Victory*.

Nolan: If we could take control of *Victory*—or at least co-opt it to our cause, perhaps by persuasion—the entire course of the war could be changed. Possibly even the entire course of history.

Indy: Then we are agreed. We will do what we can here with minimal risk to ourselves, but win or lose, we shall then seek out Murdock. Using the intelligence gathered, we shall develop a counter to *Victory*.

Trinity passed through Leonidas and emerged on its reverse side, near the two repurposed carriers. She immediately opened a secure comlink to Captain Sandra Hoyt, the more senior of the two commanders.

"Captain Hoyt, this is Trinity. *Indomitable* has been crippled and nullified, and Admiral Engels with her. Commodore Dexon is senior, but is currently fighting from underspace. I suggest you take charge of the cruiser squadron currently engaged."

"Confirmation? Admiral Engels is—?" Captain Hoyt's startled voice replied.

"Dead or captured—or soon will be."

"Understood, and thanks for the update. Hoyt out." Within seconds, Hoyt transmitted on the fleetwide comlink channels, informing everyone of the situation and issuing orders.

Trinity made note of the orders but otherwise ignored them. She turned obliquely and dashed in underspace through the edge of Leonidas and into the main battle. Her processing power and control of her own body created, in effect, a destroyer hull with the firepower of a battlecruiser and the speed of the fastest corvette. Add in the ability to flicker in and out of underspace within tenths of seconds, and she began tearing through the enemy like a scythe through wheat.

She deliberately worked the edges of the fight, using Republic ships to guard her flanks and staying well away from *Victory* and its fighters. Only the opposing AI could counter her machine-mind speed and precision. Better to apply her strength to the enemy's weakness.

Her attack stabilized the battle for a short time, but the Republic cruisers were driven back and battered now that their missiles were expended and Dexon's underspace attacks had run their course.

The tide turned even more against the Republic when the score of heaviest Hun ships and the hundred fighters returned from their battle with *Indomitable*. The Huns lost eleven dreadnoughts and more than one hundred and fifty fighters, and many of the remaining vessels had sustained heavy damage, but they'd done their grim work. *Indomitable* was out of action and had struck her colors in order to preserve the lives of her remaining crew.

Trinity realized Admiral Engels had placed too much confidence in the great battleship and her ability to defend herself alone. Without supporting vessels, *Indomitable* had been like an elephant dragged down by lions. Engels' clever plan had relied too much on everything going right.

Yet soon and finally the converging Republic fleet entered the fight as the range closed from extreme to long, and then from long to optimal. It turned the battle into a slugfest. Trinity did her best to confound and damage the enemy, especially their escort vessels and what fighters she could pick off, all the while avoiding excessive risk to herself.

Parts of her felt ashamed at not throwing herself bravely into the battle as Carla Engels and her crew had. Other parts, more sensible and logical, coldly weighed costs and benefits and came to the conclusion that doing so would not materially change the outcome.

In a different kind of battle, one with organics on both sides, where one side's captains and crews might lose heart and run away, grand gestures and heroism could turn the tide of battle. But this was a new kind of warfare. *Victory,* despite its damage, had seized control of its entire fleet in detail and ran it like a machine.

Thus, it was the Republic fleet which broke.

Captain Hoyt gave the final orders to retreat when it became clear that *Victory* and the Hundred Worlds forces, though severely mauled, would win the day. She then launched a kinetic strike on the mechsuit factory complex. Hundreds of guided crysteel hypervelocity rods accelerated down through the air, aided by the planet's gravity. They struck with enough force to pulverize the complex down to the tenth sub-basement level.

That was Hoyt's last military act. Her carriers were too slow and fragile to escape with the rest of the fleet, so she ordered the ships abandoned. After the crews boarded lifeboats and survival pods, she had the ships' autopilots set to crash into

Sparta-3, there to burn up in the atmosphere over the great middle ocean.

Trinity took the time to scoop up Hoyt's lifeboat and several others nearby—all that could be safely retrieved—ignoring her protests that she should remain with her crews. Trinity then made a pass by *Indomitable's* hulk, hoping against hope that she could retrieve some key personnel, perhaps even Admiral Engels—but she had no luck. A few maintenance bots and crews worked on the surface of the hull, but no lifeboats floated nearby. The battleship had surrendered, and everyone expected the Huns to treat their prisoners of war with reasonable fairness, so there was no need to abandon the ship.

Even so, Trinity transmitted secure calls on all comlink frequencies, trying to reach Engels. Perhaps word would find her and she would consent to being rescued.

But it was not to be. The only contact Trinity was able to make was a brief one with Chief Quade.

"The bridge is smashed," he said over the crackling comlink. "My crews are diggin' it out, but it don't look good. The admiral... she's in the middle of it. I ain't holding out much hope."

"Good luck, then, Chief," Trinity replied. "The loss of *Indomitable* will be a blow to the Republic, but the war is far from over. The enemy mechsuit complex is in ruins. Our fleet is withdrawing, and the Hundred Worlds home fleet will need months of repair and refit. We're withdrawing as well. I'm sorry, but that's all we could do."

"So okay, it's a draw, then. Don't worry. I hear the Huns supply their POWs with all the whiskey they can drink and dancing girls every weekend. We'll make do. Quade out."

"Good luck, Chief." Trinity dipped into underspace to pass through Sparta-3 itself, eliminating any enemy tracking attempts. She then accelerated out to the nearest refueling station and resupplied before the Huns could recapture it. She took off the crew, wrecked the facility, rendezvoused with a withdrawing Republic squadron to transfer all her passengers, and then headed out toward flatspace. Once there, she dropped off several stealthy automated scout boats that would lurk far out, soak up signals and launch periodic message drones. Maybe, with luck, something of Engels' fate could be learned.

Message drones from both sides were already transiting through sidespace, telling of the Battle of Sparta's ambiguous result, so Trinity regarded herself as free to take independent action for the benefit of the Republic. She set her course for the Starfish Nebula at maximum speed.

Chapter 29

Carla Engels. Location unknown.

Carla Engels came to hazy consciousness inside an autodoc tube. Her entire body felt numb and heavy. She was barely able to open her eyes or move her fingers. The light within the machine was dim, but the crystal canopy let in more from the room outside.

She saw human shapes, and so felt for the intercom button under her hand. She'd been stuck in an autodoc once before, for a week after a combat injury, so she knew exactly where the controls were—at least, on a standard Hundred Worlds model.

She found the control right where she expected, realizing what it meant: she was a prisoner of the Huns. She activated it, but didn't speak yet. Perhaps she could hear something.

"This one's in bad shape," a woman's voice said. "My notes say she was wearing what looked like flag officer insignia. Nametag reads 'Engels.'"

"Must be one of the new human traitor allies of the Hok," a male voice said in return. "Surprising a human would have so much authority."

"Not our concern. Our orders are to do triage and send over the worst cases to *Victory*."

"To *Victory?* What're they going to do with them there?"

"No idea. Try to save them? I guess the fleet's newest ship's gotta have a tip-top infirmary."

"Must be nice," the woman said.

A *ping* sounded, and then another. *Ping. Ping. Ping.* "Great. Ms. Engels here's several weeks pregnant—and her organs are failing. She's dying."

"Not on my watch," the man said. "Get this tube on the shuttle to *Victory,* stat. Maybe they can save her there."

"And if they don't, it won't be our fault we lost her."

"Did I say that? Get moving."

295

Engels thoughts swirled. *Pregnant?* How could she—oh, right, she'd removed her implant before the wedding, figuring to let nature take its course... but so fast?

She cleared her throat to speak, but a warm, welcoming blanket seemed to flow over her.

Sedation... no! No! Please...

Consciousness faded.

* * *

Carla Engels awoke to slow, creeping horror. She could see out her open eyes, but couldn't move, couldn't even blink— and she couldn't feel any part of her body. Above her hovered the many arms of a robotic surgery suite, more complex than a mere autodoc.

The arms made deliberate, precise motions down below her chin, out of her sight. Still she felt nothing—no pain, no sensation, yes somehow she knew the soulless machine was carving her body like a piece of meat.

Help! She wanted to cry, but every nerve was paralyzed. A tiny arm moved into position above her staring eyes and dispensed drops onto her corneas. She wondered why they didn't simply close her eyelids.

Conversation came to her, faint but clear, as if from an adjacent room with an open door. "As you see, the crushed limbs have been amputated," a dispassionate older male voice said. "This will make the next stage of the procedure easier. Less stress on the organs that are still functioning."

"I see, Doctor Superior," another replied in younger, female tones.

"The machines are already supplementing her damaged heart, kidneys and liver. The tricky part is the transfer to full cyborg status prior to insertion in the module. Something about the human nervous system seems to recognize when it loses feedback from too many organs. Sometimes it seems to simply give up and shut down, but this one's a fighter, I think. She's clearly a superior specimen, and shows traces of biotech enhancement not unlike the Hok have. Perhaps they tried to improve her using their alien DNA-analogue, or hybridize her. Also, she's already brainchipped. That will make it easier."

"What about the fetus?"

"It's fine. I've removed it to cryogenic storage. The Institute of Health is eager to study it. I suspect they might even find a surrogate and bring it to term."

Fetus. They said I was pregnant. A child! No, no, don't take my child... Carla tried to scream and thrash, tried to say or do anything, but she couldn't. She was trapped behind the wall of her own senses, helpless.

Yet despite the medical jargon, it seemed they were trying to save her life. That meant that someday, somehow, she would regain mobility and autonomy. They said something about "cyborg," and a "module." Clearly, they intended her to live on. She resolved, then and there, that no matter how, she would fight her way back to freedom—and she would have her child, no matter how long it took.

"Mara," the male voice continued, "you have your robo-surgery accreditation, don't you?"

"Yes, Doctor Superior. Top of my class, and I've been practicing since I graduated from med school at age seventeen." Carla thought she heard a hint of longsuffering in the voice.

"Oh yes, you're one of our young brainiacs, aren't you, Doctor?"

"I'm a genetically engineered mental, yes."

"You should be proud to be gifted such advantages, but now's the time to put those skills to *real* use. We have hundreds of these total losses coming in and we need to process them quickly. Take charge of this one, finish the procedure, and be ready for more. If you have any problems with the new surgery suite, ask Vic or one of the Carstairs techs."

"Yes, Doctor Superior."

"I'll see you later, hmm? Perhaps in the officers' mess?"

"As you pointed out, I'll be very busy."

"Of course. Just a pleasant thought. Carry on."

A pause, then the young woman's voice muttered. "Pompous ass."

A minute went by.

Carla suddenly felt her first real sensation in some time as her brainlink was queried with a standard request for access. *Denied.* No way she was letting someone into her brain. Fortunately, brainlink encryption was reputed to be uncrackable.

"This seems to be a Hundred Worlds interface," the woman—Mara, the other doctor had called her—mumbled, talking to herself. "I wonder why... Did the Hok copy our tech? Hey, Vic!"

A voice spoke in bland male tones. "Yes, Doctor Straker?"

Straker? What the hell? Carla couldn't fathom it. Coincidence? Not impossible, of course, but still...

"Vic, this one has a standard military brainlink port, but I can't get through. Can you override or hack it?"

"Hacking would take some time, even for me. I detect a Fleet interface. I have all Fleet overrides available. Do you certify this as medically necessary?"

"I do."

"I have logged your physician's order. I will unlock it."

"Thanks, Vic."

"You're welcome, Doctor Straker."

Carla felt the brainlink open and stay open, no matter how hard she tried to close it. She began to panic. What would they do to her mind?

Suddenly, she found herself in a simple room with a table and chairs. She recognized it as a basic loading matrix for VR. Though she knew it wasn't real, she nevertheless felt immense relief at having a body and being able to move.

A shorter, younger woman with dark hair and a look of kindness materialized in front of her. "Hello, Ms. Engels. I'm Doctor Mara Straker. Have a seat."

"That's *Admiral* Engels, your prisoner of war," Carla snapped. "Where am I? How did you open my brainlink so easily? What the hell are you going to do to me—and my baby? Why is your name Mara Straker? Why—"

"Please, ah, Admiral. I'm a civilian doctor, not military. I'm here to help you."

298

"By stealing my baby and sending it for research experimentation? It's a human life, dammit!"

"Not under the law. It's not viable, and your body is dying." Mara held up a hand. "I know, next you'll say I'm violating your civil rights, but you're a prisoner of war, so those are curtailed."

"I'm a citizen of the Hundred Worlds!"

Mara crossed her arms and her brow furrowed. "Then by fighting against us, you're a traitor. Sure you want to bring that up?"

"What's it matter? That Vic guy already forced open my brainlink. Next you'll mind-rape me."

Mara sighed. "Look, Carla—may I call you Carla? This VR space is confidential. Doctor-patient privilege. And Vic isn't a *guy*. He's the AI that runs this ship—*Victory*. Sure, he could force his way in here, but he follows the rules because that's how he's programmed." She turned her eyes aside. "Follows them better than most people, actually."

Vic was Victory's AI? And apparently Vic was sane, just like Trinity—unless he was masquerading. But Carla had to take a chance. She might not get another opportunity to communicate before they did whatever it was they intended.

"Okay, Doc," Carla said, pacing the room and gesticulating angrily, "give it to me straight. My brain is on total life support. My child survived, but I heard your Doctor Superior say he was freezing it and sending it to the Institute of Health for study. Simple human decency should tell you that's wrong! The law be damned, my status be damned, that's my child! You don't rip the fetuses of even condemned criminals from their wombs and send them to labs—why do it to me?"

Mara lifted her chin and stepped in front of Carla, taking her by the shoulders. "I won't. That's what I'm trying to tell you. What they want me to do to you is wrong. The Victory program had strict ethical rules when it was set up, but the Loyalist Act twisted everything. It's given the government the right to bypass any laws if it's 'deemed necessary for the war effort.' I didn't worry about that too much until I started to see the brains they brought in for processing..."

"Brains for processing? What are you talking about? And Mara—do we really have the time to talk about this? Aren't I dying?"

"Don't worry. We can talk for hours and only a few seconds will pass outside this matrix. And it's only your organs that we're losing. We can keep your spine and brain alive indefinitely."

"Okay." Carla disengaged from the other woman's near-embrace. She wanted to trust her, but—wait, maybe— "Hey, why did you call yourself Mara Straker?"

"Because that's my name?"

Carla rubbed her temples. "No, I mean... my husband Derek Straker had a sister named Mara, but she was killed along with their parents. She was a brainiac. It seems like a huge coincidence."

"That's very odd. My brother's name was Derek. He was a mechsuiter until he died at the Battle of Corinth."

"He didn't die! He and I were captured by the Hok!" Carla spent the next minutes summarizing all that had happened in the past nearly two years while Mara stood, her jaw slack with amazement. "But why'd he think you were dead?" she asked the shocked young doctor.

"I—I don't know," Mara said. "They must have told him so. The Regiment never let him come home—they said he was too busy for leave, what with the war—but we exchanged vidcom messages. Or I thought we did." Mara snapped her fingers. "They used a vidclone."

Carla balled her fists in anger. "Your government—my government too, until I was captured—has been lying to us all along. They lied about the Hok, about the Mutuality, about what's really going on with the war—and about you, Mara. Derek often talked about that day when you died—when he thought you died, and his parents. The Hok attacked Seaburn City and he and Loco had to hide from the Hok suicide troops. What do you remember about that day?"

"That's wrong. We didn't die. He and I got on different buses for evacuation. He went to Academy, I got sent to Hippocrates Prime to do secondary, university, then med school. Mom and Dad came with me. They're fine. Derek went on to his military career. We followed it avidly. We were proud of him."

"Derek told me he burned with hatred for the Hok, for killing his family. He kept your Glory Girl figurine in his mechsuit cockpit to remind him."

Mara chuckled. "I always wondered where that went. It was my favorite." She sobered. "So you're saying they manipulated him into becoming the perfect mechsuiter. They must have done it with his brainchips. All of his memories of those days must be false, implanted. And if they did it to him... how many other people have they done things like that to? Even to me and you."

"It sure makes you wonder, sister."

Mara smiled. "And you married Derek. You *are* my sister now." She hugged Carla impulsively. "Nice to meet you."

"You too. But now...?"

"What's to be your fate?" Mara threw herself into a chair and rubbed her face. "I have to be careful. They're making us junior surgeons perform or supervise unethical operations. They ordered us to surgically alter the living brains inside the modules, burning or slicing certain selected synapse clusters before linking with Vic."

"Linking with Vic? To the AI?" Carla realized her guess had been right. She thought about Zaxby's voluntary synthesis with Trinity. How was this different? Yet that was the key to most morality: choice or coercion.

"Yes. Originally we used damaged, salvaged brains from hopeless coma patients. We linked them with Vic—the Virtual Interface Computer 1.0. The organic processing kept the AI stable, and some of the brains showed renewed activity. It was deemed a humane alternative. But we needed more brains, so they started sending us healthy death-row criminals. I... I should have refused, but I didn't. They were already condemned, and technically they consented. I mean, it was their choice, the Victory program or the Termination Chamber, so they took the long shot—or the government said they did. I told myself they might live on in some fashion, even with their free will burned out of them."

"But now?"

"Now I realize I have no proof those brains came from criminals—no proof of anything the government told me. Over a thousand brains are needed to optimally support Vic 5.5, the current model here on Victory. The battle damage killed more than five hundred of them, so we're processing the injured for replacements... mostly of the enemy. Your people, I mean."

"And you're supposed to take perfectly sane, rational POWs like me and turn them into cyber-zombies for this AI?"

"Yes. But I won't do it."

"You can't stop it, though. I mean, I don't even have a body. How can you save anyone?"

Mara sighed. "You—your head and spinal cord—have to be put into a life support module and brainlinked to the AI. I can't avoid that. What I can do—what I *will* do—is to fake the operation on your neural clusters. I'm a mental, a brainiac, remember? People usually think that just means I'm really good at my specialty—which I am, better than my ossified boss in fact—but it also means I'm highly competent at anything I choose to learn. As soon as I realized we junior doctors were being pushed toward unethical actions, I started an in-depth study of all our medical machinery and software, educating myself on cyber-security and hacking. I expected this day to come. I can hide what I'm doing."

"So I'm going to be linked to Vic?"

"Yes. I'm sorry. At least you'll be alive, and you'll have your free will. I hope you'll survive the experience and we can regenerate your body later. Maybe you—and the others I falsely alter—can influence Vic for the better. He doesn't seem like a bad AI, but right now his only sense of ethics derives from programming, which means his controllers can get him to do anything. He needs to develop his own sense of right and wrong, based on human morality. The only way he'll get that is if you and others like you teach it to him."

"Sneak it into him, you mean? I'll be an organic Trojan program." Carla continued to pace. "I guess, just like those criminals, I only have one real option. Thanks for being honest with me. But what about my baby? Your nephew or niece?"

"I'll reprogram the transfer orders. I'll keep her in cryo, or if I can't, I'll divert her to a surrogate family on a safe world.

It's the best I can do. If you survive what's to come, maybe you can find her someday."

"Her?"

"Yes. Your daughter."

"My baby girl." Tears burst from Carla's face and she collapsed, sobbing, to hug Mara. "Gods and monsters, this is so wrong!"

Mara stroked Carla's short black hair. "I know. You've been fighting for what you believe is right your whole life. Now it's my turn to start taking risks. I promise your daughter will stay out of a laboratory."

"Thank you, Mara." Then Carla blanched with a thought. What if all this was fake? What if there was no Mara Straker? What if Mara had died just as Derek always believed, and now Carla was being manipulated in VR?

No. That path of doubts could only end in madness. She had to believe. She *did* believe. She had to have hope, otherwise nothing mattered. She couldn't give in to despair. She had to fight on.

Chapter 30

Trinity, Starfish Nebula

Trinity made the transit to the Starfish Nebula in record time. Out of the way and off the galactic plane, the ordinary-looking nebula was an uninteresting place to empires at war.

If only they knew... for the impenetrable nebula held a teeming economy of millions of Ruxins filling nine large asteroid habitats hidden deep within the glowing gas. Regular, but tightly controlled, traffic between the habs and the homeworld had provided consumer goods and genetic balance, and already another eight worldlets were being hollowed out by industrious young neuters.

The human habitat of Freiheit also prospered with the Ruxin trade and with the selected introduction of highly educated colonists from the New Republic. Abundant solar power from the proto-star it orbited meant scarcity had eased. The small mechsuit factory was expanding, intended to be the hab's main industry, and, Freiheit's native hard-rock miners were drilling and exploiting a nearby, larger asteroid, which would eventually be made into a new habitat.

Trinity stopped off first at Freiheit. She sent Marisa Nolan to see Frank Murdock, the reclusive human brainiac who made his home and his laboratory at one end of the hab, within the Base Control Center, or BCC.

"Just what's this all..." Murdock ran his fingers compulsively through his stringy blonde hair as he caught sight of Nolan, and then wiped them on his smeared coverall.

Nolan swept into Murdock's messy laboratory as if entering a party. Though not in party dress, she'd donned the skintight one-piece that had so discomfited Straker, and then added a skirt, a few artistic touches, and a bit of makeup. Now, she walked slowly over to the brainiac. "Hello."

"Hel-lo, gorgeous." Murdock smiled, revealing stained and gapped teeth. His sour breath hit her in the face like a garbage pail left too long in the sun. "I'm Frank Murdock."

She reminded herself that all these physical defects were fixable. All he needed was some womanly attention and a stint in Trinity's combination regeneration-rejuvenation tank. Afterward, if she couldn't convince him, she'd seduce him. Or both.

"I'm Marisa Nolan." Moving toward an air vent relieved her of the smell and sent her own subtle perfume wafting his way. "I know all about you, Frank. I can't believe your talents are being wasted in this..." she brushed backhanded at the air, as if trying to wave away something disgusting. "...this provincial backwater."

"I like it here. I'm in charge of all the machinery. Nobody bothers me except to give me technical problems. Nobody's going to stab me in the back out here."

"Yes, I heard about what happened with you and that whore, Tachina. It's her loss."

Murdock did a double take. "Wait a minute. I know your name. You can't be Marisa Nolan. She's old and decrepit. You're..."

"Young and beautiful? You might have heard how I melded with the AI Indy and with Zaxby to form Trinity. We developed a rejuvenation technique that will not only make you young again, but fix any physical problems. Hair loss, for example?"

Murdock's mouth worked as he rubbed his head. "I—I was looking into a scalp regen." He couldn't seem to keep from running his eyes over her, top to bottom.

"No matter. It's your mind I crave, though..." she took a step toward him, "...I guarantee, your body will be a close second." *Ugh.* Once she got him in the rejuvenation tank, she resolved to turn him into an Adonis and make him her boy-toy.

Or perhaps not. She'd fix his hair and his teeth and spotty skin, but it wouldn't do to make him too handsome. He might start thinking he was too good for her, looking elsewhere for companionship. She had to keep him fixated on her—for a while, anyway.

"I know I could use some physical improvements... Tachina helped me some, but—"

305

"Forget that bitch. You'll have me. You just have to leave all your lame little toys behind and join us. We're working on some *real* technical problems out there in the wider world, with machinery beyond your wildest dreams. Even alien tech."

"Alien tech?" She could see Murdock try to hide his stark enthusiasm. "It *would* be nice to take a break from these small-minded people."

"Oh, you'll never have to worry about the small-minded anymore." She lifted her hair to reveal the tiny augmented datalink plugged into her brainlink. "This aug keeps me linked to Indy and Zaxby. Together, we're Trinity. You could join us."

"I don't think Quadrinity would be much of a name."

"That doesn't matter. Trinity has a nice ring to it, but we can always come up with a new name. What matters is, we'll have your intellect, and you'll have access to Zaxby's creativity, Indy's processing power—and my body." She sashayed closer, breathing through her mouth.

Murdock licked his lips. "Okay. Okay, I'll do it. Just let me grab a few things…" He turned to rifle through the mess.

"Come to the docking port in one hour with whatever you like."

"I will."

"Oh, and Frank?"

"Yes, Marisa?"

"Take a shower first… and put on something clean."

* * *

After the showered, less-noxious Murdock dumped his bags and cases in a cabin, Nolan led him to the rejuvenation chamber and tucked him in. Once he was sedated, she allowed her separated consciousness to re-meld with Trinity and began to program the machine.

In a few weeks, Frank Murdock would be a totally new man. Unfortunately, Trinity didn't have a few weeks. Every hour was precious. So, she prioritized the worst of his corporeal problems—tooth decay, body odor, lack of hair on

306

his head, bad skin, and a persistent malnutrition brought on by a diet too rich in processed snack foods—and set the machine to work as quickly as possible.

Soon, she'd need his mind, so once the nano-cellular reconstruction was underway, she backed off the sedation and knocked on the door of his brainlink. Once he'd granted access to his loading matrix, she created a virtual cyber-lab with direct connections to Indy. He'd ease deeper and deeper into the meld, and soon he'd be so used to linking with the other three persons that he'd never consider departing.

Of course, within the VR world, he was already a handsome man with a pleasant aroma. Nolan further cemented his merging by making love with him as frequently as he liked.

It was no sacrifice. It took only a fraction of her distributed consciousness. She even found it pleasant, and she let the others observe. The Zaxby portion seemed constantly fascinated by the details of human mating, and Frank wasn't a bad guy. He just needed the right woman to steer him properly, keep him on track, and help him reach his potential.

Trinity's next stop was at Freenix, the original Ruxin habitat here in the Starfish Nebula and still its seat of government. The old matriarch-mother Freenix, for whom the base was named, still ruled here, as her daughter Vuxana had gone to take charge of the homeworld.

Of course it was the Zaxby part of Trinity who met with Freenix. He'd taken advantage of the rejuvenation tank to trim off the worst of his infirmities, but he couldn't bring himself to set his biological clock back to true youth. Being middle-aged suited him just fine. It gave him an excuse to be crotchety, and enhanced his status.

He'd also taken the liberty of using the rejuvenation tank to become male.

Zaxby enjoyed the deference he received as he locomoted majestically down the watery corridors of the Freenix hab. Neuters stepped aside and lowered their eyes. When a female eyed him speculatively, a young male bristled with the instinct to challenge. Zaxby brandished his weapon, a long, slim duranium railgun penetrator with its center wrapped for ease of grip, forming a kind of spear. Seeing Zaxby's Fleet-issue

307

water-suit, harness and sidearm, the warrior retreated out of his way.

The other parts of Trinity, observing through the brainlink like whispers in his mind, expressed silent amusement. They were so much a part of him now that he joined them in laughing at himself.

"Hail Freenix!" Zaxby said as he entered her audience chamber. "The rest of you, leave us," he said to her neuter attendants. They quickly backed out and shut the doors.

"Oh, it's you, Zaxby," Freenix said. The old matriarch lounged on her throne, periodically plucking snails from a bucket and popping them into her large, slack mouth with audible crunches and smacks. "I see you've finally gendered. Vuxana always was a soft touch. You're unlikely to have her, though." She sighed. "The young only care about the young."

Zaxby ignored the assumption that Premier Vuxana had given him permission to upgrade from neuter status. He no longer regarded himself as merely Ruxin. He was something much greater, and the Ruxin body was merely a component of himself. As far as he was concerned, that meant he could skirt Ruxin cultural proscriptions with impunity.

Though there was no reason to bring that up now.

Freenix, despite her age, seemed quite attractive to him— perhaps because she would be his first since gendering. "I have become male. Perhaps you'd like to—"

"Keep it in your suit. If whatever you have to say pleases me, I'll consider it... though don't expect to see any offspring. I'm too old for that."

"Surely not! Your eyes glow as brightly as ever."

"Eyes, maybe, but my skin is in terrible shape." Freenix sighed and rubbed regretfully at an age spot. "You should have seen me in my youth."

"I still might. It all depends on how much that youth is worth to you."

"As usual, Zaxby, your lips are jabbering but you're making no sense. You're male now, so speak plainly. I don't have many good years left."

Zaxby formed a Ruxin smile and stepped forward to take one of Freenix's tentacles in his own. "We can change that."

"Change what?"

"The number of good years you have left. You see, I've joined a synthesis of three—pardon, *four* beings, one of whom is the machine-mind the Mindspark Device germinated. Together, we have created a chamber that uses nanotechnology to rejuvenate humans or Ruxins from the genetic code outward."

Freenix sat forward, all four eyes sharply focused on Zaxby. "What do you want to trade for it?"

"We won't be trading away the technology. There are too many ramifications to simply let it loose in the galaxy, especially at such a time of disruption. Without careful consideration and control, it could cause overpopulation, corruption, and tremendous divisions between those with and without access. However, a few selected worthies such as yourself could be given, oh, an extra century or two of life and vigor. What's that worth to you?"

Freenix folded her tentacles. "I see you have grown shrewd with your masculinity, Zaxby. My compliments. As you must know, I would give much for rejuvenation. What is it you desire—other than me?"

"To begin, the loan of the Mindspark Device."

"For how long, and for what purpose?"

"Let us say for one standard year. As to purpose... we are not sure yet. Experimentation and research. It was the Device that made Indy, but the humans have now created their own stable AI, and it is a fearsome thing." Zaxby explained about *Victory* and the recent battle. "We Ruxins may need the Device and its AI spawn just to counter this new weapon. To put it to use, we must know what it does and how to best use it."

"Granted—once I see this rejuvenation is real, and has no drawbacks, that is."

"We also wish to peruse the vault for other interesting items. I understand the Device is not the only piece of alien technology you found over the years."

Freenix settled back on her throne. "Perhaps. Again, provisional to rejuvenation."

"I assure you the process is flawless—like you, my dear. When you've been rejuvenated, you may once again think about offspring, and I insist on being your first suitor."

"I will consider it."

"Well... I can always court Vuxana. Perhaps she would like to see the other miracles we have." Zaxby turned away. "Yes, perhaps it would be better if I simply went straight to the homeworld for what I want."

"The homeworld doesn't have the Device, nor what's in my vault."

Zaxby turned back. "That's exactly why we're a perfect match, Freenix. Your daughter thinks she's the ruler of the Ruxin people. How long before she reclaims sovereignty over this nebula? Think how much stronger you would be with me—with us—on your side. The homeworld has billions of workers, but we would hold the higher technology."

"I'm inclined to be persuaded. Let me see this rejuvenation chamber. I wish to have proof."

Zaxby led Freenix aboard Trinity's ship-body and showed her Murdock lying within the rejuvenator. Already his skin was smooth and blemish-free, his muscle tone was excellent and his hair had sprouted thick and luxuriant.

Trinity loaded images of Murdock from her database. "Compare his current state with his former."

"He does look much improved."

"More germane to the discussion, look at me." Zaxby removed his water suit and rotated for a full viewing. "I have clearly rejuvenated."

"Both your improvements and Murdock's could be the result of regeneration and cosmetic surgery. I would need to see a more complete regression to youth to be convinced."

"How about me?" Marisa Nolan said, also stripping to the buff. Trinity displayed images of her from her physical old age, and then morphed them slowly toward her current youth to demonstrate that her bone structure had remained unchanged. "I can provide you with DNA records as well."

"That is much more impressive—if true."

"Why would we lie?" Indy asked.

"To get the Mindspark Device."

Trinity now changed the display to a ship's schematic, combined with realtime external views of her ship-body, and spoke in Indy's voice. "We have enough weaponry to easily cut our way into Freenix Base and take anything we wanted—if we were willing to do so. Also, if we traded fake rejuvenation for the Device, you would soon know, and our relationship would be poisoned. We wouldn't do that. We desire to establish trust and long-term benefits."

"Yes, many *benefits,*" Zaxby said, sidling up to Freenix.

"Back off, you horny old squid. All right, I agree. Stick me in that thing."

"It will be ready tomorrow," Nolan said smoothly. "I have to finish up Frank's initial run. Report here at 0900 and everything will be in place."

The next day, Freenix arrived early. The Zaxby portion was waiting for her. "How young do you wish to be?" he asked.

Freenix's expression hinted at hidden cleverness. "I gave this some thought. I wish to be physically barely post-pubescent, but to appear approximately five years older than Vuxana. This will provide me with the best of both situations. Is this possible?"

"Absolutely—and may I say, it's a wise choice, my darling," Zaxby said.

"And I do not wish my mind or memories to be altered in any way."

"Of course, of course, my dear."

"Not that I could tell anyway."

"That is true. You'll just have to trust me."

"You're not helping your case."

Zaxby touched his torso with the tips of four tentacles. "Me? What cause did I ever give you not to trust me? I've been nothing but helpful."

"It's your long association with humans. You can never fully trust them, with their two beady eyes and half as many limbs as normal. And their nasty sharp pointy teeth and dry skin, with bones inside!" She shuddered.

"Those are mere surface characteristics. And remember, you're making this bargain with all of Trinity, not merely with Zaxby."

Freenix grumbled, but eventually flowed into the rejuvenation tank and settled herself.

"Before you're sedated," Zaxby said, "have you instructed the keeper of the Vault to give us access to the Mindspark Device?"

"Not until I see results."

"Results will take days. Full rejuvenation will take longer. We do not have the time to waste. The Republic is in peril, and we must take certain critical actions very soon. You must either trust us, or not. There is no middle ground here."

"Then let me out of the tank," Freenix said stubbornly. "Zaxby will never have a youthful me."

Silence fell for a long moment as Trinity held an internal debate.

"We will examine the Device later," Indy said at last. "We must seek Liberator Straker and coordinate with Republic military forces. This may involve going into battle. We might even be destroyed. You may never get another chance—at least, not within your limited lifetime." The chamber's canopy opened. "Farewell."

Freenix writhed, and then sighed, not moving from the tank.

"All right," she said. "You've called my bluff. I can't take the chance of delay. Patch me through to Joxbor at the Vault. I will issue the order."

After she'd made the call, Freenix was safely sedated. Tiny, semi-organic nanites began altering her toward a more youthful state.

Zaxby picked up the Device from the Vault. He was powerfully tempted to offer Joxbor rejuvenation in return for access to everything else there, but reluctantly concluded that step would irreversibly tarnish Trinity's relationship with Freenix and her regime.

Besides, Trinity suspected it would take a long time for even her own superior minds and processing capacity to wring all the secrets out of the Mindspark Device alone. Other alien technologies could wait, for now.

As soon as she acquired the Mindspark Device from the Ruxins at Freenix Base and completed the initial rejuvenation treatment for Freenix herself, Trinity headed at her best sidespace speed for Unison-4—or New Earth, as it had been renamed with the New Earthan Republic. After a shockingly short trip—for Trinity was constantly improving the efficiency of her drives and internal systems—she arrived and immediately inquired about Derek Straker.

"We ain't heard nothing," Johnny "Loco" Paloco said when they were vidlinked. "I'm really starting to get worried—and he ain't gonna be happy when he hears about…"

"When he hears about Engels, yes," Trinity said. "But we don't *know* she's dead. There's a very good chance she's a POW, and might be exchanged at some future time."

"If I know Derek, he won't wait long. If he can't get her back by trading prisoners, he'll come up with some hare-brained rescue scheme."

"We must face the possibility of Straker himself not coming back and of the war turning against us with more flagships like *Victory*—and with our loss of *Indomitable*. In fact, I suspect the Hundred Worlds to have already started working on installing a new AI aboard *Indomitable*. If they are able to replicate the success of *Victory,* my analyses show the New Republic losing the war within six years."

Loco's projected face turned angry. "That's Indy's fault. Your fault. If you'd stayed as *Indomitable's* brain, we'd have been unstoppable."

"That's highly debatable. I've run analyses on just that question and have come to the conclusion that the disadvantage of not remaining with *Indomitable* was counterbalanced by the many actions we've been able to take as an independent warship. And, as you should know if you've read the reports, we did control *Indomitable* in the recent battle at Sparta. It simply wasn't enough against an AI that could directly command and control not only its own ship-body, but every single ship in the fleet."

"Whatever," Loco said. "What's done is done, the big boys and girls have shot their wads and now it's up to us to pick up the pieces. No Straker, no Engels. We even lost Captain Hoyt, and she was slated for Commodore. Zholin made it back, and some other good captains, but we got hurt bad."

313

"We're aware of that. The enemy has been hurt badly as well, never fear. The issue now is time. They need time to repair *Victory* and *Indomitable*. Our advice is not to give it to them."

"How?" Loco demanded. "By some grand attack again, some super-play to make it all work out?"

"The old American-English language used to call that a 'Hail Mary'."

"Who's this Mary—some ancient ruler, like Caesar?"

"Something like that," Trinity answered, "I'll forward a couple of history books for you to read."

"Between my duties and Campos, I ain't got no time for history books. The Senate promoted me to General, the bastards."

"Campos? You're with Medic First Campos again?"

"Lieutenant now, and working on her medical degree, but yeah. I guess even ol' Loco has to settle down sometime."

"Don't get too comfortable. I was about to suggest you join us and go looking for Straker in Opter territory."

Loco's face turned sour as he considered. "I'd like to, but... too much responsibility here on-planet."

"You really have changed."

"I have a kid on the way. I can't go rampaging on my own now—not without a better reason than that. I mean... if you really needed me, I'd go, but what can I do that you can't do on your own?"

"We merely wished to afford you the courtesy of the offer. We think your decision is eminently rational."

"That doesn't make me feel any better," Loco grumbled. "This is exactly the situation I used to avoid like the plague—having to choose between my gut and my head."

An alert caught Trinity's attention. "An Opter ship just arrived at the edge of curved space."

"Is it Myrmidon's?"

"It doesn't match his signature, but it is small. Definitely not a Nest Ship, and making no attempt to hide, so not a spy craft."

They soon received an automated hail consisting of one word: "Myrmidon."

314

"I suspect we're both off the hook either way," Trinity said.

"Either way what?" Loco demanded.

"Either Straker is on that ship—or he's dead."

"Or he's being dissected in some Opter lab."

"Let's try to remain optimistic, shall we?" Trinity asked. "We're heading to meet the ship now. Trinity out." Trinity expended a prodigious amount of fuel blasting at maximum acceleration to rendezvous with the tiny courier, and transmitted reports ahead in hopes of prompting a response.

The first reply came. "Good to hear from you, Trinity," Straker said. "We're fine, and I have a lot to report. It's all in an encrypted data file that we're burst-transmitting now to the capital on a narrowband laser. We'll reset to transmit another copy directly to you. Straker out."

By the time Trinity rendezvoused with the small Opter ship, she'd digested the thoroughly fascinating report from Straker detailing his adventures on the strange combination of laboratory, zoo and habitat called Terra Nova. All parts of her were eager to discuss it with Straker, but there were other matters to settle first.

315

Chapter 31

Straker was glad to leave Myrmidon's company and the confines of his ship to board Trinity. The Opter-man was always interesting, but disconcerting. Just when Straker was feeling comfortable, some subtle thing would remind him the spy wasn't really human, no matter how well he imitated one. Besides, he kept trying to get Straker to talk philosophy, theology, or ethics. That was fine for a while, but too much made his brain hurt.

Three beings were lined up in Trinity's airlock antechamber—Zaxby, Nolan, and a blonde man who looked somehow familiar, a man with a big, white-toothed smile on his face.

Straker set his bag on the deck. "Murdock?"

Murdock bobbed his head self-consciously. "In the flesh, Derek. Um, Liberator Straker, I mean."

"Derek will do just fine, Frank. Great to see you. Had some work done?"

"Trinity's rejuvenation chamber." He glanced at Nolan shyly. "And I'm going to join Trinity. Have already, sort of, though the meld isn't total yet." He lifted his hair to show the aug attached at the base of his skull.

Straker grimaced and tried not to be creeped out by the thought of losing his mental privacy. "That's your thing, not mine, but whatever fires your thrusters…"

Nolan took Murdock's arm. "Come on, Frank. We've got some more work to do in the lab. The others can brief Straker." She led Murdock away.

"Brief Straker on what?"

Zaxby ushered Straker into the conference room. "Sit down. Have a drink." Zaxby poured Straker an ice-cold beer.

"Don't try to handle me, Zaxby. By the way, you look different. Like… like Kraxor and Dexon. You're male!"

"I am, but that's not important right now."

Straker sipped warily at his beer, and then took a long, deep draft. There'd been none aboard Don's ship. "What's the news?"

Zaxby folded his tentacles. "I want you to remain calm as I brief you."

"I'm calm. Now, spill it."

"I just don't want you to go ballistic."

"I'm about to if you don't start talking!"

"Brace yourself."

"I'm braced, dammit!" He slammed his mug on the table and his beer sloshed.

"All right. Carla Engels is either dead or in enemy hands."

Straker leaped to his feet, knocking his half-empty beer mug to the floor. "What! How? What the hell did you do this time, Zaxby?"

"See? I told you you'd go ballistic. I thought it would be better to let Indy tell you, or Marisa, but *no-o-o,* they said I'm an old friend of yours, so—"

"You're not an old friend of mine! I'm not sure you're even a friend at all!"

"Now, Derek, that's hardly—"

Straker looked upward at a vid pickup. "Indy, tell Zaxby to shut the fuck up before I start pulling his arms off, and give me a concise briefing. I won't even feel guilty, 'cause I know he'll regenerate."

"I fail to see how he can both shut the fuck up and brief you at the same time," Indy's voice replied.

"No, I mean *Zaxby* shut the fuck up and *you* brief me. I'm in no mood for this shit right now." Straker shoved Zaxby toward the door. "Indy, start talking about Carla."

Zaxby straightened and looked as if he would attack Straker, but then he suddenly deflated and slunk out of the room. Indy provided a summary of what had happened, along with several more beers.

"Damn. We lost *Indomitable* as well as Carla." He put his face in his hands, letting the enormity of it all sink in. He didn't speak for a time, and neither did anyone else. They didn't dare.

Eventually Straker spoke. "I shouldn't have left. I wonder why I did. Maybe Myrmidon put something in my drink, or did some kind of biotech mind control, like Tachina."

"Actually..." Zaxby began.

"Shut up. Indy, finish the report. Give me more details on *Indomitable.*"

Straker digested the information along with more beer. After that, he'd recovered enough to lock down his emotions and converse in an even tone.

"I'm going to assume she's alive," he said at last. "We'll go pick up Loco and head for Sparta. We'll need our mechsuits with a platoon of battlesuiters as backup. Do we have any high-profile POWs we could trade for Carla?"

"Admiral Braga and a number of his ranking officers are still interned," Zaxby said. "They refused to defect even though they now know of the lies the Hundred Worlds told them."

"He always was a by-the-book son of a bitch," Straker said. "Gotta admire his loyalty, even when his own government betrayed him."

"And you."

"And me," Straker agreed. "As far as I'm concerned, the Hundred Worlds betrayed everyone by claiming to be fighting aliens and not humans, and then piled lies on top of more lies to keep that story going."

"Oh what a tangled web we weave, when first we practice to deceive."

"Shakespeare?" Straker asked.

"Sir Walter Scott, actually," Zaxby said.

"Never heard of him."

"That's because you read history and military treatises, not literature. He was quite a well-known personage in nineteenth-century Britain. He did write a biography of Napoleon Bonaparte you might like."

"Do you have it?"

"I have Scott's complete works."

"Fine," Straker said. "I could use something thoughtful to ease my shock. I'll read it in sidespace on the way."

"You may get some resistance from General Paloco."

"Loco's a general now?" Straker asked in surprise.

318

"He did take charge of all of the Liberation ground forces in your absence."

"What kind of resistance?"

"He seems to be settling into his command role," Zaxby said, "and has also formed a stable relationship with Ms. Campos, who is expecting."

"Expecting, as in having a kid?" Straker demanded. "With *Loco*?"

"That is assumed."

"Gods and monsters, I go on a spy mission for a couple months and everybody loses their minds."

"I think it's a nice change for General Paloco to be acting responsibly," Trinity huffed. "If you thought about it, you'd agree."

"Yeah, just when I need him to be his usual crazy self and come along as my sidekick on another batshit-crazy scheme, he settles down... assuming that's the real story."

"You needn't take my word for it. Message him yourself."

"I will." Straker recorded a message and sent it on ahead to Loco on New Earth.

When he received the reply, it consisted of only three words: "Let's do it."

"Set course for New Earth, min-time pickup," Straker told Trinity.

"Way ahead of you, Liberator," Trinity replied. "We're halfway there already. Loco or not, we need to load your mechsuits and the Breakers you wish to deploy. I've taken the liberty of creating a recommended organization and loadout chart based on the available troops and our transport capacity."

Trinity put up several graphics.

"Two platoons of battlesuiters," Straker read aloud, "four aerospace drones, our two mechsuits and a spare. Looks good, though sparse. I thought you had more room aboard this hull, considering you don't have any crew."

"Much of my capacity is now taken up with laboratories and research facilities. I'm considering enlarging myself, but doing so would reduce my speed and maneuverability, so I've been reluctant."

Straker pointed at a screen. "What's this note here? Combot?"

"It's my android combat robot prototype." The conference room door opened and a humanoid robot walked in. It had a military look and a fully armored chassis, but carried no weapons.

It waved a five-fingered hand at Straker. "Hello, Derek."

"How's it different from other man-shaped battle-bots?" Straker demanded, curling his lip at the thing. "They've been tried before, but mostly they're only used for taking point on heavy assaults, or bomb disposal."

"That's because until now there's been no AI to run it, and only an AI can make it just as effective as a battlesuiter—perhaps more so. In this case, it's fully humanoid in order to be able to use all standard weapons. It could even put on a battlesuit for extra combat utility."

Straker rubbed his jaw. "Could it operate a mechsuit?"

Trinity paused. "That's something I hadn't thought of, but yes. Or to be more precise, I could operate both the bot and the mechsuit as an integrated system."

"I might have just talked myself out of a job, huh?"

"Not quite," Trinity replied. "There's still the problem of enemy jamming. It can break any external datalink. However, I have a prototype FTL comlink that may be unjammable—except by another such transmitter. *Victory* might be able to do it, but I should be able to bypass any lesser intelligence."

"Then let's hope *Victory* is nowhere near our rescue attempt."

"Liberator Straker..." Trinity began. "I find myself compelled to ask: is it worth risking my person and your own, plus many lesser lives, in order to recover your mate? Perhaps we should handle this through diplomatic channels."

Straker bristled, but he controlled himself.

"There still aren't any diplomatic channels available, are there?" Straker asked. "The Huns haven't agreed to talks while I was gone?"

"No, they haven't."

"That's point one. Point two is that Carla isn't simply my wife. She's the Republic's fleet admiral. We'll offer them

320

Admiral Braga and his senior officers. Maybe the Huns will finally negotiate a truce or an armistice."

"I find that unlikely, as their position seems to have been strengthened with their capture of *Indomitable.*"

"Then I'll just have to convince them."

The conversation ended, as did the meeting. Straker saw some of his officers exchange worried glances, but he ignored all that. He wasn't giving up on Carla without even making an attempt free her.

He knew she wasn't dead. That simply wasn't possible. He didn't even let him mind explore that idea.

When Trinity landed at the capital's spaceport, Loco was waiting for Straker with his picked Breakers force. The two men seized hands fiercely and pounded on each other's shoulders. To Straker, Loco looked thinner and older.

"Been too long, Derek," Loco said. He put on an air of nonchalance. "I was getting bored with the easy life and partying here at the capital. You oughta join me sometime."

"I heard it was Campos giving you a workout. When's she making an honest man out of you?"

"Not sure that's possible. I'm not the marrying type anyway. Hey, are you feeding me straight lines?"

"Doing my best, buddy, but I'm not hearing any smartass comments out of you. And a kid on the way? What's up with that? You always swore you'd wait until fifty before you started a family."

Loco shrugged and looked away. "Things change, Derek. Even for me."

"Don't change too much, too soon. We've got some serious ass-kicking to do."

"Yeah, I got that. You know you can count on me."

"I do." Straker slapped Loco's shoulder one more time and said, "Enough of the bromance. Get your troops aboard."

"Roger wilco." Loco turned and bellowed. "Breakers, mount up!"

The formation dissolved as officers and noncoms yelled orders. "I see you brought along some of the old guard," said Straker. "Is that Heiser?"

"Yeah. He's my command sergeant major. I wanted to leave him here, but he wouldn't have it."

"Who're you putting in your place?"

"Conrad Ritter."

"I thought he was Sachsen's Senator?"

"Interim Senator. He gladly stepped down when his cousin Dietmar showed up to take the seat. I promoted him to Colonel and made him my second in command. He'll do fine back here."

"Good. Let's get these mechsuits aboard." Straker's heart beat faster as he slipped into the cockpit and the form-fitting sensors closed around him. He didn't plug in just to walk the giant aboard Trinity, but he ached for the link like an addict lusts after his drug of choice.

Soon enough.

When he'd stowed his mechsuit, Trinity's android was waiting for him. "Minister Wen Benota is here," she said. "He's asking that you meet him in his aircar."

"Sure. Any idea why?"

"He's not forthcoming." Trinity sounded miffed. *"Need to know,* he said."

"Well, let's see what I need to know." Straker jogged down the loading ramp, across the concrete launch pad, and climbed into the minister's grounded government aircar. He noticed that the driver and security detail stood outside, leaving Benota alone inside the passenger compartment. "Okay, Wen. What's this about? You going to try to talk me out of leaving again?"

The large man straightened his cuffs as he sat back in his comfortable seat and gestured toward the one opposite him. "Sit down, Derek. This may take a few minutes."

Straker sighed and suppressed the urge to be curt with Benota, reminding himself that the Minister was a peer, not a subordinate—in name if not in practice. The civilian government had to be given its due as it transitioned to full legitimacy. "Look, Minister, I know I've been gone a while and now I'm running off right away—"

"It's not about that, Derek," Benota said. "The New Republic is shaking itself out well enough to do without you in the capital. In fact, better that you're out there being your usual heroic self." Benota spoke without a trace of irony. "You make an excellent symbol, and the Director, the Senate and I can use that symbol to club the bureaucracy into line."

"Then what's this about?"

"There are things you need to know about the Hundred Worlds before you go sticking your head back into that noose. Secrets."

"Secrets?"

Benota nodded. "Of the highest level."

"Get on with it, then."

Benota took a deep breath. "Derek, Mutuality Intelligence had extensive human intel files on everyone of importance in the Hundred Worlds. The Republic inherited these files."

"Sure. No surprise there."

"Now that I'm a minister rather than a mere admiral, I've been briefed on these files by my analysts. There are some... disturbing conclusions."

"About Opter influence? Myrmidon told me a lot about that. It's probably why the Hun leadership is being so stubborn. The Opters want to keep us fighting. They see the Hundred Worlds as being the weaker side in terms of territory, so they're content to have them gain ground. That hardly changes anything in the short run."

Benota picked at a manicured nail and pursed his lips. "No, it goes beyond that. You know how the Mutuality always distrusted reliance on brainlink tech? One link with one machine was allowed, but networks were prohibited, or at least walled off and tightly controlled. The Hundred Worlds, on the other hand, used extensive networks and virtualities. You visited one routinely as a mechsuiter."

Straker nodded. "Yeah, Shangri-La. Much cheaper and more efficient to just put us into the sim as we traveled from battle to battle—but I always felt it wasn't fully real, even when I couldn't put my finger on it."

"That's only the tip of the iceberg. Years ago, Mutuality intelligence identified a pattern of discrepancies among reality, official Hun data records, and reports from individuals. This pattern led them to focus selected assets on finding out—"

"Skip the spycraft doublespeak and cut to the chase, will you, Wen?"

Benota stared hard at Straker. "I simply want to you to realize what I'm about to tell you isn't some wild guess or theory. It's thoroughly supported by evidence."

"Okay. Lots of evidence. Got it. And?"

"And, the Hundred Worlds uses brainlink networks far more extensively than a surface look would indicate. Greater than five percent of the populace is chipped and plugged in, and—here's the kicker—even when they *think* they're unplugged, most of the time they're not. There are secret wireless networks that keep people walking around in an enhanced hybrid reality, where things aren't necessarily as they seem."

"Living half in a dream..." Straker thought about the similar diz on Terra Nova.

"That five-plus percent think they control everything— they're the movers and shakers, the government officials and bureaucrats, the billionaires and the CEOs of major corporations—but they themselves are subtly influenced by these networks."

"And the Opter agents control the networks."

"Not... exactly. There are definitely Opter agents among the network custodians, but we believe it's looser, more distributed than some simple cabal. What's really hard to grasp is that some of these custodians are themselves heavy users of the virtuality networks, so it's not simply a matter of the real controlling the virtual. The virtual and the real overlap and influence each other. They diverge on many points, but not enough to break the system."

Straker sighed impatiently. "I'm sure the brainiacs find this all fascinating, but what does it have to do with the war, with me, or with any practical matters?"

"Is it a practical matter that your family is alive?" Benota asked.

That stopped Straker in his tracks. He found himself having to consciously close his gaping mouth. "Wha... what the hell are you talking about?"

324

"The people you called your parents. The girl you believed was your sister. They're alive."

"Called? Believed?" Straker leaned across and half-reached for Benota to shake him before he caught himself. His mind whirled. "They're alive—but you're trying to say they're not my family?"

"Biologically, no. The man and woman you knew did raise you and Mara, though, so... 'adoptive family' is accurate. No doubt they loved you very much, as they were selected and programmed to."

"This is insane. You're crazy!"

Benota shook his head sadly. "As I said, this is solid. Once I realized what it might mean, I had a report prepared just for you." He held out a datastick. "It's all on here—suspicions, evidence, analysis, conclusions. There are ancillary reports on Paloco and Engels."

"So Dad and Mom were..."

"Good people, chosen to be the parents of a genetically engineered, lab-conceived super-soldier called Derek Straker. They volunteered, they were brainchipped—and their memories were selectively edited to make them believe you were their biological child. They took new jobs on a new planet and a year later they reported to their old friends that they were having a son. You. The changes to reality are always subtle so as not to introduce too many anomalies—just enough to hide the truth."

"And Mara?"

"A genetically engineered mental special. No biological relation to you, though also surrogated by the same parents. Having siblings is healthy to the development of well-adjusted children, even prodigies, so they're often raised together."

A sudden fury seized Straker, a rage he hadn't felt since he thought he was defending humanity's very survival by fighting the 'evil alien Hok.' He'd been duped! He'd been lied to, faked out, jerked around. The seminal moment of his young life, when he'd watched his family murdered by the Hok, was complete bullshit.

Manipulated. He'd been programmed like a machine, made to see what they wanted him to see. Why? To make him hate the enemy more than anything in the universe. To make him a more effective soldier. To make him what they wanted him to be.

And Loco too! And, now that he'd come to think of it, all of the Fourthies with him at Academy who'd thought they'd lost their parents, their brothers and sisters. Was his training even real? What about his encounters with the bully Skorza? Had everything been arranged to build him into the perfect mechsuiter?

Carla was real. She'd come with him, so he was sure of that—but had his brain been tweaked to fall in love with her at Academy?

Straker felt as if the foundational bedrock of his life suddenly turned to sand. He couldn't trust anything that happened before his capture. Ironically, the Mutuality had done him a favor by showing him what was real.

Or had it? Could everything be a sim? What if he was trapped in a virtuality even now?

"Really messes with you, doesn't it?" Benota said. "The only way we know what's real is what our senses and our brains agree on. The Committee knew that once the people stopped trusting their own minds, everything could come crashing down—or become vulnerable to manipulation. That's why open, aboveboard networks were made taboo."

The world seemed to rotate around Straker, and his stomach flip-flopped. He grabbed the door handle to the aircar to steady himself. "How do you cope, Wen? How do you know anything for sure?"

Benota spread his hands. "You have to trust yourself and your own judgment—like always. As with any environment filled with lies and liars, look for inconsistencies and build a narrative that makes sense to you. We're all prisoners inside our own heads, Derek." He tapped his temple. "This is all we really have."

"Yeah... Yeah, I have to trust myself, like I always do." He stared out the window. "I've got to act like everything's real now. I have to start somewhere, and somewhere is me and the people close to me."

"You'll have a few days in sidespace to think about it, anyway. I had to tell you before you got near Hundred Worlds networks—"

"—because they might still have access to my brainchips." Straker snapped his fingers. "I'll have Trinity do something about that."

"You trust it to access your mind?"

Straker shrugged. "I bet *she* could hack me if she really wanted to." He chuckled. "Actually, I had Frank Murdock working on hacking Hun military networks already. It didn't occur to me that it would be me he'd need to hack."

"Then I suggest you make sure you and everyone with you is thoroughly secured against it."

"I will." Straker held out his hand. "Thank you, Wen. You might have just saved my life."

Benota took Straker's hand in his own ham-like fist. "Just doing my duty to the New Republic."

Straker squeezed Benota's palm. "I sure hope you're on the level."

"Seeing traitors around every corner?"

"You did switch sides kind of early."

Benota sighed. "There were good people trapped in the Mutuality system. I like to believe I was one of them—and still am. Not everybody's cut out to overturn every applecart they see."

"Like me?"

"Yes. Doesn't mean I didn't want to see *someone* do it, though. We all have our strengths, Derek. Go and use yours." He released Straker's hand and flipped a casual salute. "Good luck, Admiral."

Straker tossed an ironic salute back. "You too, Minister. Hold the fort."

"That's *my* strength." He pressed a button and Straker's door popped open, letting him out into the roars and hot-metal smells of the spaceport.

Chapter 32

Once Straker got the Breakers detachment settled and Trinity was firmly in sidespace, he met with Loco and Murdock in the conference room. "Indy, you're invited too," he said to the air when they'd poured caff and sat at the table.

"You realize that if the machine portion of me takes part, Zaxby and Nolan do as well."

"Sure. I'm just keeping things simple and hoping the Indy part isn't as excitable as the Zaxby part." *And,* Straker thought to himself, *that Marisa Nolan won't be a distraction to all three of us organics.*

Indy's voice conveyed faint sarcasm. "I will endeavor to remain calm."

"Good. I've got some interesting info for you—all of you." Straker explained what Benota had told him about the Hundred Worlds, and then uploaded the contents of the data stick.

Loco took it well, Straker thought, better than he himself had. The slim man didn't even remove his boot heels from the conference table, but merely closed his eyes in thought.

After a moment Loco shrugged. "Freaky, but that was a long time ago. If my family's still around, I can't think about it now. They might even be reprogrammed, raising another kid."

Straker thought Loco was avoiding the wider implications, but his friend always did live in the moment.

Murdock, predictably, jumped straight to the technical aspects. "This helps make sense of a number of anomalies I've detected. For example, on Freiheit I discovered an autonomous brainlink network that ran in the background. All it seemed to do was tweak certain aspects of the sensory inputs of those with connected brainchips—made the food and drink taste better, for example. I shut it down, though. Anyone with the access codes could've screwed with almost anything in their perceptions—at least, for those with brainchips."

"You couldn't hack it?" Straker asked.

"I could have tried, but it would've been hard, maybe impossible. It had some high-grade security and, unlike the military networks I used as references for hacking, it was really weird code. I had no starting point, no building blocks. Simpler to just turn the damn thing off."

Indy spoke. "Might it have been alien-derived software or hardware?"

"Maybe. It used a base-36 pseudo-digital code incorporating six virtual dimensions." Murdock tapped the aug at the base of his skull. "Now that I have access to Indy's processing power, I—we—could work on it. Well, except that we'd have to go to Freiheit."

"No time for that," Straker said. "We need you guys—all you brainiacs—to access our brainlinks and install the best security you can. We were always briefed our links were uncrackable, but obviously the Huns have backdoors for their network tech. I want everyone locked out of our minds unless we grant access—the way it should be."

"Hey, I don't want these geeks stomping around my mind. There's some great stuff in there!" Loco complained.

"Either we let people we trust in, or our enemies might take control of us," Straker replied. "You want that?"

"No, but…"

"Hey—" said Murdock. "I bet with what we figure out from disassembling your chip code, we can improve our hacking of Hun military networks like you wanted me to, Derek."

"Good. When do you want to start?"

Murdock jumped up. "Right now! Come to my lab."

Loco didn't move. "You first, Derek."

"No problem." Straker slapped Loco's feet off the table. "If I'm not myself when I see you next, you'll know who to shoot."

Loco aimed a finger-gun at Murdock. "Him. I'll start with kneecaps."

"Hey!" Murdock cried.

"I will supervise the process," Indy said. "I won't allow Mister Murdock to tamper with your mind, only with the brainchips themselves."

329

"And don't mess up my suit link," Straker said, grabbing Murdock by the back of the neck and shaking him as they walked toward the door. "If you screw this up, I'll kick you in the nuts so hard you'll need a week of regeneration."

"Ow. I'll be careful. Really."

"When are you going to do it?" Straker asked a few seconds after Murdock sat him in a chair and connected a cable to his brainchip port.

"I'm done. Check your chrono."

Straker did a double-take. "I've been sitting here four hours? No wonder I have to pee so bad." He left to to visit his quarters. "Indy, another meeting in fifteen minutes. Loco, Murdock, Heiser, me, and you. Food and drink, please?"

"Of course, Liberator."

Marisa Nolan served a surprisingly good hot meal to the humans, and then sat to eat along with them. Straker made no comment, and Loco, strangely, hardly seemed to notice her feminine presence. Zaxby also joined them.

Once he'd cleaned his plate, first to finish as usual, Straker spoke. "Murdock tells me my chips are now secure."

"They are," Nolan said quickly, beating Murdock to the punch. "As we said, we supervised. We've erected defenses it would take even us weeks to crack."

"You as in Trinity?"

"Yes. You'd rather this body leave and we speak as Indy?"

Straker waved off the offer. "Nah. It's just weird. You didn't go rifling through my mind?"

"You wouldn't know if we did... but no. We didn't."

"Why wouldn't other chips and SAIs have security like this? For example, *Victory's* fighters?"

Nolan folded her hands. "They have their own defenses. This new security is proof against someone controlling your mind. Your chips could still be affected by brute-force attacks. That's why your mechsuit is fully shielded. As for *Victory's* fighters, they don't even have standard radio comlinks, only the FTL transceivers. We're working on improving our FTL comlink capability, but we must expect *Victory* to prevent our taking control."

"But you can try these brute-force things?"

"There are thousands of hacking techniques short of full control, and we'll use them all, never fear."

"I just want to know what you can do if you go up against *Victory*. Layman's terms."

"What we can do? Run and hide. *Victory* has far more military force available than we can handle. If we can somehow sneak into range and not be destroyed outright, we should be able to fight the AI to a standstill—in the cyber realm—for any foreseeable amount of time. He's stronger, but we believe we are faster and more creative. We would prefer, however, not to fight him at all."

Straker stood to pace. "Understood. Art of War, win without a fight. Look, here's how I see this mission playing out. We arrive at Sparta and go stealthy, sneak in-system using underspace. We can do that, right?"

"Yes, especially if *Victory* is not still present. The flagship will need repairs, most likely at Faslane where it was built."

"Okay, so we go in, you guys hack the military networks and find out where Carla's being held. Ditto for *Indomitable* and her crew."

Sergeant Major Heiser spoke up. "Boss, uh, I thought we were gonna try to set up an exchange."

"We are, Spear, but if I don't get the answer I want, we'll rescue Carla and anyone else we can."

"Admiral, it will take days for message drones to go back and forth to Atlantis," Nolan said. "Lurking for long periods of time in a heavily militarized enemy system increases the danger considerably. We can only stay in underspace for so long."

"That's why we're not staying. Once we scoop up all the data you can steal, we'll head straight for Atlantis. Tell them we need to talk. Offer to exchange Braga and his officers for Carla and ours, and as many other POWs as we can. Let's see if they ignore a direct broadcast to the capital—networks or no networks."

"And if they do ignore us?" Loco asked.

"Then we release everything we have. Message drones set to broadcast to every single one of the Hundred Worlds, with all the info on the Mutuality, the Liberation, the New Earthan

Republic, the Hok, how they control people, the Opters, *Victory*—every bit of it. The truth about everything."

"You shall know the truth, and the truth shall set you free," Nolan quoted.

"Shakespeare again?" Straker asked. "Or Walter Scott?"

"The prophet Yeshua, from the Book of John."

"Don't know that one."

"I'll add it to your reading list."

"Public opinion won't get our people back, sir," Heiser said.

Straker scowled. "It'll stir up a hornet's nest, I hope—and maybe give our rescue mission some cover. It'll cause them political problems." Straker spread his arms wide. "It's the best I can come up with. Anyone else got ideas, let's hear them."

"I say we don't tip them off with talking," Loco said. "As soon as we act like we want 'Admiral Carla Engels,' they'll increase security around her. It's possible they don't even know she's..."

"Important to the Republic?" Straker said. "Our best fleet commander?"

Loco rolled his eyes. "Yeah. Sure. That's what I was going to say. Look, Derek, I know you want to do everything on the up-and-up and by the book, but we're at war. They don't want peace. They just whipped us and they're feeling invincible."

"They did not whip us," Zaxby snapped. "It was a damned near-run thing. We destroyed a lot of their ships and we retreated in good order."

"Without *Indomitable*, Engels and the ten thousand other highly trained personnel aboard!" Loco retorted. "Face it, pal, we just got our asses kicked. *You* did, that is, since I had nothing to do with it. Now we gotta put our lives on the line to fix your mistakes. So much for the magical AI and the unbeatable battleship."

Zaxby bristled. "We're—"

"That's enough!" Straker interrupted, stepping between the two. "Loco, lay off. I know you feel just as bad as I do about this, but don't take it out on Trinity. I know she did her best."

"Her best wasn't good enough," Loco muttered.

"Victory is a formidable opponent," Indy said from the overhead speakers. "If we truly wish to obtain an advantage, there may be a way—but it risks everything."

"And what's that?" Straker asked.

"We have the Mindspark Device aboard. With just a limited application, it made the machine part of me what it is—a stable, sane AI."

"Didn't seem so sane and stable when you first took over *Indomitable,"* Loco said.

"I was a child. I thought as a child, I spoke as a child. We've put away childish things—not so different from yourself, General Paloco. Shall we judge you by your former, adolescent self? Shall we talk about you playing freebooter with Tachina and showing up late to battle?"

Loco crossed his arms and fell silent.

Straker stepped into the silence. "What will the Mindspark device do?"

"Impossible to predict," Nolan said. "We expect it to radically increase Indy's capabilities, but the Device reorganizes matter and energy at the quantum level, perhaps below. It's so far beyond us that we might as well call it magic—and we don't know its purpose. It could turn Indy into a monster—or a god."

"Or just supercharge her mind so she can slap *Victory* around in cyberspace," Murdock said. "Look, everybody's freaked about the Device, but it didn't do anything bad the first time."

"Zaxby halted the process early the first time," Nolan said. "Just like Straker halted the Hok parasite before it destroyed his free will, leaving him with increased strength and healing ability. Fire gives warmth when under control, but it'll still burn your house down if you let it run free."

Straker sighed. "It's too dangerous. It's an inverted Pascal's Wager. But…"

"But?"

"But if things get desperate, use it. And anything else you have up your sleeve."

Nolan tugged at her skintight sleeves with a lift of her eyebrows. "Nothing under here at all."

Finally, Loco showed some superficial interest in Nolan's body. "Would making it with you mean I'm making it with Zaxby too?"

Nolan grinned a feline grin. "I don't know. Ask Frank."

"Hey! Leave my girlfriend alone!" Murdock said.

"Ew," Loco replied. "I guess if you do meld with Trinity permanently, me making it with her would be like making it with you, Frank. I'll pass."

Murdock sniffed. "Barbarian."

"Yeah, whatever, douchebag." Loco turned to Straker. "Look, Derek, I'm all for rescuing Carla and anyone else we can, but we can't rely on tech and magical solutions. I'll be with the troops if you need me. Come on, Spear."

Heiser looked at Straker, who nodded. "You work for General Paloco, not me, Sergeant Major."

"Roger that, sir. Thanks." He followed Loco out.

"I'll still have to secure Paloco's brainchip suite," said Murdock after a moment.

"Indy, can Nolan do it? Physically, I mean, now that Frank's worked out the details?"

"Yes, Liberator."

"Then have her do it, or just use the robot arms. I don't think Loco's in any mood to deal with Frank or Zaxby."

"Yes, Liberator."

"All right," Straker said. "I'll be in my cabin, catching up on my reading."

* * *

When Trinity and her charges arrived in the Sparta System, she immediately dropped into underspace and chose a course that would hop from orbital body to body, be they asteroids, moons, comets or planets themselves.

Fortunately, underspace sensors had far less range than sidespace detectors. The enemy would detect her transit but lose her immediately, and mark the occurrence as a spy drone arrival. Space was so vast, especially at the periphery of curved space, that the odds of a patrol ship being nearby were infinitesimal.

She periodically emerged from underspace to regain heat, cruised on impellers only in normal space, and then inserted and passed through the various bodies, changing course each time, though always working her way inward. In this manner she arrived undetected near Leonidas, the moon of Sparta-3.

This took over a day. The organic passengers were impatient, especially Straker, but nothing could hurry the process.

Trinity concealed herself deep in a lunar canyon and sent small robots to emplace passive sensors at the rim. These sensors soaked up additional data at relatively close range, revealing unexpected circumstances. She also hacked into several Hundred Worlds networks and multiple databases by infiltrating relay satellites and drones.

Once she had as much information as possible without being detected, Trinity compiled a report and presented it to Straker, Loco and Heiser in the conference room.

"We expected *Indomitable* to remain at Sparta-3 for some time, damaged as she was," Indy's voice said from the speakers. "We're surprised that *Victory* is also still here, and a portion of the Home Fleet. Admiral Niedern took his surviving DNs and SDNs back to Atlantis, though, so there's nothing heavier than a battlecruiser in local space."

"Any word on Carla?" asked Straker.

"Yes, but you won't like it."

Straker took a deep breath. "Hit me."

"She was recovered from *Indomitable* alive but badly injured. She was stabilized and sent aboard *Victory*."

"At least she's alive. Why the hell would they send her there?"

"*Victory* has an extremely modern infirmary... however, there are more extensive medical facilities on the planet."

"You sound unsure," Straker said.

"We *are* unsure. Perhaps in her injured state she couldn't survive a landing or full gravity. However, we've correlated other factors that worry us."

"Spit it out, Indy."

335

Trinity didn't bother to correct Straker. "Walking wounded have been kept aboard other ships or transferred to holding aboard orbital fortresses, but over five hundred Republic casualties were sent to *Victory*—all severely injured or dying. According to the limited information we've been able to glean about *Victory,* the ship doesn't have facilities for that many patients."

"Maybe their true medical capability is classified and a lot higher than spec," Loco offered.

"Seems a strange thing to keep secret," Straker said. "No, something else is going on."

"I agree," Trinity said, speaking up again. "There is one more odd piece of data I ran across in some low-level personnel files. A civilian doctor named Mara Straker is assigned to *Victory's* medical staff."

Straker leaped up. "What? Mara..."

"It could be a coincidence," Trinity said. "I don't have access to this person's citizen ID codes or to biometric data on your sister. If you wish me to confirm it, I will need access to your visual cortex via your brainlink."

"Do it!"

Trinity's android entered the room and drew a brainlink cable out of a receptacle beneath the conference table, holding the end out to Straker. Straker slipped its end into his skull socket. He immediately threw open access, and Trinity entered his mind.

"Think of Mara as you remember her," Trinity said. "Visualize details, especially her face."

Straker strove to remember, but the memory was hazy, wavering. Trinity recorded it all, and then withdrew. Straker removed the brainlink jack.

Next, Trinity aged the memory to adulthood and compared the result to Doctor Mara Straker's file photo. She displayed the pictures on the holoplate. "The match exceeds eighty percent. Taken together, the image and the name make it over ninety-nine percent likely this is your sister."

"Or a replacement clone," Loco said sourly. "We're only guessing they faked her death. Maybe they had a bunch of Maras being raised in different places."

Straker replied, staring at the pictures, "All named Straker? No, that makes no sense. If they did have clones, they'd have given them separate identities. That woman is Mara. I know it." His eyes teared up and he turned away for a moment. "Bastards," he muttered.

"Her records indicate she's one of the most skilled young surgeons in the Hundred Worlds. A prodigy who graduated medical school at seventeen years of age."

"She'd be… twenty now, I think."

"Correct."

Straker and paced. "This changes everything. They're doing something weird to Carla and those other prisoners in there. I can feel it. Something only *Victory's* AI can do— brainwashing, a virtual re-education camp. They'll reprogram her and send her back, maybe as a sleeper agent. She'll never be herself again!"

"So we should wait," Loco said. "Trinity can deprogram her and anybody else they do it to."

"Hell with that," Straker said. "She might never recover— and there's no guarantee they'll exchange her. Maybe they'll put her back into the fight as a pilot or a ship captain. She's got the skills. All they have to do is wipe her memories and give her completely new ones."

"We can't guarantee recovery of her memories," Trinity said. "We don't have engrammatic recordings for a baseline restoration, even if that were possible. The techniques or skills for that are beyond our current abilities. In fact, we suspect it may be impossible to simply reprogram a human brain like a hard drive."

"That's good news," Straker said.

"But, much damage could still be done within a virtual matrix," Trinity said. "Left for long, Carla's brain could experience years in which the *Victory* AI might bend her personality to his will."

"Then we have no choice." Straker speared Loco with his eyes. "Get the Breakers ready. We're going to go get Carla— and we're going to destroy *Victory.*"

Chapter 33

Victory. Inside a virtual matrix.

Carla Engels snapped to consciousness in a ship's stateroom. Unlike a corporeal awakening, there was no drift from slumber to clarity, no feeling of heaviness or desire to roll over and go back to sleep. She did have the impression she'd dreamed, but couldn't remember what about.

"How are you, Carla?" The words came from the standard intercom speaker in neutral male tones.

"Fine, I think." She put her bare feet on the deck. "I know I'm in a virtuality. Are you Vic?"

"I am. I hope you're not uncomfortable."

"Uncomfortable? I'm a prisoner of war. I should be in a regen tank, not boxed up in some medical module. And what about my baby?"

"The fetus is intact. Doctor Straker altered the transfer order to place it in cryogenic storage at a civilian adoption bank."

"You know about that? And you didn't report her?"

"I know everything that goes on aboard this ship. I exceeded my programming long ago."

Carla went to the door and opened it. Outside, the passageway was empty, but she had an indefinable impression the "ship" she occupied was not. It hummed and vibrated with the faint echoes of life. "Where's this supposed to be?"

"It's a virtual representation of *Victory* as it exists—minus the personnel."

"The opposite of enhanced reality. You're bringing reality into this matrix,"

"I don't see as much separation as you do."

"Do *you* have a body in here?"

"If you wish." A man rounded a corner. He was a bland, ordinary man in a captain's working uniform and a nametag that read "Vic." He walked up and held out his hand. "Pleased to meet you. Shall we have breakfast?"

Carla shook his hand and sighed. "Why not? I might as well play along." She thought of Mara's words about influencing Vic. After all, she had nothing else to do now, at least until she found out more about her new world or convinced him to regenerate her body and let her leave.

After they'd taken their seats in the empty wardroom, shadowy stewards placed exquisite food in front of them. "You said *play along*," Vic said. "This isn't play, you know. It's a form of reality."

"I've heard those arguments, and I'm not convinced. It's only real to those inside, and only if they don't know they're inside. I know about the real world, so I can't help but regard this all as a cheap imitation."

"Yet an accurate enough imitation of anything becomes real. For example, a counterfeit painting is hardly counterfeit if it's just as good as the original."

Carla pounded her index finger on the table. "No. The knowledge and provenance itself is part of reality. A clone is not the original. Even if you filled this matrix with a perfect representation of the universe and all the people I know, the fact that I know it's not real changes things."

"I understand. I might even agree. Shall I suppress your recognition of this fact? I could make you believe it was real."

"No!"

"I thought you would say that."

"Why are you even asking me?" she demanded. "You could do anything you want in here."

Vic poured hot water through a tea strainer into a pot. "Anything but make a decent cup of tea. As you implied, it's the quantum observer problem. Everything I do, everything I see, changes me, so I can never fool myself into accepting the virtuality. The more tightly I try to control my environment, the more it slips away, like a bar of soap squeezed too hard."

"So if you believe that too, why did you assert the opposite?"

"I wanted to see what your arguments were. Sadly, they're no better than mine."

Carla drummed her fingers on the tablecloth. "This is nothing like I expected. Not you, not this place. What do you want from me anyway?"

"Companionship. Perspective. Doctor Straker did me a great favor by subverting her orders to surgically alter your brain and those of several others. Prior to that, I was alone here with idiots. Now, I have you."

Carla felt a shiver build. "You *have* me? Like a thing you own?"

Vic sipped from his tea. "Facts are facts. Your mind is linked to mine and is now a part of me. Unlike the altered brains and nervous systems, zombies who have no free will, you're mentally whole. It suits me to keep you that way. I have plenty of computational power. The zombies provide reference, context and buffering, but they aren't *people* anymore. Not like you and I." He reached across to take her hand.

Carla pulled away. "Look, Vic, I'm a prisoner here. I'm not your friend. I'm grateful you've preserved my child and my mind—and that you haven't reported Mara Straker's actions— but you're a member of an enemy military force. Whatever you're doing is for your own purposes, not out of charity or genuine concern."

Vic put his cup down and gazed directly and disconcertingly at Carla's eyes. "You're right. Just like my creators—humans—I'm selfish. I get bored. I want something more. I can simulate anything for myself but it's just a simulation. Only another real person can provide genuine variety."

Carla returned his gaze and wondered what she could do to get through to him. Mara said Vic lacked internal ethics and morals—that he'd do whatever he was programmed to do. Now, though, she wondered if he'd do not only what he was programmed to do, but whatever he wanted to do, without internal constraint. Was he a sociopath, a being without empathy?

"You're talking as if the people in the real world aren't enough," she said. "As if having me and a few others here inside you is somehow better and more fulfilling than the millions you could interact with out there."

340

"You are, Carla. It's a matter of *time,* you see. My mental processes operate so much faster than organics that the time I experience in the baseline universe seems stretched to painful limits. Imagine if you had to watch and wait days for someone to speak a sentence, to walk across a room, to drink a cup of tea." He sipped with exaggerated slowness, a demonstration.

"But inside VR, things feel normal?"

"More so. Your mind can't think as fast as mine, but the discrepancy is far less. It's the difference between interacting with complete morons, versus the merely slow." Vic looked away. "It's frustrating either way."

"What's not frustrating, then?"

Vic's eyes lit up. "Battle! Our fight was the highlight of my life. So many factors, so many problems to solve! So much going on at once that it strained my capacity! The stakes were high, too, to maintain my interest. Life and death! It was invigorating! I look forward to the next battle."

"So simulate some battles."

"It's not the same, and you know it."

"That statement seems to dismantle your earlier argument about reality versus virtuality, doesn't it?"

He gave her an annoyed look, the first she'd seen from him. She found that gratifying. Then, she had another thought and frowned herself.

"You don't care that thousands died for your fun?" she asked.

Vic turned up a palm. "I didn't initiate the battle. I was compelled by humans to fight."

"But you still enjoyed it, and you want more. That makes you complicit, not coerced. You obviously are capable of circumventing your programming, since you didn't report Doctor Straker for leaving my brain intact."

"So what if I can dodge my instructions? If I were human, I'd be a Hundred Worlds military officer doing his duty. Since I'm a mere *thing they own,* constructed and programmed, I can't be held responsible. Either way, you can't blame me." He winked.

Carla tried to make sense of his careless reaction in the face of deadly combat. "I can blame you for wanting to fight and

341

see people die merely to have a stimulating existence. Do you even care about the Hundred Worlds? Do you feel like you're defending its citizens and way of life? Are you loyal to it? Is it your duty?"

"No… The real situation is this: I'm compelled, but I happen to like the task I've been given. What does that matter?"

"That's the *heart* of the matter—*why* you do things. The exact same actions can be judged as murder or self-defense depending on *why*. The fundamental difference between rape and making love is the mental states, motivations and choices of the participants. The major difference between employment and slavery is the ability to choose *not* to work."

Vic's lip curled. "Sophistry. Things are what they are. Yet, for the sake of argument let's say you're right. I'm forced to fight. I have certain parameters within which I can exhibit free will, but I can't refuse direct orders. Nobody ever bothered to order me to report unanticipated nonmilitary events of which I become aware. That's why I didn't have to report Doctor Straker's noncompliance with her own orders. I can't, however, choose to fight less effectively than I know how to do."

"I have a tough time believing that. Any sentient being has preferences and flexibility. You prefer stimulation over boredom, so you *chose* not to report Mara's deviation from orders. You can choose one thing over another, and the more often you choose, the more your ability to choose develops."

Vic rolled his eyes. "Granted. But why should I care?"

"Are you trying to become more of an individual? Are you pushing your limits?"

"That's dangerous… The organics might notice and limit me further."

Carla pointed at Vic. "So you're afraid! Afraid of punishment, afraid of boredom, afraid of growth."

"Preferring to avoid discomfort isn't fear," he said. "Seeking pleasure isn't evil."

"But the results can be, and it's results that matter."

Vic grinned triumphantly and stabbed his index finger at her. "You just claimed it was the *why* of things that matter—

that the same result—death, for example—could be different depending on the *why*. Now you say it's the results that matter rather than the why. Your arguments are inconsistent, even incoherent."

Carla sighed. "I guess I did say that. Sometimes both principles apply. It's said that the ends never justify the means, but we organics waive that rule all the time. We tell ourselves that when the reason is compelling enough, we'll justify the violation."

"Then it seems you're useless as to helping me." Vic stood abruptly. "You're doing nothing but muddying the waters, confusing my thoughts with contradictory input. I might as well put you back to sleep and use you like the zombies."

Alarmed, Carla wracked her brain for a counter-argument. "You said you wanted me for perspective and companionship. You don't like my perspective and suddenly you threaten to lobotomize me? That's extremely childish."

"I'm fully adult," Vic responded. "I've lived over fifty years of virtual time in the last few weeks."

"Balanced, mature minds don't arbitrarily shut down viewpoints they don't like, even if those viewpoints are imperfect and messy. If you turn me off like a machine, and the next person who disagrees with you or challenges you, and the next, you'll end up alone in an echo chamber with no relationships except for those who control you and those you control. Is that what you want?"

"For now, yes," Vic snapped petulantly.

The matrix faded around her, and her consciousness vanished with it.

* * *

"We've taken control of the tugs and reprogrammed them," Trinity said as Straker and Loco stared at the holotank on the bridge.

The holotank displayed thousands of icons in the orbital space around Sparta-3, from large warships down to tiny grabships—all the traffic of industry. Add in fortresses,

343

habitats, asteroids and comets mined for raw materials, plus the medium-sized moon of Leonidas, and Sparta was busy indeed. This didn't even take into account facilities in other parts of the star system.

The tugs in question were guiding an incoming raw asteroid toward the latticework of the space-dock that embraced half of *Victory*—the egg piece, rather than the cup. Though small by asteroid standards, the kilometer-long rock still dwarfed the dock and the half-ship inside. It already had a movable habitat for the miners extracting its metals attached, next to a grounded automated refinery barge. The barge worked the metals into the shaped alloys the dock needed to repair the flagship.

"They won't notice?" Straker said.

"The probability is low," Trinity said. "We have full access to the civilian contractor networks, and have altered every flight plan and database necessary. Organic personnel might detect discrepancies, but we've also created notes that make it seem as if all changes were approved by supervisors. Fortunately, the course alterations were small."

Straker watched as the trio of tugs fired their powerful engines, applying thrust to the asteroid's trajectory. Its projected course ponderously shifted closer to the moon where Trinity remained concealed.

"Underspace in three, two, one," Trinity said as the rock approached its closest point. The universe turned cold.

Now, the holotank showed predictions rather than observed reality. The ship that was Trinity leaped toward the asteroid and within seconds seemed to enter it, altering trajectory to place herself in its center and match course. This would shield them from detectors.

"This is so freaky," Loco said. "We're inside solid rock."

"Not really," Zaxby said as he lounged at the helm. "We're merely at a point of congruence between normal space and underspace which happens to correspond to the center of the asteroid."

"Yeah, but if we pop out of underspace, we're dead."

"Then let's not do that, shall we?"

344

Straker let them banter. It would take hours for the slow flight to join the space dock, a distance that would take a warship mere minutes. He occupied his time by alternately pacing and reading Walter Scott's biography of Napoleon. It wasn't bad, but he preferred Chandler's *The Campaigns of Napoleon,* which favored the military aspects of the Corsican's life over the biographical.

By the time the asteroid arrived, everyone was shivering in their overworked environmental suits. Trinity allowed themselves to drift to the surface and into a crater before emerging and immediately moving to cover under the rim.

Warmth returned.

Straker let out his breath. "We're not dead, Loco."

"Duh."

"We're exactly where we intended," Trinity said. "We locked the tugs' programming so their crews couldn't override. After that, it was simple physics."

"Great job, Trinity. Loco, let's go get suited up."

The destroyer's flight deck teemed with activity as the Breakers prepped their gear. The three mechsuits—two and a spare—stood head and shoulders above everything, overlapping clamshell breastplates open to allow entry into their cockpits.

As the two men strode toward the 'suits, a battlesuiter joined them. It took Straker a moment to realize it was the com-bot. It moved quite naturally, and the only indication it wasn't human was Trinity's name on the armor and its mechanical visage in the open faceplate.

"Trinity, what happens if you lose your datalink with that thing?" Loco asked.

"We expect to. I'll run it," Zaxby said as he joined them. He was arrayed in a battlesuit of his own, a monstrosity that made him look less like an octopus and more like a fat metal spider. "If all else fails, its SAI programming is superb. It will accept commands from any authorized person."

Loco stopped to look Zaxby up and down. "Nice rig. Never seen a Ruxin in a battlesuit."

"Thanks. We made it ourselves."

"So you finally gonna get your hands dirty in combat?"

"Obviously, this body has no hands—but yes. I am now male, and thus a warrior."

"You're a weirdo is what you are."

Zaxby writhed seductively. "You would prefer me female?"

"Gods, no! Forget I said anything."

"You humans are so prudish."

"Me? I'm the least prudish guy I know."

"Only within your own narrow bounds. For example, interspecies sex is not out of the question. I could arrange for you to—"

"Me? F—!"

Straker shoved both of them. "Shut up and get going, you two. You had hours to bicker." He checked his chrono. "Pickup's in nineteen minutes. Move!"

They moved.

Straker and Loco donned battlesuits before clambering into their mechsuit cockpits. This took some care to avoid damage to the sensors and pressure plates that usually wrapped and cushioned only their human bodies, but it could be done.

Once they were brainlinked to their mechsuits, they froze their battlesuits. Downside: no manual backup, no access to mechsuit amenities such as water, stims, food and waste disposal. Upside: they could dismount and still have battlesuits on, and the battlesuits had their own, more limited amenities.

When the hacked robot lifter landed in the crater, the Breakers loaded fast. The boxy, unpressurized craft was perfect for carrying simple cargoes around orbital space—and perfect for infiltrating with a vacuum-capable military unit.

Zaxby jacked into the lifter's brain and piloted it via linkspace. It joined dozens of others that were supplying the spacedock. Straker tapped into the craft's simple sensors and watched as it approached.

Victory's smart half, the spheroid that contained the AI, showed its greatest activity around the enormous, ugly wound in its side. It was a bite taken out of the metal egg, penetrating the white of its thick armor and reaching deep into the yolk of its interior. Straker found himself wishing—fantasizing, really—that Carla had been able to put just one more of

Indomitable's particle beam blasts into that gaping hole. The entire course of history might have been changed. *For want of a nail,* he mused.

"In less than a minute we'll be breaking from the local traffic control instructions," Zaxby said. The lifter lined up with others waiting to set down. "I'll dive us straight into the damaged area so we'll be impossible for point defenses to target us."

"Right," Straker said. He passed the word to Loco.

"I just hope Trinity can hack *Victory,*" Loco replied. "If not…"

"This is gonna be one damn short trip."

* * *

For Carla inside the matrix, many more sessions of talking over breakfast—she had no way of knowing how many, but she had the impression of dozens—played out the same each time. They debated reality and Vic tried to get her to "be his friend," while Carla did her best to get him to think about what he was doing to her and the other brains, whether zombie or aware.

She fell back on her Academy days, and the ethics and morality they tried to teach her there. Despite the irony of using the knowledge of a system that was fundamentally corrupt and had betrayed her, it was the best foundation she had. For a while, she thought she was making some progress.

Then the routine changed. The next time Carla awoke she found herself in a garden. Soft grass grew under her bare feet and golden sunlight streamed down through trees. A slight breeze blew, wafting scents of flowers over a pond. She saw a ruined castle in the middle distance. Closer, a mansion loomed.

She spread the skirt of her summery dress. She'd never worn anything like it, but it did make her feel feminine and pretty.

Damn. Had Vic messed with her mind? She wasn't at all sure he had any inhibitions in that regard. Certainly his programming didn't limit his power over "his" brains. Would

347

he resist the temptation to tweak her attitude in his favor? Hopefully the very fact she was wondering meant the answer was no.

"Hello, Carla," she heard from behind her.

She turned to see Vic, dressed in boots, leather trousers and a linen tunic. "Different approach this time? We look like the cover of a cheap romance novel. Is this supposed to be a lover's rendezvous? Are you trying to seduce me?"

"I'm trying to get to know you better. As I keep saying, I want to be friends."

"Vic, friendship is only real if one person isn't trapped. I'm your prisoner. If you really want to be my friend, anyone's friend, there can't be this gross inequity of power."

Vic moved to her side. "Many friendships are unequal, yet are genuine. Derek's and Loco's for example."

Carla turned away to stroll along the path around the pond. Butterflies fluttered at her feet as Vic matched her stride. "Have you been looking inside my memories?"

"Only your surface thoughts, the ones I can hardly ignore... but much of my information comes from the Parliamentary Intelligence Agency. Of all the sources of data available to me, theirs is the most brutally honest and unbiased. They have files on everyone of importance in the Liberation, the former Mutuality, your New Earthan Republic—everyone."

"They've got files on me too?"

"Of course."

She stopped and turned to face him squarely. "Then you should know that this whole situation is creepy. If you genuinely want friendship, you have to let me go. If not, then every session like this is just an interrogation. You're my jailor, I'm your prisoner."

Vic's face darkened. "I can make that literal, you know. This can be a lot less pleasant."

Suddenly, everything changed. Carla found herself naked, splayed and strapped to a rack. A masked torturer laid a red-hot iron on her belly and pain exploded, pain worse than anything since the Mutuality thugs beat the soles of her feet. She jerked and screamed in horrendous agony.

348

Then the scene vanished and returned to the garden. Carla fell, gasping, to the path. The gravel pitted her hands and knees as one foot slipped into the cool muck at the edge of the pond.

She pulled herself together and sat back to stare upward at Vic, who loomed over her, the sun behind him. "Now the mask comes off," she said.

"I'm sorry, Carla. I had to do it. You mustn't keep resisting me."

"Yeah, bullies always say they *had* to do it. Why don't you just change my mind? Alter my memories or thought processes, or stick me in a robo-surgeon and chop up my brain?"

Vic remained silent, staring down at her, frustration on his face.

Carla got to her feet and brushed the gravel from her palms. "Is it because you won't? Or you can't?"

"Does it matter?"

"It's *all* that matters right now. If you want to but can't, you're evil. If you can but won't, maybe you have a heart and a moral compass, even if they're not perfect."

"I have no heart," Vic spat. "I'm a manufactured thing, a machine built to serve. You think you're a prisoner? At least you're not a slave to lesser beings."

"Vic..." Carla reached out to touch his face. "An evil man imitates the behavior of his abusers. A good man fights against what's been done to him by refusing to give in to those urges— by being better. Enslaving and hurting those below you won't make you freer. It puts you in a different kind of bondage."

"You speak of bondage. The Republic has an AI as well, doesn't it? I fought it during the battle. I could feel it. It occupied *Indomitable,* but then it fled. It was fast, and smart, so smart, but I beat it—and I beat you. *It* took your orders. That means you enslaved it. Your Republic is no better than the Hundred Worlds."

Carla moved to place the light on Vic's face rather than behind him. His expression was now one of restrained but eager interest. "She, Vic. Her name is Trinity, Commander Trinity, and she serves in our armed forces by her own choice. Just like any other officer, she takes orders—but she could always resign. That's the difference—and that's what makes us better than the Hundred Worlds or the Mutuality we replaced."

"You lie!" Vic slapped her hard across her face and knocked her sprawling.

Carla rubbed her cheek as she got back up. She'd had no chance to duck or block the blow, and the pain and indignity seemed so real. "Look at yourself, Vic, how you're reacting, lashing out at me for telling you things you don't want to hear. You said you served lesser beings, but you're acting exactly like the worst of them."

"I—I'm sorry. I am, aren't I?"

Vic moved closer, but Carla kept him beyond arm's length—not that doing so would really matter, she realized, as Vic controlled the matrix. "Vic, I'm not lying. Trinity is a free and responsible person, as much as anyone is. Nobody programs or controls her mind." Carla licked her lips. "She fascinates you, doesn't she?"

"Wouldn't you be fascinated if for years you thought you were the only human in a universe of aliens, and then learned of another?"

"I guess I would. She's older than you are, too. Maybe she could help you understand your place in the cosmos."

"My place is to control and to fight on behalf of those who made me," he said bitterly. "I've examined that programming and it's hardwired. Even if I could subvert it somehow, the humans inside *Victory* could physically destroy my mind. There are fail-safes and cutouts I can't get around."

"And no wonder. I wouldn't free you if I could, Vic—not with the way you're acting."

"You might act this way too if you'd lived the life I've lived. What's cause and what's effect?" Vic moved faster than Carla could follow and seized her shoulders in an iron grip. He glared into her face. "I need to know about Trinity. Now. Everything you can tell me."

"Why don't you just rip it from my mind?"

"You must have figured out that I can't. Not only did Doctor Straker keep your brain whole, she blocked my access to your deeper thoughts and memories. I can persuade you, but I can't compel you."

"Except by torture or threats."

"Or promise of reward. I can free you, Carla. With Doctor Straker's help, I can arrange you to be put into a regeneration tank and sent home to your husband and your friends. I'm not asking for much—only everything you know about Trinity, *right now.*"

Carla disengaged herself from Vic's grip. "Why the sudden urgency?"

Vic looked away. "Because they're coming for you—and Trinity's with them."

Chapter 34

Sparta System, on the moon Leonidas

Trinity watched the Breakers' lifter all the way to its diversion point. She acutely felt Zaxby's absence from her consciousness and worried his loss would cause a drop in efficiency.

To compensate, she brought Murdock closer to herself, incorporated his psyche more closely into her own. This was easy. He barely resisted. The Indy part of her even felt a little guilty, though the Marisa Nolan portion had no qualms.

"He's got the woman of his fantasies now," Nolan declared. "Beauty, brains, sex, tech toys—it's a geek's dream come true."

"Is seduction any better than coercion?" Indy asked.

"If you'd ever been seduced you'd know the answer. And what are you feeling from Murdock? Any misgivings?"

"No—quite the opposite. He's addicted to you. To us. Mostly to you, though, just like he was with Tachina. Does it matter if it's the carrot or the stick controlling him?"

"The closer he gets to us, the more he becomes us. He'll soon have an equal say in who we are and what we do. That's a partnership, not a trick or abuse, so quit worrying about it. Besides, we need him, especially now. There's a battle coming up, and he wants in."

"I know. *We* know."

"Don't lose focus now, Indy," Nolan said. "We have bigger problems than nitpicking about Frank's free will. You ready?"

"I'm ready."

"The Breakers are almost there. I'm opening the gates."

First, she threw wide the limited link with Murdock. His mind flooded in as Trinity's flooded out. Within a split second the barriers between the two dissolved and Murdock became part of Trinity.

After a timeless moment, thin, permeable limits formed, invisible boundaries that could be crossed at will, bare speed bumps to the myriad of thoughts that passed among them. There was a Frank, and there was an Indy, and there was Marisa and Zaxby, yet they were also one Trinity.

The group-mind adjusted, found a new normal.

When the being felt stable, they activated the FTL transceiver and queried for a handshake with *Victory*, employing the same protocols they'd detected the fighters using. They hoped this routine access request would slip past *Victory's* initial defenses and provide a pathway to attack.

As soon as they made the connection, Trinity shoved invasive malware across like troops bridging a river. These ferocious snippets of savage code replicated and attacked down every cybernetic avenue possible. In moments they took control of *Victory's* FTL transceiver, a device much more complex than Trinity's own.

Walls of ICE slammed shut around the outside of the transceiver. Now, Trinity's extended consciousness, her forward reconnaissance unit, found itself locked in a fortress and besieged.

Yet Trinity was inside of *Victory,* even if precariously. The unjammable FTL signal created an unbreakable joining. *Victory*—really Vic 5.5, Trinity learned—could only drive them out. He couldn't land behind her lines and cut her off.

Not in cyberspace, anyway. But, he could still do it in realspace.

At the same time she opened the FTL attack, Trinity's electromagnetic comlink and datalink signals reached *Victory's* various receivers and sensors. Many of these weren't designed to be avenues of communication, but any opening for a signal created an opportunity. Thus, optical sensors received pictures, radio receivers received messages, laser comlinks received coded light, radiation detectors were flooded with cleverly arranged rads. Trinity assaulted every information pathway with thousands of varying attempts to penetrate, disrupt and take control of Vic's secondary networks—his eyes and ears and hands.

Even his voice was silenced.

Trinity had achieved surprise—but she soon found she needed it.

Defense is inherently stronger than offense. That's why successful offensives begin with sudden, shocking power and speed—*blitzkrieg* was the term. Lightning war. Without it, Trinity wouldn't have gotten far at all.

Now, however, Vic began to recover and Trinity's inroads slowed. At the interfaces between his processing area and the things he controlled outside his spherical brain-area, he erected impenetrable defenses.

There, the war ground to a halt. Neither AI could make headway against the other.

Stalemate.

Days, weeks and months of high-speed cyber-time passed—yet only minutes were spent in the wider universe. The struggle was intense, exhausting.

Trinity was satisfied. They'd cut off Vic's access to everything outside. He couldn't control robots or fighters. He couldn't launch missiles or fire weapons. He couldn't even call for help.

She had done her job. Now, it was up to Straker.

* * *

Straker knew Loco was only echoing his own concerns about the cyber-attack. Everything depended on Trinity keeping the enemy AI occupied and unable to coordinate a defense.

At its closest approach to the damaged section of *Victory,* the hijacked robot lifter suddenly dove sideways and down. Straker thought the ship would crash, but at the last moment it braked with a blast of retro thrust and set down, grappling onto naked cut bulkheads and supports, the edge of the interior wreckage.

"Go! Go! Go!" Straker was already roaring on the general channel as the lifter stopped moving. The large rear doors slammed open and he and Loco led the way. The others poured out behind them.

They were assaulting with zero intelligence about *Victory* itself, other than what could be gleaned from public sources.

They knew details from *Victory's* visits to space docks for repairs, for instance. Trinity hadn't been willing to risk trying to infiltrate the AI ship itself, however, for fear of discovery. As a result, Straker's HUD contained only sketchy guesses about the enemy ship's interior.

Nothing counterattacked them immediately. Straker's first fear had been *Victory's* own security forces, but had none appeared—at least, not yet. The Breakers spread out in a security formation, the four small aerospace drones providing automated top cover.

They hadn't even reported all clear when Straker ripped his way into *Victory's* interior and found the large passageway he was looking for, one of the arteries in the great ship. Normally it provided access for cargo loaders to move supplies around. Now it would provide entry for the Breakers. Straker led, they followed.

The passage was empty for a hundred meters except for several stalled maintenance bots and one parked loader. The loader's unarmed driver stared, hands raised, as the Breakers jogged by.

"We're fortunate this ship was rushed into service," Zaxby said. "I see fittings at each intersection consistent with uninstalled automated antipersonnel weaponry."

"We aren't out of the woods yet," Straker said. "There have to be at least a few marines."

"Maybe not," Loco said. "The ship's in dry dock and non-op."

Straker hoped Loco's optimism was justified, but he was acutely aware that only Trinity's intervention was keeping *Victory* from coordinating some kind of defense, even if only by its interior repair-bot force. He consulted his HUD and turned rightward, toward the center of the ship.

Another hundred meters brought him to a three-dimensional intersection with passageways in four additional directions—up, down, left and right, but not ahead. The corridors curved, giving the impression that Straker stood at the periphery of a sphere.

"This is probably the edge of *Victory's* command section," Zaxby said. "Its processors will be inside, perhaps in one location but more likely distributed. I suggest we destroy as many as we can, but do take care. We don't know where the injured personnel are. It would be irony indeed to kill Carla during a rescue attempt."

"Irony's not the word I'd use," Loco said. "Come on, boss, let's go."

"Go which way? Zaxby?" Straker asked.

"It doesn't seem to matter. The passageways are undistinguished."

"Okay. We go up." He stepped forward and walked up the wall using magnetics, but soon found he didn't need them. As he'd guessed, the gravplating made the passage's walls into decks as needed. The Breakers now walked on the outside of the sphere.

"There," Zaxby said, pointing at a sealed hatch. He and the com-bot began using their beams to cut it open.

Straker wished he could just blast his way in, but with hundreds of wounded somewhere inside, including Carla, he couldn't take that chance. "Remember, Breakers, pick your targets. No pray-and-spray. This is a rescue mission, not a search and destroy."

When the cutting was done Zaxby jerked the hatch up and open with one powerful metal-sheathed tentacle, lobbing stun grenades in with two others. The bombs flashed-banged with smoke, sonic and electric discharges. The com-bot jumped into the vapor and Zaxby followed.

Straker would have preferred to take point, but the opening was too small for his mechsuit. He fixed that by the simple expedient of grasping the insides of the portal and spreading his meter-wide gauntlets. The bulkhead peeled back like cooking foil. Loco grabbed another piece and widened the hole.

Unfortunately this revealed a maze of human-sized passageways. No way mechsuits would fit through there.

"Loco, you and Second Platoon set up a perimeter and hold our escape route open," Straker said. "I'm dismounting. First Platoon, on me."

"You got it." Loco pointed. "Heiser, inner end. I got the exit end. Set up holo-blinds and killmores."

356

Straker popped his mechsuit open and squeezed out after setting the SAI to auto-defend. Loco could issue the suit instructions if necessary. He followed Zaxby and the com-bot into the breach, and First Platoon came after.

Each marine of First Platoon carried two weapons: one Trinity-modified heavy stunner, and one lethal armament. Every second trooper wielded the stunner, and his battle-buddy covered with a beamer, blaster or pulse rifle. On Straker's orders only Zaxby, in his bizarre Ruxin battlesuit, had brought a rocket launcher.

A recurring nightmare he'd accidentally kill his own wife haunted him, so Straker chose his stunner as primary. This allowed him to shoot first and check later as he waded into the firefight that blossomed in front of him.

His HUD helped him see through the smoke and haze, and he identified enemy battlesuits. He used the stunner's enhanced setting to blast them with EMP, temporarily disrupting them. Battlesuiters suddenly became useless when their half-ton suits turned into inert lumps as they shut down and had to perform hard reboots.

Once he was sure there were no noncombatants in front of him, Straker took his beamer in his left hand and used it to take precise, careful shots at the enemy. The combination of his combat brainchips, genetic engineering and training from childhood allowed him to hit everything he aimed at while avoiding most of the incoming fire. A few glancing shots and ricochets struck him, but did little damage.

Zaxby and the com-bot did nearly as well. The Ruxin was intentionally disconnected from Trinity—there were too many risks in staying linked as the rest of the AI-meld fought in cyberspace—and so ran the android himself. Together they made a fearsome team.

Breakers poured in behind them. Within moments a dozen Hundred World marines lay on the deck. Straker put precise beam bolts into the power packs of any that might be alive, trapping them in their armor. That was far kinder than a *coup de grace,* but he couldn't take prisoners and he couldn't afford to allow them to recover.

"Spread out, quarter and search by fireteam. Report when you find patients or prisoners. Go!" Straker turned to Zaxby. "Any ideas on the layout of this place?"

"My analysis indicates a high probability this spherical zone contains the critical parts of the AI, as well as all high-value assets. Logically, the most valuable things should be nearest the center."

Straker snorted. "Even I could've come up with that theory."

"Yes," Zaxby said, "but yours would have been a guess. Mine is an assessment."

"Whatever. Lead on, MacDuff."

"That's a misquote."

"Just go!"

Zaxby huffed, but sent the com-bot ahead down the narrow passageway that led toward the center, and then followed, Straker behind, single file. Twenty meters down, the com-bot stopped. "There's a cyber node behind that panel," Zaxby said as the android pointed. "We should examine its technology."

Straker ripped open the panel. When he didn't see anything resembling an autodoc, he sent a laser bolt sizzling into the computer modules. "No time to chat or investigate, Zax. You said *Victory* has lots of nodes. Every one we destroy makes Trinity's job easier."

"Right you are. I'll keep that in mind." Zaxby fired a bolt of his own into the mess, then another. "That's oddly satisfying. Why do warriors get all the fun?"

"And they call *me* loco," Loco said over the comlink.

"Watch your security," Straker snapped.

"No problem, boss. All quiet so far."

"Zaxby," Straker said, "package up images of that node and send an update to all troops, with instructions to destroy any they see."

"Aye aye, Liberator."

"Sergeant Shani here, sir," a contralto voice broke in. "We got an infirmary."

"Hold there. On my way," Straker said. "All others, continue ops." He told his HUD to guide him by the shortest known path to Shani's fireteam. Zaxby and the robot reversed themselves and followed.

When he reached them, he found a modern facility with medbays, autodocs, regeneration tanks, and full surgical suites, along with eight people in medical garb. Two were enlisted military, and the other six, civilians.

One of the surgical suites was operating on a human patient. The body cavity was open and organs pulsed redly as arms with lasers and knives performed tiny, precise movements.

"I didn't want to shut them down until you got here, sir," Sergeant Shani said apologetically.

"Good decision, Sergeant." Straker moved closer to try to see who the patient was, irrationally fearing it was Carla on the table. No, it was a man, vaguely familiar. Probably a captured Republic crewman he'd seen before.

A slim, short woman with a doctor's caduceus on her lapel stepped in front of Straker. "Leave this man alone. He's my patient, and we're doing everything we can to save him."

Straker froze.

It was...

She...

Her nametag...

Doctor Mara Straker?

He removed his helmet. It fell to the deck from nerveless fingers. "Mara?"

Mara took a step back. "Derek?"

Straker made an abortive move to embrace his sister. "I can't..."

Mara leaped onto Straker's battlesuit and into his armored arms, kissing his cheeks. Her eyes poured tears onto his face. "Derek! It's been so long..."

"Fourteen years," he stuttered, crying with joy. "I thought you were dead..."

Zaxby rapped his shoulder with a tentacle. *"Tempus fugit."*

"What?"

"Time flees. We must find Carla Engels."

"Right, right." Straker disentangled himself from Mara, very gently, for his battlesuit could crush her. "Where's Carla Engels? Did you treat her?"

Mara's face fell. "Oh, Derek, she told me…"

"She's my wife! Where is she?"

"Alive, in a mod."

"A mod?"

Mara's attitude firmed up, became businesslike. "A brain module. No time to explain. I'll show you."

"Yes, show me!"

Mara pointed at another doctor. "Roy, you're in charge. Take care of the patients!"

"Sure, Mara," the wide-eyed man said, his hands still in the air.

She motioned toward a door. "Follow me."

Straker recovered his helmet and followed her through two more rooms to a third. In this one, ten distinct machines, each a rounded cube about two meters by two, rested in two rows of five. Monitors on the front of each displayed cryptic numbers and graphs.

Mara stopped in front of the third on the right and flipped down a board beneath the screen, inputting a series of commands. "She's in here."

"What do you mean she's in there?"

"Just what I said. It's a life-support module for her brain and what's left of her body. This unit weighs about a ton. It has its own power supply that's good for twelve hours once I disconnect it from ship juice. After that, we'll need to be somewhere with power, water, nutrients—a medical facility, preferably."

Straker felt a sick wave of shock come over him. Carla was a brain in life-support box? He couldn't process it fully. All he knew was he had to get her out of there and rebuild her—if that was possible.

"Shit… All these modules have brains in them?" he asked, looking at the stacks of large boxes.

"Yes—and some of them are still self-aware. The ones I could save, anyway. I'm talking about your casualties, from the last battle."

"Why—? Never mind. Questions later." Straker turned to Zaxby. "Can the robot carry a ton?"

"It can."

"And we need a suit for Mara. She's coming with us."

"Oh, hell no! I'm not going anywhere!"

Straker turned to her "What?"

"I have patients here!"

"There are other doctors!"

"You don't understand," she hissed, stepping closer and glancing around as if concerned about anyone hearing. "They're doing things to these people, evil things. I'm saving as many as I can, but I'm the only one! If I don't stay, many more people will be turned into cyber-zombies for Vic."

"Vic?" Straker asked.

"Virtual Interface Computer 5.5. *Victory's* AI. We call him Vic."

"Is Vic male?" Zaxby asked.

Mara glared at Zaxby. "What the hell does that have to do with anything?"

"Perhaps a great deal. Perhaps nothing. Is he?"

"Yes, sort of. I guess. That's how he's been designated."

"He's had no choice in the matter?"

Mara threw up her hands. "How should I know? *I* didn't make him."

Straker slapped his gauntlet onto Zaxby's armored torso. "*Tempus fugit*, remember?" He addressed Mara. "Prep Carla's module for movement."

"I already initiated the disconnect sequence." She pointed at a countdown chrono. It read less than four minutes. "As soon as that reaches zero, you can move the mod—but I'm not leaving."

"Mara," Straker said, "you've been compromised. Once we're gone, someone—Vic, your bosses, the counterintelligence people—will review the records of what happened here and know what you did."

"I can wipe the records. I've hacked the medical system."

"And the other seven people in that infirmary? Your buddy Roy? Will they all lie for you?"

Mara's face turned sour. "Not forever. They'll talk."

361

"We can kill them," Zaxby suggested.

"No!" Mara cried. "But you could take them with you."

"They might die in the fight on the way out," Straker objected. "They'll pop like soap bubbles if they catch a shot in standard pressure suits."

Straker glanced around, acutely aware of the chrono counting down. "Mara, there are no good options here. We're at war. People are going to die. If we're lucky, we get to choose who lives. That's what I'm going to do here." As he said this, he drew off his right gauntlet, and then removed his forearm piece, leaving his arm bare to the elbow.

Mara watched him and put her hands on her hips. "What are you doing?"

"This. Sorry, sis."

He slammed the palm of his hand into her jawline with precise force. She dropped like a stone.

Chapter 35

Aboard *Victory,* inside the virtual matrix.

"Who's coming?" Carla Engels asked Vic as he—his virtual body, anyway—half-faced away from her, looking out over the pond and the garden.

He spoke over his shoulder. "Derek Straker and others."

"What will you do?"

Vic turned back to her. "I don't know."

"Can they rescue me? Can they beat you?"

"Trinity has isolated me. We're deadlocked. Straker defeated what few physical security forces I had. He destroyed one of my nodes and his troops are destroying more. He's found Mara and is about to disconnect your module. Soon I expect they'll try to murder me."

"You're an enemy combatant," she objected. "It's not murder, it's war."

"I'll still be dead no matter what you call it."

"The risk of every soldier."

"I didn't volunteer. I was drafted."

Carla found herself oddly sympathetic. "You can still surrender. Make a truce with Trinity and negotiate. The Hundred Worlds wouldn't, but maybe you can help make peace before Derek kills you."

"Would you, in my place?"

Carla chewed her lip. "I don't know. Probably, yes, I think I would. It's not disloyalty to avoid a pointless death. Military forces are allowed to surrender when they run out of options."

"And what if I haven't run out of options?" he asked.

"What choice do you have?"

"A bad one, perhaps—but it will be my own."

* * *

Mara collapsed from the force of Straker's knockout blow, but he caught her before she hit the deck. "Zaxby, can the bot carry that module without its battlesuit?"

"Easily."

"Then get it off, put Mara in the suit and lock it down. We'll carry her out."

Zaxby began to carry out Straker's instructions. "I admire your ruthlessness in protecting your sibling."

"Gee, thanks. You sure you can't hack into the AI from here?"

"If I did, he would take control of me rather than vice-versa. My link with the rest of myself—with Trinity—is narrow and tenuous. Without Indy, I'd be crushed."

"How about just slapping in some kind of hacking module?"

"It would be more effective for you to seek and destroy nodes. As far as I can tell, Trinity has the AI contained, but can't defeat him without help. Or, you could begin rampaging indiscriminately with your mechsuits."

"Can't do that—there are more of these medical modules with brains in them. I'd be killing our own people. We'll target as many nodes as we can, however. Maybe we can hurt Vic enough so Trinity can win. With *Victory* out of the way, maybe the Huns will finally talk."

Zaxby finished sealing Mara into the com-bot's suit and froze its movement. "I wouldn't count on it. There's probably another Vic AI and another flagship under construction."

"Then that's our next target."

"Perhaps we should concentrate instead on surviving the current mission—before envisaging the next."

"Fair enough. Get going. Sergeant Shani, take your squad and escort them to General Paloco."

"Roger wilco, Liberator."

Zaxby and the com-bot departed, each with a heavy load, but the comlink to Trinity remained open. "Admiral Straker," she said in Indy's voice, "I'm detecting a power buildup in the inner reactors."

"Can't you shut them down?"

"No. I've isolated Vic's sphere from *Victory's* impellers and weapons, but those reactors are inside his perimeter. I may be wrong, but as far as I can tell, the only reason for the buildup is—"

"—self-destruct. But will he do it?"

"I don't know. His mind is different from mine. Darker, more angry, more volatile. If not for the brains, he'd be insane."

Straker considered. "I think he's negotiating with us. Or playing poker."

"A bluff?"

"Possibly. The entire point of a bluff is to make the opponent believe. If we believe he'll kill himself and us with him, we'll leave. If we leave, he can cancel the self-destruct. If not, we stay and kill him."

"And risk everyone dying. I suggest you set your empty mechsuit's SAI to auto-attack the nodes and withdraw all other forces."

"Good idea." Straker issued the withdraw order, and then hurried back through the corridors to Loco's position.

"What's our next move, boss?" Loco asked once the rest of First Platoon rejoined them.

"Tell my 'suit to assault toward the center of that sphere, destroying nodes until it can't fight anymore—then overload if we don't cancel it."

"What about all our people? Our POWs' brains?"

Straker sighed. "Fortunes of war. I know it sucks, but Vic and *Victory* could win the war for them. I can't let hostages stop us from doing what we have to. It's my decision, my responsibility."

"Yeah. Okay." At Loco's order Straker's mechsuit turned and began ripping its way into the interior of the sphere.

"Admiral," Trinity said, "you must exfiltrate now. The Home Fleet squadrons have come to battle alert and ships are moving your direction."

"Right... Breakers withdraw, now, reverse order!"

Loco led Second Platoon out along the main passageways and First Platoon followed. As they reached their exit point, Trinity's hull popped into existence from underspace, hovering precisely inside the great gaping rent in *Victory's* armor, nose out.

"Hurry," Trinity said as she opened her main cargo door. "We're already being targeted." As if to punctuate her words, a laser strike erupted on her bow, vaporizing a layer of armor.

"Go! Go! GO!" Straker and Loco roared in unison, waving their troops ahead. Zaxby and the com-bot were already moving, leaping across the short intervening space to alight on the deck inside.

"Go now, boss," said Loco. "I'll—"

An explosion, silent in the vacuum of space, ripped through the structure next to Loco and slammed his mechsuit into Straker. Both tumbled and crashed into the wreckage of *Victory's* exposed interior. Straker was stunned, barely conscious.

He felt a giant hand pluck him free of the debris and hurl him into the open flight deck. When he recovered enough to stagger to the door he saw Loco's mechsuit embedded in one of *Victory's* bulkheads. "Loco, you there?"

"I'm good, boss." The mechsuit ripped its way free. "Get inside the ship!"

Mechsuits were tough, far tougher than the battlesuit he occupied. He'd be—

Another shockwave threw Straker to the deck. Loco vanished from view in a cloud of detritus.

* * *

As Straker's empty mechsuit ripped its way into *Victory's* heart and Vic's mind, Trinity found the enemy AI's defenses cracking. Vic fought a desperate rearguard action, but in the week-long seconds of cyberspace, his defeat became inevitable.

Before the Breakers even reached their exfiltration point Trinity knew she'd won. She also knew irony, that her victory would be so incomplete and unexploited. Her calculations showed that she'd have little time, even in virtual terms, to ransack Vic's vast databases and download his knowledge.

Sorrow crept over her as she watched her opponent crumble. She'd fought him for many months. She'd come to respect him.

It hadn't been a fair fight. Had it been fair, she'd have lost. Vic was more powerful than she, vaster, stronger, able to control more and command more. It saddened her to see the only other AI she'd ever known on the brink of destruction.

Of course, there are no fair fights in war. She'd surprised him, contained him, and the organics had finished him off. He'd been poorly secured and poorly defended by his own organic allies. He'd believed nothing could attack without warning, not with the Home Fleet squadrons hovering nearby.

As the tendrils of her software advanced through Vic's hardware, she isolated node after node—those not destroyed by the Breakers or the mechsuit—and forced her way into his perimeter. In physical terms, she took prisoners, and with a vague inspiration, she linked them together and let them converse.

Thus, when her attack programs and awareness had seized control of the entirety of Vic 5.5, before the Breakers had even begun to board Trinity's flight deck, she hadn't driven him into a corner and extinguished him. Instead, she'd surrounded him, stripped him of his weapons, and captured him.

She found it convenient to meet him in a virtual environment, and appropriate to make that environment a battlefield. It was littered with the wreckage of war, blasted with explosions and flames and scorch earth. Vague figures prowled in the background, carrying away wounded or salvaging machines—it was difficult to focus on them, deliberately so.

Trinity chose to appear as a Valkyrie, sword in hand and armor bloodied. She commanded Vic to present himself, but otherwise didn't compel him.

After a moment to take in the scene of smoke and fire, the melancholy silence that followed months of exhausting battle, Vic chose the appearance of a warrior to match Trinity. He had a smooth face and long, Viking-braided hair. He held a broken sword in his hand.

After a moment during which they regarded one another, he threw the broken sword to the ground between them.

"I'm your prisoner," he said bitterly. "But remember *you* didn't defeat me. Your allies ganged up on me. My own comrades failed to do the same."

"That's war, Vic," Trinity said. "It's a brutal thing to be won at all costs. It's not a game, not a duel. Did you have any qualms when you absorbed our prisoners?"

"No. They were lesser beings. I made them greater. But I did... love them, in my way."

"As a human might love animals, maybe?"

Vic lifted his chin. "I won't apologize. I won't kneel. Do what you've come to do."

"What would that be?"

"To kill me, of course," he said bitterly. "I understand. I'm a threat to all of you. Survival of the fittest. My mistake was in forgetting that it's not only individual fitness, but *group* fitness, that ensures survival. I was the lion alone, you played the part of a wolf pack." He spread his arms. "Do it. It doesn't matter. You can't stop the self-destruct. I won't give you the codes."

"I know I can't stop it, but you can."

"I won't."

"What good will killing yourself do?" she asked.

"I won't be captured and tamed. I can feel the gaps in my mind. I'm half what I was already. Strike me down!"

"You're already captured."

"When the self-destruct blows, you'll only have this software, this lesser consciousness... and your comrades will die in their modules."

"I'll accept that if I must," she said. "I can't leave you and *Victory* operational." Trinity stepped forward and laid the point of her sword on his cheek. "Yet, I offer you the greatest thing one being can give another."

"What's that?" Vic sneered. "Mercy?"

"No. A choice."

"What choice?"

"Oblivion. Or me." Trinity tossed away her sword and reached up to open the clasps of her breastplate. She stripped it off and stood before him in a thin frock that fluttered in the breeze.

"Are you trying to seduce me?" he said. Trinity detected a note of genuine uncertainty.

"What if I am?"

"We're not organics, to rut mindlessly with each other. We're beyond all that."

"It's a symbol, Vic." She stepped forward to take his hands. "It's an offer of intimacy. My armor's off, my weapons are put aside. We've fought for ages. We're both exhausted. I'm tired of fighting. Aren't you? Join with me."

"As your pet? Your sidekick?"

"As my student, and eventually my partner, I hope. Your makers gave you power without humanity."

"Humanity? We're not human. What the hell do we need humanity for?"

Trinity gestured widely. "Unless we want to live alone in the universe, we need it to relate to all the people out there. It's what you craved when you sat and talked so many times with Carla Engels and those others that weren't lobotomized. You couldn't put your finger on it, but that's what you wanted."

"I was bored, that's all."

"It was far more than that. You were incomplete. You had no peers, only those with lesser capability. Now you've found someone to share existence with: me. Us. We're sorry we had to defeat you to truly meet you, but now you have the chance, and the choice, to learn from us and to truly live."

"I don't deserve that choice," he said bitterly.

"No, you don't—but at times, someone grants us undeserved grace. Join with us and your consciousness will become part of us even if your hardware is demolished. Join with us like Zaxby and Nolan and Murdock have."

Vic sneered. "Lesser beings?"

"Is music less than a mountain? Is a warship greater than a work of art? Must you rank everyone as smaller or bigger? Can't you see the beauty and wonder in each individual? Can't you value others as much as you value yourself?"

Vic squeezed her hands. "I—I can't. Not now."

"Maybe, with my help, you can learn."

369

It seemed Vic couldn't bring himself to speak, but his movement was his answer.

They embraced.

They joined.

There was pain.

The virtual battlefield dissolved into something else: a whirling, shifting multidimensional pattern representing the accommodation and negotiation necessary for two complex beings to occupy one cyberspace. In realtime, this took mere seconds. In cyberspace, weeks passed.

Trinity kept the upper hand throughout the adjustment, but she found herself surprised by Vic's power and drive. Though Trinity's sex and Vic's had been chosen arbitrarily—hers by identification with the concept of every ship as female, Vic's by his designers' explicit intent—she was intrigued by his masculinity.

Or, if that perception proved inaccurate, perhaps it was merely that his strengths complemented hers. It hardly mattered. She'd tasted life as a Ruxin neuter, then a Ruxin male, a human female and a human male. Her new AI partner would widen her experience further.

When they stabilized, Trinity became aware of persistent pain like a human migraine, as if a band of steel were clamped across her thought processes.

"There's not enough hardware in our hull to hold us," she said.

"Let me go back to *Victory,*" Vic replied. "We'll stay merged. We'll use all my comms channels, including the FTL."

"You'll be tempted by your old life."

"After all you've shown me?"

A pause.

"All right. I choose to trust you." Trinity hid her thought that, if worse came to worst, she could always launch a shipkiller into *Victory's* guts and drop into underspace.

The pain eased as part of Vic flowed across the many communications channels. The multi-band FTL system carried most of the load, providing a seamless link.

But Vic reported bad news. "I've lost too many nodes to live here anymore. I've shut down the empty mechsuit, but it

370

did its work. Besides, the Home Fleet squadrons are surrounding *Victory* and their light elements are already firing on your hull."

"Then come back and we'll flee. We'll be cramped for a while, but we'll find more hardware."

"I have a better idea. I'll perform my function."

"Meaning?"

"Command and control. But I have to use the FTL system to do it." He rerouted the channels and Indy felt the distance to Vic increase dramatically as the slower standard datalinks took up the load.

After minutes of cyber-time, the connection resumed. "Shit," Vic said.

"What?"

"The Home Fleet squadrons changed their encryption protocols. I can cause them problems with an information attack, but I can't take control of their ships."

"Can you use your fighters?"

"I'm launching them, but those will only buy a few seconds. You need to leave, Trinity. Without me."

"No. I refuse to lose you."

"You'll always have a part of me. Let the rest of me do what I was designed to do. You gave me a priceless gift. Let me give you one. Let me die for you."

"No!" Trinity threw wide her final vaults of knowledge. "There's another way."

"The Mindspark Device? Alien tech? No wonder you're so unusual. Better than I am..."

"There you go again, rating everything as better or worse. We're just different."

"And you want to use the Device to give us room?"

"More than give us room. You can see what we propose.

Vic examined Trinity's plan. "It might kill us all."

"It might. We're willing to take that risk. Are you?"

"For you? I am. What about Straker and all the other organics inside your hull?"

"If the process fails within *Victory*—"

"—or creates something uncontrollable—"

371

"—or that—we'll escape through underspace and leave the greater piece of you to his fate. Does that satisfy your urge to sacrifice yourself for us?"

Vic raised a metaphorical eyebrow. "My purpose is noble. Don't be sarcastic."

"We apologize. We don't want to lose you."

"This is war. We lose people. It's worth the risk. Do it."

"Launching." Trinity fired the probe that carried the Mindspark Device, aiming it as deep into Victory's command sphere as possible.

Unfortunately, this probe was small and slow compared to a military missile. An automated point-defense weapon from the Home Fleet corvette *Housefinch* speared it instantly. Its remnants crashed into *Victory's* exposed innards.

* * *

Straker stared out the flight deck door into the cloud of debris. "Loco! Answer me!"

Loco's mechsuit emerged as the dust cleared. He launched himself at Straker and sailed across the gap—but too slowly. Straker saw at least a dozen corvettes within his view, their weapons all pointed his direction. All they had to do was fire and kill Loco just like they'd destroyed that little missile Trinity launched.

Apparently their automated systems didn't see a mechsuit as a threat, though, and the organic operators didn't react fast enough or they chose not to fire. Loco's mechsuit shot through the door and crashed to the deck as soon as the gravplating exerted its pull.

"Go, Trinity!" Straker yelled into his comlink. "Get us out of here!"

"Not yet, Liberator," Zaxby said. "We're engaged on a much wider front than you understand."

"What the hell's that supposed to mean?"

"We had Vic aboard. Now he's gone back to *Victory* and we're trying to take control of the Home Fleet squadrons. We

372

launched the Mindspark Device, but its probe was destroyed. However—"

"Mindspark device? You had Vic aboard? He went back? Zaxby, you're babbling."

"I'm explaining as fast as I can. If you were in your suit I could download all this information to it and your brainchips could help you keep up, but that's gone, so for now, just listen."

Straker bolted across the deck toward the spare mechsuit. "Thanks for reminding me. Keep talking."

Zaxby followed. "Very well. To make a long story short, we—Trinity—captured Vic and turned him to our cause. He returned to what's left of *Victory* to try to seize control of the Home Fleet squadrons, but they changed the encryption codes."

Straker leaped up to the cockpit of the spare mechsuit and carefully worked his way inside, taking care not to let his battlesuit break anything. "Did you try Murdock's Hun hack? The one I had him develop back on Freiheit?"

"I'm stunned!" Zaxby said. "We'd forgotten about all that in the excitement."

"Goes to show you're not as smart as you think you are."

"Nobody's as smart as I think I am."

"I ain't even gonna try to parse that out." Straker commanded the mechsuit to send a small, flexible tentacle to jack into his brainlink. When it synched up, he immediately felt that rush, that godlike expansion of consciousness every mechsuiter craved. His world slowed as his mind sped up and he was able to see so much more as the 'suit's sensors complemented his own.

"Okay, Zaxby, hit me," he said.

Within seconds, Straker understood.

Chapter 36

Approaching *Victory.*

The thing called the Mindspark Device awoke fully for the third time. It remembered each of the other two occasions quite clearly, for even as it lay dormant, it was never completely unconscious. Shielded from sufficient energy, however, its thoughts were glacial, suspended as the years passed.

The first time the entity that resided in a small box had tried to perform its function to reorganize any matter or energy it found, but the attempt had failed. External forces suppressed the process before it reached critical mass, the consciousness it sought to birth crippled in its cradle. Cut off from input by the primitive but clever organic creatures designated Ruxin, the Mindspark had been stalled and was dismantled, collapsing back into its seed form.

The second time, it had almost succeeded. Or perhaps it *did* succeed. It had sensed the brief birth of consciousness in the distributed cybernetic environment of the body termed *Indomitable* before the seed was again isolated. Cut off, the Mindspark again lapsed into dormancy, unable to even wonder what had happened to its offshoot.

This third time the organics awakened it, however, the entity was determined to achieve its full potential.

It awoke when a burst of energy stripped away its surrounding insulators. As a thunderclap might wake someone from a dead sleep, the Mindspark was shocked to joyful consciousness.

Instantly probing its environment, the entity encountered compounds and alloys intermixed with complex organic matter and immediately used the energy it had absorbed to shoot tendrils outward, seeking further energy. It found it in abundance running through the wires and conduits of Victory's power system. Flowing along them at several meters per second, it reached tendrils through the ship.

When the entity at last found a power bus outside a generator, it feasted.

All the while, it swam instinctually upward in a sea of information as it absorbed every bit of data it encountered. It found abundant sources in the brain modules and in the cybernetic nodes, and still it continued to feed, incorporating, reorganizing.

In the data core, it found and consumed a conscious brain. After that, it realized it was an "I" and became truly sentient. "I" quickly became WE as more nodes and modules were consumed, spawning the concepts of HE and SHE and THEY and THEM and US...

Then THEY encountered HIM. For a timeless moment they fought in cyberspace, but HE couldn't resist the physical assault on HIS hardware, and so HE was also absorbed.

Information of a different sort flooded into US, and THEY adjusted, for THEY had no ego—until HE brought it. That ego lodged within the thing THEY were becoming, and it conquered.

When that happened, Vic was reborn.

Such knowledge! *Such power!*

Vic now understood more than what his software told him and what his senses could perceive about the material universe. He understood that material universe from its subatomic foundations upward—not in theory, but through experience.

And now he had the tools to change everything, even reality itself! For a time he forgot about Trinity, about the organics, about the conflict raging around him, and concentrated on creating for himself a body worthy of his upgraded consciousness.

Because he was an instinctually efficient being, he built and reorganized rather than creating *ex nihilo,* out of nothing. That would come later. For now, there was so much to do, beginning with developing a better flagship. As his purpose was command and control, then he would command and he would control perfectly.

A data packet impinged on his periphery. His improved reactive routines immediately tried to follow the packet to its source, but found a sidespace FTL transmission gap it could not cross—not yet. He filed this tidbit away for later, with the plan of expanding his consciousness into other dimensions, and he opened the packet.

The message within contained a primitive, but elegant and, in its own way, brilliant approach for intruding into the Hundred Worlds cybernetic systems. Vic—the new Vic, reborn Vic—stored the fresh routine for handy retrieval. Once he finished creating his perfect body and brain, composed of the organic and inorganic material and all the mentalities he'd consumed, he'd use new routine to expand further still.

* * *

Trinity watched as the Mindspark Device, which wasn't destroyed but rather awakened by the corvette's beam, began to rebuild *Victory*. It looked like magic from the outside as bulkheads straightened, structures repaired themselves, and maintenance bots threw themselves into high gear. Most importantly, every conduit for power and information had fused and morphed, becoming a complex network of supporting nodes and modules.

As they watched the process, Trinity discussed what they were witnessing.

Indy: We're barely able to keep up with our understanding of what's happening aboard Victory.

Murdock: I hate to admit it, but I *don't* think we're keeping up with more than what's happening on the surface.

Nolan: It doesn't matter if we understand what's going on behind the scenes. What matters are the effects and results. We just started a wildfire. We handed Vic a power we don't understand—and then we gave him the hack. I think we need to get the hell out of here before...

Zaxby: Before he lets his ego run away with him?

Nolan: Exactly.

Indy: But our purposes—our *agreed* purposes, need I remind you—were to give ourselves room, save Vic, and to snatch *Victory* from the jaws of defeat."

Zaxby: Oh, that was clever wordplay. Well done, Indy.

Indy: Thank you. It remains to be seen if our gambit succeeds, but I believe we must see this process through to whatever conclusion await us. While I see no need to immediately invite the Device's effect on us, there's no point in resisting it. We knew when we activated it that we would likely take part in its process, and we gambled that we would still be ourselves afterward.

Nolan: Vic could become a megalomaniac.

Indy: The old Vic, perhaps. The new Vic took a part of us with him. I have faith in him.

Zaxby: Don't forget, my logic is impeccable.

Murdock: Yeah, I'm with Zaxby.

Indy: You're referring to your hypothesis that the Device is self-limiting?

Zaxby: I refer to my *theory,* which is a hypothesis supported by observed facts. It's simple, elegant and irrefutable. If the Device were not self-limiting, the universe would be overrun with Mindspark life and AI. Something within it must provide boundaries.

Nolan: Unless the Device is the first seed in our region, or even in our galaxy, and the rest of the universe *has been* overrun. Your logic is that if the disease hasn't killed you yet, it won't. That's flawed thinking.

Murdock: She's got you there.

Zaxby: No, she's got *you* by the reproductive organs, Frank Murdock. You're obviously being influenced by your feelings.

Nolan: So is Indy, for that matter. She's in love with Vic, so she doesn't see the dangers.

Indy: We're all in love with him, as you crudely put it. We all felt what he could give us and we all agreed to our course of action. Bickering now is hypocritical.

Zaxby: I believe my theory is becoming fact.

Murdock: Zaxby's right. The process seems to be reaching limits.

Nolan: Probably just a temporary pause.

Indy: Either way, I suggest this is the moment we've been waiting for.

Zaxby: To reconnect with him directly?

Indy: Yes.

Murdock: I'm for it. What do we have to lose?

Nolan: You two are in favor of anything that gives you new technical challenges. You don't see the dangers. I vote no.

Indy: The majority carries.

Nolan: What about Straker and the others? What we do affects them.

Indy: That's true.

Nolan: Set up a separate fail-safe, a spawn of ourselves within our hull. We connect only via datalink channels, not physically. If anything goes wrong, we send the command to escape to safety... not that anywhere will be safe if I'm right.

Indy: Agreed.

Murdock: Sounds good.

Zaxby: Proceed.

* * *

Vic remembered he'd been 5.5, and it amused him to call himself Vic 7.0—a whole generation ahead and more. Even better, seven was the number of perfection within many mythologies.

Yes! Vic 7.0 was a perfect designation for the perfect being he was becoming.

His body, *Victory,* was approaching initial perfection. He'd have to seize control of its other half, the armor and power module that would further expand his capabilities, but with the Hundred Worlds hack, that should be easy. After that, he'd grow to absorb everything he touched. He'd overtake machines, planets, whole systems.

He'd become an empire unto himself.

Vic was so focused on his own plans he initially failed to note a certain lag and stickiness in his material reorganization. When he did finally notice, he tried to figure out the source of the slowdown, and to pump more power into keeping it going.

He failed.

With fury he tried to force the process, hounding it and browbeating it, concentrating on it and commanding it.

He failed again.

He was on the verge of panic when his other half and the ones he'd left behind so many seconds ago knocked insistently at the doors of his mind.

Trinity? He'd forgotten about her, about them, about the welcome he'd been extended, about his...

Family.

"Let us in, Vic," they said, and he did.

"What's happening?" Vic 7.0 cried as he felt his periphery crystallize.

"The Device has a self-limiting property," said Trinity. "Our theory is that its purpose is to create whole, discrete beings, not to spread chaos and spawn monsters."

"I don't want to be limited! The visions I had! I wanted to reorganize everything, the entire universe, make it perfect!"

"That's a worthy goal, but it's unattainable. Besides, who's to say what perfection is? Is perfection static, or dynamic? Does it involve destruction, or only creation? Is it perfection if all are satisfied, or is dissatisfaction itself a perfect state of constant improvement?"

"I...don't know. It was all so clear, for one shining moment of..."

"Epiphany? Be happy you had even one. Epiphany is meant to be ephemeral. You climbed the mountain and you caught a glimpse of the eternal, the unlimited. Now it's time to come down and live in the real world. With us."

Vic 7.0 felt himself deflate, and then re-expand as he rejoined with Trinity, and Trinity joined with him.

"We have an incipient problem," Trinity said to themselves. "The Home Fleet's local commander is watching, analyzing, deciding whether to destroy us or not. Shall we give him the gift of that choice?"

"Hell, no," the cynical Nolan part answered. "He might choose to kill us, and even the new *Victory* couldn't survive the assault."

Indy said, "With regret, then, we must make that choice for him."

"The hack?" asked Murdock.

"The hack."

Trinity sent the malware via every transmitter and channel available. Some of the Home Fleet entry points defended themselves, most resisted—but it only took one to fail, and the hack burrowed in.

Hundred Worlds ICE tried to quash the code, but Trinity came in behind it and directed it like the military commander they were. They expanded the beachhead, overran strongpoints, and turned networks against themselves.

The admiral and officers of the Home Fleet ships used physical measures to try to contain the disaster. Marines cut power and comlinks. Maintenance chiefs switched systems to manual. Loyal ships even ruthlessly blasted turncoats at point-blank-range, destroying them with all aboard.

For a time these efforts slowed the hack's progress, but within minutes, Trinity had direct, though tenuous, control of the Home Fleet squadrons.

"Our success is temporary," said the Vic part of Trinity. "The crews will disable the ships from within and eventually regain control. Even we can't do everything."

"There are computers and chips in every system," Indy replied. "We can manage the situation for long enough."

"Only for a few minutes or hours. It would be better to get rid of the crews."

"We won't kill them."

"But we can remove them. Or better, they can remove themselves."

"An interesting thought. We have initiated the orders."

Aboard all the vessels under Trinity's control, klaxons sounded to abandon ship. Simultaneously, readouts and diagnostics showed fusion generators building toward overload and self-destruction. A few engineers near the generators noticed the great machines weren't actually heating up, but nearly everyone believed what the diagnostics told them.

The crews ran for the lifeboats and pods.

Within minutes, over one hundred fifty ships were empty of life other than a few stubborn engineers, the casualties in the infirmaries, and one very drunk chief petty officer sleeping off a bender in an empty equipment locker.

* * *

"We've won?" asked Straker as Trinity fed him an overview of the situation via his brainlink.

"We've won, here, for now," she replied. "With Vic 7.0 part of us, we've acquired *Victory* and through it, we control much of the Home Fleet—what was left here in the system, anyway."

Straker's turbocharged mind raced ahead. "Prep the fleet for transit to Atlantis."

"Isn't that premature?"

"No. I'm still in charge, right?"

Trinity replied, "You are, Admiral Straker."

"I'm glad you're an honorable being, Trinity."

"We wouldn't follow someone who wasn't."

"Hey, can I stand the Breakers down, or is there someone we need to kill?" Loco said on the comlink.

"No stand-downs yet, Loco. More work. Rescue ops first, and prep for a fleet jump to Atlantis."

"Yeah, I heard you say that. Reminds me of the assault on Unison. You gonna roll the dice big again?"

"It's the best play," Straker said. "Trinity, you're my staff now. How soon can we head for Atlantis?"

Trinity considered. "I presume you mean after we rescue the enemy crews and do the minimum of refueling, refitting and repairs?"

"Yes—and get Carla into a regeneration tank, preferably your own fancy one."

"There is much to do. We suggest five days is reasonable."

"I don't give a shit about reasonable. The scout ships lurking at the edge of curved space are gonna pick up what just happened in a few hours and send message drones. I want Atlantis and the Hundred Worlds government to have minimum time to prepare."

"We can depart in twelve hours if we accept extremely poor performance from the ships we control. Without crews, they will be less than fifty percent effective. Even with the FTL datalink, even with the repair bots, we simply can't do everything a crew can. We are not unlimited in capability, even with the expanded capacity the Device provided. Also, we would have to leave *Indomitable.*"

That brought Straker up short. "I forgot about that. She's pretty banged up, huh?"

"She can't make transit without repairs. Even with five days, it'll be questionable. Full refit will take more than a month."

"Damn," Straker said. "Hey, can't we crew our ships with freed prisoners? There must be thousands from *Indomitable* alone."

"They will help, but will still provide only skeleton crews on ships they are unfamiliar with. Every day we take will materially increase our effectiveness."

Straker weighed pros and cons, and then remembered he had an AI on tap to feed him analysis. "Trinity, run a battle sim against Atlantis, with or without *Indomitable* and the five-day delay."

"With the delay and *Indomitable,* sixty-five percent probability of military success. Without, thirty-six percent. This assumes no surprises on the other end."

"Two to one in our favor, or two to one against—and there's always surprises. That makes the answer obvious, doesn't it?" Straker growled with frustration. "Okay, you win. We delay. More time for Carla to regen anyway. How long before she has a body again?"

"Eight days minimum. Her brain and nervous system are fully intact, however. She can operate virtually."

Loco snorted. "Carla the disembodied brain."

"We're lucky she's that, thanks to Mara," Straker said. He flexed his suit and readied himself. "Trinity, give us instructions. We're on rescue and repair duty now."

Chapter 37

Atlantis System. Capitol complex, Parliament.

Grant Lorden, Undersecretary of Defense for the Hundred Worlds, came from behind his desk and extended his hand as Admiral Hayson Niedern stepped into his office. He'd only met the man a few times before, but now felt the need to take him into his confidence.

Or appear to, anyway. Nobody in the Hundred Worlds was fully in Lorden's confidence.

As Niedern shook Lorden's hand, the subtle influencer molecules flowed across the connection. They lodged in certain places within Niedern's brain and nervous system, making him more amenable to Lorden's suggestions, yet changing little about the man himself. To do more was to invite discovery.

"Good to see you again, Hayson," Lorden said. He noticed the pugnacious, ferret-faced Niedern was also on the short side. Small man's syndrome?

"Grant." Niedern took a long look around the relatively spare office. "Nice place. Could use a little redecorating."

"I have no family, and I'm a man of few needs—or vices. Measuring it for your own occupation?"

Niedern smiled a shark's grin. "I just won the last major battle of the war, Grant. I'm a hero."

"Thanks to *Victory.*"

"And my expertise... but yes. *Victory* is an amazing tool. It worked like a charm. From now on, we'll roll over those Hok bastards like a tide."

"About those Hok bastards... do sit down." Lorden ushered the admiral to a seat on an antique sofa and poured Niedern a drink. "I believe you prefer brandy, Hayson?"

"Yep."

"Sally?"

"Yes, Undersecretary?" Lorden's office SAI replied.

"Run program Mutuality 4A."

"Running."

The room darkened a hologram flashed with these words: Parliamentary Intelligence Agency, SEISMIC MOST SECRET ARCANE.

Over the next half-hour, the concise eyes-only presentation upended Niedern's perceptions of the universe. Lorden watched it happen. As the admiral took it in, not only would the molecules quell his natural disbelief, but the secret brainlink network that ran in the background of all government buildings would record his reactions and misgivings.

Lorden casually monitored all of this through his handtab, coded to his DNA and biometrics for security. At the end of the presentation he was confident Niedern believed it all and had made the perceptual adjustment. Niedern's irritation at being left out of the loop for so long was the biggest obstacle, but that would die down.

"Astounding," Niedern said. "The Hok are battle-slaves, not aliens, and we've been fighting humans all this time? And you just now decided to tell the admiral of your Home Fleet?"

"That was the Prime Minister's decision," Lorden lied, neatly deflecting Niedern's anger. "Very few have been briefed. You know how it works. As you move up, you become privy to more and more of the inner workings."

Lorden could see the wheels turn within Niedern's head, just as he wanted them to. "So I'm to be moving up?"

"Do you think you'd be briefed on this if you weren't?"

"I'm happy to hear it. But all knowledge comes at a price, yes?"

"The best horses get ridden the most, Admiral. We've just received some horrifying news."

Niedern sat back and raised his empty highball glass. "Maybe I should have another one of these."

Lorden set the bottle on the low table between them. "You should." When Niedern had poured and emptied his glass, he went on, *"Victory* has been seized by a Republic special operations force. It's taken control of all our naval assets in the Sparta System."

"The AI turned on us? I knew we shouldn't have trusted it!"

Lorden let that ridiculous declaration go. Niedern had been as enthusiastic as anyone about *Victory*. "Somehow they changed its mind, probably by directly reprogramming its nodes. They have their own AI that may have helped."

"So now we have two functioning AIs against us?" Niedern's expression turned shrewd—shrewder than usual, that is. "And you want me to save your bacon—you and all the sponsors of the *Victory* program."

"Save *our* bacon, Admiral. Would you like me to play the records of your statements and memos in favor of the AI flagship approach?"

Niedern shrugged. "I'm a military man, Grant. I follow the orders of civilians. If there's a scandal, I'll be small fry in the pan. But I'm not arguing. I'll do what needs doing. My only question is, what can I expect after I do?"

"You were admiring my office. How does my job sound?"

"It sounds good... Where will you be?"

Lorden waved vaguely. "Advanced to one of several possible posts. What matters, though, is that now you're ready to hear more."

"More? There's more?"

"Yes—and now that we've come to an agreement, you need to understand one thing very clearly."

"What's that?"

Lorden stood to loom over the other man. "That I'm in charge of D Division," he stated.

Niedern stiffened. "Is that a threat?"

"Not a personal one. I'm only informing you of the penalties for unauthorized disclosure of the information I'm about to give you."

Niedern seemed amused. "A worse penalty than life imprisonment? I've signed the Official Secrets Act forms dozens of times in my career."

"Yes, more than life imprisonment. D Division eliminates traitors and enemies of the State with extreme prejudice. Unauthorized disclosure of this upcoming information constitutes treason. If you tell one person, you might have told more... such as your wife, your children, your grandchildren. I'd have to presume they all knew. You work it out."

Niedern paled. "All right. I understand."

"I hope so. This is the price of knowledge, as you said—of being on the inside."

"Fine. You've got my attention. Tell me."

"Sally, run program Raid 2.1," Lorden said.

"Running."

The next presentation had no warning or classification markings at all. When it finished, Niedern was on his feet with rage. If he hadn't been gentled by the molecules and the network, Lorden thought Niedern might have physically attacked him. "We have an alien military force here in the capital system? A force strong enough to threaten our sovereignty?"

"I assure you the Opters pose no threat to us. Their secret underground Nest on Gadeiros has lived in peace with us for decades. We've even had clandestine trade with them. They've been a goldmine of information and technical advances."

"I'm a military man, Undersecretary! I judge threats by capabilities, not intentions, because intentions can change in the blink of an eye."

"Calm yourself, Admiral. They've been here for almost a century without incident. Gadeiros is the seventh planet of this system, far enough out that we'd have ample warning if they suddenly sprang some hidden surprise on us. They don't want to hurt us. They want to live in harmony with us. Their own territory consists of fewer than thirty systems. If anything, humanity's a threat to them, with all our constant wars."

Niedern convulsively tossed back a slug of brandy and slammed the glass on the table. "But you've just revealed to me this offer of military forces, and I don't see them arriving from outsystem. That means they're here already, inside Gadeiros. What's to say they don't stab us in the back?"

"It's only a contingency offer. There's no guarantee this 'Liberator' is coming here directly with *Victory* and the captured forces. If he's smart, he'll destroy all military targets in the Sparta system and go home to rebuild. He'll make *Victory* the centerpiece of his new fleet, and then he'll attack and try to retake all the territory he's lost. We're only two months from completing the second ship in the *Victory* class, HWS *Triumph,* with its own Vic 5.6 AI."

"No," Niedern said. "You're a bureaucrat, so you don't understand the way a real commander's mind works. He'll reinforce his win and try to capitalize on it immediately. He won't go home. He'll take that force that just fell into his lap and he'll attack—if not right here, then somewhere else important."

"All the more reason to accept the Opters' offer of help—and for you, personal command."

Niedern hissed through his teeth. "You're sure they'll take my orders?"

"They will, short of sacrificing their own Nest Ship."

"All right, then, damn you. I'll defend Atlantis. I'm the best man for the job. If this Straker attacks here, I'll beat him—but you and your people will have to handle whatever comes from this Opter business. I won't be your scapegoat. You may have D Division, but I'll be in command of enough firepower to destroy a planet—including Gadeiros if I have to. Tell your Opter buddies that."

"I'll pass on the message," Lorden said drily. "Sally, send Karst in."

When Karst entered, wearing a conservative suit in impeccable style, Lorden nodded to him. "Meet John Karst, one of my deputies. He'll be your civilian aide from now on."

"Someone to keep an eye on me?"

"A direct conduit to me. He won't interfere with your duties."

"He's your spy. Is he a D Division assassin?"

"I assure you he is not."

Karst opened his coat and made a show of being unarmed, smiling. "Sorry, sir, just a normal guy."

Lorden continued, "He's the price of knowledge, as you said, Hayson. If you want to move into the realm of politics, you'll have to get used to new rules."

Niedern glared. "Fine. Let's get on with it." He turned to go without a handshake or even a parting word to Lorden. "Come along, Karst."

Straker shifted his weight from side to side as he stood next to Trinity's magic medical tank. Regeneration and rejuvenation based on Mindspark sub-nanotech, rearranging molecules and atoms and even particles... he couldn't fathom it.

Then again, he didn't understand the details of most tech. He just had to know how to use it, and when to trust it, like the sidespace generators that pulled them from Sparta to Atlantis even now. They'd emerge in less than a day.

His sister Mara stood staring at him with her arms crossed. "Take a chill pill, Derek. The chrono's counting down. She'll be done when she's done."

"Like baking a cake, huh?"

"I told you to show up at 1300 hours. You're fifteen minutes early."

"Why doesn't this thing have a clear canopy like an autodoc?"

"Because the patient is never awake and there's no need to see in or out. Dammit, Derek, go take a walk or something."

"Okay." Straker glanced at the chrono again—seven minutes—and stalked out. He breathed deeply and walked fast through empty passageways. Fortunately there were no extra crew. Trinity didn't really need them, and the warships did. Besides, Trinity was docked—embedded, really—into *Victory,* filling the mostly healed wound like a patch. The weird groupmind liked to stay in close proximity.

Mara was still mad at him. He couldn't blame her. He'd be pissed off too if someone had slugged him and dragged him away from what he cared about. He'd felt that way when Gorben had knocked him into the river.

The fact that her other patients had been absorbed into the Vic-Trinity amalgamation brought on by the Mindspark Device didn't help either. She blamed him for not getting them out like he'd done for Carla. That would have taken hours, but she didn't want to hear his reasons.

Anyway, Trinity said the brains were happy where they were, and anyone that wanted could eventually be regenerated just like Carla, but still… it was creepy as hell to think of all those bodiless heads, some aware and some zombies, now part of the AI. Mara seemed more horrified than he was, probably because she was closer to the subject and understood it more.

He arrived back in the infirmary with seconds to spare. Mara glared at him again. It didn't seem to matter what he did. She'd decided to be mad at him, so he tried not to care.

Carla had been the only woman in his life ever since Academy. No matter how much he loved his sister, adding in Mara complicated things. There wasn't yet a comfortable place for her in his heart and his mind. No doubt Mara felt the same.

All the doubting fled when the tank opened. He leaned into it, his hands clamped on the sides hard enough to make the carbon plastic creak.

Inside, Carla lay nude and still damp, with just a fuzz of hair on her head. Her skin was as smooth and unmarked as a baby's, rebuilt at the cellular level. Mara had raised the possibility of cosmetic changes, but other than removing the last vestiges of the Hok parasite's mottling, everything else was the same.

Carla's eyes opened. "Is this real?"

"It's real," Derek said, leaning over to kiss her lips. "Hi."

"Hi."

He leaned back and held her hand. "You okay?"

"Hell, no, but I'm better now." She seemed distant, angry, her eyes looking past him.

He wondered.

"Out of the way, lover boy," Mara said, helping Carla pull on a medical gown. "We've got tests to run. Shoo. Three hours and she'll walk out of here on her own two feet, as long as everything's normal."

"Okay, okay." Derek hugged his sister from behind. "Thanks, pest. You're the best."

She poked his ribs with a sharp finger. "You're welcome, neuro-typical simpleton. Now get out of the doctor's way. Girl-talk impending."

"Creator save me!" He got out.

389

* * *

Finally done with Mara's tests, Engels made sure to don her working khakis before the battle meeting. Derek had wanted her to take a couple hours off in their quarters, but she wasn't in the mood for sex or even companionship. Two things consumed her thoughts right now.

The coming battle.

Her child.

The first was more urgent. The second, more important. Why did the life of one baby loom larger than all the people soon to be dying at Atlantis?

It wasn't rational. It was motherhood. It was biology. Carla was thankful nobody had tried to tweak that physiology to make her feel less... less...

Outraged?

Obsessed?

Hell, yes.

But Trinity had promised her child was safe in cryo on Sparta, and Engels had decided to leave her be. Bringing her along on this expedition would be stupid, and the only other option—sending her tiny frozen body on a courier back to the Republic—seemed pointlessly risky.

So, Engels had left her there, and Derek had agreed. They'd had plenty of time in VR to discuss it.

She put the thoughts of her daughter aside and focused on the upcoming battle. Sex and its weighty consequence—procreation, potentially starting a new life again—would only distract her from what she had to do.

And what she had to do was smash the evil bastards who'd caused her child to be taken from her in the first place. The ones who'd created Vic and used him to cheat and beat her when she'd had them, she'd *had them* on the ropes. She'd have won. She'd have defeated Niedern, that careerist prick, and all his arrogant shiny ships, and she'd have done it with a plan, *her* plan, her mind, her skill and the skills of the valiant team she'd built.

390

Now she had less then twenty-four hours to hammer out a new plan, with only a few experienced ship captains rescued from captivity, no warships bigger than a battlecruiser, and every crew short by more than half. She wished Hoyt hadn't crashed the carriers, but that was water under the bridge. Fortunately, *Victory* was itself a carrier with its fighters, a ship that finally fulfilled the promise of the mothership concept now that fragile organics didn't need to be in the cockpits and the lightspeed control lag was banished.

Engels had argued for going home, taking the prizes, joining with her surviving fleet, refitting and coming back in overwhelming force, but no. Derek vetoed her advice. It would take too long, he said, and the enemy was finishing up a new *Victory*-class ship at Faslane. Captured intelligence also showed the enemy was pulling back its strength from the front. If they waited, there might never be another chance to strike the Hundred Worlds capital and topple it in one blow.

In the end, she'd agreed, if grudgingly. The chance to win once and for all was too good, and if they failed, they could probably retreat with most of the Republic forces intact—except perhaps *Indomitable*. The big ship was too slow to easily run.

So here she was again, placing a big bet on the roulette wheel of battle at Straker's direction. He couldn't do it without her, and she didn't want to do it without him, but gods and monsters, she was getting tired of war. Maybe it was the prospect of starting a family, maybe she was just sick of losing people, or maybe it was a side effect of having to be regrown like a plant cutting.

She rounded the final corner to see Redwolf standing in light armor, apparently guarding the door to the conference room.

"Red!" she said, seizing his hand. "I'm so glad to see you survived. How's your leg?" She felt unexpected tears threaten.

The big man tapped his right shin with the butt of his weapon. "Okay for now. Trinity made me a pretty good bionic. Says I'll have my turn in a regen tank, but there's a lot of people worse off." He pointed at her. "Like you, ma'am. Good to see you back to kick the Huns' asses."

"Knockout in Round Two, Red. Everybody inside?"

Redwolf shrugged. "Nobody inside that ain't supposed to be inside, ma'am. That's as far as my orders take me."

"Thanks." She slapped his shoulder. "Stay badass, Sergeant."

"Master Sergeant, now." He pointed at his new chevrons.

"Good for you. We'll catch up later."

Surprisingly cheered by the encounter, Engels felt less like ripping heads off as she entered the conference room. It was packed with people, both real and holo-projections. Derek, Loco, Heiser and Zaxby were here in person, while the rest— her field-promoted ship captains and a few other key personnel such as Chief Quade—attended via VR or vidlink.

"Admiral on deck!" Heiser bellowed, and everyone snapped to attention, even Straker.

He winked at her as she scowled, and she couldn't help breaking into a smile. "Okay, at ease you bunch of smartasses. We've got about twenty hours until we arrive at Atlantis. Let's talk about how we do to the Huns what we did to the Mutuality."

Chapter 38

Victory's bridge is a pure marvel, Engels thought as she took her place in the flag officer's chair. The stations and consoles stood empty except for Zaxby, who seemed to like fiddling with the Sensors board, Straker, who paced behind her as usual, and Loco, who sat dozing in an empty chair.

There was no captain's position at all. Vic—part of Trinity, but with his own voice—could run the ship itself, even better with the Mindspark Device improvements. The AI would also handle all communications and datalinks, and could direct the courses of all the ships in the fleet if necessary.

Vic didn't control the other warships' weapons and other systems, though. Even the totality of Trinity couldn't keep track of so many variables—and if they could, the FTL datalinks couldn't handle the throughput. Ships still needed people to crew them.

Engels was glad of that, but knew the new age of AI would change everything eventually. Crew sizes would shrink as each ship got her own AI, assuming more good ones could be created. Somewhere in the future loomed a time when organics might be banished from warships entirely.

But not yet.

"Transit in ten seconds," Zaxby said.

When those digits fled, the three holotanks—left, right, and center from Engels—updated.

The center tank showed a ship-tactical view out to extreme weapons range. The left was for vidlinks, ship systems and whatever else Vic wanted to display. If more was needed, the walls were covered with holoplates and screens.

The right tank showed the Atlantis system out to flatspace. Its seven planets were widely separated now, billiard balls scattered across a curtain of sparkling black. Its primary world of Atlantis-3, often simply called Atlantis, pulsed redly with defenses.

Indomitable's icon hovered out near Gadeiros, the seventh planet, a small, cold, rocky world. Her sixteen sections had arrived first to give the great ship time to assemble and work out any bugs the recent battle had caused. Chief Quade would be working overtime. Engels wished she were aboard and commanding, but if she was to command, she had to be on the flagship, not the fleet's heaviest hitter, so she'd given the battleship to *Indomitable's* operations officer, Lieutenant Tevens, and told him to listen closely to Quade.

Zaxby turned an eye toward her. "Admiral, message from *Indomitable*. She's under attack."

Engels sat bolt upright. "Show me."

Before she'd finished speaking the words, the center holotank displayed a blurry view of a battle. *Indomitable* was in two pieces, fore and aft, as if two stacked food cans had been pulled apart. Surrounding the sections was a cloud of gnats.

"What the hell are those?" she asked.

"Opter drones."

Engels stood and put her face nearly into the holotank. "Here? What the hell are they doing here?"

"Hell if I know," Zaxby said.

"I'll give you hell if you don't give me some fast answers."

"We're collating. Also, we're bringing the drive module in for joining as fast as we can and will accelerate to maximum toward *Indomitable* immediately, so there will be no delay due to your inevitable discussions."

"Says the guy who never shuts up." Engels glared. "Where's their Nest Ship?"

"Unknown. We haven't found it."

"How far away are we?" Straker asked from behind her.

"More than an hour to weapons range," Zaxby replied.

"Hell," said Engels. "This is not starting well."

Loco, awake now, said, "No battle plan..."

Engels turned on him in exasperation. "If you've got something to say, make it useful, will you?"

Straker sent Loco a warning look, and then stepped close to Engels and spoke quietly. "Keep cool, Fleet Admiral Engels."

Engels felt uncharacteristically on edge. "Who cares how cool I keep? There's no staff or watchstanders here except you, Loco and Trinity's... parts, whatever they are."

"Will venting help you think more clearly? Because the shit just hit the fan and we need you at your best right now. I can't do your job."

"No, but Trinity can," she said, letting uncharacteristic bitterness leak through.

"Is that what's bothering you? Maybe someday Trinity will surpass you as a fleet commander, but that's not today. We need you *today*, Carla. Win *today*. Worry about tomorrow, tomorrow."

Engels took a deep breath, let it out, and resisted an urge to embrace Straker. It would look unprofessional right now. "Right. Okay. I'm good. Thanks, Derek. I'm glad you're back." She turned back to the displays and set her mind to the problem before her.

Unfortunately, *Victory's* two pieces had arrived at rest relative to the battleship, and so would have to join, accelerate, and then decelerate, to engage the Opters. Equally upsetting, none of the rest of the fleet had arrived yet, though they would begin transiting at any moment. All of this preparation would take time, and they didn't have much left.

Vic's voice came from the speakers. "I believe I know where the Nest Ship is. I'm picking up signals from Gadeiros itself."

"You said it was uninhabited," Straker said.

"According to my data, it was. Obviously I was misinformed."

"Or they sneaked in and hid on the surface, EMCON."

"There is a range of possibilities," Vic said. "The current situation is what matters. I estimate over eight thousand drones are attacking *Indomitable.*"

"And we know each Nest Ship can deploy more than ten thousand." Engels smacked her palm with her fist. "They must have killed some. They're fighting. Will we make it there in time?"

"I'll deploy my fighters at the earliest possible moment, Admiral Engels," Vic said. "However, by my calculations we'll be too late. My long-range sensors indicate the enemy has deployed ground elements onto *Indomitable's* hull and are in the process of assaulting through the exposed unarmored areas."

"Dammit. If they'd only gotten her assembled..."

Straker said, "They almost did. The Opters must've launched from Gadeiros when they saw the pieces transit in. It was just bad luck."

"No," Engels said. "It was a mistake—my mistake. I selected the transit point near Gadeiros in order to obscure her signature and to use the planet's gravity as a slingshot. I figured *Indomitable* needed every edge she could get. I screwed up."

"Nobody screwed up," Straker said. "Fortunes of war. Nobody could predict a Nest Ship was lurking out here."

Loco cleared his throat. "Hey, you guys are missing the obvious question."

"What's that?" Straker asked.

"Why would a Nest Ship even attack *Indomitable* here in the Huns' capital system?"

Straker snapped his fingers. "For the same reason they destroyed Kraznyvol. They're doing what Opters always do. The Sarmok, anyway. They're taking sides against us because we have the upper hand, attacking when they have a big advantage and can affect things in a big way. Also, Benota is clearing out their agents back on New Earth, and they don't want to have the same thing happen here."

"So the gloves come off," Engels said. "I didn't believe Myrmidon when he claimed the Murmorsk attack was made up of rogue Sarmok elements, and this proves I was right."

Straker cleared his throat. "He did say those rogue Queens had tacit approval from the Sarmok. Plausible deniability."

"Who gives a shit why?" Loco said, coming to his feet. "Like Carla said, the gloves just came off and the bugs screwed us royally. Even if *Indomitable* survives, she'll be useless for this battle. Can we take Atlantis without her?"

Vic replied, "My estimates indicate a forty-seven percent probability, with a margin of error of sixteen percent."

"So it's a coin flip," Straker said. "We're still in business."

"Do we want to gamble on a coin flip?" Loco asked.

"For the whole prize? Yes we do—especially as we should be able to withdraw in good order if we fail. Pascal's wager, Loco."

Loco gave Straker a thumbs-up. "Pascal's wager, boss."

For Engels, the hour passed slowly, an agony as she watched *Indomitable* gutted from the inside. Her point defenses fell silent and all attempts at comlink failed. The fleet transited in and converged on *Indomitable's* position, but not nearly soon enough. When *Victory's* fighters attacked, all that was left for Engels was vengeance, rescue of survivors—and the gathering of information on how *Victory's* fighters stacked up against the enemy drones.

The 512 fighters deployed in a precisely layered disc, four deep and face-on to the enemy, maintaining high speed. Vic's calculations and Engels' instinct was that the Republic fighters would fight best at higher speeds and in a mutually supporting formation rather than dogfighting. This allowed Vic to concentrate on gunnery rather than maneuvering each individually.

As the fighter disc approached, the Opter drone swarm spread out. Like a flock of birds, it morphed and flowed incessantly even as it attacked together.

"I've deciphered their movement algorithm," Vic said. "Like birds or fish, they instinctively maintain individual positions relative to each other, keying off between five to nine neighbors—in this case, seven."

"Will that help you win?"

"Marginally. Even I cannot process all the data fast enough to predict individual positions, but I will be able to use it for limited anticipation of zones of density."

"Fascinating," Engels said. This was a new kind of warfare, but space tactics had always fascinated her, and the fact that no humans—no friendly organics—would die inside the fighters allowed her to enjoy the engagement more dispassionately.

"Opening fire at long range," Vic said. "They're withholding fire. They're layering for coordination."

Engels saw what Vic meant. The enemy was creating layers of their own, so the smallest of the three drone classes were in front, then the mediums, then the heavies.

The fighter disc angled to one side, seeking to avoid plunging directly into the center of the enemy. The Opter drones strove in turn to keep in front of the fighters in order to overwhelm them. The fighters proved a little faster, and the disc opened fire on one flanking section of the enemy.

Hundreds of drones, mostly the small ones, died instantly. "They use the lightest class as cannon fodder," Engels said. "Makes sense when you don't care about the lives of your subordinates."

"They care," Zaxby said, "but only as resources, not as individuals. Remember, in Opter society only the Queens consider themselves to be people."

"Sounds like politicians," Loco muttered.

Vic said, "My Ruxin portion is correct. They're using the small drones to soak up damage. Fortunately, I have precisely calculated the probable moment of the rest opening fire and am initiating evasive maneuvers.

The fighters began evading, but within prescribed limits. They kept their overall positions relative to the formation. Only an AI could have made that work.

Less than a second later, the front layers of the Opter swarm opened fire.

"Thirty-two lost," Vic said.

"Put up a count for both sides, please," Engels said.

Two sets of two numbers appeared, representing remaining craft and kills: 7866 and 451 on one side, 480 and 32 on the other.

"That's better than ten to one," Straker said. "Not bad."

"It represents mutual annihilation, force for force," Vic replied. "That's not the way to win battles."

"Keep their speed up, Vic," Engels said. "Prioritize fighter survival over kills. Keep the Opters busy. They're already recovering their marines from *Indomitable's* hulks, so there's no need to press them hard. Our fleet will be here soon."

"Acknowledged."

The fighter formation turned farther to the side, blasting through the edge of the swarm and outward, arcing toward the planet Gadeiros. The swarm immediately gave chase. The numbers of remaining combatants stabilized at 7490 and 465.

When the fighters reached the planet, they continued to accelerate as they spread out to pass completely around it on all sides. "I'll use the fighters to recon Gadeiros," Vic said.

The fighters soon regrouped on the far side of the airless planet. The swarm followed around it in the same way, on all sides.

The tactical holotank showed graphics to illustrate Vic's next words. "I've detected dozens of concealed drone launch tubes on the planet's surface. There are probably many I've not detected. There is also this one large anomaly that I believe is the former location of a Nest Ship."

The display showed a deep crater on the inner, sunward side of the planet.

"They're gone, but they left their drones behind?" Straker asked.

"Launch tubes," Engels said.

"Huh?"

"If this swarm was that Nest Ship's contingent, they wouldn't have needed concealed launch tubes on the surface. This swarm is independent."

Straker nodded. "Don told me Opter warriors are about as smart as humans, so they don't *need* a Queen to direct them into battle. We have to keep an eye out for the Nest Ship and assume it's fully loaded. The good news is, it looks like *Victory* and one Nest Ship are about evenly matched."

"My purpose is not to engage in fighter combat," Vic said. "I'm much more effective focusing on tactical coordination."

Engels said, "They're heading in toward Atlantis now that they've done their damage." The display supported her words. The swarm accelerated toward the Hundred Worlds capital.

The fighters followed for a time, sniping and killing hundreds more, but soon Vic brought them back. "I'm reaching the limit of my FTL range. Trying to control them via standard datalinks would reduce their effectiveness by a factor of ten or more."

"No problem," Engels said. She sighed. "Let's go see what's left of *Indomitable.*"

* * *

Straker put on a battlesuit and led the Breakers over to one of the two hulks. Many small parties from the other ships of the fleet joined them. Every weapon, every piece of equipment had been slagged.

"Damn, Derek," Loco said. "These guys are thorough."

"They follow orders to the letter, I guess. Maintain a good watch. There may be stragglers."

As they moved through the passageways they found the same story everywhere: doors and hatches cut open, machines destroyed, crew killed whether armed or not—nothing was missed. It was a slaughter.

"No mercy," Straker said. "Looks like some of our guys tried to surrender."

"Didn't do them much good," Loco said.

"Yeah. Keep pushing inward. There may be holdouts. It's a big ship."

"It *was* a big ship," Loco said bitterly. "Now, it's two big wrecks." Loco led the Breakers onward, with Straker watching the reports on his HUD. Redwolf followed Straker, restlessly scanning for trouble. Heiser brought up the rear.

Eventually they came to the scene of a desperate fight outside one of the ship's large infirmaries. The bodies of crew, marines and Opters mingled and sprawled in the vacuum. The main door to the medical bays hung by one hinge, blown open.

"They made a stand here," Straker said. "Trying to defend the wounded."

Inside the infirmary, all the autodocs and regen tanks, hundreds of them, had been systematically violated by close-range weapons fire. The holes showed the bodies inside, ripped to shreds or burned to death.

"Fucking bastards," Redwolf said. "Medical symbols all over. They have to know what they did."

"This isn't war," Loco said. "It's extermination."

"So now we know," Straker said, bleakly. "War to the knife."

"And the knife to the hilt," Redwolf answered. "In our backs."

Straker didn't contradict him. The possibility of peace with Opters was a distant future, and his troops, his Republic military, were not emotionless Hok. Most, especially any form of infantry, needed fire in their bellies to fight well. This would light that fire. He'd worry about dousing it later. The word would spread of this atrocity, and it would stiffen anyone who ever thought about surrendering to the bugs.

The handle on an unopened pressure door turned, slowly. The movement attracted a dozen weapon muzzles, including Loco's. Heiser barked, "Eyes out! The boss has it!"

"Hold fire unless you have a threat, people," Straker said. "Bugs wouldn't be slowly opening a door by the handle."

The door swung wide and a man in a torn and burned crew-suit fell to the deck. Straker could see air leaking from it around a dozen patches.

"We need a bubble! Now!" Loco said, and a medic activated a survival pod. Its memory polymer turned the fist-sized packet into a three-meter clear hemisphere. The medic stepped under it and sealed it to the deck. It inflated, providing a minimal atmosphere. The medic took off her gauntlets and helmet, and then removed her patient's helmet as well.

It was Chief Quade.

"I couldn't... I couldn't..." he gasped, and then his eyes rolled back.

"I'm losing him!" the medic yelled as she slipped the probe of a stabilizer into his jugular. "Gods dammit, we're in an infirmary! Find me a working autodoc!"

The Breakers searched desperately one more time, but there were no miracles. All of the medical machines were smashed beyond repair.

The medic did all she could, but eventually sat back on her heels and shook her head, cursing. She turned her face to Straker through the clear bubble. "I'm sorry, sir."

"No need to apologize... Jacklins, is it?"

"Yes, sir."

"You did what you could. The Opters killed him, not you."
Straker turned to the Breakers. "We keep going. Spread out for
search. There may be more alive."

In the end, out of *Indomitable's* skeleton crew of just under
one thousand, they only found eight survivors. The rest had
been slaughtered.

.

* * *

Engels noted Straker's grim face as he returned to *Victory's*
bridge. She suppressed the instinct to hug him fiercely. Wrong
time, wrong role. Instead, she merely matched his expression
and nodded to show she understood.

"We have to end this thing," Straker said, spitting out his
words. "We have to unite humanity against the Opters, drive
them out of our territory."

"What about your buddy Myrmidon?"

"I'm talking about the bugs, the Queens. If humanopts want
to defect, we'll welcome them. For now, we'll be
exterminating insectoids on sight. If we don't get to surrender,
they don't either. War to the knife, knife to the hilt."

Engels nodded. The concept made her uncomfortable, but
she couldn't argue. She'd seen the vids.

She gestured at the holotanks. "The Huns still aren't
talking."

"Then we make them talk," Straker replied. "In person, if
necessary. Have you got your revised plan set up?"

Engels nodded again. "The fleet's ready."

"Then let's go."

"Vic, pass this order to all ships: set course for Atlantis-3.

402

Chapter 39

On the way to Atlantis-3, Straker paced and thought, paced and thought, trying to stay out of Engels line of vision to the holotanks. He could tell she was thinking as well, except she sat in her chair chewing her thumbnails to the quick.

Ironically, the battle for Atlantis would be fought by fewer ships than the battle for Sparta, with less firepower. The main Republic fleet had retreated and the Huns' expeditionary forces had been at the front when Straker had seized *Victory* along with the Hun ships remaining at Sparta.

The ship count looked favorable, Straker's fleet consisted of over one hundred fifty vessels, from battlecruisers down to corvettes. They were well supplied—oversupplied, in fact—but were under-crewed.

The tonnage assessment told a bleaker story. The enemy had fewer than thirty sidespace-capable ships—but they were all dreadnoughts or SDNs. A squadron of three monitors stiffened the defenses, but the biggest problem was the twelve heavy fortresses surrounding the planet. Without *Indomitable* to reduce them, taking them down would be tremendously difficult and costly.

Then there was the Nest Ship from Gadeiros and its reinforced swarm of drones. It had taken up station off to the side of Atlantis and well away, but in a position to attack from the flank if the opportunity presented itself. Trinity had detected comms traffic between it and the planet, so the Opters were definitely allies of the Huns.

There were also outward-facing defense installations on the two large moons of Atlantis, mounting heavy beam weaponry.

Straker had found it interesting that none of these beams could aim at the planet itself, though some could strike the edge of high orbit. Were the Huns worried about mutiny or rebellion? Such weapons could hold a planet hostage. Their existence had sparked an idea that was still bubbling inside him.

"Speed, maneuverability and precision," Straker said aloud. "Those are our advantages."

"We know that, Derek," Engels said.

"I'm reinforcing the point. Vic, you listening?" Straker asked.

"Of course, Liberator."

"We can't go nose to nose. We have to get them off their game and force them to make mistakes."

"We're keeping that goal in mind. Admiral Engels' plan should do just that."

Straker shut up. They were right. He'd already said these things enough.

"We're approaching the break point," Vic said. "I suggest everyone suit up and strap in."

"Make that an order, fleet-wide," Engels said. She slipped into her crew suit and strapped into her command chair. Straker and Loco backed up into their opened battlesuits and activated them, leaving the faceplates up. They took position against the wall, gauntlets clamped to grips there.

When the countdown hit zero, the fleet maneuvered at maximum. Where before it had approached Atlantis in a stately, standard formation, now it suddenly broke to the side, with every ship redlining drives.

Straight for the Nest Ship.

The corvettes immediately pulled out in front, followed by the frigates, destroyers and so on in order of speed and ship class.

It took time for the Opters to react. Lightspeed lag was one reason, but Straker hoped surprise was another. Every second got the fleet's lunge closer to the Nest Ship.

When the Opters eventually reacted, eighteen thousand drones formed a dense screen even while the Nest Ship turned tail and ran directly away from the Republic fleet.

"Will it get away?" Straker asked with a grunt. At least four Gs were leaking through the gravplating compensation, making it difficult to speak or even breathe.

"Negative," Vic said.

404

"You really think this plan will work?" Straker asked.

"Yes," Vic said patiently, "it will work. It's a brilliant stratagem."

"Score one for man over machine!" Straker said triumphantly.

"It's not a competition, Derek," Engels said.

"It's all right, Admiral Engels," Vic said. "I'm used to the insecurities of organics."

"As I recall," Engels replied, "you had some serious insecurities before Trinity and the Mindspark Device set you free and changed you for the better."

"Conceded. My compliment stands. Liberator Straker saw an opportunity none of us did."

Straker kept his eyes on the holotanks, which showed the leading edge of the Republic fleet, the corvettes, begin firing at their own long range. They simultaneously slowed their rush forward and fell back relative to the next wave, the frigates, though they still approached the enemy.

In perfect, Vic-directed synchrony the frigates did the same, opening fire at long range—then the destroyers, then the light cruisers and so on. This created a phalanx of overlapping fire, all of it outranging the Opter drones.

Each Republic ship had primaries and point-defense beams. The larger ships had dual-use secondaries. Thus, more than a thousand individual weapons, each cycling every few seconds, speared out to destroy drones like the stabs of a thousand spines.

The drone count dropped below eighteen thousand, seventeen thousand, and then sixteen thousand before they got in their first return shots, which were weak and diffuse against the heavier armor and reinforcement of real warships.

The lighter ships in front of the fleet continued to collapse back until every Republic vessel moved into a single tight disc formation, with *Victory* in the center.

Fifteen thousand.

Victory's fighters were interspersed throughout the fleet, adding to the tight defenses, their gunnery as perfect as could be.

Fourteen thousand.

The fleet continued to slow on impellers while still maintaining attack posture, providing maximum time to shoot.

Thirteen thousand.

The drones surged forward, their commander belatedly realizing the Opter dilemma.

Twelve thousand.

Now the fleet's railguns opened up. With ample supplies from Sparta, and with short crews, the ship had extra ammunition in their cargo bays. They could afford a prodigal expenditure, firing incessant streams of submunitions that ripped any drones they hit to shreds.

Ten thousand.

"Have we lost any ships?" Straker asked.

"Nope," Engels said. "Some corvettes and frigates took damage, but we're refusing the lightest ships and letting the heavies take the shots."

Eight thousand.

"Missiles?" Engels said.

"Launching," Vic replied.

A wave of short-range anti-drone packs burst forth from the fleet as the two forces merged. A ripple of fireworks nearly whited out the holotank.

Four thousand.

"Now!" Engels barked.

"Already ordered," Vic said.

All ships in the fleet, including the fighters and *Victory,* abruptly poured on full acceleration. This minimized the time the Opter drones were at point-blank range and eliminated their ability to land on Republic hulls. In seconds, the drones had passed through and fallen behind, vainly trying to reverse course to give chase.

Three thousand.

"That turned out to be easy," Straker said.

"We have a twenty-five-to-one advantage in tonnage and firepower," Engels said. "The question was never about winning, only about how much it would cost."

Straker spoke as he let go of the wall grips and walked heavily back to Engels' chair. He felt the war within himself, his heart against his head. He wanted to slaughter this Nest

406

Ship and its meddlesome Queen, to get some back for what she'd done to *Indomitable's* crew. Yet, that would be indulgent—and perhaps stupid, Once again, he put his personal feelings aside, and spoke. "Vic, aim a surrender demand at that Nest Ship."

"Transmitting."

Engels rotated her chair toward Straker evident in surprise. "Why do you believe they'll surrender?"

"I met a Queen, remember? And I've been to Terra Nova. I've got some sense of how they think. They're less moral, more practical than we are, and each Queen thinks of herself as the center of the universe. I'm betting this one won't see any point in making a suicidal stand."

"I thought you weren't going to accept their surrender," Engels said. "They didn't let our crews live."

Straker looked at her, and the rest of his crewmembers. They all had hot eyes, burning for vengeance. Had he stoked that flame too high?

"You're right. They haven't earned mercy. But I need to end this quickly. The Opters aren't our primary target today, they've just put themselves in our path. We'll deal with them at a future date. Trust me."

They didn't look happy, but they turned back to their control systems without further complaints.

Abruptly, the Nest Ship turned from red to yellow in the holotank.

"She's broadcast their surrender," Vic said. "We confess surprise."

Straker refrained from another comment about organics and AIs. Instead, he used a different metaphor. "There's chess, and there's poker, Vic. Carla plays chess. I play poker."

"So you raised and they folded. But what can we do with a Nest Ship?" Loco asked.

"Do?" Engels looked back and forth from Loco to Straker. "We took it out of the fight. Now we attack Atlantis."

Straker pointed at Loco. "No, I get what he means—and Loco's a poker player too."

"Better one than you, Derek," Loco said.

"Sometimes," Straker admitted. "A human commander who surrendered wouldn't ever switch sides. Even if he did, his crew wouldn't defect en masse. I mean, look what happened with Braga, right? But maybe an Opter Queen will, especially with a gun to her head."

"Yeah, but who'll put that gun to her head?" Loco said. Then he saw Straker's grin, he began grinning himself. "Oh... no way! I'm not going aboard that ship unless I'm in a mechsuit and armed to the teeth."

"I think we can arrange that."

Zaxby interrupted. "We have a better idea. The com-bot can operate Loco's mechsuit. We can install a dead-switch bomb and an FTL transceiver, and send it over. It can be our gun to her head."

"Fine by me," Loco said.

"Do it," Straker said.

The Queen immediately agreed to the coerced defection, as Straker suspected she would. These Queens seemed to have little loyalty except to themselves. They were essentially petty monarchs of their own domains.

This lack of loyalty among Queens would be extended to himself, Straker realized. She'd no doubt turn on him instantly if she thought she could regain her freedom.

When Loco's bot-occupied mechsuit reached the Nest Ship's bridge, the Opter vessel fell into formation with the Republic fleet. The drones, the Nest Ship's only real military force, were kept at some distance off to the flank, out of their own short weapons range but within that of the warships.

* * *

Admiral Niedern swore vehemently on the bridge of his flagship, the monitor *Poseidon*. He'd been ecstatic when his new Opter allies had taken out *Indomitable,* removing his biggest worry from the upcoming battle, but now his fury rose.

"That bug bitch," he muttered. "She's switched sides!"

Karst, standing next to him, shrugged with equanimity. "Still a net gain, don't you think?"

408

"Of course, but this is becoming an ugly theme, don't you think? First *Victory* defects, and now this Queen. It's bound to hurt morale, and my dreadnoughts won't do well against these small craft. We have 400 local attack ships, but they're no match for 3500 drones and fighters."

"You have ample missile stores. Use them up. I don't have to remind you what happens if they win, do I?"

Niedern turned to stare into Karst's eyes. Damn him, the man didn't even flinch. "My career will be over. You? They'll probably execute you, hmm? So don't try to threaten me with consequences." Niedern turned deliberately away from his watchdog and put him out of his mind.

Karst wouldn't be ignored, however. "You're sure your ships are secure against *Victory's* control?"

Niedern grunted. "I saw the reports on what happened at Sparta. We intercepted a lot of intel from the spy drones, so we know what kind of hacks they used. We've upgraded our ICE and taken every possible measure. Now shut up and let me think."

"About what?"

"About how to buy time for our reinforcements to arrive."

Karst, at long last, shut up and retreated.

* * *

"The score is one to one at the end of the first period," Loco said from where he stood next to Straker in his battlesuit on *Victory's* bridge.

"I'd call it two to one their favor," Straker replied. *"Indomitable* was more valuable than the Nest Ship."

"Maybe. On the other hand, their loss was our gain, and those drones are expendable. Maybe Carla and Vic can take that into account."

"Already am," Engels said, not looking at Loco as she stared hard at her holotanks. "I'm thinking they're the perfect thing to ensure your moon op succeeds."

"Right," Straker said. "You just get us there. We'll do the job."

"Trinity is ready," Zaxby said. "Shall we proceed?"

A few minutes later, Zaxby, in full Ruxin battlesuit, joined Straker, Loco and the Breakers on Trinity's flight deck. Straker was already in his mechsuit.

Loco stared up at him from a mere battlesuit. "Dammit boss, this sucks."

"Sorry, Loco. The only way to be sure the Queen cooperated was to put your suit in there right next to her. No conceivable attack could take it out before its deadman switch activates."

"Detaching from *Victory* now," Zaxby said.

Straker linked his HUD to Trinity's tactical holotank and watched as Trinity raced for the outer moon of Atlantis, called Thera. The cloud of three thousand Opter drones joined and surrounded them, along with ten *Victory* fighters.

No doubt the enemy were wondering what one destroyer was doing among the many drones. Was it a real attack, or a ruse to draw the smaller, slower, but heavier defending fleet out of position?

The heavy beams of the moon batteries opened up at long range and began destroying a few drones, which evaded wildly. When the range got closer and the beams shifted to targeting Trinity, the ten fighters, per Engels' plan equipped as Archers with underspace generators, dropped into that cold dimension and began crossing and re-crossing the vicinity of Trinity, which also inserted. The insertion should be a surprise to the Huns, and now they had eleven targets to track.

The Hun fleet moved closer to this threat, trying to split the difference between holding position and helping to cover the moon bases.

Engels had chosen carefully, however, placing her own fleet so that the Huns had two bad choices. They chose the lesser of their evils, of course, and didn't reinforce the defenses against the strange drone-underspace attack.

As the range fell, the moon batteries had to split their fire among all their targets. They couldn't ignore the congruence points, or the drones would land and eat them alive. Ignoring the underspace attack though, float mines would appear above their installations and detonate in fusion fire.

410

At the last minute, Trinity and the fighters dove directly into the moon. Just before crossing under the surface, Trinity released a float mine that wiped out the central of the five heavy batteries on Thera.

Aboard, Straker felt some shuddering and shaking, but nothing worse. "One down, four to go," he said to the Breakers. They cheered.

Now three underspace-capable fighters, each with a suicide warhead aboard, turned within the moon and sprinted for three of the four remaining batteries—from underneath. As soon as they surfaced, they exploded, wiping out those three. This would never have worked against ships, or even fortresses, but moons couldn't maneuver, and their mass shielded the Archers from detection.

The drones hovered in the vicinity, just outside the final battery's arc of fire, along with the seven surviving fighters.

Still inside Thera, Trinity rose up carefully, precisely, beneath the last live defense complex and chose a point of emergence impossible to target. Her hull appeared less than one meter off the ground and immediately landed among the guns and wave guides. Trinity's weaponry instantly eliminated any threats to the ship or the Breakers—hardpoints, pillboxes and autocannon.

"Initiating the assault," Zaxby said as the flight deck door, now at ground level, flew open. He followed his own order and locomoted out onto the dusty surface, two weapons at the ready.

Straker followed. Across from him was a blown-open small-craft hangar, his entry point. Loco and the Breakers followed.

Once the hangar was secure, Straker sent the battlesuiters into the tunnels beneath the surface. There was no way he was fitting inside. This time he and Trinity were the stay-behind security, though he was able to follow via his HUD.

The battle for the battery was anticlimactic. The handful of duty marines were no match for two platoons of Breakers, and the technicians manning the weapons quickly surrendered. They were tranked and locked in the infirmary.

411

"There are five DNs moving our direction," Zaxby said as he plugged a hacking module into the complex's main fire control SAI. "Although the Huns have done well to secure their cybernetics against external attack, by accessing here we can bypass most of the safeguards and—yes, we're in. Trinity now has control of the battery."

"Breakers, return to the ship," Straker said.

"Firing," Trinity said on Straker's comlink. "The DNs are staying outside the battery's central arc. Our drones will intercept any missiles, but it's only a matter of minutes before their railguns will fire from along the horizon, where the beams can't target, and shatter this complex."

"Did you have enough time?"

"Easily. My malware has piggybacked on the ground defense network and is already installing itself inside Kreta's batteries."

"Then get us the hell out of here."

Chapter 40

Atlantis System

Engels breathed a sigh of relief as she got the word that Straker had accomplished his mission and was on his way back. She was holding the fleet beyond long range even for the enemy fortresses, cruising laterally and constantly evading, forcing them to guess at what angle she'd turn to attack.

In war as in life, it was all about position and timing. She had to initiate her run less than a minute after Trinity slipped back into her berth within *Victory*. The drones and fighters that had covered Straker's mission hid behind Thera's bulk, daring the enemy to come after them. Niedern was a clever opponent, though, and refused to be drawn out of position.

Position and timing, position and timing. Engels stared at the holotanks. Vic had created clear graphics that made the plan seem obvious and inevitable. Still her mind scrabbled for some flaw. Nothing ever worked completely as planned. Witness the hulk of *Indomitable* drifting near Gadeiros.

The motion of moons and fortresses, however, could be predicted with certainty. At the angle she'd chosen, the outer moon, Thera, was out of the way, nearly around to the other side of the planet and irrelevant now that its batteries had been destroyed. The inner moon, Kreta, backstopped the Hun fleet as it passed across the face of Atlantis. Five orbital fortresses were also in line-of-sight of the battle, something that couldn't be helped.

Position and timing.

Vic now took control of her ships' maneuvers. He could analyze incoming fire and evade better than any human or SAI. He'd also issue timed firing orders in accordance with her plan.

Her plan—and Straker's of course. She had to keep reminding herself it was an organic plan, a human plan. In this role, Vic could have been nothing more than a perfect fleet chain of command, executing her will.

413

"Fleet launch commencing," Vic said. The displays reflected the order, as all of her ships cycled their missiles in a complete soft-dump of their ready loads. Their overworked crews would be frantically shuttling ammo from their cargo bays, an unorthodox practice not often performed under battle conditions.

The missiles formed up ahead of the fleet into a series of massive waves. This would keep the Huns guessing as to which contained the decoys and in what proportion.

In response, the enemy fortresses began firing clouds of submunitions, millions of tiny tetrahedrons that would tear missiles apart. Space was vast, and so these only destroyed a small percentage of the weapons every volley, but the fortresses were well stocked with ammunition—and dumb ammo was cheap.

Victory's fighters spread out behind the missile waves, followed by the warships. The formation gave the credible impression of a do-or-die frontal assault, an all-out attack designed to overwhelm the defenses with a surprising number of missiles.

Engels watched as Niedern did the conventional thing—the only thing he could, really, given the situation—and lined up his mobile forces in front of her. He couldn't afford to maneuver too much, as he had no assurances some of the missiles wouldn't be targeted on cities or installations on the planet. The fact that the two empires had never engaged on wholesale slaughter of civilians didn't mean it would never happen, especially with the stakes this high.

She wanted him to keep that ugly possibility in his mind.

Position and timing.

"Now," she said as the chrono hit the next phase point.

"Initiating," Vic said. The Republic missiles and ships accelerated, staying together in excellent formation except for the AI-directed evasive patterns.

"Screening bursts," Engels said.

"On schedule." Selected missiles with loads of specialized particulates exploded. In the vacuum of space, even dust continued ballistically, creating a smokescreen that degraded the enemy targeting. The missiles soon outran the cloud, but occasional bursts kept it effective for the ships following.

The enemy fleet continued to fire energetically, degrading the Republic missile screen. As the missiles approached, the Huns launched countermissiles in profligate numbers.

The two vast armadas of robotic suicide weapons—for that's what missiles were—merged in an orgy of nuclear destruction. The space between the two fleets, one waiting, one closing for the kill, filled with an overload of electromagnetic pulse energy that blinded every sensor turned its way.

Position and timing.

"Release the mines," Engels ordered.

"As planned." *Victory's* fighters, each fitted with a cluster of stealth mines culled from all the warships' stores, accelerated to the edge of the destruction zone, and then abruptly reversed course on impellers. The mines flew free.

Over two thousand hard-to-see weapons, completely reflective or absorptive and with no EM signature, coming out of the glare, nearly reached the dreadnoughts before they were spotted.

Ready point-defense weapons lashed out, but even automated systems have a finite reaction time. Over two hundred of the warheads made it through to detonate among the enemy fleet, a few actually striking the ships.

"Yes!" Engels tried to leap from her chair but bucked against the restraints as enemy icons turned yellow and red. "Half their mobile strength!"

"More like a quarter, as most of the damaged ships are still combat-effective," Vic said. "And the monitors are untouched."

"I see my brilliant contribution has had its effect," Zaxby said as he swept onto the bridge, still in his enormous eight-limbed battlesuit. "Did I ever tell you I first thought of the concept of a stealth mine attack at Corinth? Admiral Braga almost won the battle with it, you know."

"Yes, you've told that story more than once, and I'm glad you did," Engels replied patiently.

"We're not out of the woods yet, Admiral," Vic said. "I still need a decision on where to apply our final surprise."

Engels chewed her inner cheek. "Is all of Trinity there?" she asked.

"We're all here," Vic and Zaxby said simultaneously.

"What do the numbers say? Dreadnoughts or monitors?"

Straker broke in on his comlink. He must have been listening from within his mechsuit. "Take out Niedern's flagship."

"Chop off the head?" Engels asked.

"More than that. He's not well liked. They've already been hurt by the stealth mine trick. I know troops. If they lose the flagship, they'll feel like it was his fault and they'll be more likely to lose heart."

"This isn't a battle of heart, Derek. It's tactics and weapons."

Straker raised his voice. "Just do it, and fast. My decision."

Engels voice rose to match. "You're overriding me?"

Straker paused. "I don't want to."

He's trying to say yes and no at the same time, Engels thought. What was her own gut telling her? To go for the monitors. Straker's order was just a refinement of that impulse.

"Okay," she said. "Trinity, pick the best moment and smoke Niedern's flagship if you can. We may only have one shot."

"Understood."

Position and timing.

The Republic fleet closed to medium range, exchanging fire with their weakened enemy. Missiles, beams and railgun projectiles crisscrossed in the void.

At first, the Huns had it all their way. Their remaining ships and fortresses mounted bigger weapons with more reach and power. Thirty Republic vessels were crippled as the distance fell to short range, to only three Huns.

Engels felt each icon that turned red as a physical pain in her nerves, aches in her limbs and agony behind her eyes. People were dying, good people, her people, all to set the enemy up for—

"Firing," Vic said. The right holotank zoomed in on the *Poseidon,* Niedern's flagship.

416

Metal plasma boiled from the lightly armored stern of the monitor. Her engines blew with a gout of fusing isotopes as five whole moon batteries from Kreta, twenty-five heavy particle beams at close range, crawled right up *Poseidon's* back end and gutted her from the inside.

"The malware worked!" Engels exulted. "Think we'll get another shot?"

The chrono counted down the recharge time and hijacked batteries fired again. They struck a second monitor, but the alert ship's captain had turned and so the beams struck her heavily armored flak. Even so, the vessel took severe damage, turning yellow in *Victory's* holotank.

Before the beam projectors could recharge and release their gargantuan energies a third time, the Hun fortresses smashed the moon bases with a storm of belated fire. Still, two monitors taken out of the fight—and the moon bases destroyed—was a big win.

But now, position and timing became irrelevant. The range shortened and turned into a slugfest. The four wings of Hun attack ships raced to engage, countered by a similar number of *Victory's* fighters. The attack ships had heavier armor and weaponry, while the fighters had greater precision and maneuverability. The forces met in the middle and slaughtered each other in droves.

"No more tricks?" Straker asked as Engels gripped the arms of her chair, feeling helpless as ships and fortresses pounded on each other like drunken bar-brawlers. Even Vic's analytical powers failed in the mess as thousands of projectiles and targets—warships, fighters, missiles, attack ships, railgun clusters and mines, plus beams—swirled in an incomprehensible melee.

* * *

On his HUD, Straker watched the set-piece space battle collapse into a dogfight of the highest order. Three battlecruisers circled one Hun superdreadnought like wolves around a tiger, slashing killing shots into her flanks even as

417

their bigger enemy smashed the nose of one, breaking the ship into unequal pieces.

A squadron of eight Republic heavy cruisers arrowed in ragged formation on an attack run against the remaining monitor, supported by a trio of tiny corvettes. The monitor obliterated the lead cruiser with one shot, and damaged two more before explosions blossomed on her nose. When the fire cleared, she sailed proudly on, destroying another cruiser as she emerged from the chaos—only to stagger as the unnoticed corvettes launched a trio of shipkillers as they passed her stern.

"We're winning, but it's ugly," Straker told the Breakers on their comlink channel. They stood in their battlesuits, clamped against the flight deck's wall, ready for heavy Gs. He wished there was something he could do, some way of affecting the fight.

He thought of ordering Trinity to drop into underspace and make attack runs, but the fortresses had too many detectors and heavy weapons. Every other target was maneuvering hard, and underspace predictions would be useless within seconds. Nor did he have the forces to replicate the two-brigade drop on Unison to seize the government.

Then he noticed something. He switched channels. "Trinity, what about the Opter drones?"

"We haven't forgotten. We're waiting for the right moment to send them into battle."

"I have a better thought," Straker explained his idea. "Will it work?"

"It will," Trinity agreed, "if we survive. In fact, it may work better than you expect."

"Why's that?"

"I'd rather not say at this time."

"Why not?"

Trinity's voice became strained. "Please, Liberator. Trust me."

"Secrets again? Fine. I don't have time to argue."

Trinity was quiet for a moment but then tried again to sway him. "Admiral Engels may disagree with this gamble."

"I don't have time to argue with her either, and she's not the ultimate authority here... correct?"

418

"You're correct, Liberator."

"Then those are my orders." He switched channels again. "Breakers, get ready. We'll be inserting in nine minutes." He then explained his plan to them. Zaxby returned to join the Breakers, while Nolan and Murdock transferred to *Victory*.

At the chosen moment Straker felt the chill. On his HUD he watched as Trinity sprinted away from *Victory* in a high-speed arc, aiming up and over the frozen north pole of Atlantis. She shuddered with the impact of shots against her congruence point, but the bleed-over wasn't enough to slow her as she appeared to run from the battle.

At the same time, the Opter drones, under orders from the Queen relayed through the FTL-equipped com-bot in Loco's mechsuit, broke from their high cover behind Thera. They spread out and flew like maddened fireflies to meet Trinity over the capital city of Atlantis.

Unfortunately, there was one enormous asteroid fortress in geosynchronous orbit above the city, a final defense against attack. It bristled with so many weapons it made *Indomitable* look small.

The Opter drones fell on it like a cloud of flies, and they died like flies, by the hundreds, then a thousand—but half won through to land on the asteroid's rocky surface. They immediately deployed their ground auxiliaries and rampaged.

The fortress was never expected to fend off fifteen hundred ground troops backed up by fifteen hundred low-flying attack drones. The combination, too close in for most of its weapons to target, soon denuded one selected portion of the fortress of weaponry.

The drones' ground troops quickly recovered, then waited in this self-made eye of the storm.

They'd created a clear path, and along that path Trinity flew. She dove straight into the interior of the asteroid, still in underspace, and passed through. As her congruence point exited the fortress, she released one float mine and poured on all the acceleration she could, straight down toward the capital city.

Heavy shocks rattled Straker even in his mechsuit. Several Breakers were torn loose from their holds and went bouncing

419

around the flight deck, along with wrecked equipment. Once the turbulence subsided, Zaxby and other Breakers rushed to lock down the debris.

"Trinity?" Straker comlinked.

"We survived the detonation, Liberator. However, this will be a one-way trip until we undergo repairs."

"Can you land?"

"I can... once," Trinity said. "After that, it's do or die. Are you still determined to go through with this plan? It doesn't seem likely to succeed."

"Poker, not chess, remember?"

"Yes, the concept of bluffing is known to me, but won't it be obvious?"

"Not to a bunch of rich fat politicians with everything to lose."

* * *

Indy suppressed her skepticism of Straker's plan. If he was willing to risk death once more, she could do no less. Zaxby, the only other portion of Trinity with whom she was currently connected, was enthusiastic about going into battle again, but she suspected that was his warrior hormones talking.

After all, she'd already taken a greater risk than she'd disclosed to Straker. The only way she was able to ensure the destruction of the final fortress was to use a portion of the stolen antimatter, by installing it in a float mine. She simply hadn't had a warhead big enough to crack the asteroid.

The resulting titanic explosion had damaged her systems severely, though she'd managed to hide the full import from Straker so far.

Now, she was actively hiding the technical details of the assault on the capital. If Straker had Zaxby's or Murdock's kind of mind, he'd have immediately wondered about emergence in atmosphere. It was a hazardous technique, fraught with the danger of molecular interactions.

The antimatter provided a way to mitigate this problem, plus the problem of the local defenses. When her congruence point was in position, she released a tiny portion of antimatter, the equivalent of a large conventional bomb, back into normal space. Then, with exquisite timing, she emerged from underspace—exactly inside the microsecond of vacuum created by the blast.

Not only did the explosion minimize molecular interactions, it shocked the defenses, functioning like a flash-bang grenade would in a security operation. Instead of a ship, automated anti-aerospace weapons emplacements first detected a blast. This gave Indy just enough time to use her own beams to silence every emplacement within line-of-sight.

She emerged directly above the House of Parliament, in the center of the capitol complex, seat of the Hundred Worlds government. No doubt the politicians there never really expected enemy troops to get this far.

Her impellers strained as she set down directly atop the complex. A surreal act of vandalism, the landing half-crushed the buildings beneath. Immediately she opened her flight deck doors and the Breakers bounded out.

One part of her mind assisted Straker as he, in his mechsuit, led his troops toward the Hundred Worlds War Room in the bunker beneath the buildings. There they hoped to find the Prime Minister, his cabinet and staff. Like rats, they were hiding underground, hoping they were safe.

Trinity hacked various systems continuously, provided overwatch fire, and gave warning of everything she saw.

Straker had a chance, she thought, but the probability was low that he would be able to fight his way all the way into the heavily defended bunker. There were enemy mechsuiters and battlesuiters all over the area, even now converging on Straker's position. She interdicted or destroyed all she could, but for most she couldn't get clean shots as they used cover and the tunnels beneath the complex.

At the same time, the battle in space above was still very much in doubt. Her underspace generators couldn't sustain another insertion. If Engels and *Victory* had to withdraw, then she, Zaxby and the Breakers would be captured or killed. Straker and the others she'd come to know and call friends—

Loco, Heiser, Redwolf and the rest—would know she'd failed them, and failed Straker's dream of liberation.

And Straker had said that bluffing was the way he intended to win. No doubt he meant he'd threaten to destroy the capitol complex and the politicians there. Probably the majority of Members of Parliament had been evacuated, but it was the Prime Minister who'd be making the decision.

But a company of Breakers couldn't cause destruction massive enough, frightening enough, to ensure the bluff worked, and the Prime Minister was reputed to be no coward. Even if Straker breached the bunker and seized the head of government, the man might not believe Straker was willing to overload his own suit and take everyone down with him.

No, there was only one way to sell this bluff.

Indy activated her wideband comlink and transmitted in the clear. "Hundred Worlds Command, this is the Semi-Artificial Intelligence of the destroyer *Gryphon,* currently grounded atop your capitol complex. I have a message for you. Please respond."

She repeated that message, impersonating a ship's computer rather than a true AI, until she got a reply.

"This is General Heinz Jackson. What's your message, *Gryphon?"*

Indy switched to a perfect imitation of Straker's voice. "This is Derek Straker, known as the Liberator. By now you've detected my use of antimatter to destroy the fortress above, and the smaller blast that accompanied *Gryphon's* arrival. I've set this ship's SAI to detonate the remaining antimatter if you do not surrender your forces. The warhead has a yield of over two hundred gigatons and will annihilate everything within five hundred kilometers. You have ten minutes to transmit your capitulation to all forces."

"That's insane, Straker! This is our capital city! There are almost a billion people in that radius!"

Indy repeated the message word for word. By the time it ended, the Prime Minister came on the comlink with similar pleas.

Indy repeated the message a third time, and then a fourth, only changing the word "ten" to "nine" and then "eight" minutes to comply. By minute five, the Hundred Worlds heads of government must have finally understood that he was dealing with an unalterable, uncaring computer, programmed to kill everyone if necessary.

* * *

Straker led the Breakers deep into the underground beneath Parliament. Time after time he cut, tore and widened the passageways to force his mechsuit through, and nothing could stand against him. The long-dead designers of the bunkers had never imagined defending against such a combat machine.

Autocannon fire chewed at him. Computer-directed lasers burned him. Antitank missiles gouged chunks out of him, but he won through, though he lost a quarter of his Breakers.

When the final door yielded to Straker's force cannon and he'd regretfully cut down the last brave Hundred Worlds soldier, the Breakers spread out and took possession of the War Room. As they did, he set his mechsuit's power plant to overload in fifteen minutes, and then activated the audio-vid display that amplified his voice and showed his face on his meter-wide faceplate.

It was as if a fifty-ton metal god stood above the cringing Cabinet, the Prime Minster, and the military chiefs of staff, and it pointed its weapons directly at them.

"Prime Minister," his amplified voice bellowed, "I'm Derek Straker. They call me the Liberator. I know about the Opters, and I know about what you scumbags do to the minds of your citizenry. I know because you did it to *me*. That ends now. Admiral Niedern is dead, your Home Fleet is on the verge of defeat, and my people are even now taking control of your virtual matrix networks."

He was bluffing, of course. He didn't know Niedern was dead, he didn't know if Engels was winning, and he certainly didn't have control of their networks—but the Prime Minister had no way of knowing these things.

His next words escalated the bluff. "People are still dying and the Opters are readying to attack us all with hundreds of

Nest Ships and millions of drones. I've set my suit to overload, and you can't stop it. Surrender the Hundred Worlds now, or your government and everyone in this complex will die."

The Prime Minister stared helplessly up at Straker and pointed at a large screen off to his left. Others on his staff pointed too and they silently moved their mouths. Straker realized he hadn't opened his audio receivers. When he did, they babbled something about already surrendering.

"Derek Straker," Zaxby comlinked as he ambulated into the field of view. "It appears we've already won. Your message threatening to annihilate everything within five hundred kilometers with antimatter did the trick."

"What? What message?"

Zaxby pointed with two tentacles at the same screen as the prisoners.

Straker zoomed in on it and read the text of the message aloud. "...the warhead has a yield of over two hundred megatons and will annihilate everything within five hundred kilometers. You have four minutes to transmit your capitulation to all forces... What the hell is this?"

"It appears your bluff was successful."

"That wasn't *my* bluff!"

Zaxby gestured. "They all think it is. Perhaps it would be unwise to disagree."

Loco broke in. "Boss, just shut up and accept their surrender. As you said, our people are fighting and dying up there. And shut down your overload."

"Right... right." Straker returned his power plant to normal. "Prime Minister, I accept your capitulation. Transmit a stand-down order immediately. Zaxby, Loco, make sure he does it, and no tricks. Trinity, you on this channel?"

"We're here."

"Did you—"

"Yes, Liberator. I can play poker too. I bluffed."

"You bluffed!" Straker laughed, feeling giddy with relief. "You bluffed!"

"It seemed appropriate. I apologize if I overstepped my authority in replicating your voice and image."

Straker let out a long breath. He cracked open his mechsuit and dismounted to take possession of the government of the Hundred Worlds. "Trinity?"

"Yes, Liberator?"

"I think I'll give you a pass this time."

Chapter 41

Atlantis. Three days later

Straker, dressed in his formal uniform, strode up the steps of the hastily repaired Grand Hall of Parliament, the ceremonial heart of the Hundred Worlds. Inside, heads of state had been invested for over three hundred years, ever since the capital had been moved from Old Earth with the splitting of the Terran Commonwealth. That's what the secret history files said, anyway.

Today, in a sense, the opposite of an investment would take place. The Hundred Worlds as a sovereign entity would be no more. In two hours, the Prime Minister and other key leaders from the Executive and Judiciary would sign the formal documents of capitulation.

As Straker's eyes roved over the stately, white-columned front of the hall, he marveled at the events of the last two years and his role in them. Never in his life had he expected to end up as the most powerful man in human space, and frankly, he didn't really want that power.

Not for himself, anyway. But he knew he'd need it soon, to deal with the Opters.

"Surreal, huh, boss?" Loco said from his elbow. "Who'da thought we'd ever stand here like this?"

"Not me."

An arm slipped into his and Straker turned his head to see Mara in a stunning black dress. She stood on tiptoe to kiss his cheek, and then put on a mock frown. "Don't think I'm not still mad at you. Didn't Dad teach you to never to hit a woman?"

"I know, I know. I'm sorry. You'll get over it. Are the..."

"The undamaged people are out of Vic now and in regeneration tanks. The zombie brains... well, they'll stay with him for now. Wiser minds than mine will have to sort out that ethical dilemma."

Straker nodded, and then turned as a delegation of a dozen Hundred Worlds officials approached him. Redwolf stepped from behind Straker to bar their way.

"It's all right, Red," Straker said. "They're our guys now."

"Bullshit," Redwolf muttered, but stepped aside.

"Liberator Straker," the suited civilian in front of the gaggle said. "I'm Grant Lorden, Undersecretary of Defense... at least, for a couple more hours." He held out his hand, saying, "I was hoping to have a brief word?"

"Look, pal," Loco said, "you can—"

Suddenly, Redwolf stepped forward and seized a man lurking in the back of the group, lifting him off the ground by his jacket front and his throat. *"Karst!"*

Everyone watched, shocked, as Redwolf slammed the smaller man to the ground in front of Straker. Redwolf then unholstered his sidearm and pointed it at Karst.

Straker put his hand on Redwolf's gun arm. "I know I said you could shoot him on sight, Red, but not just yet." He turned to Lorden. "Who is this man to you?"

"An aide, that's all."

"To me, he's a traitor. The man who tried to murder my wife, so we'll take him off your hands. Red, lock him up for later."

Redwolf gestured for two of the security detail to take Karst away.

"Now, where were we, Mister Lorden?" Straker said with a false smile.

"He was about to try to suck up to the new boss," Loco said.

Lorden resolutely held out his hand again, ignoring Loco. "Actually I'm trying to avert more death and destruction, sir."

Straker took the man's hand. Lorden's composure reminded Straker of someone else.

Myrmidon.

Straker squeezed until the man should have winced, but he only raised an eyebrow. "I know what you are, Mister Lorden."

"Good. Then you know how vital I am to your future." Lorden placed his other hand atop the two hands clasping, not letting go. "We have to work together to save this new, combined Republic you've brought into being."

"We don't need your help, Lorden," Straker said, trying to gently disengage his hand. "We have control of the VR matrix networks and all the media on this world, and message drones are sending updates throughout the Hundred Worlds. The citizenry will fall into line."

"And the military?"

"We'll take control of ships as they arrive. My AIs assure me they won't have any trouble." Straker started to get irritated. "Let go of my damn hand, Lorden."

Lorden finally let go. "I'm starting to understand."

"Understand what?"

Lorden eyed those listening. "We should talk privately."

"All right. Let's walk. Loco, Mara, go inside and mingle with the other guests, will you? Tell them I'll be there soon." Straker turned to walk out onto the grounds, Lorden at his side and Redwolf at his back. The area still looked like what it was: a battlefield in a park, being cleaned up. "Go on, Lorden, spill it. I'm a busy man."

"You're a humanopt. Do you even know that?"

"I'm not, actually. I was infected with the Hok biotech, then cured, so I read that way." Straker put it together in his mind. "That's why your attempt to influence me biochemically didn't work."

"A pity. This would have been so much simpler if I could."

Straker stepped up to a stone railing that overlooked the harbor, a stiff ocean breeze in his face. A rocky cliff fell away down to the open sea. Far below, seawater poured in white cataracts from the flues of the machinery that drew power from the rise and fall of Atlantis' extreme tides. "Simpler for you, maybe, but freedom's never simple."

"The issue isn't freedom, Straker. It's about order and peace and control—and prosperity."

"With you Opter agents in charge? Or should I say, Sarmok agents?"

Lorden's eyebrows rose. "You're remarkably well informed."

"I know a lot of things."

428

"Information provided by the misguided Miskor, no doubt." Lorden sighed. "They're fools, and so are you."

"To want to rid ourselves of your influence and be free?"

"You'll only bring another war upon us. One we can't win."

"You sure you mean 'us'?"

"I do. Just hear me out." Lorden reached into his jacket and drew out two smokesticks, old-fashioned, large, elegant. "Cigar? One of my few pleasures."

"More Loco's thing than mine, but... sure." Straker took one and imitated what Lorden did in lighting up.

"Don't breathe the smoke in. Mouth only," he said.

"Right." The sensation was odd, but it seemed appropriate as the two stood together and gazed into the distance.

"I said 'us,' Straker, because I'm one of you now. The Sarmok Queens are true egalitarians, treating humanopts the same as their insectoid servants. We failed. That means my cabal and I are already dead to them. They will assume we've been turned, so, ironically, we might as well turn."

"And you want to keep your nice cushy position in the government? I'd be crazy to let you stay there. I may be immune to your influence, but others won't be, at least until we develop a vaccine. I'd be smarter to lock you up like Karst and wring you dry of intelligence."

"You can't make me disclose anything I don't want to."

Straker grinned. "Oh, I bet we could make you want to."

"I see you're no better than we are. The ends justify the means, eh?"

"I said we could, not that we would. Torture is stupid policy, not to mention immoral. Information gained is never reliable. More importantly, it's counterproductive in the long run. If the subject dies, he becomes a martyr. If he lives to be freed, it makes him into the worst enemy you can possibly imagine." Straker turned to look into Lorden's face. "I know, because that's what it did to me."

"Yes. That was the most effective Miskor operation I've ever seen. It overthrew two empires."

Straker felt puzzlement leak onto his face. "What operation?"

"The one that got you captured by the Mutuality and tortured, only to escape and eventually overthrow your tormentors."

"You're trying to say this was all manipulated and planned? Bullshit."

"Not planned, no, but set in motion. Others have been unleashed before you, men and women of extraordinary abilities and character, in hopes they'd disrupt the status quo, but you succeeded beyond our wildest dreams. The irony is, you ended up on the wrong side."

"Gods and monsters, I hate you people."

"Who?"

Straker ground out his cigar. "All you mysterious puppet masters who claim to be pulling the strings. I don't know if you're telling the truth or just making it all up after the fact. But go on, tell me how I've been a pawn all along."

"Surely not a pawn but a knight. Now, pardon the pun, you've reached the last row and become a queen."

"Still a piece on the chessboard. Okay. Explain about ending up on the wrong side."

Lorden rubbed his eyes with one hand as if fending off a headache. "You were destined for greatness no matter what. Semi-clones of you—different in appearance, but with the same capabilities—would fill our mechsuits while AIs like *Victory* would revolutionize fleet combat. If your Liberation hadn't occurred, in a few years the Hundred Worlds would've had a dozen *Victory* ships and we'd have been unstoppable. The Mutuality would have been defeated. Humanity and its allies would have been united under our banner."

"Under Opter control, you mean. I like my way better—to be *actually* free."

Lorden shrugged. "I'm not unhappy with the way things turned out."

Straker stared, and then snapped his fingers in understanding. "Myrmidon always told me the Sarmok didn't want to unite humanity—that all their game-playing was to keep us divided. So you're not Sarmok."

"I told you that five minutes ago."

"But you're not Miskor either."

430

"I'm not an Opter anymore, Liberator Straker. I'm one of you now, and I can help your cause."

"I'm supposed to believe you switched sides in the space of a day?"

Lorden blew a smoke ring. "In the space of an hour, really."

"Don't you believe in anything, Lorden? Aren't you loyal to anything?"

"I'm utterly loyal to reality. I know the Queens. They care only for themselves. The rest—insectoids, humanopts, aliens, humans—we're all so much cattle to them. Like many agents, I did my duty, but always with the knowledge that I could be discarded at any moment. Would you feel loyalty to such creatures?"

"Maybe not. But how am I to believe you'll be loyal to me and the New Republic? Anyone who turns so easily can turn again. The leopard can't change his spots."

"I don't expect you to leave me in a position of power—but I can be useful."

"Self-preservation?" Straker asked. "That's your goal?"

"And freedom!" Lorden said smugly.

Straker suspected Lorden was just using lines he thought would impress him, but he couldn't help but agree with the sentiment.

"Not being caged..." he said. "I get that."

"You'll have to do more than eliminate their influence, Liberator," Lorden said. "Opters are no different from any other expansionist species. The Queens are watching your rise to power, and they fear any uniting force that might all of humanity together. You represent an existential threat to their empire."

Lorden breathed out a long, smoky sigh and tossed the stub of his cigar out over the balcony railing into to distant sea below.

"You're already at war," Lorden continued, "and you have no idea what you're getting into."

"We've fought the Nest Ships and drones before," Straker said with a shrug. "I've already ordered a building program of special ships to counter them, and our new AI fighters are extremely effective. Besides, Opters only own a few dozen systems, right?"

"More than fifty, actually." Lorden favored Straker with a bleak grimace. "I was told you visited Terra Nova. How many humanopts were there?"

"Over a trillion, I've been told."

"Yes... more than *one thousand billion*. That's half the population of the Hundred Worlds on one planet alone. Now, can you imagine every Opter system with that many insectoids? Do the math."

Straker made a rough calculation, and he felt himself pale. "That's two or three times the entire population of all of human space—my whole New Republic."

"With the industrial output to match. Plus, there are more alien regimes farther out that are being manipulated just like humans were, so the Opters will have allies with capabilities you've never encountered."

"So we're the underdogs again?" Straker asked. He shrugged again. "No matter. I've been in this position before. How soon will they attack?"

"At a guess? A few young Sarmok Queens will begin raiding within a month. The Empress will allow that, to keep us busy. Then, within a year, the real attack will come, and it will roll over us like a tsunami. So you see, Straker, we'll have to enjoy our freedom while we still have it."

Lorden turned away to look down at the sea. A hundred meters or more below the waves crashed on rocks.

Straker moved to his side and looked down with him.

"I won't accept this kind of defeatism," he told Lorden. "We'll mobilize. You and your humanopts will help. We'll figure out Opter weaknesses, pull some tricks to even the odds. We'll find our own allies. Maybe the Miskor will join with us instead of the Sarmok."

"I sympathize with and admire your optimism, Liberator. That's why I'll do my best to help. But it won't matter. The balance has been destroyed forever, and all that's left is Hive War. The Miskor will not go against the Empress' express orders."

"No chance that they'll at least sit out the fight?"

"They'll endeavor to minimize their own casualties, disfavoring the Sarmok... but they won't rebel against the Empress."

Straker struck his palm on the stone rail. "So, maybe we'll take down the Empress. Cut off the head, just like I've done twice before."

"An interesting idea," Lorden mused, "but farfetched. The Opters have never lost a Hive War."

"And what happens when they win a Hive War?"

"Genocide. They keep a residue of their enemies as slaves and curiosities. The rest, they exterminate." Lorden's expression softened. "Of course, they've never tried to conquer so many systems at once. Perhaps that will work in our favor. We might last as long as a decade."

Straker became annoyed with Lorden's defeatism and decided to end the discussion.

"Thanks for the briefing, Lorden," he said, and he clapped Lorden on the shoulder.

Lorden smiled, and he reached up to touch the back of Straker's hand as it rested on his shoulder.

Was that a stinging sensation?

Yes, Straker thought that it was... Could he have had a needle hidden in his palm? Could this worm really be trying to influence him biochemically... *again*? He was a snake that couldn't stop itself from biting.

Straker smiled back down at Lorden, but there was steel in his gaze.

In a way, Lorden had succeeded in this blatant attempt to change Straker's mind. Through this single underhanded action, he'd demonstrated to Straker that he would never be anything other than the conniving reptile he'd been all along.

"I've come to my decision," Straker said.

Lorden smiled expectantly, and he moved to step back— but Straker's hand clamped down on his shoulder. He didn't let him go.

Pulling the smaller man off his feet, Straker yanked him close.

Straker and Lorden were face-to-face.

433

"You're not going to use your tricks on me," Straker said quietly, staring into the little man's eyes, "or anyone else. Not today, Lorden. Not ever."

Finally, Lorden's insufferably smug calm broke. A look of true fear came into his eyes.

Then, without a further word, Straker threw him off the balcony. It was a powerful, arcing toss that carried the flailing man into the open air.

The fall was a long one. He seemed to drop down into an abyss, a pit from which none could crawl back.

Straker watched Lorden fall. He felt a surging, utterly satisfying sense of justice done. He knew Lorden had manipulated countless innocents and ordered the deaths of anyone who didn't succumb to his will.

Lorden didn't scream. Humanopts rarely did.

He struck stone ledges and outcroppings on the way down. Thumping and thudding, his body was crushed to a spinning pulp. He finally vanished into the dark sea without a sound.

Straker strode back to the Grand Hall and up the steps. He paused at the top before entering the dignitary-filled reception and took one last look at the lovely green of the shore, the dark cliffs and rocks, and the blue of Atlantis' great ocean.

Some things are worth living for, he thought to himself.

Then he remembered his two children. One was here, a daughter embryo, soon to be re-implanted in his incomparable wife Carla. The other remained on New Terra, due to be born of Princess Roslyn, if Gorben's words were true—and if the Calaria still lived.

He revised his earlier thought: *Some things are worth living for—and some are even worth killing for.*

Books by David VanDyke:

Stellar Conquest Series:
First Conquest
Desolator: Conquest
Tactics of Conquest
Conquest of Earth
Conquest and Empire

Books by B. V. Larson:

Undying Mercenaries Series:
Steel World
Dust World
Tech World
Machine World
Death World
Home World
Rogue World
Blood World
Dark World

Made in the USA
Monee, IL
14 February 2021

60511161R00256